Pride and Prejudice

The WILD and WANTON Edition

Annabella Bloom and Jane Austen

Avon, Massachusetts

The source material, *Pride and Prejudice* by Jane Austen, referenced
for this book can be found at *www.gutenberg.org/etext/1342*.

Published by
Adams Media, a division of F+W Media, Inc.
57 Littlefield Street, Avon, MA 02322. U.S.A.
www.adamsmedia.com

ISBN 10: 1-4405-0660-4
ISBN 13: 978-1-4405-0660-4
eISBN 10: 1-4405-1128-4
eISBN 13: 978-1-4405-1128-8

Printed in the United States of America.

10   9   8   7   6   5   4   3   2   1

Library of Congress Cataloging-in-Publication Data
Bloom, Annabella.
Pride and prejudice : the wild and wanton edition / Annabella Bloom and
Jane Austen.
p. cm.
ISBN-13: 978-1-4405-0660-4
ISBN-10: 1-4405-0660-4
ISBN-13: 978-1-4405-1128-8 (e-book)
ISBN-10: 1-4405-1128-4 (e-book)
1. Social classes—England—Fiction. 2. Young women—England—Fiction.
3. Sisters—Fiction. 4. Courtship—Fiction. 5. England—Social life and
customs—Fiction. I. Austen, Jane, 1775–1817. Pride and prejudice. II. Title.
PS3616.I46P75 2011
813'.6—dc22
2010039470

*This book is available at quantity discounts for bulk purchases.
For information, please call 1-800-289-0963.*

PRAISE FOR *PRIDE AND PREJUDICE:* *THE WILD AND WANTON EDITION*

"It is a truth universally acknowledged that the romance of Eliza Bennet and Mr. Darcy is told with a clever intelligence and great wit. Now it is also a work of captivating passion. Michelle Pillow [writing as Annabella Bloom] has honored Austen's original novel while giving readers an intimate view of this classic love story, taking the romance from the parlor into the bedroom. Do not miss this book."

—ALISON KENT, bestselling, award-winning author
of over thirty works, *www.alisonkent.com*

"Fans of Austen's classic will find the same great story, expertly embellished into this 'Wild and Wanton' edition that's sure to please readers who enjoy a spicier tale. If you ever wanted to know what Mr. Darcy was really thinking, check out this book!"

—MEGAN HART, award-winning author of
Pleasure and Purpose, www.meganhart.com

"A sensual take on a favorite classic. You'll never look at Mr. Darcy the same way! Michelle Pillow [writing as Annabella Bloom] heats up the pages and makes the romance burn with passion. Unforgettable!"

—CYNTHIA EDEN, award-winning author
of *Deadly Fear, www.cynthiaeden.com*

"We've never seen a hotter Mr. Darcy. I couldn't tell where Austen ended and Pillow [as Bloom] began . . . or put it down."

—CANDACE HAVENS, bestselling and award-winning author
of *Dragons Prefer Blondes, www.candacehavens.com*

ACKNOWLEDGMENTS

*H*OW CAN I POSSIBLY SAY a big enough thank you to the wonderful people in my life? Your love and support have been a true source of inspiration. To my mother, who nurtured my creativity, stood up to teachers who tried to doubt it, and let me raid her library. To my father, who instilled in me a great sense of honor and a love for learning, who also encouraged my artistic side when he gave me my first camera. To my husband, you are my knight in colorful armor. To my beautiful, talented, wonderful B, I know you will conquer the world. To my many sisters and the poor brother who had to live with us. To Carol, who has a generous spirit and an open kitchen filled with goodness. To Jean and Dave, who inherited me and did not throw me back. To Mandy M. Roth, a very talented writer and artist. I couldn't ask for a better friend, writing buddy, or sister. Thank you for being there for me. I love you all.

To my agent, Laura Bradford of the Bradford Literary Agency, thank you for believing in me. You are a pleasure to work with. Also, to those who helped make this book possible: AE Rought, Gina Panettieri from Talcott Notch Literary, my editor Paula Munier, Meredith O'Hayre, and the people at Adams Media for giving me the chance to play in Jane Austen's world. And, of course, the talented Jane Austen, the grandmother of all us modern day romance authors.

NOTE FROM ONE
OF THE AUTHORS

*W*HEN I WAS FIRST APPROACHED to work on this project, I was thrilled at the prospect of being allowed to play in Jane Austen's world. I've been a fan of Austen's since I discovered her books hidden on the shelves of the high school library, and have the greatest respect for her talent and imagination. The love story of Elizabeth Bennet and Mr. Darcy is easily one of the greatest romances ever written and I, like many *Pride and Prejudice* fans, long to know more, to peek behind the veil of this complicated relationship into the lives and private thoughts of these beloved characters—especially the enigmatic and often misunderstood Fitzwilliam Darcy.

Though nothing can compare to the true originality of Jane Austen's work, it has been an honor working on this project. I hope you enjoy my peek into this world as much as I enjoyed writing it. Visit *www.MichellePillow.com*, where you can find deleted and expanded scenes and download free *Pride and Prejudice: The Wild and Wanton Edition* wallpaper and banners.

Happy Reading!
Michelle Pillow

Pride and Prejudice

CHAPTER ONE

*I*T IS A TRUTH UNIVERSALLY ACKNOWLEDGED that a single man in possession of a good fortune must be in want of a wife. However little is known of the feelings or views of such a man upon his first entering a neighborhood, this truth is so well fixed in the minds of the surrounding families, that he is considered the rightful property of one or another of their daughters.

It is a truth *not* so universally acknowledged, that a young woman understands more about the ways of the world than she ought to know. In those unintentional lessons, rarely articulated but often learned, a woman understands she must be clever if she is in want of a desirable husband. Society expects this woman to be the picture of virtue and perfection, but men rarely fall in love with statues, which is why there is a vastly unspoken difference between the public and private thoughts of young ladies. Whereas public opinion makes ladies untouched by anything resembling the erotic, it was not unheard of to discover in the private diaries of these ladies that secrets of intimacy had passed between them and a fiancé. For a fiancé was as good as a husband and few saw reason to wait beyond such a happy occasion as a proper engagement, and these ladies only felt truly condemned if the act was not with a man of such position. In fact, it had been hinted nearly one out of every three brides gave birth to their first child a few months early.

When it came to the business of marriage, Mrs. Bennet often said to her daughters, "When you are married, you will see the way things are. That is why you must trust your parents to such a serious affair. We have the foresight to make a decision of such importance—and though I myself have had my share of flirtations, I pride myself on my wisdom of such things." Despite this comment, it was not a statement Mrs. Bennet had enforced upon herself in girlhood concerning her own marriage. Mr. Bennet, having been captivated by youth and beauty, and that appearance of good humor which youth and beauty generally give, had married a woman whose weak understanding and illiberal mind had very early in their marriage put an end to all real affection for her. Respect, esteem, and confidence had vanished forever; and all his views of domestic happiness were overthrown. But Mr. Bennet was not of a disposition to seek comfort for the disappointment which his own imprudence had brought on, and did not partake of any of those unseemly pleasures which too often comfort the ill-fated.

Luckily for their second eldest daughter, Elizabeth, the education into the female arts did not rest solely upon the dear Mrs. Bennet's shoulders, but rather on the secret books circulated among their peers and the gossip of the maids. In improving her mind, she had come to expect much more in a man than simple fortune and social standing could give. Elizabeth put importance on love, happiness, laughter, and companionship; in finding a

true match to her playful heart and generous spirit. In this she was irrevocably encouraged by her father who believed no man would ever be good enough for his Lizzy. So thus educated in the ways of catching a husband, she did not intend to use her education. To her thinking, such marital scheming was best left to her mother who, though loved by her five daughters, was silly enough to be ignored by them.

"My dear Mr. Bennet," his excited lady said to him one day when she believed them to be alone, "have you heard that Netherfield Park is let at last?"

Mr. Bennet replied he had not.

"But it is," she insisted, "for Mrs. Long has just been here, and she told me all about it."

Mr. Bennet made no answer.

"Do you not want to know who has taken it?" his wife demanded impatiently.

"You want to tell me, and I have no objection to hearing it."

This was invitation enough.

"Why, my dear, you must know, Mrs. Long says that Netherfield is taken by a young man of large fortune from the north of England. He came down on Monday in a chaise and four to see the place, and was so delighted with it that he agreed with Mr. Morris immediately. He is to take possession before Michaelmas, and some of his servants are to be in the house by the end of next week."

"What is his name?"

"Bingley."

"Is he married or single?"

"Oh, single, my dear, to be sure! A single man of large fortune—four or five thousand a year. What a fine thing for our girls."

Mr. Bennet pretended not to hear the giggling of eavesdroppers outside his window. "How so? How can it affect them?"

"My dear Mr. Bennet, how can you be so tiresome?" **His wife moved about the room in a well practiced show of exasperation.** "You must know that I am thinking of his marrying one of them."

"Is that his design in settling here?"

"Design! Nonsense, how can you talk so? But it is very likely that he *may* fall in love with one of them, and therefore you must visit him as soon as he comes."

"I see no occasion for that. You and the girls may go, or you may send them by themselves, which perhaps will be still better for as you are as handsome as any of them, Mr. Bingley may like you the best of the party."

"My dear, you flatter me. I certainly have had my share of beauty, but I do not pretend to be anything extraordinary now. When a woman has five grown-up daughters, she ought to give over thinking of her own beauty." **Mrs. Bennet caught her wavy reflection in a windowpane and smiled briefly at herself.**

"In such cases, a woman has not often much beauty to think of."

Mrs. Bennet's attempt to hide her pleasure at his compliment failed. "But, my dear, you must indeed go and see Mr. Bingley when he comes into the neighborhood."

"It is more than I engage for, I assure you."

"But consider your daughters. Only think what an establishment it would be for one of them. Sir William and Lady Lucas are determined to go, merely on that account, for in general, you know, they visit no newcomers. Indeed you must go, for it will be impossible for us to visit him if you do not."

"You are over-scrupulous, surely. I daresay Mr. Bingley will be very glad to see you. I will send a few lines by you to assure him of my hearty consent to his marrying whichever he chooses of the girls. Though, I must throw in a good word for my little Lizzy."

"I desire you will do no such thing. Lizzy is not a bit better than the others, and I am sure she is not half so handsome as Jane, nor half so good-humored as Lydia. But you are always giving her the preference."

"None of them have much to recommend them," he replied. "They are all silly and ignorant like other girls, but Lizzy has something more of quickness than her sisters."

"Mr. Bennet, how can you abuse your own children in such a way? You take delight in vexing me. You have no compassion for my poor nerves."

"You mistake me, my dear. I have a high respect for your nerves. They are my old friends. I have heard you mention them with consideration these last twenty years at least."

Mr. Bennet was so odd a mixture of a fast mind, sarcastic humor, reserve, and caprice, that the experience of three-and-twenty years had been insufficient to make his wife understand his character. Her mind was less difficult to develop. She was a woman of mean understanding, little information, and uncertain temper. When she was discontented, she fancied herself nervous. The business of her life was to get her daughters married, its solace was visiting and news.

Mr. Bennet was among the earliest of those who waited on Mr. Bingley. He had always intended to visit him, though to the last assuring his wife he should not go, and till the evening after the visit was paid she had no knowledge of it. It was then disclosed in the following manner. Observing his second daughter employed in trimming a hat, he suddenly addressed her with, "I hope Mr. Bingley will like it, Lizzy."

"We are not in a way to know *what* Mr. Bingley likes," her

mother said resentfully, "since we are not to visit."

"But you forget, mamma," Elizabeth said. "Mrs. Long promised to introduce him at the assemblies."

"I do not believe Mrs. Long will do any such thing. She has two nieces of her own. She is a selfish, hypocritical woman, and I have no opinion of her."

"No more than I," said Mr. Bennet, "and I am glad to find that you do not depend on her serving you."

Mrs. Bennet deigned not to make any reply, but, unable to contain herself, began scolding one of her daughters. "Do not keep coughing so, Kitty, for Heaven's sake! Have a little compassion on my nerves. You tear them to pieces."

"I do not cough for my own amusement," Kitty replied fretfully, before making an effort to turn the attention away from herself. "When is your next ball to be, Lizzy?"

"Tomorrow fortnight."

"Aye, so it is," cried her mother, "and Mrs. Long does not come back till the day before. It will be impossible for her to introduce him, for she will not know him herself."

"Then, my dear, you may have the advantage of your friend, and introduce Mr. Bingley to *her*."

"Impossible, Mr. Bennet, when I am not acquainted with him myself. How can you be so teasing?"

"I honor your circumspection. One cannot know what a man really is by the end of a fortnight. But if we do not venture somebody else will. After all, Mrs. Long and her daughters must stand their chance. Therefore, as she will think it an act of kindness, if you decline to take the responsibility, I will take it on myself."

The girls stared at their father. Mrs. Bennet said only, "Nonsense, nonsense!"

"What can be the meaning of that emphatic exclamation?" he asked. "Do you consider the forms of introduction, and the stress that is laid on them, as nonsense? I cannot quite agree with you there. What say you, Mary? For you are a young lady of deep reflection, I know, and read great books."

Mary wished to say something sensible, but knew not how.

"While Mary is adjusting her ideas," he continued, "let us return to Mr. Bingley."

"I am sick of Mr. Bingley." **His wife shook her head in dismay, growing more flustered with each passing second.**

"I am sorry to hear that, but why did you not tell me that before? If I had known as much this morning I certainly would not have called on him. It is very unlucky but, as I have actually paid the visit, we cannot escape the acquaintance now."

The astonishment of the ladies was just what he wished, with that of Mrs. Bennet surpassing the rest. Though, when the first tumult of joy was over, she began to declare that it was what she had expected all the while.

"How good it was of you, my dear Mr. Bennet, but I knew I should persuade you at last. I was sure you loved your girls too well to neglect such an acquaintance. It is such a good joke, too, that you should have gone this morning and never said a word about it till now."

"Now, Kitty, you may cough as much as you choose." Mr. Bennet left the room, fatigued with the raptures of his wife.

"What an excellent father you have, girls," their mother said, when the door was shut. "I do not know how you will ever make amends to him for his kindness; or me, either, for that matter. At our time of life it is not so pleasant, I can tell you, to be making new acquaintances every day, but for your sakes we would do anything."

The rest of the evening was spent in speculating how soon Mr. Bingley would return Mr. Bennet's visit, and determining when they should ask him to dinner.

CHAPTER TWO

*N*OTHING MRS. BENNET, with the assistance of her five daughters, could ask on the subject was sufficient to draw any satisfactory description of Mr. Bingley. They attacked Mr. Bennet in various ways—with barefaced questions, ingenious suppositions, and distant surmises—but he eluded the skill of them all, and they were at last obliged to accept the second-hand intelligence of their neighbor, Lady Lucas. Her report was highly favorable. Sir William had been delighted with him. He was quite young, wonderfully handsome, extremely agreeable, and, to crown the whole, he meant to be at the next assembly with a large party. Nothing could be more delightful! To be fond of dancing was a certain step towards falling in love, and very lively hopes of Mr. Bingley's heart were entertained.

"If I can but see one of my daughters happily settled at Netherfield," said Mrs. Bennet to her husband, "and all the others equally well married, I shall have nothing left to wish for."

In a few days Mr. Bingley returned Mr. Bennet's visit, and sat about ten minutes with him in his library. He had entertained hopes of being admitted to a sight of the young ladies, of whose beauty he had heard much, but he saw only the father. The ladies were somewhat more fortunate, for they had the advantage of ascertaining from an upper window that he wore a blue coat, and rode a black horse.

"He carries himself well," Jane remarked, giving a shy smile. Though, a compliment from Jane was not a rare thing. She generally thought of something nice to say about everyone.

"Very well," Elizabeth agreed with an enthusiastic nod, inclined by the nature of their relationship to agree with her sister on most things. If she had been forced to choose, she would have named Jane her favorite. Luckily, Kitty and Lydia were too self-absorbed to notice the preference, and Mary was too preoccupied with her own thoughts to care.

"He looks as if he could seat a horse bareback," Kitty whispered a little too loudly to Lydia, to which that sister replied in a quieter voice, "It is she who has the thighs to seat a horse bareback." The two giggled, believing themselves to be very clever in repeating the shocking wit of a soldier they had overheard in town. The remaining three sisters were content to ignore them, and their mother chose not to hear that which she did not wish to think upon.

An invitation to dinner was soon afterwards dispatched, and Mrs. Bennet had already planned the courses that were to do credit to her housekeeping when an answer arrived which deferred it all. Mr. Bingley was obliged to be in town the following day, and, consequently, unable to accept the honor of their invitation. Mrs. Bennet was quite taken aback. She could not imagine what business he could have in town so soon after his arrival in Hertfordshire. She began to fear that he might be always flying about from one place to another, and never settled at Netherfield as he ought to be. Lady Lucas quieted her fears a little by starting the idea of his being gone to London only to get a large party for the ball. A report soon followed that Mr. Bingley was to bring twelve ladies and seven gentlemen with him to the assembly. The girls grieved over such a number of ladies, but were comforted the day before the ball by hearing, that instead of twelve he brought only six with him from London—his five sisters and a cousin. And when the party entered the assembly room it consisted of only five altogether—Mr. Bingley, his two sisters, the husband of the eldest, and another young man.

Immediately an introduction was sought by Mrs. Bennet, and Sir William was applied to for procuring it. She ushered her girls before the eligible Mr. Bingley. "May I present Miss Bennet," Sir William said, gesturing toward the eldest, Jane, before moving on. "Miss Elizabeth, Miss Mary, Miss Lydia, and Miss Catherine Bennet." As they were singled out to the newcomers, each girl bowed her head.

"Delighted," said Mr. Bingley, smiling.

Mr. Bingley was good-looking and gentlemanlike with a pleasant countenance, and easy, unaffected manners. His brother-in-law, Mr. Hurst, merely looked the part of the gentleman. His sisters were fine women, with an air of decided fashion. **They lacked the openness of their brother when greeting the Bennets. Elizabeth noted with both amusement and joy that Mr. Bingley's shy gaze lingered a few seconds longer on Jane than anyone else. Jane appeared completely unaware of the attention, at least to those who were not so intimately acquainted with her moods as her dear sister. Elizabeth detected instantly the slight flush that threatened the composure of Jane's face, as well as the quick lift of her chest as she inhaled, holding her breath several seconds too long.**

This small exchange was soon lost on Elizabeth as her attentions turned to Mr. Bingley's friend. Mr. Darcy soon drew the attention of the room by his fine, tall person, handsome features, noble mien, and the report which was in general circulation within five minutes after his entrance, of his having ten thousand a year. Elizabeth was less impressed with his fortune and the rich cut of his jacket, though both tended to invoke an instant respect, and the general desire to like such a person. What she found striking were his blue eyes—deep and soulful, fixed with a kind of studious attention and profound knowledge seen only in the most worthy of men. As they were introduced and his attention fell upon her, she felt a stirring of interest inside her chest. Her heart beat quickened; her breath caught. He did not speak, merely nodded, the slight gesture showing neither pleasure nor disdain.

Afterwards, when they were away from him, she imagined him to glance in her direction, finding her foremost among her sisters, even before the widely acknowledged beauty of Jane. So preoccupied, she barely heard Jane comment on the politeness in which Mr. Bingley and his sisters spoke, and she almost missed the carefully calculated shrewdness of her mother in suggesting they stand in full view of the eligible gentlemen. She nodded, apparently answering both to satisfaction, though she would be hard pressed to repeat herself upon later contemplation.

Mr. Darcy turned, the movement giving way to the gracefulness of his limbs and trimness of his body. Unlike some men, he did not need padding to add the appearance of health beneath his clothes. The stiff material moved in such a way to suggest that the bulge of muscles were completely natural. Elizabeth was no fool. She had read things in books not meant for the eyes of young women, at least not till after they were married; but those passages, once so mysterious in their descriptions of attraction and the exploration of love suddenly felt very clear and extremely clever. Her heart beat quickened once more and warmth spread throughout her stomach. She forced her eyes to move, scanning the room before finding their way once more to the object of her interest. Mr. Darcy's back was to her, and now that she did not have the distraction of his eyes, she found the breadth of his shoulders, squarely set, and the unmistakably mesmerizing shift of his hips beneath his jacket. A tingling warmth erupted beneath her flesh, rising in a blush across her cheeks.

When Mr. Bingley spoke, Mr. Darcy turned and his lips curled ever so slightly into a smile. The expression broke into the seriousness of his face. She imagined him to be a great many things in those first moments—a graceful dancer, an intelligent mind, a wild spirit, an amiable companion, a handsome and considerate man searching for the woman who might turn not only his head but his heart. As the heat continued to spread throughout her limbs, she silently willed him to look at her, to come across the room and ask her to dance, to touch her hand so that she may assure herself that he was real, to hold her a little too close during a waltz so the other women would know not to bother trying to turn his head—though some still found such close dancing improper. Had she allowed it, her mind would have taken the daydreams further—to a private walk, a lingering look, a hand upon her cheek tilting her lips to his, and to a sweet, stolen kiss while the laughter of the party faded into the background. Fortunately, the arrival of her dear friend, Charlotte Lucas, distracted such wanderings of the mind and she did not find herself foolishly blushing for all to see.

At first, her daydreams of Mr. Darcy's character were affirmed most readily by those in attendance. The gentlemen pronounced him to be a fine figure of a man, the ladies declared he was much handsomer than Mr. Bingley, and he was looked at with great admiration for about half the evening. **It was then the true nature of this quickly esteemed gentleman began to reveal itself.** His manners gave a disgust which turned the tide of his popularity for he was discovered to be proud, to be above his company, and above being pleased; and not all his large estate in Derbyshire could then save him from having a most forbidding countenance, and of being unworthy to be compared with his friend. **Elizabeth did not want to acknowledge the crushing truth, till she found herself the subject of his unwarranted disdain.**

Elizabeth had been obliged, by the scarcity of gentlemen, to sit down for two dances. During part of that time, Mr. Darcy had been standing near enough for her to hear a conversation between him and Mr. Bingley, who came from the dance for a few minutes, to press his friend to join it.

"Come, Darcy," he said, "I must have you dance. I hate to see you standing about by yourself in this stupid manner."

Elizabeth might have looked pleasantly at the dancers, but her attention was fully fixed upon the conversation. She held her breath, not wanting to miss a single word.

"I certainly shall not. You know how I detest it, unless I am particularly acquainted with my partner. At such an assembly as this it would be insupportable. Your sisters are engaged, and there is not another woman in the room whom it would not be a punishment to me to stand up with."

"I would not be so fastidious as you are for a kingdom!" Mr. Bingley cried. "Upon my honor, I never met so many pleasant girls in my life as I have this evening, and there are several who are uncommonly pretty."

"You are dancing with the only handsome girl in the room," said Mr. Darcy, looking at the eldest Miss Bennet. **Elizabeth's smile faltered and she felt as if someone pushed her into a cold lake.**

"She is the most beautiful creature I ever beheld! But there is one of her sisters sitting down just behind you, who is very pretty, and I daresay very agreeable. Do let me ask my partner to introduce you."

Elizabeth forced the smile back to her mouth, and lifted her hands to clap in time with the lively music. Perhaps the gentleman had forgotten about her when he made his generalized comment about the lack of beauty in the room.

"Which do you mean?" Turning round he looked for a moment at Elizabeth, till catching her eye, he withdrew his own and coldly said, "She is tolerable, but not handsome enough to tempt me. I am in no humor at present to give consequence to young ladies who are slighted by other men. You had better return to your partner and enjoy her smiles, for you are wasting your time with me."

And, then again, perhaps not. Elizabeth took a deep breath, and her smile became forcibly fixed upon her face.

Mr. Bingley followed his advice. As Mr. Darcy walked off, Elizabeth remained with no very cordial feelings toward him. She told the story, however, with great spirit among her friends for she had a lively, playful disposition, which delighted in anything ridiculous. **It was easier to laugh at the nature of the slight than admit to the true depth of the wound.**

Mr. Bingley had soon made himself acquainted with all the principal people in the room. He was lively and unreserved, danced every dance, was angry that the ball closed so early, and talked of giving one himself at Netherfield. Such amiable qualities must speak for themselves. What a contrast between him and his friend! Mr. Darcy danced only once with Mrs. Hurst and once with Miss Bingley, declined being introduced to any other lady, and spent the rest of the evening in walking about the room, speaking occasionally to one of his own party. His character was decided. He was the proudest, most disagreeable man in the world, and everybody hoped that he would never come there again. Among the most violent against him was Mrs. Bennet, whose dislike of his general behavior was sharpened into resentment upon hearing he had slighted one of her daughters.

Lydia Bennet loved attending balls. She was a stout, well-grown girl, with a fine complexion and good-humored countenance. She was a favorite with her mother, whose affection had brought her into public at an early age. **For this she could never fully express her gratitude and pleasure. Often Elizabeth would watch Lydia's behavior with mortification. She was convinced Lydia wanted only encouragement to attach herself to anybody. Sometimes one gentleman, sometimes another, had been her favorite, as their attentions raised them in her opinion. Her affections had continually been fluctuating but never without an object. The mischief of neglect and mistaken indulgence towards such a girl were often acutely felt by her sisters.**

Mr. Bennet often observed of this particular daughter, that it was from these affections of her mother that she had become sillier than the rest of them. Knowing such, he did not take pains to correct her behavior and Lydia was left to decide for herself the pleasures that were to be taken. And, since she did not feel it necessary to neglect herself any of life's pleasures, she gave herself great leeway to enjoy them to the fullest.

It was with this innately selfish pursuit that she found herself sneaking away from the assembly. In truth, it was not difficult to do, for she had much practice at slipping away undetected in such crowded places, and the thrill of getting away with her aim was just as exciting as the reason for the deception. Mr. Daniels

would be eagerly waiting, for nearly half-an-hour, excited to the point of explosion. Oh, how she did enjoy making him wait!

She had been looking forward to this meeting for nearly a week, for there had been little time to slip away from the constant watchfulness of Kitty, who when lacked distractions of her own would follow Lydia wherever she went. Love Kitty as she did, there were some secrets she did not allow even that sister to know. For, if she understood anything, she understood that what she was about would be frowned upon, and whereas she did not worry about the lectures of society except where they would make it necessary to take her from the societal pleasures she now enjoyed.

Knowing just where Mr. Daniels waited for her, she quickened her pace. The sound of music became a faint backdrop to the dark night. She hurried around the building, her heartbeat quickening with her steps. Already her body was moist with desire. As she turned the corner to a section of the building encased with shadows, she grinned. Mr. Daniels was excited indeed, for he had already taken the liberty of unfastening his pants. His hand fisted his arousal, pumping until he saw her approach. His hand stopped.

"There you are. I worried you could not get away this time." The husky passion in his tone caused her to shiver. "Did you have any trouble?"

"I was stopped by your wife," she lied, for she generally avoided that unpleasant woman. For a moment her lover looked worried, until she laughed gaily. "She does not suspect a thing, I assure you. We both have reason to keep our arrangement quiet. You for your in-laws' money and me for my reputation."

As she said the last words, she leaned down to lift her skirts, showing him her lack of undergarments. She never wore such things under her dresses, for it excited her to go without. His breathing deepened visibly and he reached to pull her against his body. His hands fumbled, giving away his excitement.

"I would leave her to run away with you, my darling," he whispered. "You have but to say the word. You know my marriage was arranged. My wife does not let me touch her, and I am sure she has lovers of her own. I see how she looks at the stable hand. We could be off to France. There I would marry you, for you are well past the age of consent. My passion for you has ruined you for other men. I have taken your innocence, I—"

Lydia quieted him with a kiss, thrusting her tongue into his mouth as he had taught her to do. She would not consider running away with him, for he was not anything she wanted in a husband. He was not the handsomest of men, nor the most charming. What made him suited to her pleasure was his situation—an ill-tempered wife from a well-off family. He would keep their secret and give her whatever she wished.

Daniels pressed her into the building and tugged up her skirts. The urgency of the moment filled them. She could not stay away from the ball for too long or someone might notice. There was no waiting. He brought himself to her, thrusting his turgid shaft to take claim once more. The pressure felt good and she gasped. He pumped his hips, impaling her; kissing her neck as if he would devour her with his body.

"Do not stop until I am finished this time," she ordered in breathless pants, "or else I will make you finish the job with your mouth and then your wife shall taste me on you when you kiss her goodnight."

Her naughty words made him thrust faster. Lydia gasped, greedily taking what she wanted from him. The tension built with each rock of their bodies. The hard wall pressed into her back and snagged bits of her hair. In that moment, it did not matter. Release was within her grasp. Suddenly, she came, climaxing with a great jerk of her body. Mr. Daniels, sensing the glorious moment, instantly withdrew himself to spill his seed against her inner thigh. As he lowered her down, she gave a soft laugh.

"I must get back."

"Can you not stay a moment longer?" he pleaded.

Lydia smiled, laughing lightly as she ignored his entreaty. "Did you bring me the present you promised?"

"I could not manage it."

Suddenly, Lydia's pleasure was dampened. No gift? And after what she had done for him! She straightened her skirts and artfully tugged at her hair to right it. "I did not want to have to tell you this, but I cannot see you again. It is not right." Then, mumbling something about his wife and propriety, she quickly left him before he could protest. Within moment, she was back amongst the dancers, taking Kitty's arm as if she had never left. No one suspected her, and the one person who could ruin her left soon after under the guise of being too under the weather to stay. That man's wife hardly missed him.

The evening altogether passed off pleasantly to the whole family. Mrs. Bennet had seen her eldest daughter much admired by the Netherfield party. Mr. Bingley had danced with her twice, and she had been distinguished by his sisters. Jane was as much gratified by this as her mother could be, though in a quieter way. Elizabeth felt Jane's pleasure. Mary had heard herself mentioned to Miss Bingley as the most accomplished girl in the neighborhood, and Catherine and Lydia had been fortunate enough never to be without partners, which was pretty much all that they had yet learned to care for at a ball. They returned in good spirits to Longbourn, the village where they lived, and of which they were the principal inhabitants. They found Mr. Bennet still up. With a book he was regardless of time, and on the present occasion he had a good deal of curiosity as to the events of an evening which had raised such splendid expectations. He had rather hoped that his wife's views on the stranger would be disappointed, but he soon found out that he had a different story to hear.

"Oh, my dear Mr. Bennet," she said, as she entered the room, "we have had a most delightful evening, a most excellent ball. I wish you had been there. Jane was so admired, nothing could be like it. Everybody said how well she looked, and Mr. Bingley thought her quite beautiful. He actually danced with her twice and she was the only creature in the room that he asked a second time. First of all, he asked Miss Lucas. I was so vexed to see him stand up with her, but he did not admire her at all— indeed, nobody can, you know. He seemed quite struck with Jane as she was going down the dance. So he inquired who she was, and got introduced, and asked her for the two next. Then the two third he danced with Miss King, and the two fourth with Maria Lucas, and the two fifth with Jane again, and the two sixth with Lizzy, and the Boulanger—"

"If he had had any compassion for *me*," her husband broke in impatiently, "he would not have danced half so much. For God's sake, say no more of his partners. Oh, that he had sprained his ankle in the first dance so I would not have to hear of all his partners."

"My dear, I am quite delighted with him. He is so excessively handsome and his sisters are charming women. I never in my life saw anything more elegant than their dresses. I daresay the lace upon Mrs. Hurst's gown—"

Here she was interrupted again. Mr. Bennet protested against any description of finery. She was therefore obliged to seek another branch of the subject, and related, with much bitterness of spirit and some exaggeration, the shocking rudeness of Mr. Darcy.

"But I can assure you," she added, "that Lizzy does not lose much by not suiting *his* fancy. He is a most disagreeable, horrid man, not at all worth pleasing. So high and so conceited that there was no enduring him! He walked here and there, fancying himself so very great. I wish you had been there, my dear, to have given him one of your set-downs for I quite detest the man."

CHAPTER THREE

HEN JANE AND ELIZABETH WERE ALONE in their shared bedroom, the former, who had been cautious in her praise of Mr. Bingley before, expressed to her sister how very much she admired him.

"He is just what a young man ought to be," said she. **She danced around the room, twirling in her long nightgown till it billowed about her legs.** "Sensible, good-humored, lively, and I never saw such happy manners—so much ease, with such perfect good breeding!"

Elizabeth sat on the bed, pleased to see her sister so happy. "He is also handsome, which a young man ought likewise to be, if he possibly can. His character is thereby complete."

Jane sighed, and all the excitement she felt shone from her sparkling eyes. "I was very flattered by his asking me to dance a second time. I did not expect such a compliment."

"No? I did for you. But that is one great difference between us. Compliments always take *you* by surprise and *me* never. What could be more natural than his asking you again? He could not help seeing that you were about five times as pretty as every other woman in the room. No thanks to his gallantry for that. Well, he certainly is very agreeable, and I give you leave to like him. You have liked many a stupider person."

Jane grabbed her sister by the hands, and leaned close. "Dear Lizzy!"

"Oh, you are a great deal too apt to like people in general." **Elizabeth pressed her forehead to Jane's. Their words became a whisper.** "You never see a fault in anybody. All the world is good and agreeable in your eyes. I never heard you speak ill of a human being in your life."

"I would not wish to be hasty in censuring anyone, but I always speak what I think."

"I know you do, and it is that which makes the wonder." **Elizabeth fell back onto the bed, kicking her feet lightly as they dangled over the edge.** "With your good sense, to be so honestly blind to the follies and nonsense of others. Affectation of candor is common enough—one meets it everywhere. But to be candid without ostentation or design, to take the good of everybody's character and make it still better, and say nothing of the bad, belongs to you alone. And so you like his sisters, too, do you? Their manners are not equal to his."

"Certainly not—at first. But they are very pleasing women when you converse with them. Miss Bingley is to live with her brother to keep his house, and I am mistaken if we shall not find a very charming neighbor in her."

Elizabeth listened in silence, but was not convinced, for Mr. Bingley's sisters' behavior at the assembly had not been calculated to please in general. With more quickness of observation and less pliancy of temper than her sister, and with a judgment too unassailed by any attention to herself, she was very little disposed to approve them.

Mr. Bingley's sisters were in fact very fine ladies, not deficient in good humor when they were pleased, nor in the power of making themselves agreeable when they chose it. Though proud and conceited, they were rather handsome. They had been educated in one of the first private seminaries in town, had a fortune of twenty thousand pounds, were in the habit of spending more than they ought, and of associating with people of rank, and were therefore in every respect entitled to think well of themselves, and meanly of others. They were of a respectable family in the north of England, a circumstance more deeply impressed on their memories than that their brother's fortune and their own had been acquired by trade.

Mr. Bingley inherited property to the amount of nearly a hundred thousand pounds from his father, who had intended to purchase an estate, but did not live to do it. Likewise, Mr. Bingley intended it; however, as he was now provided with a good house and the liberty of a manor, it was doubtful to those who best knew the easiness of his temper, whether he might not spend the remainder of his days at Netherfield, and leave the next generation to purchase.

His sisters were anxious for his having an estate of his own. Though he was now only established as a tenant, Miss Bingley was by no means unwilling to preside at his table—nor was Mrs. Hurst, who had married a man of more fashion than fortune, less disposed to consider his house as her home when it suited her. Mr. Bingley had not been of age two years, when he was tempted by an accidental recommendation to look at Netherfield House.

He did look at it and into it for half-an-hour, before deciding he was pleased with the situation and the principal rooms, satisfied with what the owner said in its praise, and took it immediately.

Between him and Darcy there was a very steady friendship, in spite of great opposition of character. Bingley was endeared to Darcy by the easiness, openness, and ductility of his temper, though no disposition could offer a greater contrast to his own, and though with his own he never appeared dissatisfied. On the strength of Darcy's regard, Bingley had the firmest reliance, and of his judgment the highest opinion. In understanding, Darcy was the superior. Bingley was by no means deficient, but Darcy was clever. He was at the same time haughty, reserved, and fastidious, and his manners, though well-bred, were not inviting. In that respect his friend had the greatest advantage. Bingley was sure of being liked wherever he appeared, Darcy was continually giving offense.

The manner in which they spoke of the Meryton assembly was sufficiently characteristic. Bingley had never met with more pleasant people or prettier girls in his life, and everybody had been most kind and attentive to him. There had been no formality, no stiffness, and he had soon felt acquainted with all the room. As to Miss Bennet, Bingley could not conceive an angel more beautiful. Darcy, on the contrary, claimed he had seen a collection of people in whom there was little beauty and no fashion, for none of whom he had felt the smallest interest, and from none received either attention or pleasure. Miss Bennet he acknowledged to be pretty, but she smiled too much.

Mrs. Hurst and her sister agreed, but still admired and liked her, and pronounced her to one whom they would not object to know more of. Miss Bennet was therefore established as a sweet girl, and their brother felt authorized by such commendation to think of her as he chose.

What Darcy refused to comment on during the carriage ride home was Miss Elizabeth Bennet. Though he could think of no reason as to why she should enter his thoughts, he found her there for much of the ride. When pressed about his mood, he was content to let the others think him generally dissatisfied, and Bingley being accustomed to his friend's quiet temperament readily carried on the conversation without him.

Only when he was alone, unable to sleep, did Darcy allow the improbability of Miss Elizabeth to enter his thoughts. The very ridiculousness of her mother and the impropriety shown by her sisters made courting her out of the question, had he even been inclined toward courtship. But, to consider her as a lover? He had taken them before, but never a woman from the country, never one without experience, never one with her eyes. Gentlemen never lacked for female company while in London. Servants and prostitutes were always willing to do the job, should he have an inclination, though it had been many long years since he had walked the grounds near Covent Garden. Women like Elizabeth Bennet were raised to be wives, not mistresses. Darcy could not find fault with it. Wives needed to be virtuous, whereas mistresses did not. He accepted this order of things. Yet, when the woman had looked upon him, he felt her gaze trying to see into his very thoughts, and he was torn between the impertinence of her daring and the bravery that she should try to see within his soul.

"Nonsense," said he to the subtle hint of his reflection in the glass. It occurred to him that perhaps he had consumed too much port upon returning to Netherfield Park. How else could he explain the fanciful path his thoughts now wandered?

Candlelight flickered on the wall, the subtle dance of the flame pulling his eyes from the window where he stared at the dislodged cravat over the linen of his shirt. His discarded jacket lay over the back of a chair, his boots forgotten on the floor. Darcy curled his toes against the carpet, all too aware of his arousal, even more aware of how long it had been since he had taken care of the more private needs of his body. Duty and responsibility had borne down hard upon him in recent months, taking precedence over passion.

"Elizabeth," he whispered as if coming to a decision. He thought of her dark eyes under the sweep of long lashes. It was a fantasy he would never admit to, not out loud and barely to himself. He undressed; and crossed to the large, empty bed; and climbed naked beneath the covers. Awareness filled his senses with the soft mold of the mattress along his backside, the softer caress of the covers along his front, the warmth of liquor in his veins, the feel of his hand creeping down his stomach to the stiff arousal awaiting his fingers. Again he wondered why such a woman should tempt him to this level of madness. It was a well-quoted fact that those young ladies meant to be the wives of gentlemen lacked the passions of mistresses.

Even so, Darcy took himself in hand, stroking to thoughts of the dark eyes of a young lady who had been slighted by other men. As it often happens, the momentary pleasure of the flesh overtook reason and logic. He tightened his fist; and dug in his heels; and worked his hips; and gasped for a breath he could not catch. He imagined Elizabeth above him in such a way that could never happen, turning her into a temptress of little breeding and hungry appetites, and in doing so removed her from the real world of propriety and manners into an acceptable realm of pleasure and playthings.

Darcy met with gratifying release. His body stiffened, his muscles quivered and tightened beneath the flesh, and his seed spilled forth unto his stomach. And as the haze of sleep overtook his suddenly relaxed mind, one word whispered through his unaware thoughts, "Elizabeth."

CHAPTER FOUR

ITHIN A SHORT WALK of Longbourn lived a family
with whom the Bennets were particularly intimate. Sir
William Lucas had been formerly in trade in Meryton, where he
had made a tolerable fortune, and risen to the honor of knighthood by an address to the king during his mayoralty. The distinction had perhaps been felt too strongly. It had given him a
disgust to his business, and to his residence in a small market
town; and, in quitting them both, he had removed with his family to a house about a mile from Meryton, denominated from
that period Lucas Lodge, where he could think with pleasure of
his own importance, and, unshackled by business, occupy himself solely in being civil to all the world. For, though elated by
his rank, it did not render him supercilious. On the contrary, he
gave his attention to everybody. By nature inoffensive, friendly,
and obliging, his presentation at St. James's had made him
courteous.

Lady Lucas was a very good kind of woman, not too clever to be a valuable neighbor to Mrs. Bennet. They had several children. The eldest of them, a sensible, intelligent young woman, about twenty-seven, was Elizabeth's intimate friend, Charlotte Lucas.

That the Miss Lucases and the Miss Bennets should meet to talk over a ball was absolutely necessary, and the morning after the assembly brought the former to Longbourn to hear and to communicate.

"You began the evening well, Charlotte," said Mrs. Bennet with civil self-command to Miss Lucas. "You were Mr. Bingley's first choice."

"Yes, but he seemed to like his second better."

"Oh, you mean Jane, I suppose, because he danced with her twice. To be sure that did seem as if he admired her. Indeed I rather believe he did. I heard something about it, but I hardly know what." **Mrs. Bennet paused, pretending to consider her thoughts.** "Something about Mr. Robinson."

"Perhaps you mean what I overheard between him and Mr. Robinson?" Charlotte said. "Did I not mention it to you? Mr. Robinson's asking him how he liked our Meryton assemblies, and whether he did not think there were a great many pretty women in the room, and which he thought the prettiest? And Mr. Bingley answering immediately to the last question: 'Oh, the eldest Miss Bennet, beyond a doubt. There cannot be two opinions on that point.'"

"Upon my word! Well, that is very decided indeed; however, it may all come to nothing, you know."

"My overhearings were more to the purpose than yours, Eliza," said Charlotte. "Mr. Darcy is not so well worth listening to as his friend, is he? Poor Eliza, to be only just *tolerable*!"

"I beg you would not put it into Lizzy's head to be vexed by his ill-treatment, for he is such a disagreeable man, that it would be quite a misfortune to be liked by him. Mrs. Long told me last night that he sat close to her for half-an-hour without once opening his lips."

"Are you quite sure, ma'am? Is not there a little mistake?" inquired Jane. "I certainly saw Mr. Darcy speaking to her."

"Aye, because she asked him at last how he liked Netherfield. He could not help answering her, but she said he seemed quite angry at being spoken to."

"Miss Bingley told me that he never speaks much, unless among his intimate acquaintances," Jane said. "With them he is remarkably agreeable."

"I do not believe a word of it, my dear. If he had been so very agreeable, he would have talked to Mrs. Long. Everybody says that he is eat up with pride. I daresay he heard Mrs. Long does not keep a carriage, and had come to the ball in a hack chaise."

"I do not mind his not talking to Mrs. Long," said Charlotte, "but I wish he had danced with Eliza."

"I say again, Lizzy," instructed her mother, "I would not dance with him, if I were you."

"I believe, ma'am, I may safely promise you never to dance with him." **Elizabeth assured herself she meant every word. Though, whenever she thought of the disagreeable man, she thought of that smile he bestowed on Mr. Bingley, and could not help but remember how she felt in those first moments of introduction, and of all the things she imagined him to be. A dull ache centered in her chest as she longed for that fictional ideal. If only she could find all of those fine qualities in one man.**

"His pride," said Charlotte, "does not offend me so much as pride often does, because there is an excuse for it. One cannot wonder that so very fine a young man, with family, fortune, everything in his favor, should think highly of himself. If I may so express it, he has a right to be proud."

"That is very true," Elizabeth replied, "and I could easily forgive his pride, if he had not offended mine."

"Pride," observed Mary, who piqued herself upon the solidity of her reflections, "is a very common failing, I believe. By all that I have ever read, I am convinced that it is very common indeed. Human nature is particularly prone to it, and there are very few of us who do not cherish a feeling of self-complacency on the score of some quality or other, real or imaginary. Vanity and pride are different things, though the words are often used synonymously. A person may be proud without being vain. Pride relates more to our opinion of ourselves, vanity to what we would have others think of us."

"If I were as rich as Mr. Darcy," said a young Lucas, who came with his sisters, "I should not care how proud I was. I would keep a pack of foxhounds, and drink a bottle of wine a day."

"Then you would drink a great deal more than you ought," scolded Mrs. Bennet. "And if I were to see you at it, I should take away your bottle directly."

The boy protested that she should not, she continued to declare that she would, and the argument ended only with the visit.

CHAPTER FIVE

*T*HE LADIES OF LONGBOURN soon waited on those of Netherfield, and the visit was returned in due form. Miss Bennet's pleasing manners grew on the goodwill of Mrs. Hurst and Miss Bingley, even though the mother was found to be intolerable, and the younger sisters not worth speaking to, a wish to be better acquainted was expressed towards the two eldest. By Jane, this attention was received with the greatest pleasure, but Elizabeth still saw superciliousness in their treatment of everybody, hardly excepting even her sister, and could not like them. Though their kindness to Jane, such as it was, arose in all probability from the influence of their brother's admiration.

It was generally evident whenever they met that Mr. Bingley did admire Jane. To Elizabeth it was equally evident that her sister was yielding to the preference which she had begun to entertain for him from the first, and was in a way to be very much in love. Elizabeth considered with pleasure that it was not likely to be discovered by the world in general, since Jane united, with great strength of feeling, a composure of temper and a uniform cheerfulness of manner which would guard her from the suspicions of the impertinent. She mentioned this to Charlotte.

"It may perhaps be pleasant to be able to impose on the public in such a case," replied Charlotte, "but it is sometimes a disadvantage to be so very guarded. If a woman conceals her affection with the same skill from the object of it, she may lose the opportunity of fixing him. It will then be but poor consolation to believe the world equally in the dark. We can all begin freely, a slight preference is natural enough, but there are very few of us who have heart to be really in love without encouragement. In nine cases out of ten a women had better show more affection than she feels. Bingley likes your sister undoubtedly, but he may never do more than like her, if she does not help him on."

"But she does help him on, as much as her nature will allow. If I can perceive her regard for him, he must be a simpleton, indeed, not to discover it too."

"Remember, Eliza, that he does not know Jane's disposition as you do."

"But if a woman is partial to a man, and does not endeavor to conceal it, he must find it out."

"Perhaps he must, if he sees enough of her. But, though Bingley and Jane meet tolerably often, it is never for many hours together; and, as they always see each other in large mixed parties, it is impossible that every moment should be employed in conversing together. Jane should therefore make the most of every half-hour in which she can command his attention. When she is secure of him, there will be more leisure for falling in love as much as she chooses."

"Your plan is a good one," replied Elizabeth, "where nothing is in question but the desire of being well married, and if I

were determined to get a rich husband, or any husband, I daresay I should adopt it. But these are not Jane's feelings. She is not
acting by design. As yet, she cannot even be certain of the degree
of her own regard nor of its reasonableness. She has known him
only a fortnight. She danced four dances with him at Meryton,
she saw him one morning at his own house, and has since dined
with him in company four times. This is not quite enough to
make her understand his character."

"Not as you represent it. Had she merely *dined* with him,
she might only have discovered whether he had a good appetite,
but you must remember that four evenings have also been spent
together—and four evenings may do a great deal."

"Yes. These four evenings have enabled them to ascertain
that they both like Vingt-un better than Commerce, but with
respect to any other leading characteristic I do not imagine that
much has been unfolded."

"Well," Charlotte mused, "I wish Jane success with all my
heart. If she were married to him tomorrow, I should think she
had as good a chance of happiness as if she were to be studying his character for a twelvemonth. Happiness in marriage is
entirely a matter of chance. If the dispositions of the parties are
ever so well known to each other or ever so similar beforehand,
it does not advance their felicity in the least. They always continue to grow sufficiently unlike afterwards to have their share of
vexation. It is better to know as little as possible of the defects of
the person with whom you are to pass your life."

"You make me laugh, Charlotte, but you know it is not
sound, and that you would never act in this way yourself."
**Elizabeth lowered her voice to ensure they were not overheard.
"You speak of felicity and growing vexation, but you say nothing of passion. Should not a woman know her feelings before she
marries? Should not she at least enter the marriage with more**

than a probability of love? Do you not want passion with your husband? Romance? Do you not wish to be swept away in emotion, and feel your heart race every time he looks at you?"

"Eliza, you speak like you are a character in one of those silly novels, but I suspect you know as well as I that a probability of love is all many can hope for. Those who are swept away, as you so put it, often find themselves the victim of their own stupidity and keepers of a ruined reputation. I am a practical woman and I would consider myself lucky to have that much, but when I marry it will be a practical matter, and for a good and comfortable home. I have given up on passion. I would advise you to do the same, but I know that you will not."

Occupied in observing Mr. Bingley's attentions to her sister, Elizabeth was far from suspecting that she was herself becoming an object of some interest in the eyes of his friend. Mr. Darcy had at first scarcely allowed her to be pretty, and had looked at her without admiration at the ball. When they next met, he looked at her only to criticize. **Yet this did not erase the haunting memories he had unintentionally created in imagining her as his lover.** But no sooner had he made it clear to himself and his friends that she hardly had a good feature in her face, than he began to find it was rendered uncommonly intelligent by the beautiful expression of her dark eyes. To this discovery succeeded some others equally mortifying.

Though he had detected with a critical eye more than one failure of perfect symmetry in her form, he was forced to acknowledge her figure to be light and pleasing; and in spite of his asserting that her manners were not those of the fashionable world, he was caught by their easy playfulness. **He found her** delicate flaws more attractive than that of perfection, for they added a realism and charm difficult to render by even the most competent of artists. The more he looked, the more he found reason to keep looking, and the unfolding realizations only added tinder to the fire smoldering beneath his flesh. Darcy prided himself on his good sense, and the constant drifting of his mind to matters of a sordid nature only served to exasperate him.

One night at Sir William Lucas's, where a large party had been assembled, he found himself again thinking about her to the point of distraction. With what had become a late night routine fixed firmly in his mind, he began to wish to know more of Miss Elizabeth. Perhaps it was the lack of entertainment in the country, or that of refined company, but he found his thoughts preoccupied with catching a glimpse of her. He followed her progress around the room with his eyes, never looking for too long, waiting for the perfect moment to move closer. She laughed often, smiling gaily as she addressed friends. Her manners were too relaxed to be proper, but in an infectious way that captivated. Finally, as a step towards conversing with her himself, he attended to her conversation with others. His doing so drew her notice.

Of his thoughts Elizabeth was perfectly unaware. To her he was only the man who made himself agreeable nowhere, and who had not thought her handsome enough to dance with. Or, rather, that is what she told herself on the matter. He was a proud and disagreeable man, without doubt, but that did not stop her from noticing the blue of his eyes or the subtle, yet brief, drumming of his long fingers against his outer thigh. The movement was only one in a perfected ritual that was Mr. Darcy. Each bow of the head, each proud lift of the chin, each cutting glance of the eyes, had been bred into him from boyhood, as much a part of his character as breathing.

"What does Mr. Darcy mean," Elizabeth whispered to Charlotte, "by listening to my conversation with Colonel Forster?"

"That is a question which Mr. Darcy only can answer."

"But if he does it any more I shall certainly let him know that I see what he is about. He has a very satirical eye, and if I do not begin by being impertinent myself, I shall soon grow afraid of him."

On his approaching them soon afterwards, though without seeming to have any intention of speaking, Charlotte defied her friend to mention such a subject to him. This immediately provoked Elizabeth to do it, and she turned to him. "Did you not think, Mr. Darcy, that I expressed myself uncommonly well just now, when I was teasing Colonel Forster to give us a ball at Meryton?"

"With great energy, but it is always a subject which makes a lady energetic."

"You are severe on us." **Elizabeth shot her friend an impish look and tried not to laugh. When she again looked at the gentleman, she had managed to compose her face.**

"It will soon be her turn to be teased," said Charlotte. "I am going to open the instrument, Eliza, and you know what follows."

"You are a very strange creature by way of a friend—always wanting me to play and sing before anybody and everybody! If my vanity had taken a musical turn, you would have been invaluable. As it is, I would really rather not sit down before those who must be in the habit of hearing the very best performers."

On Charlotte's insistence, however, she added, "Very well, if it must be so, it must."

"I am sure your talent is adequate," Mr. Darcy allowed.

Elizabeth was taken by surprise by the half-compliment, so did not acknowledge it. Her performance was pleasing, though by no means capital. After a song or two, and before she could reply to the entreaties of several that she would sing again, she was eagerly succeeded at the instrument by her sister Mary, who, in consequence of being the only plain one in the family, worked hard for knowledge and accomplishments, and was always impatient for display.

Mary had neither genius nor taste, and though vanity had given her application, it had given her likewise a pedantic air and conceited manner, which would have injured a higher degree of excellence than she had reached. Elizabeth, easy and unaffected, had been listened to with much more pleasure, though not playing half so well. Mary, at the end of a long concerto, was glad to purchase praise and gratitude by then performing Scotch and Irish airs at the request of her younger sisters, who, with some of the Lucases, and two or three officers, joined eagerly in dancing at one end of the room.

Mr. Darcy stood near them in silent indignation at such a mode of passing the evening, to the exclusion of all conversation, and was too engrossed by his thoughts to perceive that Sir William Lucas was his neighbor, till Sir William thus began, "What a charming amusement for young people this is, Mr. Darcy! There is nothing like dancing after all. I consider it as one of the first refinements of polished society."

"Certainly, sir. It has the advantage also of being in vogue amongst the less polished societies of the world. Every savage can dance."

Sir William only smiled. "Your friend performs delightfully," he continued after a pause, on seeing Bingley join the group, "and I doubt not that you are adept in the science yourself, Mr. Darcy."

"You saw me dance at Meryton, I believe, sir." **He glanced over the room, hoping to catch a glimpse of Elizabeth.**

"Yes, indeed, and received no inconsiderable pleasure from the sight. Do you often dance at St. James's?"

"Never, sir."

"Do you not think it would be a proper compliment to the place?"

"It is a compliment which I never pay to any place if I can avoid it."

"You have a house in town, I conclude?"

Mr. Darcy bowed.

"I had once had some thought of fixing in town myself, for I am fond of superior society, but I did not feel quite certain that the air of London would agree with Lady Lucas." He paused in hopes of an answer, but his companion was not disposed to make any. Elizabeth at that instant was moving towards them, and he was struck with the action of doing a very gallant thing. "My dear Miss Eliza, why are you not dancing? Mr. Darcy, you must allow me to present this young lady to you as a very desirable partner. I am sure you cannot refuse to dance when so much beauty is before you." And, taking her hand, he would have given it to Mr. Darcy who, though extremely surprised, was not unwilling to receive it, when she instantly drew back.

With some discomposure to Sir William, she said, "Indeed, sir, I have not the least intention of dancing."

"You excel so much in the dance, Miss Eliza," insisted Sir William, "that it is cruel to deny me the happiness of seeing you. Though this gentleman dislikes the amusement in general, he can have no objection, I am sure, to oblige us for one half-hour."

"I entreat you not to suppose that I moved this way in order to beg for a partner," Elizabeth said. **Unable to help herself, she added mischievously, "I would not have Mr. Darcy tempted into an amusement he finds merely tolerable."**

The words drew a small reaction from Mr. Darcy, but she merely smiled politely and pretended not to notice the subtle reference to his slight upon her character. When Sir William looked expectantly at the gentleman in question, Mr. Darcy, with grave propriety, requested to be allowed the honor of her hand. It was in vain for Elizabeth was determined.

"Mr. Darcy is all politeness." **Elizabeth smiled in earnest now that she knew her clever barb had been well placed. Let the prideful man know his remark had been heard, remembered, and that she was unaffected by it.**

"He is, indeed," Sir William agreed, "but, considering the inducement, my dear Miss Eliza, we cannot wonder at his com-plaisance—for who would object to such a partner?"

Sir William did not shake her purpose by his attempt at persuasion.

Elizabeth looked archly, and turned away. Her resistance had not injured her with the gentleman, and Mr. Darcy was thinking of her with some complacency, when thus accosted by Miss Bingley, "I can guess the subject of your reverie."

"I should imagine not."

"You are considering how insupportable it would be to pass many evenings in this manner, in such society, and indeed I am quite of your opinion. I was never more annoyed. The insipidity, and yet the noise—the nothingness, and yet the self-importance of all those people. What I would give to hear your strictures on them."

"Your conjecture is totally wrong, I assure you. My mind was more agreeably engaged. I have been meditating on the very great pleasure which a pair of fine eyes in the face of a pretty woman can bestow."

Miss Bingley immediately fixed her eyes on his face, and desired he would tell her what lady had the credit of inspiring such reflections.

Mr. Darcy replied with great intrepidity, "Miss Elizabeth Bennet."

"Miss Elizabeth Bennet!" repeated Miss Bingley. **She was hard pressed to hide her amusement.** "I am all astonishment. How long has she been such a favorite? And pray, when am I to wish you joy?"

"That is exactly the question which I expected you to ask. A lady's imagination is very rapid. It jumps from admiration to love, from love to matrimony, in a moment. I knew you would be wishing me joy."

"Nay, if you are serious about it, I shall consider the matter as absolutely settled. You will have a charming mother-in-law, indeed. Of course, she will always be at Pemberley with you."

He listened to her with perfect indifference while she chose to entertain herself in this manner, and as his composure convinced her that all was safe, her wit flowed long.

Sleep did not come quick or easy for Elizabeth, and she found herself walking through her darkened home in the early hours of morning. She liked the stillness of night and the way the shadows and moonlight transformed the ordinary, everyday objects of her family's existence into a fanciful garden. She traced her fingers over the mantel, around the wide body of a vase, along the curving paths of oval paintings. She recognized each item from memory and did not need the light to discern their details. This gave her thoughts leave to wander where they willed, and where they willed was the deep blue eyes of Mr. Darcy, for it was always his eyes that first came to her before the memory of his handsome face, then the breadth of his shoulders and length of his arms. He was attractive, would be more so if he smiled and laughed; there were a great many gentlemen of Mr. Darcy's social stature that managed as much. What was it about Mr. Darcy that caused him to be the most

rigid soul of propriety? Wealth commonly brought with it a reserve of character and pride, understandably so, but Mr. Darcy embodied both traits a little too perfectly.

She had imagined once she pointed out her knowledge of his hurtful words, she would sever the ties that kept him tethered to her mind. This was not to be. Despite his proclaiming her to be merely tolerable as a dance partner, he had been easily persuaded by Sir William to change his mind. She could not make out his character; could perceive no reason as to why Sir William should persuade him when his good friend Mr. Bingley had not. Had something changed since that first meeting?

Elizabeth touched her face, seeing the ghostly reflection of herself in the window. The blue light caused her features to pale. Many had told her she was pretty, not so beautiful as Jane, but more blessed than others. Though conscious of her looks and figure, she did not obsess about them as some women were wont to do. She much preferred to apply her thoughts to the gaiety of friends, the fanciful worlds in novels, and the application of her mind.

Her lips parted and she reached for the window, tracing the reflection. The cool glass slid beneath her fingertips. Bringing the chilled fingers to her mouth, she closed her eyes, and whispered, "Mr. Darcy."

A small shiver of pleasure and longing passed over her, even as part of her wished to deny the attraction. Any feelings she harbored were certainly owed more to the mystery of the brooding gentleman than any comprehensible logic. When she opened her eyes, she detected a shadow to move beyond her reflection. Instantly, she stepped back, banishing the fanciful thoughts from her as she hurried once more into the sanctuary of bed.

CHAPTER SIX

*M*R. BENNET'S PROPERTY consisted almost entirely in an estate of two thousand a year, which, unfortunately for his daughters, was entailed, in default of heirs male, on a distant relation. Their mother's fortune, though ample for her situation in life, could but ill-supply the deficiency of his. Her father had been an attorney in Meryton, and had left her four thousand pounds. She had a sister married to a Mr. Philips, who had been a clerk to their father and succeeded him in the business, and a brother settled in London in a respectable line of trade.

The village of Longbourn was only one mile from Meryton, a most convenient distance for the young ladies, who were usually tempted to go there three or four times a week, to pay their duty to their aunt and to a milliner's shop just over the way. The two youngest of the family, Catherine and Lydia, were particularly frequent in these attentions for their minds were more vacant than their sisters', and when nothing better offered, a walk to Meryton was necessary to amuse their morning hours and furnish conversation for the evening. However bare of news the country might be in general, they always contrived to learn some from their aunt. At present, indeed, they were well supplied both with news and happiness by the recent arrival of a militia regiment in the neighborhood. It was to remain the whole winter, and Meryton was the headquarters.

Their visits to Mrs. Philips were now productive of the most interesting intelligence. Every day added something to their knowledge of the officers' names and connections, and their lodgings were not long a secret. At length, they began to know the officers themselves. Mr. Philips visited them all, and this opened to his nieces a store of felicity unknown before. They could talk of nothing but officers; and Mr. Bingley's large fortune, the mention of which gave animation to their mother, was worthless in their eyes when opposed to the regimentals of an ensign.

After listening one morning to their effusions on this subject, Mr. Bennet coolly observed, "From all that I can collect by your manner of talking, you must be two of the silliest girls in the country. I have suspected it some time, but I am now convinced."

Catherine was disconcerted, and made no answer. However, Lydia, with perfect indifference, continued to express her admiration of Captain Carter, and her hope of seeing him in the course of the day, as he was going the next morning to London. **The very mention of the Captain's name set the two girls to giggling, a condition they were not easily cured of.**

"I am astonished, my dear," said Mrs. Bennet, "that you should be so ready to think your own children silly. If I wished to think slightingly of anybody's children, it should not be my own."

"If my children are silly, I must hope to be always sensible of it."

"Yes, but as it happens, they are all very clever."

"This is the only point, I flatter myself, on which we do not agree. I had hoped our sentiments coincided in every particular, but I must so far differ from you as to think our two youngest daughters uncommonly foolish."

"Mr. Bennet, you must not expect such girls to have the sense of their father and mother. When they get to our age, I daresay they will not think about officers any more than we do. I remember the time when I liked a red coat myself very well—and, indeed, so I do still at my heart. If a smart young colonel, with five or six thousand a year, should want one of my girls I shall not say nay to him. I thought Colonel Forster looked very becoming the other night at Sir William's in his regimentals."

Mrs. Bennet was prevented from further comment by the entrance of the footman with a note for Miss Bennet. It came from Netherfield, and the servant waited for an answer. Mrs. Bennet's eyes sparkled with pleasure, and she was eagerly calling out, while her daughter read, "Well, Jane, who is it from? What does he say? Make haste and tell us, make haste, my love."

"It is from Miss Bingley," said Jane, and then read it aloud. "My dear friend, if you are not so compassionate as to dine today with Louisa and me, we shall be in danger of hating each other for the rest of our lives, for a whole day's tete-a-tete between two women can never end without a quarrel. Come as soon as you can on receipt of this. My brother and the gentlemen are to dine with the officers. Yours ever, Caroline Bingley."

"With the officers?" Lydia cried. "I wonder why my aunt did not tell us of that!"

"Dining out," said Mrs. Bennet with a disappointed shake of her head, "that is very unlucky."

"Can I have the carriage?" asked Jane.

"No, my dear, you had better go on horseback."

"Horseback?" Elizabeth demanded, looking out the window. "But it is likely to rain!"

"And so it shall," Mrs. Bennet agreed. "And then, Jane, you must stay all night."

"That would be a good scheme," said Elizabeth, "if you were sure that they would not offer to send her home."

"Oh, but the gentlemen will have Mr. Bingley's chaise to go to Meryton, and the Hursts have no horses to theirs."

"I had much rather go in the coach." **Jane frowned in worry. Such schemes were not in her nature and felt a little too much like deceit.**

"Your father cannot spare the horses, I am sure. They are wanted in the farm, Mr. Bennet, are they not?"

Mr. Bennet had been listening with quiet interest while pretending to be occupied by his book. "They are wanted in the farm much oftener than I can get them."

"But if you have got them today," Elizabeth said, "my mother's purpose will be answered."

She did at last extort from her father an acknowledgment that the horses were engaged. Jane was therefore obliged to go on horseback, and her mother attended her to the door with many cheerful prognostics of a bad day. Her hopes were answered. Jane had not been gone long before it rained hard. Her sisters were uneasy for her, but her mother was delighted. The rain continued the whole evening without intermission, and Jane certainly could not come back.

"A lucky idea of mine, indeed!" said Mrs. Bennet more than once, as if the credit of making it rain were all her own. Till the next morning, however, she was not aware of all the felicity of her contrivance.

Breakfast was scarcely over when a servant from Netherfield brought the following note for Elizabeth, which she promptly read aloud, "My dearest Lizzy, I find myself very unwell this morning, which, I suppose, is to be imputed to my getting wet through yesterday. My kind friends will not hear of my returning till I am better. They insist also on my seeing Mr. Jones. Therefore do not be alarmed if you should hear of his having been to me, and, except a sore throat and headache, there is not much the matter with me. Yours, Jane."

"Well, my dear," said Mr. Bennet, "if your daughter should die, it would be a comfort to know that it was in pursuit of Mr. Bingley."

"People do not die of little trifling colds. She will be taken good care of. As long as she stays there, it is all very well. I would go and see her, if I could have the carriage."

Elizabeth, feeling really anxious, was determined to go, though the carriage was not to be had. As she was no horsewoman, walking was her only alternative. She declared her resolution.

"How can you be so silly," cried her mother, "as to think of such a thing, in all this dirt? You will not be fit to be seen when you get there."

"I shall be very fit to see Jane, which is all I want."

"Is this a hint to me, Lizzy," said her father, "to send for the horses?"

"No, indeed, I do not wish to avoid the walk. The distance is nothing when one has a motive; only three miles. I shall be back by dinner."

"I admire the activity of your benevolence," observed Mary, "but every impulse of feeling should be guided by reason."

"We will go as far as Meryton with you," said Catherine and Lydia. Elizabeth accepted their company, and the three young ladies set off together.

"If we make haste," Lydia said, as they walked along, "perhaps we may see something of Captain Carter before he goes."

Near Meryton they parted. The two youngest continued into town with the plan that they were to walk along the main street, before repairing to the lodgings of one of the officers' wives. Kitty hoped to see if their favorite shop carried new ribbons. Lydia had every intention of finding a replacement for Mr. Daniels. He had bowed to her once while in town, but she had not the slightest interest in him now that there were officers to be had. She knew he would dare no more than that, and chose to think of him no more. Seeing a private named Sykes nearby in his regimentals, she knew she had found her latest target. An overly ambitious young man, he would not want a scandal attached to his name, nor did he seem to be in the market for a wife. Rumor had him set to be engaged to a daughter of a family friend whom he had never met. Still more, there was a coarseness to his manners that were in great want of breeding. And, to make him perfect, he was not to stay in Meryton for long, a week at most.

Losing Kitty would prove no easy task, for her sister liked to stay close to her side. Luckily, though, Sykes did not miss the subtleties of her flirting, nor the practiced lick of her mouth and it was not long before his responses were more than she could hope for. She pointed Kitty to the far end of the store to discover the most perfect of green ribbons amongst the many, knowing her sister would never discover that which did not exist. Then, with Sykes walking at an artful distance, she led him away, through the narrow side streets where no one would venture during that time of day.

Leaning against a tight inlet between two ill fitted buildings, she waited for him to pass by. The moment that she saw him, she bid him to her with a giggle. He came, hesitating as he glanced back and forth through the alley.

"It is true you are to leave soon?" she asked with a bat of her lashes.

He replied that it was.

"But you have only just arrived here, and I was so looking forward to having you at the next ball." Lydia parted her lips, liking the way he looked at them. When he began to answer, she grabbed him by his shirt collar and jerked him around so that he was fitted into the tight space. "I suppose that I must simply settle on having you now."

Unlike the others, she found no reason to pretend she was innocent. The perfection in such a lover was that he was temporary. Her hand instantly went to his member, stroking the hard length in her palm. She tilted back her head and laughed.

"There is a good soldier, ready and at attention!" She made quick work of his pants, exited by the idea of his taking her there in the open air, surrounded by buildings. Oh, how Kitty would worry when she realized Lydia had slipped away from her. But, her sister would not know what to do and would simply pretend to browse the shop while worrying in silence.

"And what are my orders?" he managed, his voice harsh.

Lydia pulled at her skirt, revealing an ankle. "To take the enemy territory by any force necessary."

He growled low in the back of his throat. His hand gripped tight to her breast, as if he had every right to squeeze it tight. "Turn around, so that I may show you how well I wield my quimstake."

Lydia had never heard that particular term for a man's cock and did not have a ready answer. She did not need one. There was nothing gentle in the way he lifted her skirts and flung her around to face the building. Her hands splayed as she was forced to bend over, braced against the tight space. Sykes fumbled with his breeches, freeing himself just enough to join his body to hers.

He grunted, throwing up her skirts to find her naked and ready. Without testing her resolve, he gave her what she wanted, thrusting hard into her sex. Taking up her hips, he rode her to his pleasure, not caring about her any more than she cared about him.

"There's a good cunny," he grunted. "It knows to be wet for a man."

Lydia had not expected such a rough show, but then she had never tried to seduce a man with so little manners before. She found herself enjoying the role of his lover. Climax came for them both, and he pulled himself from her at the last moment. Breathing hard, he slapped her along her backside before righting his clothes. Flushed and a little dazed, Lydia watched as he reached into his pocket. Dropping two coins on the ground, he said, "Tell no one of this. I cannot have rumors attached to my name."

As he stumbled away, she would have been offended if not for the money catching her eye. She pushed down her skirts and quickly picked up the coins. Oh, the many ribbons she would be able to buy! Kitty would be so jealous. She stood for a moment longer, settling her appearance before sneaking back towards the street.

CHAPTER SEVEN

*E*LIZABETH CONTINUED HER WALK ALONE, crossing field after field at a quick pace, jumping over stiles and springing over puddles with impatient activity, and finding herself at last within view of the house, with weary ankles, dirty stockings, and a face glowing with the warmth of exercise.

In this disheveled state, she was shown into the breakfast-parlor, where all but Jane were assembled, and where her appearance created a great deal of surprise. That she should have walked three miles so early in the day, in such dirty weather, and by herself, was most incredible to Mrs. Hurst and Miss Bingley to the point that Elizabeth was convinced that they held her in contempt for it. She was received, however, very politely by them. In their brother's manner there was something better than politeness, there was good humor and kindness. Mr. Darcy said very little, but she hardly expected it to be otherwise. **The gentleman's somewhat expressionless gaze conveyed his feelings on her** appearance all too readily. Mr. Hurst said nothing at all, thinking only of his breakfast, which held his attention more than such a thing ought to.

Her inquiries after her sister were not very favorably answered. Miss Bennet had slept ill, and though up, was very feverish, and not well enough to leave her room. Elizabeth was glad to be taken to her immediately. Jane, who had only been withheld by the fear of giving alarm or inconvenience from expressing in her note how much she longed for such a visit, was delighted at her entrance. She was not equal, however, to much conversation, and when Miss Bingley left them together, could attempt little besides expressions of gratitude for the extraordinary kindness she was treated with. Elizabeth silently attended her.

"It is very kind of Miss Elizabeth to attend her sister, is it not?" Mr. Bingley asked Mr. Darcy. Though the surrounding landscape was wet, the sun had dried the stone balcony on which the two men now found themselves. Bingley busied himself with looking towards the window where Miss Bennet now resided, not bothering to hide the pleasure he felt at having her under his roof, even if the circumstances were not the best. Though, if the lovely lady must be sick, he found he liked being able to provide comfort for her. And, the proximity of her room did allow for many visits between the two of them, though propriety dictated he not enter the chambers alone.

Darcy merely nodded in response. Unlike his friend, he refused to look up, instead choosing to focus his attention on a distant, solitary tree. His thoughts were divided between admiration of the brilliancy which exercise had given to Elizabeth's complexion, and doubt as to the occasion's justifying her coming so far alone.

"There is something to be said for a woman who comes from close family," Bingley continued, though Darcy suspected his friend was finding more reasons to like Jane than the argument of such logic would allow.

"That would depend on the family," Darcy answered.

"Miss Elizabeth looked well, did she not?"

"She should not have walked so far alone."

"I think it's a testament to her love for a sister." Bingley finally drew his eyes away from the window. He could see nothing anyway.

"And I think it's a testament to her foolish impulses."

"Would you not walk ten times as far if it were Georgiana who were ill?"

Darcy's frown deepened. "That argument is faulty for I am not a young woman."

"I should say not," Bingley laughed, unwilling to let Darcy's mood infect his own. "You know I have not thought once of the charms of other ladies since first meeting Miss Bennet? I could be walking in Covent Garden right now and the prettiest of doves would not tempt me with their wiles."

"Perhaps you should aim higher in a mistress," Darcy said gruffly. It had been far too long since he had been with a woman, and having his late night obsession now under the same roof did not help. Miss Elizabeth Bennet. Just thinking of her flushed cheeks and dirty hem caused a stirring deep within his stomach. His back stiffened, as if in doing so he could hide the arousal now forming beneath his tight trousers.

"Who can think of a mistress when I am imaging a wife?" Bingley asked.

"Have your feelings developed to such a state?" Darcy did

not try to hide the worry in his voice. Whereas he found little fault with Jane, he did not observe the same level of commitment within the lady that his friend seemed to feel. However, he did not worry about it yet. Bingley had such a nature that allowed him to fall in love easily, for he was apt to like people in general.

"Do not look at me like that!" cried Bingley. "Till you have found yourself flown away by the face of an angel, you cannot possibly understand."

"The only angel I'm sure to be flown away by will assuredly appear over my deathbed."

Bingley's disbelieving laughter was his only answer, as he made his way back into the house.

Now alone, Darcy took a deep breath. His eyes turned upward, to the window that had captured his good friend's attention. His thoughts were not so pure as Bingley's. When he imagined Elizabeth, it was not marriage that came first and foremost to his mind, but a more sordid affair filled with impossibilities and improbabilities.

Whenever he was near her, he felt beside himself, nervous and thick of tongue. Afterwards, he would think of a great many things he could say to her, but whenever he stood in her presence, he found himself without the proper tools of discourse. He attributed part of this to his attraction for her, and part to his own genuinely reserved nature. Whereas people like Miss Elizabeth and Mr. Bingley had the ease of character to make new acquaintances into quick friends, Darcy did not.

The full force of his desires clouded his judgment and he knew he would never calm himself if he continued to stare at her window like a lovesick Romeo waiting for his Juliet. A brisk walk later brought him to the privacy of his room and the delinquency of his thoughts. Part of him hated her for making him feel such longings; but as he thrust his hand down into the front of his

trousers, he gave up on trying to fight the temptation. Resistance was not in him, not when it came to his desire for Elizabeth Bennet.

When breakfast was over Elizabeth and Jane were joined by Mr. Bingley's sisters. Elizabeth began to like them herself, when she saw how much affection and solicitude they showed for Jane. The apothecary came, and having examined his patient, said, as might be supposed, that she had caught a violent cold, and that they must endeavor to get the better of it. He advised her to return to bed, and promised her some draughts. The advice was followed readily, for the feverish symptoms increased, and her head ached acutely. Elizabeth did not leave her room for a moment, nor were the other ladies often absent for the gentlemen were out, and they had nothing to do elsewhere.

When the clock struck three, Elizabeth felt that she must go, and very unwillingly said so. Miss Bingley offered her the carriage, and she only wanted a little pressing to accept it, when Jane testified such concern in parting with her, that Miss Bingley was obliged to convert the offer of the chaise to an invitation to remain at Netherfield for the present. Elizabeth most thankfully consented, and a servant was dispatched to Longbourn to acquaint the family with her stay and bring back a supply of clothes.

CHAPTER EIGHT

*a*T FIVE O'CLOCK THE TWO LADIES RETIRED to dress, and at half-past six Elizabeth was summoned to dinner. To the civil inquiries which then poured in, and amongst which she had the pleasure of distinguishing the much superior solicitude of Mr. Bingley's, she could not make a very favorable answer. Jane was by no means better. The sisters, on hearing this, repeated three or four times how much they were grieved, how shocking it was to have a bad cold, and how excessively they disliked being ill themselves; and then thought no more of the matter. Their indifference towards Jane when not immediately before them restored Elizabeth to the enjoyment of all her former dislike.

Their brother was the only one of the party whom she could regard with any complacency. His anxiety for Jane was evident, and his attentions to herself most pleasing. His attitude prevented her from feeling too much like an intruder. Miss

Bingley was engrossed by Mr. Darcy, her sister scarcely less so. As for Mr. Hurst, by whom Elizabeth sat, he was an indolent man, who lived only to eat, drink, and play at cards, and who, when he found her to prefer a plain dish to a ragout, had nothing to say.

When dinner was over, she returned directly to Jane. Miss Bingley began abusing her as soon as she was out of the room. Her manners were pronounced to be very bad indeed, a mixture of pride and impertinence; she had no conversation, no style, no beauty. Mrs. Hurst thought the same, adding, "She has nothing to recommend her, but being an excellent walker. I shall never forget her appearance this morning. She looked almost wild."

"I could hardly keep my countenance. Very nonsensical to come at all. Why must she be scampering about the country, because her sister had a cold? Her hair, so untidy, so blowsy!"

"Yes, and I hope you saw her petticoat, six inches deep in mud, and the gown which had been let down to hide it not doing its duty."

"Your picture may be very exact, Louisa," Bingley said, "but this was all lost upon me. I thought Miss Elizabeth Bennet looked remarkably well when she came into the room this morning. Her dirty petticoat quite escaped my notice."

"*You* observed it, Mr. Darcy, I am sure," said Miss Bingley. "I am inclined to think that you would not wish to see your sister make such an exhibition."

"Certainly not."

"To walk three miles, or four, or five, whatever it is, above her ankles in dirt, and quite alone! What could she mean by it? It seems to me to show a most country indifference to decorum."

"It shows an affection for her sister that is very pleasing," said Bingley.

"I am afraid, Mr. Darcy," observed Miss Bingley in a half

whisper, "that this adventure has rather affected your admiration of her fine eyes."

"Not at all," he replied. **He hid his annoyance at her continually assuming to know what he was thinking.** "They were brightened by the exercise."

A short pause followed this speech, and Mrs. Hurst began again, "I have an excessive regard for Miss Jane Bennet. She is really a very sweet girl. I wish with all my heart she were well settled, but with such a father and mother, and such low connections, I am afraid there is no chance of it."

"I think I have heard you say that their uncle is an attorney in Meryton."

"Yes, and they have another, who lives somewhere near Cheapside."

"That is capital," added her sister, and they both laughed heartily.

"If they had uncles enough to fill all Cheapside," defended Bingley, "it would not make them one jot less agreeable."

"But it must materially lessen their chance of marrying men of any consideration in the world," Darcy replied. **His friend may be flown away with emotion, but that only meant Bingley needed to consider the logic of his choice all the more. Darcy was sure logic would triumph over Bingley's latest inclination of love.**

To this speech Bingley made no answer. Nevertheless, his sisters gave it their hearty assent, and indulged their mirth for some time at the expense of their dear friend's vulgar relations.

However, with a renewal of tenderness they returned to her room and sat with Jane till summoned to coffee. She was still very poorly, and Elizabeth would not quit her till late in the evening when she had the comfort of seeing her sleep. When she did go downstairs, it was because she thought it more right than pleasant that she make an appearance. On entering the drawing room she found the whole party at loo, and was immediately invited to join them. Suspecting them to be playing high she declined. Making her sister the excuse, she said she would amuse herself with a book for the short time she could stay below.

Mr. Hurst looked at her with astonishment. "Do you prefer reading to cards? That is rather singular."

"Miss Eliza Bennet," said Miss Bingley, "despises cards. She is a great reader, and has no pleasure in anything else."

"I deserve neither such praise nor such censure," admonished Elizabeth. **She did her best not to meet the probing gaze of Mr. Darcy.** "I am *not* a great reader, and I have pleasure in many things."

"In nursing your sister I am sure you have pleasure," said Bingley, "and I hope it will be soon increased by seeing her well."

Elizabeth thanked him, and then walked towards the table where a few books were lying.

He immediately offered to fetch her others—all that his library afforded. "And I wish my collection were larger for your benefit and my own credit, but I am an idle fellow, and though I have not many, I have more than I ever looked into."

"I can suit myself perfectly well with what is before me," Elizabeth assured him.

"What a delightful library you have at Pemberley, Mr. Darcy," said Miss Bingley.

"It ought to be good," he replied. "It has been the work of many generations."

Elizabeth was now forced to acknowledge him, though she said nothing.

"And then you have added so much to it yourself," Miss Bingley continued, "you are always buying books."

"I cannot comprehend the neglect of a family library in

such days as these." **Mr. Darcy glanced at Elizabeth's hands and she felt compelled to hide her selection from his studious view.**

"Neglect! I am sure you neglect nothing that can add to the beauties of that noble place. Charles, when you build your house, I wish it may be half as delightful as Pemberley." **Miss Bingley gave Elizabeth a superior look, and in that moment Elizabeth understood the woman desired her to know how very intimate she was of the details of Mr. Darcy's life. Elizabeth concealed a laugh. Why should she care if Mrs. Bingley had her sights on Mr. Darcy? It was not as if Elizabeth entertained thoughts of marrying Darcy herself.**

"I wish it may," Bingley agreed.

"But I would really advise you to make your purchase in that neighborhood," his sister persisted, "and take Pemberley for a kind of model. There is not a finer county in England than Derbyshire, or better families."

"With all my heart," Bingley assured her, "I will buy Pemberley itself if Darcy will sell it."

"I am talking of possibilities, Charles."

"Upon my word, Caroline," he answered, "I should think it more possible to get Pemberley by purchase than by imitation. **I do not have the lifetimes to match the generations of Darcy's family, nor the great discipline to see it through.**"

Elizabeth was so caught with what passed, as to leave her very little attention for her book. Soon she laid it wholly aside, drew near the card table, and stationed herself between Mr. Bingley and his eldest sister to observe the game.

"Has Miss Darcy grown much since the spring?" inquired Miss Bingley. "Will she be as tall as I am?"

"I think she will," said Mr. Darcy. "She is now about Miss Elizabeth's height, or rather taller."

Elizabeth felt a small chill as he said her name.

"How I long to see her again." **Miss Bingley's voice lifted in her raptures.** "I never met with anybody who delighted me so much. Such a countenance, such manners, and so extremely accomplished for her age! Her performance on the pianoforte is exquisite."

"It is amazing to me," said Bingley, "how all young ladies can have the patience to be so very accomplished."

"All young ladies accomplished? My dear Charles, what do you mean?"

"Yes, all of them, I think. They all paint tables, cover screens, and net purses. I scarcely know anyone who cannot do all this, and I am sure I never heard a young lady spoken of for the first time, without being informed that she was very accomplished."

"Your list of the common extent of accomplishments," said Darcy, "has too much truth, but I am very far from agreeing with you in your estimation of ladies in general. The word is applied too generously, and I cannot boast of knowing more than half-a-dozen, in the whole range of my acquaintance, that are really accomplished."

"Nor I, I am sure," said Miss Bingley.

"Then," Elizabeth observed, "you must comprehend a great deal in your idea of an accomplished woman."

"Yes, I do comprehend a great deal in it." **Darcy's blue eyes met hers and she held his gaze boldly. She wondered at his straightforward attention.**

"Oh, certainly!" cried his faithful assistant to draw their attention once more to herself. "A truly accomplished woman must have a thorough knowledge of music, singing, drawing, dancing, and the modern languages, to deserve the word. And she must possess a certain something in her air and manner of walking, the tone of her voice, her address and expressions, or the word will be but half-deserved."

"All this she must possess," agreed Darcy, "and to all this she must yet add something more substantial, in the improvement of her mind by extensive reading."

"I am no longer surprised at your knowing only six accomplished women." **Elizabeth forced herself to smile though she was not sure if she felt somewhat of a slight at the comment, or a challenge. Something within her wanted to challenge him, to irritate him just to see if she could raise his temper and crack the calm façade that normally graced his features, much like one could crack an expensive vase upon the floor.** "I rather wonder now at your knowing *any*."

"Are you so severe upon your own sex?"

Was she mistaken, or did she see a playful light enter his eyes? Was he teasing her? Surely, not. Elizabeth ignored the others in the room, captivated by the look. "I never saw such a woman. I never saw such capacity, and taste, and application, and elegance, united as you describe."

Mrs. Hurst and Miss Bingley did their part in breaking the small spell when they both protested the injustice of her implied doubt. They both claimed to know many women who answered this description. Mr. Hurst called them to order with bitter complaints of their inattention to their cards. As all conversation was thereby at an end, Elizabeth soon afterwards left the room, glad for an excuse to leave their company.

Darcy was no less affected by the brief moment that passed between them, and watched with some small regret as she went to her sister's bedside. Though he hardly agreed with her ideas, he found himself interested in how she expressed them.

"Elizabeth Bennet," said Miss Bingley, when the door was closed, "is one of those young ladies who seek to recommend themselves to the other sex by undervaluing their own. With many men, I daresay, it succeeds. But, in my opinion, it is a paltry device and a very mean art."

"Undoubtedly," Darcy replied, to whom this remark was chiefly addressed, "there is a meanness in all the arts which ladies sometimes condescend to employ for captivation."

Miss Bingley was not entirely satisfied with this reply and did not continue the subject.

Elizabeth joined them again only to say that her sister was worse, and that she could not leave her. Bingley urged that Mr. Jones be sent for, and it was settled that the apothecary should come early in the morning if Miss Bennet were not decidedly better. Bingley was quite uncomfortable. His sisters declared they were miserable; however, they solaced their woes by duets after supper, while he could find no better relief to his feelings than by giving his housekeeper directions that every attention might be paid to the sick lady and her sister.

CHAPTER NINE

*E*LIZABETH PASSED THE NIGHT in her sister's room, and in the morning had the pleasure of being able to send an acceptable answer to the inquiries which she very early received from Mr. Bingley by a housemaid, and some hours afterwards from the two elegant ladies who waited on his sisters. She requested to have a note sent to Longbourn, desiring her mother to visit Jane, and form her own judgment of her situation. The note was immediately dispatched, and its contents as quickly complied with. Mrs. Bennet, accompanied by her two youngest girls, reached Netherfield soon after the family breakfast.

Had she found Jane in any apparent danger, Mrs. Bennet would have been very miserable, but being satisfied on seeing her that her illness was not alarming, she had no wish of her recovering immediately, as her restoration to health would probably remove her from Netherfield. She would not listen, therefore, to her daughter's proposal of being carried home; neither did the apothecary, who arrived about the same time, think it at all advisable. After sitting a little while with Jane, on Miss Bingley's appearance and invitation, the mother and three daughters all attended her into the breakfast parlor. Bingley met them with hopes that Mrs. Bennet had not found Miss Bennet worse than she expected.

"Indeed I have, sir," was her answer. "She is a great deal too ill to be moved. Mr. Jones says we must not think of it. We must trespass a little longer on your kindness."

"Removed!" cried Bingley. "It must not be thought of. My sister, I am sure, will not hear of her removal."

"You may depend upon it, Madam," said Miss Bingley, with cold civility, "that Miss Bennet will receive every possible attention while she remains with us."

Mrs. Bennet was profuse in her acknowledgments, before adding, "If it was not for such good friends I do not know what would become of her, for she is very ill indeed, and suffers a vast deal, though with the greatest patience in the world, which is always the way with her, for she has, without exception, the sweetest temper I have ever met with. I often tell my other girls they are nothing to her. You have a sweet room here, Mr. Bingley, and a charming prospect over the gravel walk. I do not know a place in the country that is equal to Netherfield. You will not think of quitting it in a hurry, I hope, though you have but a short lease."

"Whatever I do is done in a hurry," he replied honestly, "and therefore if I should resolve to quit Netherfield, I should probably be off in five minutes. At present, however, I consider myself as quite fixed here."

"That is exactly what I should have supposed of you," said Elizabeth.

"You begin to comprehend me, do you?" he asked happily, turning towards her.

"Oh, yes! I understand you perfectly."

"I wish I might take this for a compliment, but I am afraid it is pitiful to be so easily seen through."

"It does not follow that a deep, intricate character is more or less estimable than such a one as yours."

"Lizzy," cried her mother, "remember where you are, and do not run on in the wild manner as you are inclined to do at home."

"I did not know," continued Bingley immediately, "that you were a studier of character. It must be an amusing occupation."

"Yes, but intricate characters are the most amusing." She gave a pointed glance at Mr. Darcy. "They have at least that advantage."

"The country," said Darcy, "can in general supply but a few subjects for such a study. A country neighborhood is a very confined and unvarying society."

"But people themselves alter so much," Elizabeth said to the contrary, not that she so much believed it as she liked disagreeing with him. "There is something new to be observed in them forever."

"Yes, indeed," stated Mrs. Bennet, offended by his manner of mentioning a country neighborhood. "I assure you there is quite as much going on in the country as in town."

Everybody was surprised, and Darcy, after looking at her for a moment, turned silently away.

Mrs. Bennet, who fancied she had gained a complete victory over him, continued her triumph. "I cannot see that London has any great advantage over the country, for my part, except the shops and public places. The country is a vast deal pleasanter, is it not, Mr. Bingley?"

"When I am in the country," he replied, "I never wish to leave it. When I am in town it is pretty much the same. They have each their advantages, and I can be equally happy in either."

"Aye, that is because you have the right disposition. But that gentleman," Mrs. Bennet looked at Darcy, "seemed to think the country was nothing at all."

"Indeed, Mamma, you are mistaken," said Elizabeth, blushing for her mother. **It was one thing for her to debate Mr. Darcy, for she fancied herself more adapt at forming logical arguments, but quite another for her mother to do it. Not for the first time in her life she wished she could will the woman to be quiet.** "You quite mistook Mr. Darcy. He only meant that there was not such a variety of people to be met with in the country as in the town, which you must acknowledge to be true."

"Certainly, my dear, nobody said there were, but as to not meeting with many people in this neighborhood, I believe there are few neighborhoods larger. We dine with four-and-twenty families."

Nothing but concern for Elizabeth could enable Bingley to keep his countenance. His sister was less delicate, and directed her eyes towards Mr. Darcy with a very expressive smile. Elizabeth, for the sake of saying something that might turn her mother's thoughts, now asked her if Charlotte Lucas had been at Longbourn since her coming away.

"Yes, she called yesterday with her father. What an agreeable man Sir William is, Mr. Bingley, is he not? So much the man of fashion, so genteel and easy! He always has something to say to everybody. *That* is my idea of good breeding. Those persons who fancy themselves very important, and never open their mouths, quite mistake the matter."

"Did Charlotte dine with you?" **Elizabeth refused to look at Mr. Darcy, but could not help wonder at his silence. Perhaps he** knew it was pointless to argue with a woman such as Mrs. Bennet. Or, perhaps, he felt the conversation was now beneath him and did not deign to rejoin it.

"No, she went home. I fancy she was needed to make the mince-pies. For my part, Mr. Bingley, my daughters are brought up very differently. I always keep servants that can do their own work and they are never expected in the kitchen. But everybody is to judge for themselves how to raise their children, and the Lucases are a very good sort of girls, I assure you. It is a pity they are not handsome. Not that I think Charlotte so very plain, but then she is our particular friend."

"She seems a very pleasant young woman," Mr. Bingley offered.

"Oh, dear, yes," Mrs. Bennet insisted, "but you must admit she is very plain. Lady Lucas herself has often said so, and envied me Jane's beauty. I do not like to boast of my own child, but to be sure, Jane—one does not often see anybody better looking. It is what everybody says. I do not trust my own partiality. When she was only fifteen, there was a man at my brother Gardiner's in town so much in love with her that my sister-in-law was sure he would make her an offer before we came away. But, he did not. However, he wrote some verses on her, and they were very pretty."

"And so ended his affection," said Elizabeth impatiently. "There has been many a love, I fancy, overcome in the same way. I wonder who first discovered the efficacy of poetry in driving away love."

"I believe many to consider poetry as the food of love," said Darcy, turning his attention back to the conversation.

"Of a fine, stout, healthy love it may. Everything nourishes what is strong already. But if it be only a slight, thin sort of inclination, I am convinced that one good sonnet will starve it entirely away."

Darcy only smiled. **The expression, directed solely at her, took her by surprise; and thus ended any further comment she would make on the subject.** The general pause which ensued made Elizabeth tremble lest her mother should expose herself again. She longed to speak, but could think of nothing to say, and after a short silence Mrs. Bennet began repeating her thanks to Mr. Bingley for his kindness to Jane, with an apology for troubling him also with Lizzy. Mr. Bingley was unaffectedly civil in his answer, and forced his younger sister to be civil also, and say what the occasion required. Miss Bingley performed her part without much graciousness, but Mrs. Bennet was satisfied, and soon afterwards ordered her carriage. Upon this signal, the youngest of her daughters put herself forward. The two girls had been whispering to each other during the whole visit, and the result of it was, that the youngest should tax Mr. Bingley with having promised on his first coming into the country to give a ball at Netherfield.

Lydia felt herself very equal to address Mr. Bingley on the subject of the ball. She had high animal spirits, and a sort of natural self-consequence, which the attention of the officers, to whom her uncle's good dinners, and her own easy manners recommended her, had increased into assurance. **"Have you settled on a date for your ball, Mr. Bingley? You will remember you promised to hold one here at Netherfield. All the neighbors have talked about it with such enthusiasm. It would be the most shameful thing in the world if you did not."**

His answer to this sudden attack was delightful to Mrs. Bennet's ear. "I am perfectly ready, I assure you, to keep my engagement. When your sister is recovered, you shall, if you please, name the very day of the ball. But you would not wish to be dancing when she is ill."

Lydia declared herself satisfied. "Oh, yes! It would be

much better to wait till Jane is well, and by that time most likely Captain Carter will be at Meryton again. And when you have given your ball, I shall insist on their giving one also. I shall tell Colonel Forster it will be quite a shame if he does not."

Mrs. Bennet and her daughters then departed, and Elizabeth returned instantly to Jane, leaving her and her relations' behavior to the remarks of the two ladies and Mr. Darcy; the latter of whom, however, could not be prevailed on to join in their censure of her, in spite of all Miss Bingley's witticisms on fine eyes.

CHAPTER TEN

THE DAY PASSED MUCH AS THE DAY BEFORE had done. Mrs. Hurst and Miss Bingley had spent some hours of the morning with the invalid, who slowly continued to mend. In the evening Elizabeth joined their party in the drawing room. The loo table, however, did not appear. Mr. Darcy was writing. Miss Bingley took a seat near him to watch the progress of his letter. She repeatedly called off his attention by relaying messages to his sister. Mr. Hurst and Mr. Bingley were at piquet, and Mrs. Hurst was observing their game.

Elizabeth took up some needlework, and was sufficiently amused in attending to what passed between Darcy and his companion. The perpetual commendations of the lady, either on his handwriting, or on the evenness of his lines, or on the length of his letter, with the perfect unconcern with which her praises were received, formed a curious dialogue, and were exactly in union with her opinion of each.

"How delighted Miss Darcy will be to receive such a letter!"
He made no answer.

"You write uncommonly fast."

"You are mistaken. I write rather slowly."

"How many letters you must have occasion to write in the course of a year. Letters of business, too. How odious I should think them!"

"It is fortunate, then, that they fall to my lot instead of yours."

"Pray tell your sister that I long to see her."

"I have already told her so once, by your desire."

"I am afraid you do not like your pen. Let me mend it for you. I mend pens remarkably well."

"Thank you, but I always mend my own."

"How can you contrive to write so even?"
He was silent.

"Tell your sister I am delighted to hear of her improvement on the harp, and pray let her know that I am quite in raptures with her beautiful little design for a table."

"Will you give me leave to defer your raptures till I write again? At present I have not the room to do them justice."

"Oh, it is of no consequence. I shall see her in January. But do you always write such charming long letters to her, Mr. Darcy?"

"They are generally long, but whether always charming it is not for me to determine."

"It is a rule with me that a person who can write a long letter with ease, cannot write ill."

"That will not do for a compliment to Darcy, Caroline," interrupted her brother, "because he does not write with ease. He studies too much for words of four syllables. Do not you, Darcy?"

"My style of writing is very different from yours."

"Charles writes in the most careless way imaginable," said Miss Bingley. "He leaves out half his words, and blots the rest."

"My ideas flow so rapidly that I have not time to express them—by which means my letters sometimes convey no ideas at all."

"Your humility, Mr. Bingley, must disarm reproof," said Elizabeth.

"Nothing is more deceitful," said Darcy, "than the appearance of humility. It is often only carelessness of opinion, and sometimes an indirect boast."

"And which of the two do you call my little recent piece of modesty?" Bingley asked.

"The indirect boast. You are really proud of your defects in writing, because you consider them as proceeding from a rapidity of thought and carelessness of execution, which, if not estimable, you think at least highly interesting. The power of doing anything with quickness is always prized much by the possessor, and often without any attention to the imperfection of the performance. When you told Mrs. Bennet this morning that if you ever resolved upon quitting Netherfield you should be gone in five minutes, you meant it to be a sort of panegyric, of compliment to yourself—and yet what is so laudable in an instance which must leave necessary business undone, and can be of no real advantage to yourself or anyone else?"

"Nay," cried Bingley, "this is too much, to remember at night all the foolish things that were said in the morning. And yet, upon my honor, I believe what I said of myself to be true."

"I am by no means convinced that you would be gone with such celerity. Your conduct would be as dependent on chance as that of any man I know. If, as you were mounting your horse, a friend were to say, 'Bingley, you had better stay till next week,' you would probably not go, and at another word you might stay a month."

Elizabeth watched Darcy carefully as he spoke, though he did not return the attention. He seemed to consider his letter, though his pen did not move over paper. To his back, she said, "Your statements have only proved that Mr. Bingley did not do justice to his own disposition. You have shown him off much more than he did himself."

Bingley grinned. "I am exceedingly gratified by your converting what my friend said into a compliment on the sweetness of my temper, but I am afraid you are giving it a turn which Darcy by no means intended. He would certainly think better of me if, under such a circumstance, I were to give a flat denial and ride off as fast as I could."

Elizabeth paused in her needlework. "Would Mr. Darcy consider the rashness of your original intentions as atoned for by your obstinacy in adhering to it?"

"Upon my word, I cannot exactly explain the matter." **Bingley gestured helplessly.** "Darcy must speak for himself."

"You expect me to account for opinions which you choose to call mine, but which I have never acknowledged." **Darcy turned from his letter.** "Allowing the case to stand according to your representation, you must remember, Miss Bennet, that the friend who requested the delay of his plan asked without offering one argument as to why it should be so."

"To yield easily to the *persuasion* of a friend has no merit with you?" **Elizabeth set her needlework aside and did not bother to pick it back up.**

"To yield without conviction is no compliment to the understanding of either."

"You allow nothing for the influence of friendship and affection. A regard for the requester would often make one readily yield to a request, without waiting for reasons. In general, between friend and friend, where one of them is desired by the other to change a resolution of no very great moment, should you think ill of that person for complying with the desire, without waiting to be argued into it?"

"Will it not be advisable, before we proceed, to arrange with rather more precision the degree of importance which is to appertain to this request, as well as the degree of intimacy subsisting between the parties?"

"By all means," cried Bingley in obvious exasperation, "let us hear all the particulars, not forgetting their comparative height and size. That will have more weight in the argument, Miss Bennet, than you may be aware of. I assure you, if Darcy were not such a great tall fellow, in comparison with myself, I should not pay him half so much deference."

Mr. Darcy smiled, but Elizabeth thought she could perceive that he was rather offended, and therefore checked her laugh. Miss Bingley warmly took up his defense by expressing her disapproval of her brother for talking such nonsense.

"I see your design, Bingley," said his friend. "You dislike an argument, and want to silence this."

"Perhaps I do. Arguments are too much like disputes. If you and Miss Bennet will defer yours till I am out of the room, I shall be very thankful. Then you may say whatever you like of me."

Elizabeth thought this too bad, for she found she perversely enjoyed arguing with Mr. Darcy. He seemed of such a character to rise to the occasion without being easily offended. Such intellectual pursuits entertained Elizabeth, all the more so when she saw how they annoyed Miss Bingley.

"What you ask," said Elizabeth, "is no sacrifice on my side. Mr. Darcy had better finish his letter."

Mr. Darcy took her advice, and did finish his letter.

When that business was over, he applied to Miss Bingley and Elizabeth for an indulgence of some music. Miss Bingley moved with some alacrity to the pianoforte; and, after a polite request that Elizabeth would lead the way which the other as politely and more earnestly refused, she seated herself.

Mrs. Hurst sang with her sister. Elizabeth could not help observing, as she turned over some music-books that lay on the instrument, how frequently Mr. Darcy's eyes were fixed on her. She hardly knew how she could be an object of admiration to so great a man, and yet that he should look at her because he disliked her was still more strange. She could only imagine that she drew his notice because there was something more wrong and reprehensible, according to his ideas of right, in her than in any other person present. The supposition did not pain her for she told herself that she liked him too little to care for his approbation. **And yet, her eyes moved to his often to see if he still watched.**

After playing some Italian songs, Miss Bingley varied the charm by a lively Scotch air. Soon afterwards Mr. Darcy, drawing near Elizabeth, said to her, "Do you not feel a great inclination, Miss Bennet, to seize such an opportunity of dancing a reel?"

She smiled, but made no answer. He repeated the question, with some surprise at her silence.

"Oh," she said, "I heard you before, but I could not immediately determine what to say in reply. You wanted me to say 'Yes,' so you might have the pleasure of despising my taste. But I always delight in overthrowing those kinds of schemes, and cheating a person of their premeditated contempt. I have, therefore, made up my mind to tell you that I do not want to dance a reel at all—and now despise me if you dare."

"Indeed I do not dare."

Elizabeth, having rather expected to affront him, was amazed at his gallantry. For a moment, her knowledge of him became mixed with her daydreams of him, and she had to remind herself of the stark difference in the two. He was not the gallant man she first pictured, but a prideful, stubborn gentleman. And the smile he bestowed upon her surely did not mean anything. It was merely a look, and his attention was because he had nothing better to attend to at the moment. She was there, convenient for the sake of his conversation, and that was all. Elizabeth did not flatter herself beyond those points.

Darcy's thoughts ran a completely different course than the object of his attention supposed. He had never been so bewitched by any woman as he was by her. There was a mixture of sweetness and archness in her manner which made it difficult for her to affront anybody. Many ladies, many men for that matter, did not dare to contradict him, and he found he enjoyed hearing her speak her mind. He really believed that, were it not for the inferiority of her connections, he should be in some danger.

He wanted to say more to her, but Miss Bingley stood from the instrument and implored Elizabeth to take her turn. Darcy withdrew, taking a seat some ways away from the pianoforte. Mrs. Hurst left her post, leaving Elizabeth to sing her song. She did not. Instead, she merely played, her eyes fixed upon the keys as if there were nothing else in the room.

Darcy watched her at his leisure, not really thinking of anything beyond the curve of her neck and shoulder in the light. Her lips moved, as if she sang softly to herself in an effort to keep a steady pace with her fingers. Resting his elbow on the arm of his chair, he lifted the back of his hand to rest against his mouth. He imagined her lips to move against his, a tender kiss that he dare not let his mind indulge before so many eyes. Seeing Miss Bingley

studying him with suspicion, he dropped his hand and endeavored to appear indifferent.

Miss Bingley saw, or suspected enough to be jealous of her rival for Darcy's attentions, and her great anxiety for the recovery of her dear friend Jane received some assistance from her desire of getting rid of Elizabeth. She often tried to provoke Darcy into disliking her guest, by talking of their supposed marriage, and planning his happiness in such an alliance.

"I hope," said she, as they were walking together in the shrubbery the next day, "you will give your mother-in-law a few hints, when this desirable event takes place, as to the advantage of holding her tongue. If you can manage it, do stop the younger girls from running after officers. **There is something off about the way Lydia looks at them.** And, if I may mention so delicate a subject, endeavor to check that little something, bordering on conceit, which your lady possesses."

"Have you anything else to propose for my domestic felicity?"

"Oh, yes! Do let the portraits of your uncle and aunt Philips be placed in the gallery at Pemberley. Put them next to your great-uncle the judge. They are in the same profession, you know, only in different lines. As for Elizabeth's picture, you must not have it taken, for what painter could do justice to those beautiful eyes?"

"It would not be easy, indeed, to catch their expression, but their color and shape, and the eyelashes, so remarkably fine, might be copied."

At that moment they were met from another walk by Mrs. Hurst and Elizabeth herself.

"I did not know that you intended to walk," said Miss Bingley, in some confusion, lest they had been overheard.

"You used us abominably ill," answered Mrs. Hurst, "running away without telling us that you were coming out."

Then taking the disengaged arm of Mr. Darcy, she left Elizabeth to walk by herself. The path just admitted three. Mr. Darcy felt their rudeness, and immediately said, "This walk is not wide enough for our party. We had better go into the avenue."

But Elizabeth, who had not the least inclination to remain with them, laughingly answered, "No, no, stay where you are. You are charmingly grouped. The picturesque would be spoiled by admitting a fourth."

Darcy watched her run happily down the path, away from them, and was sorry to see her go. He imagined she was excited at the hope of being at home again in a day or two. Her sister was already much recovered and intended to leave her room for a couple of hours that evening. Feeling a tug on his arm, he was forced to continue on with Bingley's sisters. He said nothing and they contented themselves with comments on the newly favored subject of Elizabeth and her family.

CHAPTER ELEVEN

HEN THE LADIES REMOVED AFTER DINNER, Elizabeth hurried to her sister, and seeing her well guarded from cold, attended her into the drawing room where she was welcomed by her two friends. Elizabeth had never seen them so agreeable as they were during the hour which passed before the gentlemen appeared. Their powers of conversation were considerable. They could describe an entertainment with accuracy, relate an anecdote with humor, and laugh at their acquaintance with spirit.

But when the gentlemen entered, Jane was no longer the first object. Miss Bingley's eyes were instantly turned toward Darcy, and she had something to say to him before he had advanced many steps. He addressed himself to Miss Bennet, with a polite congratulation. Mr. Hurst also made her a slight bow, and said he was "very glad." However, diffuseness and warmth remained for Bingley's salutation. He was full of joy and attention. The first half-hour was spent in piling up the fire, lest she should suffer from the change of room, and she removed at his desire to the other side of the fireplace, that she might be further from the door. He then sat down by her, and talked scarcely to anyone else. Elizabeth, at work in the opposite corner, saw it all with great delight.

When tea was over, Mr. Hurst reminded his sister-in-law of the card table, but in vain. She had obtained private intelligence that Mr. Darcy did not wish for cards. Mr. Hurst soon found even his open petition rejected. She assured him that no one intended to play, and the silence of the whole party on the subject seemed to justify her. Mr. Hurst had therefore nothing to do, but to stretch himself on one of the sofas and go to sleep. Darcy took up a book and Miss Bingley soon after did the same. Mrs. Hurst, principally occupied in playing with her bracelets and rings, joined now and then in her brother's conversation with Miss Bennet.

Miss Bingley's attention was as much engaged in watching Mr. Darcy's progress through his book as in reading her own, and she was perpetually making some inquiry or looking at his page. She could not win him, however, to any conversation. He merely answered her question, and read on. At length, exhausted by the attempt to be amused with her own book, which she had only chosen because it was the second volume of his, she gave a great yawn and said, "How pleasant it is to spend an evening in this way. I declare there is no enjoyment like reading. How much sooner one tires of anything other than a book. When I have a house of my own, I shall be miserable if I do not have an excellent library."

No one made any reply. She yawned again, threw aside her book, and cast her eyes round the room in quest for some amusement. Hearing her brother mention a ball to Miss Bennet, she turned suddenly towards him and said, "By the bye, Charles, are you really serious in meditating a dance at Netherfield? I would advise you, before you determine on it, to consult the wishes of the present party. I am much mistaken if there are not some among us to whom a ball would be rather a punishment than a pleasure."

"If you mean Darcy," said her brother, "he may go to bed, if he chooses, before it begins, for the ball is quite a settled thing."

"I should like balls infinitely better," she replied with a glance toward Darcy to make sure he heard her, "if they were carried on in a different manner. There is something insufferably tedious in the usual process of such a meeting. It would surely be much more rational if conversation instead of dancing were made the order of the day."

"Much more rational," Bingley answered, his attention still not fully on his sister's interruptions, "but it would not be near, so much like a ball."

Miss Bingley made no answer. **She smiled at Darcy with no true conception of his completely ignoring her. Her comment had, after all, been solely to impress him with the intelligent pursuits of her mind.** Soon afterwards she got up and walked about the room. Her figure was elegant, and she walked well, but Darcy, at whom it was all aimed, was still inflexibly studious. In the desperation of her feelings, she resolved on one effort more, and, turning to Elizabeth, said, "Miss Eliza Bennet, let me persuade you to take a turn about the room. I assure you it is very refreshing after sitting so long in one attitude."

Elizabeth was surprised, but agreed. Miss Bingley succeeded no less in the real object of her civility, for Mr. Darcy looked up. He was as much awake to the novelty of attention in that quarter as Elizabeth herself could be, and unconsciously closed his book. He was directly invited to join their party, but he declined it, observing, "There can be but two motives for your choosing to walk up and down the room together, either of which my joining you would interfere."

"What could he mean?" Miss Bingley asked Elizabeth, clearly dying to know. "Can you understand him?"

"Not at all, but depend upon it, he means to be severe on us, and our surest way of disappointing him will be to ask nothing about it."

Miss Bingley, however, was incapable of disappointing Mr. Darcy in anything, and persevered therefore in requiring an explanation of his two motives.

"I have not the smallest objection to explaining them," said he, as soon as she allowed him to speak. "You either choose this method of passing the evening because you are in each other's confidence and have secret affairs to discuss, or because you are conscious that your figures appear to the greatest advantage in walking. If the first, I would be completely in your way, and if the second, I can admire you much better as I sit by the fire."

"Shocking!" cried Miss Bingley. "I never heard anything so abominable. How shall we punish him for such a speech?"

"Nothing so easy, if you have the inclination," said Elizabeth. "Tease him and laugh at him. Intimate as you are, you must know how it is to be done."

Elizabeth had never been so conscious of her figure as she was at the moment. His speech hinted that he watched them in a way much more than in passing. A heat built within her stomach and she dared not look at him for fear she would see exactly where his eyes wandered. What did he think when he looked at her? Did he find pleasure in what he saw? Did he look at her often in such a bold manner? If so, his expressions never gave away his thoughts.

"But upon my honor, I do not," Miss Bingley said, drawing

Elizabeth's thoughts back to her walking companion. "I do assure you that my intimacy has not yet taught me that. I cannot tease calmness of manner and presence of mind. Should we laugh, we will expose ourselves as foolish for attempting to laugh without cause."

When she glanced at him, she found he studied them and listened to everything Miss Bingley said, for the woman was speaking loud enough for anyone who cared to hear. Elizabeth did not answer so vociferously, though she did not hide her thoughts in a whisper. "I fear then that Mr. Darcy is not to be laughed at."

"Miss Bingley has given me too much credit," said Darcy. "The wisest and the best of men—nay, the wisest and best of their actions—may be rendered ridiculous by a person whose first object in life is a joke."

"Certainly," replied Elizabeth. "There are such people, but I hope I am not one of them. I hope I never ridicule what is wise and good. Follies and nonsense, whims and inconsistencies, do divert me, I own, and I laugh at them whenever I can. But I suppose these are precisely what you are without."

"Perhaps that is not possible for anyone," said he. "But it has been the study of my life to avoid those weaknesses which often expose a strong understanding to ridicule."

"Such as vanity and pride." **Elizabeth studied him as she tried to fully determine his mysterious character.**

"Yes, vanity is a weakness indeed," he agreed. **There was something to his tone that caused a small shiver to course over her body and she delicately pulled from Miss Bingley's arm so the woman would not detect it.** Darcy continued, "But pride; where there is a real superiority of mind, pride will be always under good regulation."

Elizabeth turned away to hide a smile.

"Your examination of Mr. Darcy is over, I presume," said

Miss Bingley, moving to take up Elizabeth's arm once more. **She held tighter to it than before and turned in their stroll so they walked away from the object of their musings.** "Pray what is the result?"

"I am perfectly convinced by it that Mr. Darcy has no defect." **As they moved, she tried not to be self-conscious.** "He owns it himself without disguise."

"No," said Darcy, "I have made no such pretension. I have faults enough, but I hope they are not of understanding. My temper I dare not vouch for. It is too little yielding—certainly too little for the convenience of the world. I cannot easily forgive the follies and vices of others, nor their offenses against me. My temper would perhaps be called resentful, and my good opinion once lost is lost forever."

"That is a failing indeed," agreed Elizabeth. They turned to face him, strolling back to where he sat. "Implacable resentment is a shade in a character. But you have chosen your fault well. I really cannot laugh at it. You are safe from me. Though it is an uncommon advantage, it would be a great loss to me to have many such acquaintances for I dearly love a laugh."

"There is in every disposition a tendency to some particular evil—a natural defect, which not even the best education can overcome," he said.

"And your defect is to hate everybody."

"And yours," he replied with a surprisingly bright smile, "is willfully to misunderstand them."

Elizabeth opened her mouth to answer, completely unaware of how the eyes of the room had focused on their discussion. At some point she had wandered away from Miss Bingley and now stood close to him; not so close as to be improper, but close enough to turn away others from their conversation.

"Do let us have a little music," cried Miss Bingley, tired of a conversation in which she had no share.

Elizabeth jolted in surprise, blinking rapidly as she broke eye contact with Darcy. She took quick steps away from him toward the safety of Jane's presence. Her sister, though weak from the illness looked perfectly content to be the source of Mr. Bingley's unwavering attention. The firelight gave her a becoming glow, which probably hid the feminine blush that budding affection often brought on.

"Louisa, you will not mind my waking Mr. Hurst?" Miss Bingley asked. Her sister had not the smallest objection, and the pianoforte was opened.

Darcy watched Elizabeth move nearer her sister, sorry that their discussion was at an end. He found himself taken with the directness of her attention and the playfulness of her manner. She spoke of not being able to tease him, and yet her words had done just that. He could not be hurt by such attention from her, for there was no spite in her manner or words. When she looked at him, he felt as if they might someday be intimate friends. However, the spell he felt under her attention was successfully broken by the sound of music, and after a few moments' recollection he was not sorry for it. Intimate friends? The idea was laughable. Whatever intimacies he wanted to develop between them was not exclusive to friendship. It was best if he did not pursue such impulses. He began to feel the danger of paying Elizabeth too much open attention.

CHAPTER TWELVE

*I*N CONSEQUENCE OF AN AGREEMENT between the
sisters, Elizabeth wrote the next morning to their mother,
to beg that the carriage might be sent for them in the course of
the day. But Mrs. Bennet, who had calculated on her daughters remaining at Netherfield till the following Tuesday, which
would exactly finish Jane's week, could not bring herself to
receive them with pleasure before that time. In her letter she
added her denial that, if Mr. Bingley and his sister pressed them
to stay longer, she could spare them very well. Fearful of it being
considered that they intruded needlessly long, Elizabeth urged
Jane to borrow Mr. Bingley's carriage immediately. At length it
was settled that their original design of leaving Netherfield that
morning should be mentioned, and the request made.

The communication excited many professions of concern.
Enough was said of wishing them to stay at least till the following day to work on Jane, and their going was deferred till the

morrow. Miss Bingley was then sorry that she had proposed the delay, for her jealousy and dislike of one sister much exceeded her affection for the other.

The master of the house heard with real sorrow that they were to go so soon, and repeatedly tried to persuade Miss Bennet that it would not be safe for her, that she was not recovered enough, but Jane was firm where she felt herself to be right.

To Mr. Darcy it was welcome intelligence for he felt Elizabeth had been at Netherfield long enough. She attracted him more than he liked. Miss Bingley was uncivil to *her*, and more teasing than usual to himself. He resolved to be particularly careful that no sign of admiration should *now* escape him, nothing that could elevate Elizabeth with the hope of influencing his felicity; sensible that if such an idea had been suggested his behavior during the last day must have material weight in confirming or crushing it. This was the only way to successfully banish her from him, for any outcome of the further developing of their friendship could only complicate his feelings and devastate hers. Steady to his purpose, he scarcely spoke ten words to her through the whole of Saturday, and though they were at one time left by themselves for half-an-hour, he adhered most conscientiously to his book, and would not even look at her. **This effort it took cost him his place, and he read the same paragraph nearly twenty times without retaining a word of it.**

On Sunday, after morning service, the separation, so agreeable to almost all, took place. Now as the visit came to an end, Miss Bingley's civility to Elizabeth increased very rapidly, as did her affection for Jane; and when they parted, after assuring the latter of the pleasure it would always give her to see her either at Longbourn or Netherfield, and embracing her most tenderly, she even shook hands with the former. Elizabeth took leave of the whole party in the liveliest of spirits, excited by the prospect of going home.

After a day of being ignored by Mr. Darcy, Elizabeth was surprised by his attention when coming to see them off. When she stepped towards the carriage, it looked for the briefest of moments as if he would hand her up. Instead, Mr. Bingley extended his hand first and he delivered her safely within. Darcy's eyes fixed on her as the carriage rolled away and she found herself leaning against the window overlong to stare back. Neither of them pulled their gaze away first and it was only after the carriage turned from view that the contact was severed.

They were not welcomed home very cordially by their mother. Mrs. Bennet wondered at their coming, and thought them very wrong to give so much trouble, and was sure Jane would have caught cold again. But their father, though very laconic in his expressions of pleasure, was really glad to see them. He had felt their importance in the family circle for the evening conversation, when they were all assembled, had lost much of its animation, and almost all its sense by the absence of Jane and Elizabeth.

They found Mary, as usual, deep in the study of human nature; and had some extracts to admire, and some new observations of threadbare morality to listen to. Catherine and Lydia had information for them of a different sort. Much had been done and much had been said in the regiment since the preceding Wednesday; several of the officers had dined lately with their uncle, a private named Sykes had been flogged, and it had actually been hinted that Colonel Forster was going to be married.

Elizabeth, conscious of her sister's tired state, urged Jane to bed early. Catherine and Lydia protested that they had more news to tell, and only let Jane go after securing a promise from her to hear all about the regiment the following morning. When Jane was safely tucked away in bed, Elizabeth took a chair next

to the window to watch over her. She pulled her legs under her and wrapped a warm blanket over her shoulders, alternating her attention between Jane and the miles separating Longbourn from Netherfield.

In the quiet safety of her room, she was able at last to think in great detail about the whole of their stay at Netherfield—of what was done and what was said. Her opinion of everyone was pretty much fixed, save for one. Mr. Darcy remained somewhat of a mystery. Though she knew him to be prideful and with somber faults, as had been determined during the course of their conversations, the conviction of this knowledge did not coincide with the way he sometimes looked at her.

The more she thought of it, the more she was convinced there might have been heat within his gaze while she walked with Miss Bingley. The idea caused a curious longing within her stomach and thighs. Curious because, though she full well understood its meaning, she could not fathom why it would occur to the idea of someone she had determined to be as disagreeable as Mr. Darcy. Then, remembering how he ignored her when they were alone, but talked to her when the others were about, she determined that the heat in his gaze was not for her and that, perhaps, his conversation with her was a way to tease Miss Bingley. For, though that lady did not understand his character very well, Mr. Darcy surely understood hers.

Content at last that her assumptions of the visit were correct, she pulled the blanket tighter. Unfortunately, the ache she felt for the disagreeable gentleman did not go away. With Jane in the room, there was no hope of relieving it—not that she wanted to fantasize about Mr. Darcy. That would be a mistake, for once she allowed him to invade the intimacy of such acts, he would be forever associated with them and she would never be able to look at him in the eye again.

CHAPTER THIRTEEN

"*I* HOPE, MY DEAR, that you have ordered a good dinner today," said Mr. Bennet to his wife, as they were at breakfast the next morning. "I have reason to expect an addition to our family party."

"Who do you mean? I know of nobody that is coming, unless Charlotte Lucas should happen to call in—and I hope *my* dinners are good enough for her. I do not believe she often sees such at home."

"The person of whom I speak is a gentleman."

Mrs. Bennet's eyes sparkled. "A gentleman? It is Mr. Bingley, I am sure! Well, I shall be extremely glad to see Mr. Bingley. But, good Lord, how unlucky. There is not a bit of fish to be got today. Lydia, my love, ring the bell. I must speak to Hill this moment."

"It is *not* Mr. Bingley," said her husband. "It is a person whom I never saw in the whole course of my life."

This roused a general astonishment, and he had the pleasure of being eagerly questioned by his wife and his five daughters at once.

After amusing himself some time with their curiosity, he explained, "About a month ago I received this letter, and about a fortnight ago I answered it, for I thought it a case of some delicacy, and requiring early attention. It is from my cousin, Mr. Collins, who, when I am dead, may turn you all out of this house as soon as he pleases."

"Oh, my dear," cried his wife. "I cannot bear to hear that odious man mentioned. Pray do not talk of him. It is the hardest thing in the world that your estate should be entailed away from your own children. I am sure, if I had been you, I should have tried long ago to do something or other about it."

Jane and Elizabeth tried to explain to her the nature of an entail. They had often attempted to do it before, but it was a subject on which Mrs. Bennet was beyond the reach of reason, and she continued to rail bitterly against the cruelty of settling an estate away from a family of five daughters, in favor of a man whom nobody cared anything about.

"It certainly is a most iniquitous affair," said Mr. Bennet, "and nothing can clear Mr. Collins from the guilt of inheriting Longbourn. But if you will listen to his letter, you may perhaps be a little softened by his manner of expressing himself."

"No, I am sure I shall not. I think it is very impertinent of him to write to you at all, and very hypocritical. I hate such false friends. Why could he not keep on quarreling with you, as his father did before him?"

"Why, indeed. He does seem to have had some filial scruples on that head, as you will hear." Pausing, Mr. Bennet unfolded the letter he had brought with him to the table in preparation of this moment, and read, "Hunsford, near Westerham, Kent,

15th October."

"Oh, do get on with it!" fretted Mrs. Bennet.

"Dear Sir." **Mr. Bennet continued, as if his wife had not spoken.** "The disagreement subsisting between yourself and my late honored father always gave me much uneasiness, and since I have had the misfortune to lose him, I have frequently wished to heal the breach. For some time I was kept back by my own doubts, fearing lest it might seem disrespectful to his memory for me to be on good terms with anyone with whom it had always pleased him to be at variance." **He looked as his wife, stating, "There, Mrs. Bennet."**

"That does not change his intentions in turning us out," his wife said.

"Pray, let me finish." Mr. Bennet turned back to the letter. "My mind, however, is now made up on the subject, for having received ordination at Easter, I have been so fortunate as to be distinguished by the patronage of the Right Honorable Lady Catherine de Bourgh, widow of Sir Lewis de Bourgh, whose bounty and beneficence has preferred me to the valuable rectory of this parish, where it shall be my earnest endeavor to demean myself with grateful respect towards her ladyship, and be ever ready to perform those rites and ceremonies which are instituted by the Church of England. As a clergyman, moreover, I feel it my duty to promote and establish the blessing of peace in all families within in the reach of my influence, and on these grounds I flatter myself that my present overtures are highly commendable, and that the circumstance of my being next in the entail of Longbourn estate will be kindly overlooked on your side, and not lead you to reject the offered olive-branch. I cannot be otherwise than concerned at being the means of injuring your amiable daughters, and beg leave to apologize for it, as well as to assure you of my readiness to make them every possible amends.

If you should have no objection to receive me into your house, I propose myself the satisfaction of waiting on you and your family, Monday, November 18th, by four o'clock, and shall probably trespass on your hospitality till the Saturday sennight following, which I can do without any inconvenience, as Lady Catherine is far from objecting to my occasional absence on a Sunday, provided that some other clergyman is engaged to do the duty of the day. I remain, dear sir, with respectful compliments to your lady and daughters, your well-wisher and friend, William Collins."

"Well!" said Mrs. Bennet, as if trying to make up her mind about the gentlemen in question. She had long grown used to hating the man and found it hard to reconcile her feelings after one letter.

"At four o'clock, therefore, we may expect this peacemaking gentleman," said Mr. Bennet, as he folded up the letter. "He seems to be a most conscientious and polite young man, upon my word, and I do not doubt this will prove a valuable acquaintance, especially if Lady Catherine should be so indulgent as to let him come to us again."

"There is some sense in what he says about the girls," said Mrs. Bennet, forgetting her struggle. "However, if he is disposed to make them any amends, I shall not be the person to discourage him."

"Though it is difficult," said Jane, "to guess in what way he can mean to make us the atonement he thinks our due, the wish is certainly to his credit."

Elizabeth was chiefly struck by his extraordinary deference for Lady Catherine, and his kind intention of christening, marrying, and burying his parishioners whenever it was required. "He must be an oddity, I think. I cannot make him out. There is something very pompous in his style. And what can he mean by apologizing for being next in the entail? We cannot suppose he would help it if he could. Could he be a sensible man, sir?"

"No, my dear, I think not. I have great hopes of finding him quite the reverse. There is a mixture of servility and self-importance in his letter, which promises well. I am impatient to see him."

"In point of composition," said Mary, "the letter does not seem defective. The idea of the olive-branch perhaps is not wholly new, yet I think it is well expressed."

To Catherine and Lydia, neither the letter nor its writer were in any degree interesting. It was next to impossible that their cousin should come in a scarlet coat, and it was now some weeks since they had received pleasure from the society of a man in any other color. As for their mother, Mr. Collins's letter had done away much of her ill-will, and she was preparing to see him with a degree of composure which astonished her husband and daughters.

Mr. Collins was punctual to his time, and was received with great politeness by the whole family. Mr. Bennet indeed said little, but the ladies were ready enough to talk. Mr. Collins seemed neither in need of encouragement, nor inclined to be silent himself. He was a tall, heavy-looking young man of five-and-twenty. His air was grave and stately, and his manners were very formal. He had not been long seated before he complimented Mrs. Bennet on having so fine a family of daughters; said he had heard much of their beauty, but that in this instance fame had fallen short of the truth; and added, that he did not doubt her seeing them all in due time disposed of in marriage.

This gallantry was not much to the taste of some of his hearers, but Mrs. Bennet, who quarreled with no compliments, answered most readily, "You are very kind. I wish with all my heart it may prove so, for else they will be destitute enough. Things are settled so oddly."

"You allude, perhaps, to the entail of this estate."

"Ah, sir, I do indeed. It is a grievous affair to my poor girls, you must confess. Not that I mean to find fault with you, for such things I know are all chance in this world. There is no knowing how estates will go when once they come to be entailed."

"I am very sensible, madam, of the hardship to my fair cousins, and could say much on the subject, but that I am cautious of appearing forward and precipitate. However I can assure the young ladies that I come prepared to admire them. At present I will not say more, but, perhaps, when we are better acquainted—"

He was interrupted by a summons to dinner. The girls smiled on each other. They were not the only objects of Mr. Collins's admiration. The hall, the dining room, and all its furniture, were examined and praised. His commendation of everything would have touched Mrs. Bennet's heart, but for the mortifying supposition of his viewing it all as his own future property. The dinner too in its turn was highly admired, and he begged to know to which of his fair cousins the excellency of its cooking was owed. There he was set right by Mrs. Bennet, who assured him with some asperity that they were very well able to keep a good cook, and that her daughters had nothing to do in the kitchen. He begged pardon for having displeased her. In a softened tone she declared herself not at all offended, but he continued to apologize for about a quarter of an hour.

"You cannot mean to brood every time the ball is mentioned," said Bingley to his friend, as they waited for the grooms to bring out their horses. It was a fine evening for a ride and both gentlemen preferred any excuse to be away from Mr. Hurst and

his demands for cards. "I find my mood quite the opposite of yours. I cannot wait to dance with the lovely Miss Bennet again, and to see her well after such a dreadful illness."

"You mistake my quiet for brooding," Darcy answered. He took the reins handed to him and led the horse a few paces before swinging up on its back. "I have no opinion on your ball."

"I daresay you might enjoy yourself," Bingley, too, seated his horse and was content to follow Darcy's lead over the long drive. "I am sure you will find Miss Elizabeth more than a tolerable partner now that you are in her acquaintance. Her good humor and pleasant nature is a compliment to any gathering."

"Do not bother yourself with selecting my dance partners," Darcy said, unwilling to discuss the matter. He had made up his mind to limit his acquaintance with Miss Elizabeth and did not need any inducements to change it. The fact that his fantasies of her were only enhanced by their conversations did not bode well on his determination, and he knew he would have to be diligent if he were to strike her from his fantasies.

"But if I do not, you will not," Bingley said, allowing his horse free rein to go as it pleased. The creature had the same amiable temperament as its owner and was content to follow Darcy's stallion. "I know I said you may go to bed if it pleases you, but you will come, will you not?"

"I will," Darcy said. "I cannot imagine hiding in a room while my host entertains guests below."

"I am glad to hear it!" Bingley smiled, as if the matter had weighed greatly on his mind and now all was right in the world. "Do you think it to be too indelicate of me to ask Miss Bennet to dance three or four times? I feel we are becoming better acquainted; and though I do not wish for her illness, past or future, I am glad for the time it afforded me in her company. I find her the most delicate of females, very pleasing in every way. I am quite enamored with her, and am not hesitant to say it to you, my friend."

"As your friend, I did not need you to say it to know it was so."

"Am I so transparent, then?" Bingley laughed. "I find I do not care if I am. Oh, but if you were to find such a person as Miss Bennet to occupy your mind. Think of how wonderful it would be, the two of us, very much enamored and—"

"A race!" Darcy challenged, as he gently nudged his horse, urging it to go faster as they came to the end of the lane. He did not wish to hear more, for Bingley's compliments to the eldest Miss Bennet only forced Darcy to think of her sister. Bingley instantly complied with the idea and no more was said as they pounded their way to an unspecified finish line.

Mr. Bennet scarcely spoke at all during dinner, but when the servants were withdrawn, he thought it time to have some conversation with his guest, and therefore started a subject in which he expected him to shine, by observing that he seemed very fortunate in his patroness. Lady Catherine de Bourgh's attention to his wishes, and consideration for his comfort, appeared very remarkable. Mr. Bennet could not have chosen better.

Mr. Collins was eloquent in her praise. The subject elevated him to more than usual solemnity of manner, and with a most important aspect he protested, "I have never in my life witnessed such behavior in a person of rank—such affability and condescension, as I have myself experienced from Lady Catherine. She had been graciously pleased to approve of the discourses which I had already had the honor of preaching before her. She has also asked me twice to dine at Rosings, and sent for me only last

Saturday to make up her pool of quadrille in the evening. Lady Catherine is reckoned proud by many people, but I have never seen anything but affability in her. She has always spoken to me as she would to any other gentleman and made not the smallest objection to my joining in the society of the neighborhood or to my leaving the parish occasionally for a week or two, to visit my relations. She has even condescended to advise me to marry as soon as I am able, provided I choose with discretion. And she once paid me a visit in my humble parsonage, where she perfectly approved all the alterations I have been making, and has even vouchsafed to suggest some herself—some shelves in the closet upstairs."

"That is all very proper and civil, I am sure," said Mrs. Bennet. "I daresay she is a very agreeable woman. It is a pity that great ladies in general are not more like her. Does she live near you, sir?"

"The garden in which stands my humble abode is separated only by a lane from Rosings Park, her ladyship's residence."

"I think you said she was a widow, sir? Has she any family?"

"She has only one daughter, the heiress of Rosings, and of very extensive property."

"Ah!" said Mrs. Bennet, shaking her head. "Then she is better off than many girls. What sort of young lady is she? Is she handsome?"

"She is a most charming young lady indeed. Lady Catherine herself says that, in point of true beauty, Miss de Bourgh is far superior to the handsomest of her sex, because there is that in her features which marks the young lady of distinguished birth. She is unfortunately of a sickly constitution, which has prevented her from making that progress in many accomplishments which she could not have otherwise failed of, as I am informed by the lady who superintended her education, and who still resides with them. But she is perfectly amiable, and often condescends to drive by my humble abode in her little phaeton and ponies."

"Has she been presented? I do not remember her name among the ladies at court."

"Her indifferent state of health unhappily prevents her being in town; and by that means, as I told Lady Catherine one day, has deprived the British court of its brightest ornaments. Her ladyship seemed pleased with the idea. I am happy on every occasion to offer those little delicate compliments which are always acceptable to ladies. I have more than once observed to Lady Catherine, that her charming daughter seemed born to be a duchess, and that the most elevated rank, instead of giving her consequence, would be adorned by her. These are the kind of little things which please her ladyship, and it is a sort of attention which I conceive myself peculiarly bound to pay."

Elizabeth listened to the lengthy descriptions of Mr. Collins with both amusement and revulsion. Even Jane, whose normally docile expression could give no offense, managed a wide-eyed look at the excessive flattery.

"You judge very properly," said Mr. Bennet, "and it is happy for you that you possess the talent of flattering with delicacy. May I ask whether these pleasing attentions proceed from the impulse of the moment, or are the result of previous study?"

Elizabeth was forced to cover her mouth with the back of her hand to keep from laughing.

"They arise chiefly from what is passing at the time, and though I sometimes amuse myself with suggesting and arranging such little elegant compliments as may be adapted to ordinary occasions, I always wish to give them as unstudied an air as possible."

Mr. Bennet's expectations were fully answered. Mr. Collins was as absurd as he had hoped, and he listened to him with the

keenest enjoyment, maintaining at the same time the most res-
olute composure of countenance, and, except in an occasional
glance at Elizabeth, requiring no partner in his pleasure.

By tea-time, however, the dose had been enough, and
Mr. Bennet was glad to take his guest into the drawing room;
and, when tea was over, glad to invite him to read aloud to the
ladies. Mr. Collins readily assented, and a book was produced.
Everything announced it to be from a circulating library, and
on beholding it, he begged pardon, and protested that he never
read novels. Kitty stared at him. Lydia exclaimed. Other books
were produced, and after some deliberation he chose Fordyce's
Sermons.

Lydia gaped as he opened the volume, and before he had,
with very monotonous solemnity, read three pages, she interrupted him with, "Do you know, mamma, that my uncle Philips
talks of turning away Richard? If he does, Colonel Forster will
hire him. My aunt told me so herself on Saturday. I shall walk to
Meryton tomorrow to hear more about it, and to ask when Mr.
Denny comes back from town."

Lydia was bid by her two eldest sisters to hold her tongue.
Mr. Collins, much offended, laid aside his book, and said, "I
have often observed how little young ladies are interested by
books of a serious stamp, though written solely for their benefit.
It amazes me, I confess; for, certainly, there can be nothing so
advantageous to them as instruction. But I will no longer impor-
tune my young cousin."

Then turning to Mr. Bennet, he offered himself as his
antagonist at backgammon. Mr. Bennet accepted the challenge,
observing that he acted very wisely in leaving the girls to their
own trifling amusements. Mrs. Bennet and her daughters apologized most civilly for Lydia's interruption, and promised that
it should not occur again, if he would resume his book. Mr.

Collins, after assuring them that he bore his young cousin no ill-will, and should never resent her behavior as any affront, seated himself at another table with Mr. Bennet, and prepared for backgammon.

After it was settled, Elizabeth leaned towards Jane and whispered, "I could kiss Lydia for her insolent behavior tonight, for it saved us from such a sermon."

Jane's burst of quickly subdued laughter was her only answer.

CHAPTER FOURTEEN

*M*R. COLLINS WAS NOT A SENSIBLE MAN, and this deficiency of nature had been little assisted by education or society. The greatest part of his life had been spent under the guidance of an illiterate and miserly father, and though he belonged to one of the universities, he had merely kept the necessary terms, without forming at it any useful acquaintance. The subjection in which his father had brought him up had given him originally great humility of manner; but it was now a good deal counteracted by the self-conceit of a weak head, and the consequential feelings of early and unexpected prosperity. A fortunate chance had recommended him to Lady Catherine de Bourgh when the living of Hunsford was vacant; and the respect which he felt for her high rank, and his veneration for her as his patroness, mingling with a very good opinion of himself, of his authority as a clergyman, and his right as a rector, made him altogether a mixture of pride and obsequiousness, self-importance and humility.

Having now a good house and a very sufficient income, he intended to marry. In seeking a reconciliation with the Longbourn family he had a wife in view, as he meant to choose one of the daughters, if he found them as handsome and amiable as they were represented by common report. This was his plan of amends—of atonement—for inheriting their father's estate; and he thought it an excellent one, full of eligibility and suitableness, and excessively generous on his own part.

His plan did not vary on seeing them. Miss Bennet's lovely face confirmed his views, and established all his strictest notions of what was due to seniority. For the first evening she was his settled choice. However, the next morning he made an alteration during a quarter of an hour's tete-a-tete with Mrs. Bennet before breakfast. The conversation began with his parsonage house, and led naturally to the avowal of his hopes that a mistress might be found for it at Longbourn. This produced from her, amid very complaisant smiles and general encouragement, a caution against the very Jane he had fixed on. "I must mention, Mr. Collins, for I feel it incumbent on me to hint that my eldest daughter is likely to be very soon engaged. As to my youngest daughters, I could not take it upon myself to say, but I do not know of any prepossession."

Mr. Collins, without difficulty, changed from Jane to Elizabeth, who succeeded Jane in age and he felt was equal to the same in beauty. Mrs. Bennet treasured the knowledge, and trusted that she might soon have two daughters married. The man whom she could not bear to speak of the day before was now high in her good graces. **Though she would not mention it to Elizabeth, she did feel compelled to pull her two eldest daughters aside for that talk which every mother must someday give. And, as she did not anticipate having to wait long, she saw no reason not to give her talk in the high state of her excitement over** the pending engagements.

"I feel compelled, as all mothers of daughters must one day be, due to your age and the very likelihood of your someday—rather soon I think—getting married, to touch upon the unpleasantries. I think it is necessary to get the talk out of the way now, so as not to ruin the most happy of occasions when the day comes, as my mother did for me—only waiting until the very morning of my wedding. I can tell you I could think of little else, and did not enjoy nor remember eating my wedding breakfast for fear of what was to come."

Jane stared at her mother in shock. "Whatever did our grandmother say to make you so afraid? I do not understand what you are trying to tell us."

"Patience, dear Jane; and Lizzy, do not look at me in that manner! If you do not listen now, I will not repeat myself again and you will be on your own come that time," said Mrs. Bennet.

Her interest piqued, Elizabeth endeavored to look contrite.

Mrs. Bennet launched into her motherly duty with a look of fortitude and determination rarely witnessed by her two daughters. "The night of your wedding is like walking through a door, moving from your room of girlhood into your room of womanhood. In this new room you will discover things you cannot possibly imagine in your girlhood state. As your mother, it is my duty to inform you that your husband will come and visit. You must let him, for it is your duty to receive him as your guest. If you keep still, do not make a fuss, he will be grateful for the attention. I daresay, often early in the marriage, he will be inclined to leave you gifts. These gifts will grow to be children."

Jane shared a confused look with Elizabeth.

"A husband comes into a lady's private parlor for a visit?" asked Jane.

"Precisely. Your parlor," said Mrs. Bennet with a smart nod.

"Consider it a chore that must be performed. If you do not speak too much, he will retire from his visit with the greatest haste possible under the circumstance. If you are unfortunate, he will have a ravenous appetite, and it will be your lot to receive him often to dine at your table. But, the blessing of this is you will have many children of your own." Then, nodding as if quite proud of herself, she said, "See, that was not so bad. I must instruct you not to share this conversation with your younger sisters. Their ears are much too innocent for this story—much too young to even watch the animals' visits to their ladies' parlors."

When Mrs. Bennet left, as if chased out of the room by the devil itself, Elizabeth looked at her sister. "Did you understand our dear mother?"

"Hardly a word," Jane laughed uncomfortably. "What do you think has come over her, speaking in such a way? She acts as if she expects us to walk down the aisle tomorrow."

"Apparently, she is worried our husbands will make a nuisance of themselves by coming into our rooms to watch us sew and eat our teacakes." Elizabeth had a somewhat clearer picture of what her mother alluded to, but it was not something Jane, with all her delicate sensibilities, would care to discuss. Her sister shied away from such subjects, and at times Elizabeth wondered just how much her sister really did know about the nature of men and women. Instead of commenting further and making Jane more uncomfortable, she resolved to broach the subject with her dear aunt, Mrs. Gardiner, the next time she saw her.

Lydia's intention of walking to Meryton was not forgotten, and every sister except Mary agreed to go with her. Mr. Collins was to attend them, at the request of Mr. Bennet, who was most anxious to get rid of him and have his library to himself; for thither Mr. Collins had followed him after breakfast; and there he would continue, nominally engaged with one of the largest folios in the collection, but really talking to Mr. Bennet, with little cessation, of his house and garden at Hunsford. Such doings discomposed Mr. Bennet exceedingly. In his library he had been always sure of leisure and tranquility; and though prepared, as he told Elizabeth, to meet with folly and conceit in every other room of the house, he was used to be free from them there. Therefore, his civility was most prompt in inviting Mr. Collins to join his daughters in their walk. Mr. Collins, being in fact much better fitted for a walker than a reader, was extremely pleased to close his large book and go.

In pompous nothings on his side, and civil assents on that of his cousins, their time passed till they entered Meryton where after the attention of the younger ones was no longer to be gained by him. Their eyes were immediately wandering the street in quest of the officers, and nothing less than a very smart bonnet or a new muslin in a shop window could recall them.

But the attention of every lady was soon caught by a young man, whom they had never seen before. He was most gentlemanlike in appearance, walking with another officer on the other side of the way. The officer was the very Mr. Denny whose return from London Lydia came to inquire, and he bowed as they passed. All were struck with the stranger's air, and all wondered who he could be. Kitty and Lydia, determined to find out, made their way across the street under pretense of wanting something in an opposite shop, and fortunately had just gained the pavement when the two gentlemen reached the same spot. Mr. Denny addressed them directly, and entreated permission to introduce his friend, Mr. Wickham, who had returned with him the day before from town, and he was happy to say had accepted a commission in their corps. This was exactly as it should be, for the young man wanted only regimentals to make him completely charming.

Jane, whose attractions were decided elsewhere, greeted the new acquaintance with a sincerity that complimented her nature. Elizabeth found she was instantly charmed, and shared her new-found excitement with a secretive look to Jane—the kind of look which only the closest of sisters could understand. The introduction was followed up on his side by a happy readiness of conversation, a readiness that was at the same time perfectly correct and unassuming. His appearance was greatly in his favor; he had all the best part of beauty, a fine countenance, a good figure, and very pleasing address.

The whole party was still standing and talking together very agreeably, when the sound of horses drew their notice, and Darcy and Bingley were seen riding down the street. Elizabeth felt her breath catch in her throat. The dark countenance of Mr. Darcy was a stark contrast to the lighthearted Mr. Wickham; yet she found herself compelled, as she was often wont to do when in his presence, to watch Mr. Darcy as he approached. The sun shone against his back, framing his shoulders and casting shadows over his face. He rode with the ease of a man who had spent his life around horses, and she found her eyes drifting down to where his strong thighs gripped the beast.

On distinguishing the ladies of the group, the two gentlemen came directly towards them. When they began the usual civilities, Elizabeth forced her gaze away from Mr. Darcy's legs, and back to Mr. Wickham.

"Miss Elizabeth," Darcy acknowledged, his tone holding some amusement and she could imagine it was at her expense. She did not answer as she gave a small bow of her head.

Bingley was the principal spokesman, and Miss Bennet the

principal object. He said he was then on his way to Longbourn on purpose to inquire after her. Mr. Darcy began to corroborate it with a bow, when his eyes were suddenly arrested by the sight of the stranger. Elizabeth witnessed the countenance of both as they looked at each other, and was astonished at the effect of the meeting. Both changed color, one looked white, the other red. Mr. Wickham, after a few moments, touched his hat—a salutation which Mr. Darcy just deigned to return.

In another minute, Mr. Bingley, but without seeming to have noticed what passed, took leave and rode on with his friend.

Mr. Denny and Mr. Wickham walked with the young ladies to the door of Mr. Philip's house, and then made their bows, in spite of Miss Lydia's pressing entreaties that they should come in, and even in spite of Mrs. Philips's throwing up the parlor window and loudly seconding the invitation.

Mrs. Philips was always glad to see her nieces; and the two eldest, from their recent absence, were particularly welcome. Her civility was claimed towards Mr. Collins by Jane's introduction of him. She received him with her very best politeness, which he returned tenfold, apologizing for his intrusion without any previous acquaintance with her, which he could not help flattering himself, might be justified by his relationship to the young ladies who introduced him to her notice. Mrs. Philips was quite awed by such an excess of good breeding, but her contemplation of one stranger was soon put to an end to by exclamations and inquiries about the other. She could only tell her nieces what they already knew, that Mr. Denny had brought Mr. Wickham from London, and that he was to have a lieutenant's commission. She had been watching him walk up and down the street for the last hour. Had Mr. Wickham appeared, Kitty and Lydia would certainly have continued the occupation. Unluckily no one passed windows now except a few of the officers, who, in comparison with the stranger, had become "stupid, disagreeable fellows." Some of them were to dine with the Philipses the next day, and their aunt promised to make her husband call on Mr. Wickham, and give him an invitation also, if the family from Longbourn would come in the evening. The prospect of such delights was very cheering, and they parted in mutual good spirits. Mr. Collins repeated his apologies in quitting the room, and was assured with unwearying civility that they were perfectly needless.

Wickham.

The man's name was as distasteful to Darcy as the most rotten of fish. He watched as the object of his distaste crossed the street some distance away. The Bennets were no longer with him, but the shock of seeing the sisters with that particular man left him a little cold. He had been determining not to fix his eyes on Elizabeth when he had detected Mr. Wickham next to her. He did not miss Elizabeth's smile, but could not determine if the look was caused merely by her usual playfulness, or if it had been something special for their new acquaintance. Either way, the jealousy he felt was not welcomed.

The urge to warn her of the man's villainous nature warred with propriety, which the honor of his family name dictated he follow. Wickham was a scoundrel of the worst kind, though the truth of it was not widely known throughout the countryside, or even in London for that matter. Darcy had been careful to make sure the story was never told beyond those directly involved, nor would he be the one to speak of it now. To say what he knew of the man would be to bring dishonor to someone very dear to him. He refused to even think of the details of it lest he be spurred to anger. With the detestable man so close, it was hard not to run him down with his horse.

Reining his horse away from the man, he rode through the streets a little faster than was prudent. Bingley, undoubtedly surprised by the swift departure was soon behind him, racing beyond the buildings into the wide prairie that would lead them back to Netherfield. He wished the air hitting upon his face and chest could blow away the desires that plagued his flesh. Thinking of Elizabeth with Wickham, with any man, caused his chest to tighten and his anger to rise. He wanted to strike something, to beat his fist till the pain overtook any inkling of passion. More than this, he wanted to find Elizabeth; to pull her onto his horse, and ride away with her to some hidden alcove where they would not be discovered. There he would make love to her; claiming her so she could not go to another man; banishing the demons inside him; killing the sensations of longing that now rendered his brain feeble and his limbs weak.

He could not deny it. She had infected him like some disease, and there was only one cure for it. It was a cure he could not bring himself to take.

As they walked home, Mr. Collins expressed his gratification by admiring Mrs. Philips's manners and politeness. He protested that, except for Lady Catherine and her daughter, he had never seen a more elegant woman; for she had not only received him with the utmost civility, but even pointedly included him in her invitation for the next evening, although utterly unknown to her before. Lydia and Kitty were pleased to discuss the subject with him as they were highly anticipating the event.

Elizabeth walked with Jane behind the others, content to

let them wander far ahead, and related to that sister what she had seen pass between the two gentlemen. Though Jane would have defended either or both, had they appeared to be in the wrong, she could no more explain such behavior than her sister. **It was on the strangest of circumstances that Mr. Bingley and Mr. Darcy should happen to ride by on their way back to Netherfield, though it was by no means a direct route which the two men took.**

Upon seeing Jane, Bingley changed course and instantly offered to accompany them home since their own escort had gone on ahead. Jane agreed that he should join them for part of the distance, at least till such a point that it was prudent for him to turn home. She would not hear of him going out of his way on their behalf. Elizabeth hid her smile at Bingley's transparent excuse and Jane's ignorance of it. The ladies hardly needed a chaperone for such a short walk, one they had taken often. As he came down off his horse, leading it by the reins, he walked next to Jane. Elizabeth fell a few steps behind, letting her sister have her moment.

Mr. Darcy was slower to dismount, and rode near her for several paces. Elizabeth, who did not pride herself a fine horsewoman, inched away from the large animal. Upon seeing this, the gentleman swung down and placed himself between her and the beast.

"You do not have a fondness for horses?" he asked.

"I do not have a dislike of them. I am as fond of them as any domesticated animal." The horse neighed and snorted, as if responding to her words. She chuckled, leaning forward a small degree to look at the animal. "Though, I will profess I prefer walking to horseback. Perhaps this is because I have not had many occasions to ride."

After speaking with Mr. Wickham, Elizabeth found Darcy's long periods of silence disconcerting. Between these quiet spells,

she endeavored to draw him into conversation. She commented on the brightness of the day, to which he agreed it was, indeed, bright. Next, she mentioned the very large breadth of his horse, to which he said it was not so very different than other animals in his stables. After a few more failed attempts, she gave up and determined to enjoy the pleasure of a walk despite her brusque company.

As they neared the place where they had agreed to part ways, Elizabeth turned to take her leave of Mr. Darcy. Before she could speak, he said, "I should like to take you riding. Bingley has a horse that would suit you very well. It had a good temperament and all ladies should know something of riding. Walking will not always be prudent."

"I know how to ride," Elizabeth said, surprised by the unexpected offer. "I did not mean to imply I did not. I simply prefer to walk."

At that moment, they reached Jane and Bingley. Darcy did not pursue the proposition as he swung back on his horse. And, as the men rode away, Elizabeth did not know what to make of the offer. Dismissing it, she instead prompted Jane to tell her everything Bingley had said to her so they could examine what transpired word for word.

CHAPTER FIFTEEN

*a*S NO OBJECTION WAS MADE to the young people's engagement with their aunt, and all Mr. Collins's scruples of leaving Mr. and Mrs. Bennet for a single evening during his visit were most steadily resisted, the coach conveyed him and his five cousins at a suitable hour to Meryton. The girls had the pleasure of hearing, as they entered the drawing room, that Mr. Wickham had accepted their uncle's invitation and was in the house.

When they had all taken their seats, Mr. Collins was at leisure to look around and admire, and he was so struck with the size and furniture of the apartment, that he declared he might almost have supposed himself in the small summer breakfast parlor at Rosings. It was a comparison that did not at first convey much gratification, but when Mrs. Philips understood from him what Rosings was, and who was its proprietor—when she had listened to the description of only one of Lady Catherine's drawing rooms, and found that the chimney-piece alone had cost eight hundred pounds, she felt all the force of the compliment, and would hardly have resented a comparison with the housekeeper's room.

In describing to her all the grandeur of Lady Catherine and her mansion, with occasional digressions in praise of his own humble abode, and the improvements it was receiving, he was happily employed until the gentlemen joined them. He found in Mrs. Philips a very attentive listener, whose opinion of his consequence increased with what she heard, and who was resolving to retail it all among her neighbors as soon as she could. To the girls, who could not listen to their cousin, and who had nothing to do but to wish for an instrument, and examine their own indifferent imitations of china on the mantelpiece, the interval of waiting appeared very long. However, it was over at last as the gentlemen did approach. When Mr. Wickham walked into the room, Elizabeth felt all her admiration of him had been quite reasonable. The officers were in general a very creditable, gentlemanlike set, and the best of them were of the present party. Mr. Wickham was as far beyond them all in person, countenance, air, and walk; as they were superior to the broad-faced, stuffy uncle Philips, breathing port wine, who followed them into the room.

Mr. Wickham was the happy man towards whom almost every female eye was turned, and Elizabeth was the happy woman by whom he finally seated himself. **She felt none of the frustrations that her unnerving attraction to Mr. Darcy seemed to stir within her. With Mr. Wickham, she was completely at ease to like the agreeable man, and did not doubt that he found her pleasant in return; for a woman always has some inkling when she is liked by the opposite sex, even if she should never reveal such understandings to the gentleman in question.** The delightful manner in which Mr. Wickham immediately fell into conversation, though it was only on its being a wet night, made her feel that the commonest, dullest, most threadbare topic might be rendered interesting by the skill of the speaker.

With such rivals for the notice of the ladies as Mr. Wickham and the officers, Mr. Collins seemed to sink into insignificance. To the young ladies he certainly was nothing, but he had a kind listener in Mrs. Philips, and was by her watchfulness, most abundantly supplied with coffee and muffin. When the card tables were placed, he had the opportunity of obliging her in turn, by sitting down to whist.

"I know little of the game at present," said he, "but I shall be glad to improve myself, for in my situation in life—" Mrs. Philips was very glad for his compliance, but could not wait for his reason.

Mr. Wickham did not play at whist, and with ready delight he was received at the other table between Elizabeth and Lydia. At first there seemed danger of Lydia's engrossing him entirely, for she was a most determined talker, but being likewise extremely fond of lottery tickets, she soon grew too interested in the game, too eager in making bets and exclaiming after prizes to have attention for anyone in particular. Allowing for the common demands of the game, Mr. Wickham was therefore at leisure to talk to Elizabeth, and she was very willing to hear him, though what she chiefly wished to hear she could not hope to be told—the history of his acquaintance with Mr. Darcy. She dared not even mention that gentleman. Her curiosity, however, was unexpectedly relieved. Mr. Wickham began the subject himself. He inquired how far Netherfield was from Meryton; and, after receiving her answer, asked in a hesitating manner how long Mr. Darcy had been staying there.

"About a month," said Elizabeth. Then, unwilling to let the subject drop, added, "He is a man of very large property in

Derbyshire, I understand."

"Yes," replied Mr. Wickham. "His estate there is a noble one. You could not have met with a person more capable of giving you certain information on that head than myself, for I have been connected with his family from my infancy."

Elizabeth could not hide her surprise. **Mr. Wickham hardly seemed the type to form close connections to the likes of Mr. Darcy or his family, not that the former was unworthy but that the latter was too self-important.**

"You may well be surprised at such an assertion, Miss Bennet, after seeing the cold manner of our meeting yesterday. Are you acquainted with Mr. Darcy?"

"As much as I ever wish to be," said Elizabeth very warmly. "I have spent four days in the same house with him, and I think him very disagreeable."

"I have no right to give my opinion as to his being agreeable or otherwise. I am not qualified to form one. I have known him too long and too well to be a fair judge. It is impossible for me to be impartial. But I believe your opinion of him would in general astonish—and perhaps you should not express it so strongly anywhere else. Here you are in your own family."

"Upon my word, I say no more here than I might say in any house in the neighborhood, except Netherfield. He is not at all liked in Hertfordshire. Everybody is disgusted with his pride. You will not find him more favorably spoken of by anyone."

"I cannot pretend to be sorry," said Wickham, after a short interruption, "that he or any man should not be estimated beyond what they deserve, but with him I believe it does not often happen. The world is blinded by his fortune and consequence, or frightened by his high and imposing manners, and sees him only as he chooses to be seen."

"I should take him, even on my slight acquaintance, to be

an ill-tempered man." **The strength of her opinions was greatly affected by the pleasantness by which Wickham's delivered his.**

Wickham answered, "I wonder whether he is likely to be in this country much longer."

"I do not know, but I heard nothing of his going away when I was at Netherfield. I hope your plans will not be affected by his being in the neighborhood."

"Oh, no! It is not for me to be driven away by Mr. Darcy. If he wishes to avoid seeing me, he must go. We are not on friendly terms, and it always gives me pain to meet him, but I have no reason for avoiding him beyond what I might proclaim before all the world. I have a sense of great ill-usage, and most painful regrets at his being what he is. His father, the late Mr. Darcy, was one of the best men that ever breathed, and the truest friend I ever had. I can never be in company with this Mr. Darcy without being grieved to the soul by a thousand tender recollections. His behavior to myself has been scandalous, but I verily believe I could forgive him anything and everything, rather than his disappointing the hopes and disgracing the memory of his father."

Elizabeth found the interest of the subject increase, and listened with all her heart, but the delicacy of it prevented further inquiry.

Mr. Wickham began to speak on more general topics, Meryton, the neighborhood, the society, appearing highly pleased with all that he had seen.

"It was the prospect of constant, good society," he added, "which was my chief inducement, for I knew it to be a most respectable, agreeable corps, and my friend Denny tempted me further by his account of their present quarters, and the very excellent acquaintances Meryton had procured. Society is necessary to me. I have been a disappointed man, and my spirits will not bear solitude. A military life is not what I was intended for, but circumstances have now made it eligible. The church ought to have been my profession—I was brought up for the church, and I should at this time have been in possession of a most valuable living, had it pleased the gentleman we were speaking of just now."

"Indeed!"

"Yes. The late Mr. Darcy bequeathed me the next presentation of the best living in his gift. He was my godfather, and excessively attached to me. I cannot do justice to his kindness. He meant to provide for me amply, and thought he had done it, but when the living fell, it was given elsewhere."

"Good heavens!" whispered Elizabeth, "but how could that be? How could his will be disregarded?"

"There was just such an informality in the terms of the bequest as to give me no hope from law. A man of honor could not have doubted the intention, but Mr. Darcy chose to doubt it—or to treat it as a merely conditional recommendation, and to assert that I had forfeited all claim to it by extravagance, imprudence—in short anything or nothing. The livelihood became vacant two years ago, exactly as I was of an age to hold it, and that it was given to another man. No less certain is it that I cannot accuse myself of having really done anything to deserve to lose it. I have a warm, unguarded temper, and I may have spoken my opinion of him, and to him, too freely. I can recall nothing worse. But the fact is, we are very different sort of men, and he hates me."

"This is quite shocking! He deserves to be publicly disgraced."

"Some time or other he will be—but it shall not be by me. I must honor the memory of his father."

Elizabeth respected him for such feelings, and thought him handsomer than ever as he expressed them. **Though she** would have never guessed so horrible an action from Mr. Darcy, she could scarcely disbelieve the obvious good-nature of Mr. Wickham. Had Mr. Darcy been in attendance she might have confronted him with it. For his absence, she was grateful.

"But what," said she, after a pause, "would induce him to behave so cruelly?"

"A dislike of me, which I cannot but attribute in some measure to jealousy. Had the late Mr. Darcy liked me less, his son might have borne with me better."

"I had not thought Mr. Darcy so bad as this," Elizabeth said. After a few minutes' reflection, she continued, "I do remember his boasting one day at Netherfield of the implacability of his resentments, of his having an unforgiving temper. His disposition must be dreadful."

"I will not trust myself on the subject," replied Wickham. "We were born in the same parish. The greatest part of our youth was passed together. My father left his previous profession to be of use to the late Mr. Darcy and devoted all his time to the care of the Pemberley property. He was highly esteemed by Mr. Darcy, a most intimate friend, and did receive a voluntary promise from Mr. Darcy on his deathbed that I would be provided for."

"How strange!"

"The actions of the younger Mr. Darcy can be traced to pride, and pride has often been his best friend."

"Can such abominable pride have ever done him good?"

"Yes. It has often led him to be liberal and generous, to give his money freely, to display hospitality, to assist his tenants, and relieve the poor. Family pride, and filial pride—for he is very proud of what his father was—have done this. Not to appear to disgrace his family, to degenerate from the popular qualities, or lose the influence of the Pemberley House, is a powerful motive. He has also brotherly pride, which, with some brotherly affection, makes him a very kind and careful guardian of his sister."

"What sort of girl is Miss Darcy?"

"She is a handsome girl, about fifteen or sixteen, and, I understand, highly accomplished. I wish I could call her amiable. It gives me pain to speak ill of a Darcy. But she is too much like her brother. As a child, she was affectionate and pleasing, and extremely fond of me. I have devoted hours to her amusement. But she is nothing to me now."

After many pauses and of other subjects, Elizabeth could not help reverting once more to the first, saying, "I am astonished at his intimacy with Mr. Bingley. Do you know Mr. Bingley?"

"Not at all."

"He is a sweet-tempered, amiable, charming man. He cannot know what Mr. Darcy is."

"Probably not, but Mr. Darcy can please where he chooses. He does not lack abilities. Among those who are at all his equals in consequence, he is a very different man from what he is to the less prosperous."

The whist party soon afterwards broke up, and the players gathered round the other table. Mr. Collins took his station between his cousin Elizabeth and Mrs. Philips. The usual inquiries as to his success were made by the latter. It had not been very great for he had lost every point, but when Mrs. Philips began to express her concern, he assured her with much earnest gravity that it was not of the least importance.

"I know very well, madam," said he, "that when persons sit down to a card table, they must take their chances, and happily I am not in such circumstances as to make five shillings any object. Thanks to Lady Catherine de Bourgh, I am removed far beyond the necessity of regarding little matters."

Mr. Wickham's attention was caught. After observing Mr.

Collins for a few moments, he asked Elizabeth in a low voice whether her relation was intimately acquainted with the family of de Bourgh.

"Lady Catherine de Bourgh," she replied, "has lately given him a living. I hardly know how Mr. Collins was first introduced to her notice, but he has not known her long."

"You know of course that Lady Catherine de Bourgh and Lady Anne Darcy were sisters, consequently that she is aunt to the present Mr. Darcy."

"No, indeed, I did not. I knew nothing at all of Lady Catherine's connections. I never heard of her existence till the day before yesterday."

"Her daughter, Miss de Bourgh, will have a very large fortune, and it is believed that she and her cousin will unite the two estates."

This information made Elizabeth smile, as she thought of poor Miss Bingley. Vain indeed must be all her attentions, vain and useless her affection for his sister and her praise of himself, if he were already self-destined for another.

"Mr. Collins," said she, "speaks highly both of Lady Catherine and her daughter, but from some particulars that he has related of her ladyship, I suspect his gratitude misleads him, and that in spite of her being his patroness, she is an arrogant, conceited woman."

"I believe her to be both in a great degree," replied Wickham. "I have not seen her for many years, but I very well remember that I never liked her, and that her manners were dictatorial and insolent."

They continued talking together, with mutual satisfaction till supper put an end to cards, and gave the rest of the ladies their share of Mr. Wickham's attentions. There could be no conversation in the noise of Mrs. Philips's supper party, but his manners recommended him to everybody. Whatever he said, was said well; and whatever he did, done gracefully. Elizabeth went away with her head full of him. She could think of nothing but of Mr. Wickham, and of what he had told her, all the way home. There was no time for her even to mention his name as they went, for neither Lydia nor Mr. Collins were silent once. Lydia talked incessantly of lottery tickets, of the fish she had lost and the fish she had won. Mr. Collins described the civility of Mr. and Mrs. Philips, protesting that he did not in the least regard his losses at whist, enumerating all the dishes at supper, and had more to say than he could well manage before the carriage stopped at Longbourn House.

Elizabeth went to bed that night with thoughts of the amiable Mr. Wickham filling her head, sure that her mind had finally found an occupation to keep from speculating about Mr. Darcy. She half expected, half hoped, her dreams to be likewise filled with the pleasant man. However, her mind had other plans and instead threw her into a garden where she spent the whole night being chased through a fog by Mr. Darcy. Even though she was conscious of despising him, in the dream she could not recall why, and it was with a pounding heart that she was finally caught. The garden was not more than an impression in the dark; nor did her mind let her see the gentleman's face. She knew who grabbed her by the arm and pulled her back; felt the hard knot that sometimes formed in her stomach when he came near; experienced a rush of strong emotions that were not all against the gentleman's favor.

Then her mind did something completely unthinkable. It allowed the very unpleasant Mr. Darcy to kiss her. Elizabeth had read about kisses, and had seen them between some of the servants. That secondhand knowledge had not prepared her for what her dream imagined. The hand on her arm tightened. His lips found hers; every nerve inside her jumped at the contact. Instantly, she awoke to a hint of dawn against her bedroom walls. So vigorous was the dream that sweat adhered her nightgown to her flesh and her limbs were tangled about the covers. The hand she had thought held her arm was really her dressing gown pulled tight.

Elizabeth struggled to get out of bed, as if by moving she could erase the shameful activities of night. Why did her mind torment her so? Why, when it had Mr. Wickham to play with, did it give her Mr. Darcy? Pressing her hand to her mouth, she tried to wipe away the pleasure she had awoken with. The sting lessened; but there was no easy cure for the tingling in her stomach, nor the heat between her thighs.

"You are awake," said Jane, appearing at the door. "You missed the morning meal, but I told mother you were in a fretful sleep and that perhaps you belatedly caught my cold. We thought it best to let you sleep."

"I am well," Elizabeth assured her. "Nothing that a vigorous walk out of doors cannot cure."

CHAPTER SIXTEEN

*O*NCE SHE HAD RECOVERED SUFFICIENTLY **from her dream, Elizabeth determined to put it far from her mind and never think of kissing Mr. Darcy again. As the rising sun brought some clarity and comfort, she felt reasonably calm by the time she walked back to the house.** She related to Jane in great detail what had passed between Mr. Wickham and herself the day before. Jane listened with astonishment and concern. She could not believe Mr. Darcy could be so unworthy of Mr. Bingley's regard, and yet, it was not in her nature to question the veracity of a young man of such amiable appearance as Wickham.

"They have both," said Jane, "been deceived, I daresay, in some way or other, of which we can form no idea. Interested people have perhaps misrepresented each to the other. It is, in short, impossible for us to conjecture the causes or circumstances which may have alienated them, without actual blame on either side."

"Very true, indeed! Now, my dear Jane, what have you got to say on behalf of the interested people who have probably been concerned in the business? Do clear *them* too, or we shall be obliged to think ill of somebody."

"Laugh as much as you choose, but you will not laugh me out of my opinion. My dearest Lizzy, do but consider in what a disgraceful light it places Mr. Darcy, to be treating his father's favorite in such a manner, one whom his father had promised to provide for. It is impossible. No man of common humanity, no man who had any value for his character, could be capable of it. Can his most intimate friends be so excessively deceived in him? I think not."

"I can more easily believe Mr. Bingley's being imposed on, than that Mr. Wickham should invent such a history of himself as he gave me last night—names, facts, everything mentioned without ceremony. If it be untrue, let Mr. Darcy contradict it. Besides, there was truth in his looks."

"Are you sure it was only truth you saw in his looks?" Jane suppressed a small laugh.

"All I care to admit to at the present moment," said Elizabeth, as she, too, held back a happy giggle. "But he was exceedingly handsome and so very agreeable—much more agreeable than some."

Jane again turned serious. "It is difficult, indeed it is distressing. One does not know what to think."

"I beg your pardon, one knows exactly what to think."

But Jane could think with certainty on only one point—if Mr. Bingley had been imposed on, he would have much to suffer when the affair became public.

The two young ladies were summoned from the shrubbery, where this conversation passed, by the arrival of the very persons of whom they had been speaking. Mr. Bingley and his sisters came to give their personal invitation for the long-expected ball at Netherfield, which was fixed for the following Tuesday. The two ladies were delighted to see their dear friend again, called it an age since they had met, and repeatedly asked what she had been doing with herself since their separation. To the rest of the family they paid little attention; avoiding Mrs. Bennet as much as possible, saying not much to Elizabeth, and nothing at all to the others. They were soon gone again, rising from their seats with an activity which took their brother by surprise, and hurrying off as if eager to escape from Mrs. Bennet's civilities.

The prospect of the Netherfield ball was extremely agreeable to every female of the family. Mrs. Bennet chose to consider it as given in compliment to her eldest daughter, and was particularly flattered by receiving the invitation from Mr. Bingley himself, instead of a ceremonious card. Jane pictured a happy evening in the society of her two friends, and the attentions of their brother. Elizabeth thought with pleasure of dancing a great deal with Mr. Wickham, and of seeing a confirmation of everything in Mr. Darcy's look and behavior. The happiness anticipated by Catherine and Lydia depended less on any single event, or any particular person, for though they each meant to dance half the evening with Mr. Wickham, he was by no means the only partner who could satisfy them. A ball was, at any rate, a ball.

Even Mary could assure her family that she had no disinclination for it. "While I can have my mornings to myself, it is enough. I think it is no sacrifice to join occasionally in evening engagements. Society has claims on us all, and I profess myself one of those who consider intervals of recreation and amusement as desirable for everybody."

Elizabeth's spirits were so high on this occasion, that though she did not often speak unnecessarily to Mr. Collins, she could not help asking him whether he intended to accept Mr. Bingley's invitation, and if he did, whether he would think it proper to join in the evening's amusement. She was rather surprised to find that he entertained no scruple whatever on that head, and was very far from dreading a rebuke either from the Archbishop, or Lady Catherine de Bourgh, by venturing to dance.

"I am by no means of the opinion, I assure you," said he, "that a ball of this kind, given by a young man of character, to respectable people, can have any evil tendency. I am so far from objecting to dancing myself that I shall hope to be honored with the hands of all my fair cousins in the course of the evening. I take this opportunity of soliciting yours, Miss Elizabeth, for the two first dances especially."

Elizabeth felt herself completely taken in. She had fully proposed being engaged by Mr. Wickham for those very dances. To have Mr. Collins instead! Her liveliness had never been worse timed. There was no help for it, however. Mr. Wickham's happiness and her own were perforce delayed a little longer, and Mr. Collins's proposal accepted with as good a grace as she could. She was not pleased with his gallantry for it hinted of something more. It now first struck her that she was selected from among her sisters as worthy of being mistress of Hunsford Parsonage. The idea soon reached to conviction, as she observed his increasing civilities toward herself, and heard his frequent attempt at a compliment on her wit and vivacity. Though more astonished than gratified by this effect of her charms, it was not long before her mother gave her to understand that the probability of their marriage was extremely agreeable to *her*. Elizabeth, however, did not choose to take the hint. Mr. Collins might never make the offer, and till he did, it was useless to quarrel about him.

If there had not been a Netherfield ball to prepare for and talk of, the younger Miss Bennets would have been in a very pitiable state at this time, for from the day of the invitation to the day of the ball there was such a succession of rain as prevented their walking to Meryton once. No aunt, no officers, no news could be sought after. Even Elizabeth might have found some trial of her patience in weather which totally suspended the improvement of her acquaintance with Mr. Wickham. Nothing less than a dance on Tuesday, could have made such a Friday, Saturday, Sunday, and Monday endurable to Kitty and Lydia.

CHAPTER SEVENTEEN

*T*ILL ELIZABETH ENTERED THE DRAWING ROOM at Netherfield, and looked in vain for Mr. Wickham among the cluster of red coats there assembled, a doubt of his being present had never occurred to her. She had dressed with more than usual care, and prepared in the highest spirits for the conquest of all that remained unsubdued of his heart, trusting that it might be won in the course of the evening. But in an instant arose the dreadful suspicion of his being purposely omitted for Mr. Darcy's pleasure in the Bingleys' invitation to the officers. Though this was not exactly the case, the absolute fact of his absence was pronounced by his friend Denny, to whom Lydia eagerly applied, and who told them that Wickham had been obliged to go to town on business the day before, and was not yet returned, adding, with a significant smile, "I do not imagine his business would have called him away just now, if he had not wanted to avoid a certain gentleman here."

This part of his intelligence, though unheard by Lydia, was caught by Elizabeth, and, as it assured her that Darcy was not less answerable for Wickham's absence than if her first surmise had been just, every feeling of displeasure against the former was sharpened by immediate disappointment. She could hardly reply with tolerable civility to the polite inquiries which Mr. Darcy directly afterwards approached to make. Attendance, forbearance, patience with Darcy, was injury to Wickham. She was resolved against any sort of conversation with him, and turned away with a degree of ill-humor which she could not wholly surmount even in speaking to Mr. Bingley, whose blind partiality provoked her.

But Elizabeth was not formed for ill-humor. Though every prospect of her own was destroyed for the evening, she could not dwell on it long. Having told all her griefs to Charlotte Lucas, whom she had not seen for a week, she was soon able to make a voluntary transition to the oddities of her cousin, and to point him out to her particular notice. The first two dances, however, brought a return of distress for they were dances of mortification. Mr. Collins, awkward and solemn, apologizing instead of attending, and often moving wrong without being aware of it, gave her all the shame and misery which a disagreeable partner for a couple of dances can give. The moment of her release from him was ecstasy.

She danced next with an officer, and had the refreshment of talking of Wickham, and of hearing that he was universally liked. When those dances were over, she returned to Charlotte Lucas, and was in conversation with her when she found herself suddenly addressed by Mr. Darcy. He took her so much by surprise in his application for her hand, that, without knowing what she did, she accepted him. **Immediately following, an awkward silence passed between them. Elizabeth could not help but** think of her dream, and to her discredit she felt heat warming her cheeks. **The moment lasted but mere seconds, before he bowed politely and walked away.** She was left to fret over her own want of presence of mind.

Charlotte tried to console her, "I daresay you will find him very agreeable."

"Heaven forbid!" **Elizabeth exclaimed with a small laugh, hoping to appear completely unaffected by the man.** "That would be the greatest misfortune of all—to find a man agreeable when one is determined to hate him."

When the dancing recommenced and Darcy approached to claim her hand, Charlotte could not help cautioning her in a whisper, "Do not be a simpleton, Lizzy, and allow your fancy for Wickham to make you appear unpleasant in the eyes of a man ten times his consequence."

Elizabeth made no answer, and took her place in the set. Her neighbors looked at her in amazement, as she stood opposite to Mr. Darcy. **If she were not in better confidence with some of them, she would have thought the ladies of the ball jealous of her dance partner. This she knew to be impossible because Darcy was well-known as an unlikable man, and surely there was nothing to be jealous of.**

As soon as she thought it, reasons for their jealousy began to whisper through her thoughts. He was handsome and rich. Those two traits often recommended their master, even if he did not deserve it. Her attention drew to his mouth, unable to stop herself from examining his lips. She was not in the habit of comparing the mouths of men, but she begrudgingly allowed that his was a very fine mouth, with full lips and supported by a strong jaw. Then there were his eyes, deep and blue and full of secrets.

"I know one of your disgraceful secrets, Mr. Darcy," she thought. Charlotte's advice kept her from speaking out of turn.

They stood for some time without speaking a word. She began to imagine that their silence was to last through the two dances, and at first was resolved not to break it; till suddenly fancying that it would be the greater punishment to her partner to oblige him to talk, she made some slight observation on the dance. He replied, and was again silent. After a pause of some minutes, she addressed him a second time with, "It is your turn to say something now, Mr. Darcy. I talked about the dance, and you ought to make some sort of remark on the size of the room, or the number of couples."

He smiled, and assured her, "I will say whatever it is you wish to hear."

She made an effort not to look at him. Whenever he bestowed one of his rare smiles, it became hard not to think of his mouth. A tiny shiver of anticipation and longing filled her. Why she should feel the slightest bit of attraction for a man as detestable as Darcy was beyond her. Luckily, she was not a slave to her body, but to the logic of her mind, and could well convince her impulses to behave. "Very well. That reply will do for the present. Perhaps by and by I may observe that private balls are much pleasanter than public ones. But now we may be silent."

"Do you talk by rule, then, while you are dancing?"

"Sometimes. One must speak a little, you know. It would look odd to be entirely silent for half-an-hour together. Yet for the advantage of some, conversation ought to be so arranged, so they may have the trouble of saying as little as possible."

"Are you consulting your own feelings in the present case, or do you imagine that you are gratifying mine?"

"Both," replied Elizabeth sarcastically. "I have always seen a great similarity in the turn of our minds. We are each of us unsocial, with a taciturn disposition, unwilling to speak unless we expect to say something that will amaze the whole room and be handed down to posterity with all the éclat of a proverb."

"This is no striking resemblance of your own character, I am sure," said he. "How near it may be to mine, I cannot pretend to say. You think it a faithful portrait undoubtedly."

"I must not decide on my own performance." **Despite her better judgment, she found something wholly satisfying in bantering with him.**

He made no answer. They were again silent till they had gone down the dance. "Do you walk often to Meryton with your sisters?"

"Yes." With a cautious glance to where Charlotte Lucas stood in the crowd, she was unable to resist the temptation of adding, "When you met us there the other day, we had just been forming a new acquaintance."

The effect was immediate. A deeper shade of hauteur overspread his features, but he said not a word for many moments, and Elizabeth, though blaming herself for her own weakness, could not go on. At length Darcy spoke, and in a constrained manner said, "Mr. Wickham is blessed with such happy manners as may ensure his making friends—whether he may be equally capable of retaining them, is less certain."

"He has been so unlucky as to lose your friendship," replied Elizabeth with emphasis, "and in a manner which he is likely to suffer from all his life."

Darcy made no answer, and seemed desirous of changing the subject. At that moment, Sir William Lucas appeared close to them, meaning to pass through the set to the other side of the room. But, on perceiving Mr. Darcy, he stopped with a bow to compliment him on his dancing and his partner. "I have been most highly gratified indeed, my dear sir. Such superior dancing is not often seen. It is evident you belong to the first circles. Allow me to say, however, that your fair partner does not disgrace you, and I must hope to have this pleasure often repeated, especially when a certain desirable event, my dear Eliza," he paused and glanced at Jane and Bingley, "shall take place. What congratulations will then flow! I appeal to Mr. Darcy, but let me not interrupt you, sir. You will not thank me for detaining you from the bewitching converse of that young lady, whose bright eyes are also upbraiding me."

The latter part of this address was scarcely heard by Darcy, but Sir William's allusion to his friend seemed to strike him forcibly, and his eyes were directed with a very serious expression towards Bingley and Jane, who were dancing together. Recovering himself, he turned to his partner, and said, "Sir William's interruption has made me forget what we were talking of."

"I do not think we were speaking at all. Sir William could not have interrupted two people in the room who had less to say. We have tried two or three subjects already without success, and what we are to talk of next I cannot imagine."

"What think you of books?" he asked, smiling. **Again, the pleasantness of it took her off guard. Why was he determined to be so nice when she had determined to hate him?**

"Books—oh, no! I am sure we never read the same, or at least not with the same feelings."

"I am sorry you think so. If that be the case, there can at least be no want of subject. We may compare our different opinions."

"No, I cannot talk of books in a ballroom. My head is always full of something else."

"The present always occupies you in such scenes, does it?" He gave her a look of doubt.

"Yes, always," she replied, without knowing what she said, for her thoughts had wandered far from the subject. She said no more, and they went down the other dance and parted in silence.

They had not long separated, when Miss Bingley came towards her, and with an expression of civil disdain accosted her, "So, Miss Eliza, I hear you are quite delighted with George Wickham! Your sister has been talking to me about him, and asking me a thousand questions. I find the young man quite forgot to tell you, among his other communication, that he was the son of old Wickham, the late Mr. Darcy's steward. Let me recommend you, however, as a friend, not to give implicit confidence to all his assertions as to Mr. Darcy's using him ill. It is perfectly false. On the contrary, he has always been remarkably kind to him, though George Wickham has treated Mr. Darcy in a most infamous manner. I do not know the particulars, but I know Mr. Darcy is not in the least to blame. He cannot bear to hear George Wickham mentioned, and though my brother thought he could not avoid including him in his invitation to the officers, he was excessively glad to find that he had taken himself out of the way. His coming into the country at all is a most insolent thing, indeed, and I wonder how he could presume to do it. I pity you, Miss Eliza, for this discovery of your favorite soldier's guilt, but considering his descent, one could not expect much better."

"His guilt and his descent appear by your account to be the same," said Elizabeth angrily. "For I have heard you accuse him of nothing worse than of being the son of Mr. Darcy's steward, and of that, I can assure you, he informed me himself."

"I beg your pardon," replied Miss Bingley, turning away with a sneer. "Excuse my interference. It was kindly meant."

"Insolent wretch!" whispered Elizabeth to herself. "You are much mistaken if you expect to influence me by such a paltry attack as this. I see nothing in it but your own willful ignorance and the malice of Mr. Darcy." She then sought her eldest sister, who has undertaken to make inquiries on the same subject to Bingley. Jane met her with a smile of such sweet complacency, a glow of such happy expression, as sufficiently marked how well she was satisfied with the occurrences of the evening. Elizabeth instantly read her feelings, and at that moment solicitude for Wickham, resentment against his enemies, and everything else, gave way before the hope of Jane's being in the fairest way for happiness.

"I want to know," she said, with a countenance no less smiling than her sister's, "what you have learned about Mr. Wickham. But perhaps you have been too pleasantly engaged to think of any third person, in which case you may be sure of my pardon."

"No," replied Jane, "I have not forgotten him, though I have nothing satisfactory to tell you. Mr. Bingley does not know the whole of his history, and is quite ignorant of the circumstances which have principally offended Mr. Darcy, but he will vouch for the good conduct, the probity, and honor of his friend, and is perfectly convinced that Mr. Wickham has deserved much less attention from Mr. Darcy than he has received. I am sorry to say by his account as well as his sister's, Mr. Wickham is by no means a respectable young man and has deserved to lose Mr. Darcy's regard."

"Mr. Bingley does not know Mr. Wickham himself?"

"No. He never saw him till the other morning at Meryton."

"This account then is what he has received from Mr. Darcy. I am satisfied. But what does he say of the living?"

"He does not exactly recollect the circumstances, but he believes it was left to him conditionally."

"I have no doubt of Mr. Bingley's sincerity," said Elizabeth warmly. "You must excuse me for not being convinced by assurances alone, but I shall venture to think of both gentlemen as I did before."

She then changed the discourse to one more gratifying to

each, and on which there could be no difference of sentiment. Elizabeth listened to the happy, though modest, hopes Jane entertained of Mr. Bingley's regard, and said all in her power to heighten her confidence in it. On their being joined by Mr. Bingley himself, Elizabeth withdrew from the ballroom to take in a breath of fresh air on the balcony where she found herself quite alone.

The cool night had a calming effect on her thoughts, as she considered all she had been told of Darcy and Wickham. None of Jane's assurances as to the honorable actions of Darcy so much as dented her resolve against the man. As far as Elizabeth was concerned, he had nothing to recommend him, and not all of the money in England would induce her to think kindly of him, let alone ten thousand a year.

"Miss Bennet."

So engaged was she in her own thoughts, she had not noticed the object of them had followed her out onto the balcony. He stood some distance away, though at a very inconvenient place, for he blocked any easy retreat back into the house. To get away she would be forced to walk a wide arch around him, a feat it seemed most silly to perform. "Mr. Darcy."

She wondered at his standing there, watching her, and when he did not deign to speak again, she suddenly exclaimed, "I remember you once said, Mr. Darcy, that you hardly ever forgave, that your resentment once created was unappeasable. You are very cautious, I suppose, as to its *being created*."

"I am," said he, with a firm voice.

"And never allow yourself to be blinded by prejudice?" **She lifted her chin, staring boldly into his eyes.**

"I hope not." **He took a step closer, and then another, till he had joined her near the railing. They were hidden by shadows away from the view of the windows. The sound of laughter** and music poured from inside, but she barely heard it. All of her attention became focused on him. The darkness, the garden beyond the railing, the shadows cast upon his face—they all reminded her of her dream and she felt transfixed upon her place. She opened her mouth to speak, but Darcy chose that moment to lift his hand. His fingers hovered between them, hesitating before reaching to cup her cheek. The touch created a shock of heat to her system, opposing the cooler night. She trembled. His scent replaced that of the fresh night air, yet she found it invigorating.

Without much care to her words, she continued a little breathlessly. "It is particularly incumbent on those who never change their opinion, to be secure of judging properly at first."

"May I ask you the purpose of your questions?" His fingers did not move and yet she felt as if they ran along her entire body. She trembled again; her knees weakened, and she swayed on her feet. She parted her lips, taking in rapid, deep breaths.

"Merely to the illustration of *your* character," said she, endeavoring to shake off the sudden gravity of her predicament. "I am trying to make it out."

"And what is your success?" His breath whispered against her cheek. She perceived him to be closer, yet, without detecting him to move. There was something open about his expression, but she could not make out the details of it in her heightened state.

She shook her head, unable to force her eyes from him. She could not think but to answer honestly. "I do not get on at all. I hear such different accounts of you as to puzzle me exceedingly."

"I can readily believe that reports may vary greatly with respect to me." Suddenly, his hand was gone and he had stepped back into the light. The cast of flickering candlelight against his face through the window effectively ended the spell that he had woven with his nearness. Back was the serious Darcy she was accustomed to. "I could wish, Miss Bennet, that you were not to sketch my character at the present moment, as there is reason to fear that the performance would reflect no credit on either."

Elizabeth forced her features to harden. The effects of his touch still stung her flesh and she wanted nothing more than to rub her cheek. She resisted. "But if I do not take your likeness now, I may never have another opportunity."

"I would by no means suspend any pleasure of yours," he coldly replied.

Just when she would inquire as to his reason for seeking her out on the balcony, he bowed and walked just as quickly away. Elizabeth, in her ire, followed him, but not with the intent of chasing him down. Instead, she watched in which direction he walked so that she could go the opposite way. Her heart was still beating fast when Miss Lucas came to inquire after the pleasantness of her last dance partner. Elizabeth, still stunned that he had touched her face, and that her own body had reacted with such passion; could scarcely relate all her hearty dislike of the man before Mr. Collins came up to them, and told her with great exultation that he had just been so fortunate as to make a most important discovery.

"I have found out," said he, "by a singular accident, that there is now in the room a near relation of my patroness. I happened to overhear the gentleman himself mentioning to the young lady who does the honors of the house the names of his cousin Miss de Bourgh, and of her mother Lady Catherine. How wonderfully these sort of things occur! Who would have thought of my meeting with, perhaps, a nephew of Lady Catherine de Bourgh in this assembly? I am most thankful that the discovery is made in time for me to pay my respects to him, which I am now going to do, and trust he will excuse my not having done it before. My total ignorance of the connection must plead my apology."

"You are not going to introduce yourself to Mr. Darcy!" **Elizabeth was mortified by the idea.**

"Indeed I am. I shall entreat his pardon for not having done it earlier. It will be in my power to assure him that her ladyship was quite well yesterday se'nnight."

Elizabeth tried to dissuade him from such a scheme, assuring him that Mr. Darcy would consider his addressing him without introduction as an impertinence, rather than a compliment to his aunt. It was not in the least necessary there should be any notice on either side, and if it were necessary it was up to the discretion of Mr. Darcy, the superior in consequence, to begin the acquaintance.

Mr. Collins listened to her with the determined air of following his own inclination. "My dear Miss Elizabeth, I have the highest opinion in the world in your excellent judgment in all matters within the scope of your understanding, but permit me to say that there must be a wide difference between the established forms of ceremony amongst the laity, and those which regulate the clergy. Give me leave to observe that I consider the clerical office as equal in point of dignity with the highest rank in the kingdom—provided that a proper humility of behavior is at the same time maintained. You must therefore allow me to follow the dictates of my conscience on this occasion, which leads me to perform what I look on as a point of duty."

With a low bow he left her to attack Mr. Darcy, whose reception of his advances she eagerly watched, and whose astonishment at being so addressed was very evident. Her cousin prefaced his speech with a solemn bow and though she could not hear a word of it, she felt as if hearing it all, and saw in the motion of his lips the words "apology," "Hunsford," and "Lady Catherine de Bourgh." It vexed her to see him expose himself to such a man. Mr. Darcy was eyeing him with unrestrained wonder, and when at last Mr. Collins allowed him time to speak, replied with an air of distant civility. Mr. Collins, however, was not discouraged from speaking again, and Mr. Darcy's contempt seemed abundantly increasing with the length of his second speech, and at the end of it he only made him a slight bow, and moved another way. Mr. Collins then returned to Elizabeth.

"I have no reason, I assure you," said he, "to be dissatisfied with my reception. Mr. Darcy seemed much pleased with the attention. He answered me with the utmost civility, and even paid me the compliment of saying that he was so well convinced of Lady Catherine's discernment as to be certain she could never bestow a favor unworthily. It was really a very handsome thought. Upon the whole, I am much pleased with him."

As Elizabeth had no longer any interest of her own to pursue, she turned her attention almost entirely on her sister and Mr. Bingley. The thoughts to which her agreeable obser-vations gave birth made her almost as happy as Jane. She pic-tured her settled in that very house, in all the felicity which a marriage of true affection could bestow. She felt capable, under such circumstances, of endeavoring to like Bingley's two sisters. She plainly saw her mother's thoughts were bent the same way, and she determined not to venture near her, lest she might hear too much. When they sat down to supper she considered it a most unlucky perverseness which placed them within one of each other. She was deeply vexed to find her mother talking to Lady Lucas freely, openly, and of nothing else but her expecta-tion that Jane would soon be married to Mr. Bingley. It was an animating subject, and Mrs. Bennet seemed incapable of fatigue while enumerating the advantages of the match. His being such a charming young man, and so rich, and living but three miles from them, were the first points of self-gratulation. Then it was such a comfort to think how fond the two sisters were of Jane, and to be certain they must desire the connection as much as she. It was, moreover, such a promising thing for her younger daughters, as Jane's marrying so great a man must throw them in the way of other rich men. Lastly, it was so pleasant at her time of life to be able to consign her single daughters to the care of their sister that she might not be obliged to go into company more than she liked. She concluded with many good wishes that Lady Lucas might soon be equally fortunate, though evidently and triumphantly believing there was no chance of it.

In vain did Elizabeth endeavor to check the rapidity of her mother's words, or persuade her to describe her felicity in a less audible whisper; for, to her inexpressible vexation, she could perceive that the chief of it was overheard by Mr. Darcy, who sat opposite to them.

Her mother only scolded her for being nonsensical. "What is Mr. Darcy to me, pray, that I should be afraid of him? I am sure we owe him no such particular civility as to be obliged to say nothing he may not like to hear."

"For heaven's sake, madam, speak lower. What advantage can it be for you to offend Mr. Darcy? You will never recommend yourself to his friend by so doing!" Elizabeth frowned, wondering where her ardent need to defend Mr. Darcy came from. She tried to tell herself it was because of Jane, but as she touched her cheek she knew that was not entirely the case.

However, nothing that she could say had any influence. Her mother would talk of her views in the same intelligible tone. Elizabeth blushed and blushed again with shame and vexation. She could not help frequently glancing at Mr. Darcy, though every glance convinced her of what she dreaded. Though he was not always looking at her mother, she was convinced that his attention was invariably fixed by her. The expression of his face changed gradually from indignant contempt to a composed and steady severity.

At length, Mrs. Bennet had no more to say; and Lady Lucas, who had been long yawning at the repetition of delights which she saw no likelihood of sharing, was left to the comforts of cold ham and chicken. Elizabeth now began to revive. But the interval of tranquility was not long for, when supper was over, singing was talked of and she had the mortification of seeing Mary, after very little entreaty, preparing to oblige the company. By many significant looks and silent entreaties, did she attempt to prevent such a proof of complaisance, but in vain for Mary would not understand them. Such an opportunity of exhibiting was delightful to her, and she began her song.

Elizabeth's eyes fixed on her with most painful sensations, and she watched her progress through the several stanzas with an impatience which was ill rewarded at their close. Mary, on receiving, amongst the thanks of the table, the hint of a hope that she might be prevailed on to favor them again, after the pause of half a minute began another. Mary's powers were by no means fitted for such a display. Her voice was weak and her manner affected.

Elizabeth was in agony. She looked at Jane to see how she bore it, but Jane was very composedly talking to Bingley. She looked at his two sisters, and saw them making signs of derision at each other, and at Darcy, who continued imperturbably grave. She looked at her father to entreat his interference, lest Mary should be singing all night. He took the hint, and when Mary had finished her second song, said aloud, "That will do extremely well, child. You have delighted us long enough. Let the other young ladies have time to exhibit."

Mary, though pretending not to hear, was somewhat disconcerted. Elizabeth, sorry for her, and sorry for her father's speech, was afraid her anxiety had done no good. Others of the party were now applied to.

"If I," said Mr. Collins, "were so fortunate as to be able to sing, I should have great pleasure in obliging the company with an air. I consider music a very innocent diversion, and perfectly compatible with the profession of a clergyman. I do not mean to assert that we can be justified in devoting too much of our time to music, for there are certainly other things to be attended to. The rector of a parish has much to do . . ." **Mr. Collins said more, much more, but Elizabeth was too vexed to pay him much mind.** When finally the man concluded his speech, which had been spoken so loud as to be heard by half the room, he gave a bow to Mr. Darcy. Many stared and smiled, but no one looked more amused than Mr. Bennet himself, while his wife seriously commended Mr. Collins for having spoken so sensibly, and observed in a half-whisper to Lady Lucas, that he was a remarkably clever, good kind of young man.

To Elizabeth it appeared her family had made an agreement to expose themselves to as much ridicule as they could during the evening, and it would have been impossible for them to play their parts with more spirit or finer success. Some of the exhibition escaped Bingley's notice, as his concentration was so fixed upon Jane. Otherwise, her mortification might have been complete. That Bingley's two sisters and Mr. Darcy should have such an opportunity of ridiculing her relations, was bad enough, and she could not determine whether the silent contempt of the gentleman, or the insolent smiles of the ladies, were more intolerable. **Seeing Mr. Darcy studying her, she wondered if he silently judged her as well for allowing him to touch her cheek, and quickly made her escape from his immediate notice through the crowded room.**

The rest of the evening brought her little amusement. She was teased by Mr. Collins, who continued most perseveringly by her side, and though he could not prevail on her to dance with him again, put it out of her power to dance with others. In vain she entreated him to stand up with somebody else, and offered to introduce him to any young lady in the room. He assured her, that as to dancing, he was perfectly indifferent to it. His chief object was by delicate attentions to recommend himself to her and he should therefore make a point of remaining close to her the whole evening. There was no arguing upon such a project. She owed her greatest relief to Charlotte, who joined them often, and good-naturedly engaged Mr. Collins's conversation to herself.

She was at least free from the offense of Mr. Darcy's further notice, though often standing within a very short distance of her, quite disengaged, he never came near enough to speak. She felt it to be the probable consequence of her allusions to Mr. Wickham, and rejoiced in it. **Perhaps his touching her cheek had been merely to turn her face so he could see its expression in the dark. Surely, such an act went against the propriety of the gentleman's nature, but no matter the cause, she resolved to not care about the event and to put it far from her mind.**

The Longbourn party were the last of all the company to depart, and, by a maneuver of Mrs. Bennet, had to wait for their carriage a quarter of an hour after everybody else was gone, which gave them time to see how heartily they were wished away by some of the family. Mrs. Hurst and her sister scarcely opened their mouths, except to complain of fatigue, and were evidently impatient to have the house to themselves. They repulsed every attempt of Mrs. Bennet at conversation, and by so doing threw a languor over the whole party. This was little relieved by the long speeches of Mr. Collins, who was complimenting Mr. Bingley and his sisters on the elegance of their entertainment, and the hospitality and politeness which had marked their behavior to their guests. Darcy said nothing at all. Mr. Bennet, in equal silence, was enjoying the scene. Mr. Bingley and Jane were standing together, a little detached from the rest, and talked only to each other. Elizabeth preserved as steady a silence as either Mrs. Hurst or Miss Bingley, and even Lydia was too fatigued to utter more than the occasional exclamation of "Lord, how tired I am!" accompanied by a violent yawn.

When at length they arose to take leave, Mrs. Bennet was pressingly civil in her hope of seeing the whole family soon at Longbourn, and especially addressed Mr. Bingley, to assure him how happy he would make them by eating a family dinner with them at any time, without the ceremony of a formal invitation. Bingley was grateful, and he readily engaged for taking the earliest opportunity of waiting on her, after his return from London, where he was obliged to go the next day for a short time.

Mrs. Bennet was perfectly satisfied, and quitted the house under the delightful persuasion that, allowing for the necessary preparations of settlements, new carriages, and wedding clothes, she should undoubtedly see her daughter settled at Netherfield in the course of three or four months. Of having another daughter married to Mr. Collins, she thought with equal certainty, and with considerable, though not equal, pleasure. Elizabeth was the least dear to her of all her children; and though the man and the match were quite good enough for *her*, the worth of each was eclipsed by Mr. Bingley and Netherfield.

Elizabeth was to be married to the insufferable Mr. Collins. Darcy could scarcely believe what he had heard; though he had not meant to eavesdrop on Mrs. Bennet as she prattled on to Lady Lucas, it was not to be helped for the woman spoke very loudly

about private matters. The distaste he felt for such behavior had been made all the stronger by witnessing the excessive attention Mr. Collins bestowed upon the very person he had spent the evening observing.

The possibility that Mrs. Bennet had merely been expressing her own hopes and not the true intentions of her daughter, did not escape him. However, that idea brought him little comfort for Elizabeth had shown an unnerving interest in Mr. Wickham. The idea of either man—Wickham or Collins—possessing that which he himself would have did not set well upon him, nor did the knowledge that he had almost committed a grave impropriety.

When he had seen her go to the balcony, he had followed her with the express intention of explaining himself against some of her misconceptions, or at least that is what he told himself he would do. However, when he witnessed the gentle curves of her body caressed by moonlight, and her lips moving as if she scolded herself in some silent argument, he had been moved to act. He had wanted her then, wanted to pull her against his chest, to caress her hair, stroke her arms, and hold her close; wanted to feel the gentle press of her lips, the opening of her mouth, and the sweet, victorious moment when her resistance caved; needed the sensation of her body to his, flesh to flesh, heat to heat, sex to sex. Every inch of him stirred with desire. Had he lost another ounce of decorum he would have kissed her there on the balcony. Had he been allowed to act on pure impulse, he would have done more than kissed her. He would have thrown her over his shoulder and dragged her into the gardens, away from the music and the dancing, out of the grasp of Mr. Collins and the incessant annoyances of her family. There he would make love to her, wild and untamed, for how else could it be between them? She frustrated him, challenged him, drove him mad with distractions, and yet it only made the desires all the more forceful.

His body stirred; his arousal stiff and in need of relief. Darcy resisted his desire, not wanting to give into it once more. He should not care if Mr. Collins married her. If the whispers of the man were true it would be a good match for one of Mr. Bennet's daughters. The young ladies could do much worse than a parsonage under the patronage of his wealthy aunt, Lady Catherine de Bourgh. Still, it hardly seemed right to pair a woman of Elizabeth's natural vitality and spirit with such an insufferable man. Mr. Collins would kill the spirit he had grown to admire in her. Years of insipid and droning conversation would snuff the light from her eyes. It pained him to think of it. And, Wickham. He shivered at the very thought. That man would surely ruin her more grievously than Mr. Collins ever could. He would never allow such a match, even though such a decision was hardly his to make. However, Darcy could hardly depend upon Mr. Bennet to choose more wisely than Mr. Wickham, should the man pursue his daughter.

"I cannot have her for her family is far beneath mine, and I want no other to have her." He laughed at himself, a humorless, derisive sound that mocked his own sentiments. "What a gentleman am I to wish a spinster fate on such a woman; for, if not a spinster, I would then have her as my mistress—neither of which fates she is deserving of."

The lack of her family connections made it impossible for him to wish for much else beyond taking her as a lover, yet he would never dishonor a woman of breeding, no matter how ridiculous her parents were, or how low her prospects. Though, when he thought of Elizabeth, he did not think her so low. Confusion filled him. Never had his desires warred so fervently with his duty to his family name, and in the end he found himself seeking what physical release he could manage.

He had been a fool to think he could resist the temptation of the flesh, at least the temptation of his imagination when it came to the flesh. He could no more stop the trail of his hand down the front of his trousers than he could stop the memory of Elizabeth's heavily lidded eyes as she looked at him on the balcony. Would she have let him kiss her? She let him touch her face, caress her cheek. Even now he felt the impression of her soft skin against his fingertips. Oh, and her scent! She had smelled of flowers when he danced with her, subtle and elegant and meant to drive a man to distraction.

Darcy closed his eyes, wishing for that which could never be. He pressed a hand flat against the bedroom wall to support his weight as he lowered his head. His fist tightened, gliding over taut flesh. He would give almost anything for one night with her, one stolen moment, one secret encounter that would not end in ruin for either of them. Oh, but to have a kiss, a touch! Then, maybe she would release him of the hold she had over him; maybe he would be free of her. Maybe, maybe. . . .

Every inch of him ached to be back on that balcony, to press against her. He imagined peeling her dress from her skin, unveiling the gentle curves that haunted his erotic visions, touching supple flesh and hardened nipples. Would her eyes turn serious in such a moment? Or playful? Or challenging? Or would they close, overcome by the pleasure he could give her?

Curse her for this madness! His soul begged to be free of it. His mind taunted him with images he could not erase. His body cared naught, so long as his hand kept moving, hard and tight, propelling him onward. A plea escaped him, "Too much, too much," and his body answered with the gratifying moment of release.

Darcy groaned; gasping for breath as he let the bittersweet

pleasure overtake him. His heart beat hard and fast. Curse her fine eyes! He was immersed in madness and he knew not how to get out.

CHAPTER EIGHTEEN

THE NEXT DAY OPENED A NEW SCENE at Longbourn. Mr. Collins made his declaration in form. Having resolved to do it without loss of time, as his leave of absence extended only to the following Saturday, and having no feelings of diffidence to make it distressing to himself even at the moment, he set about it in a very orderly manner, with all the observances, which he supposed was a regular part of the business.

On finding Mrs. Bennet, Elizabeth, and one of the younger girls together, soon after breakfast, he addressed the mother, "May I solicit, madam, for the honor of a private audience with your fair daughter Elizabeth in the course of this morning?"

Before Elizabeth had time for anything but a gasp of surprise, Mrs. Bennet answered instantly, "Oh, dear, yes! Certainly, I am sure Lizzy will be very happy. I am sure she can have no objection. Come, Kitty, I want you upstairs." And, gathering her work together, she was hastening away, when Elizabeth called out, "Dear madam, do not go. I beg you will not go. Mr. Collins must excuse me. He can have nothing to say to me that anybody need not hear. I am going away myself."

"No nonsense, Lizzy. I desire you to stay where you are." And seeing Elizabeth's vexed and embarrassed looks, and her seeming about to escape, she added, "Lizzy, I insist upon your staying and hearing Mr. Collins."

Elizabeth could not oppose such an injunction and a moment's consideration made her sensible that it would be wisest to get it over as soon and as quietly as possible. She sat down again and tried to conceal her feelings, which were divided between distress and diversion. Mrs. Bennet and Kitty walked off. As soon as they were gone, Mr. Collins began.

"Believe me, my dear Miss Elizabeth, that your modesty, so far from doing you any disservice, rather adds to your other perfections. You would have been less amiable in my eyes had there not been this little unwillingness, but allow me to assure you I have your respected mother's permission for this address. You can hardly doubt the purport of my discourse; however your natural delicacy may lead you to dissemble. My attentions have been too marked to be mistaken. Almost as soon as I entered the house, I singled you out as the companion of my future life. But before I am run away with my feelings on this subject, perhaps it would be advisable for me to state my reasons for marrying, and, moreover, for coming into Hertfordshire with the design of selecting a wife."

The idea of Mr. Collins, with all his solemn composure, being run away with his feelings made Elizabeth so near laughing that she could not use his short pause to attempt to stop him, and he continued, "My reasons for marrying are, first, that I think it a right thing for every clergyman in easy circumstances, like myself, to set the example of matrimony in his parish. Secondly,

I am convinced that it will add greatly to my happiness. Thirdly, which perhaps I ought to have mentioned earlier, that it is the particular advice and recommendation of the very noble lady whom I have the honor of calling patroness. Twice has she condescended to give me her opinion on this subject, and it was but the very Saturday night before I left Hunsford, between our pools at quadrille, that she said, 'Mr. Collins, a clergyman like you must marry. Choose properly, choose a gentlewoman for my sake; for your own let her be an active, useful sort of person, not brought up high, but able to make a small income go a good way. This is my advice. Find such a woman as soon as you can, bring her to Hunsford, and I will visit her.' Allow me, by the way, to observe, my fair cousin, that I do not reckon the notice and kindness of Lady Catherine de Bourgh as among the least of the advantages in my power to offer. You will find her manners beyond anything I can describe. Your wit and vivacity, I think, must be acceptable to her, especially when tempered with the silence and respect which her rank will inevitably excite. Thus for my general intention in favor of matrimony; it remains to be told why my views were directed towards Longbourn instead of my own neighborhood, where I can assure you there are many amiable young women. But the fact is, that being, as I am, to inherit this estate after the death of your honored father—who may live many years longer—I could not satisfy myself without resolving to choose a wife from among his daughters that the loss to them might be as little as possible when the melancholy event takes place. This has been my motive and I flatter myself it will not sink me in your esteem."

Elizabeth opened her mouth to interrupt, but he did not give long enough pause and his words carried over the beginning of hers.

"And now nothing remains but for me but to assure you in

the most animated language of the violence of my affection. To fortune I am perfectly indifferent, and shall make no demand of that nature on your father, since I am well aware that it could not be complied with; and that one thousand pounds in the four percents, which will not be yours till after your mother's decease, is all that you may ever be entitled to. On that head, therefore, I shall be uniformly silent. You may assure yourself that no ungenerous reproach shall ever pass my lips when we are married."

It was absolutely necessary to interrupt him now. "You are too hasty, sir! I have made no answer. Let me do it without further loss of time. Accept my thanks for the compliment you are paying me. I am very sensible of the honor of your proposal, but it is impossible for me to do otherwise than to decline it."

"I am not now to learn," replied Mr. Collins, with a formal wave of the hand, "that it is usual with young ladies to reject the addresses of the man whom they secretly mean to accept, when he first applies for their favor; and that sometimes the refusal is repeated a second, or even a third time. I am therefore by no means discouraged by what you have just said, and shall hope to lead you to the altar ere long."

"Upon my word, sir," insisted Elizabeth, "I assure you that I am not one of those young ladies who are so daring as to risk their happiness on the chance of being asked a second time. I am perfectly serious in my refusal. You could not make me happy, and I am convinced that I am the last woman in the world who could make you so. Nay, were Lady Catherine to know me, I am persuaded she would find me in every respect ill qualified for the situation."

"Were it certain that Lady Catherine would think so," said Mr. Collins very gravely, "but I cannot imagine that her ladyship would disapprove of you. You may be certain when I have the honor of seeing her again, I shall speak in the very highest terms of your modesty, economy, and other amiable qualification."

"Indeed, Mr. Collins, all praise of me will be unnecessary. You must give me leave to judge for myself, and pay me the compliment of believing what I say. I wish you to be very happy and very rich, and by refusing your hand, do all in my power to prevent your being otherwise. In making me the offer, you must have satisfied the delicacy of your feelings with regard to my family, and may take possession of Longbourn estate whenever it falls, without any self-reproach. This matter may be considered as finally settled." And rising as she spoke, she would have quitted the room, had Mr. Collins not addressed her once more.

"When I do myself the honor of speaking to you next on the subject, I shall hope to receive a more favorable answer than you have now given me. Though I am far from accusing you of cruelty at present, because I know it to be the established custom of your sex to reject a man on the first application, and perhaps you have even now said as much to encourage my suit as would be consistent with the true delicacy of the female character."

"Really, Mr. Collins," said Elizabeth with some embarrassment for him, "you puzzle me exceedingly. If what I have hitherto said can appear to you in the form of encouragement, I know not how to express my refusal in such a way as to convince you of its being one."

"You must give me leave to flatter myself, my dear cousin, that your refusal of my addresses is merely words of course. My reasons for believing it are briefly these: It does not appear to me that my hand is unworthy your acceptance, or that the establishment I can offer would be any other than highly desirable. My situation in life, my connections with the family of de Bourgh, and my relationship to your own, are circumstances highly in my favor. You should take it into further consideration that in spite of your manifold attractions it is by no means certain that another offer of marriage may ever be made to you. Your portion is unhappily so small that it will in all likelihood undo the effects of your loveliness and amiable qualifications. As I must therefore conclude that you are not serious in your rejection of me, I shall choose to attribute it to your wish of increasing my love by suspense, according to the usual practice of elegant females."

"I do assure you, sir, that I have no pretensions whatever to that kind of elegance which consists in tormenting a respectable man. I would rather be paid the compliment of being believed sincere. I thank you again for the honor you have done me in your proposals, but to accept them is impossible. My feelings in every respect forbid it. Can I speak plainer? Do not consider me now as an elegant female, intending to plague you, but as a rational creature, speaking the truth from her heart."

"You are uniformly charming!" said he, with an air of awkward gallantry. "I am persuaded that when sanctioned by the express authority of both your excellent parents, my proposals will not fail of being acceptable."

To such perseverance in willful self-deception Elizabeth would make no reply, and immediately and in silence withdrew, determined if he persisted in considering her repeated refusals as flattering encouragement, to apply to her father, whose negative might be uttered in such a manner as to be decisive, and whose behavior at least could not be mistaken for the affectation and coquetry of an elegant female.

Mr. Collins was not left long to the silent contemplation of his successful love. Mrs. Bennet, having dawdled about in the vestibule to watch for the end of the conference, no sooner saw Elizabeth open the door and with quick step pass her towards the staircase, than she entered the breakfast room, and congratulated both him and herself in warm terms on the happy prospect of their nearer connection. Mr. Collins received and returned these felicitations with equal pleasure, and then proceeded to relate the particulars of their interview, with the result of which he trusted he had every reason to be satisfied, since the refusal which his cousin had steadfastly given him would naturally flow from her bashful modesty and the genuine delicacy of her character.

This information, however, startled Mrs. Bennet. She would have been glad to be equally satisfied that her daughter had meant to encourage him by protesting against his proposals, but she dared not believe it, and could not help saying so. "But, depend upon it, Mr. Collins! Lizzy shall be brought to reason. I will speak to her directly. She is a very headstrong, foolish girl, and does not know her own interest but I will make her know it."

"Pardon me for interrupting you, madam," said Mr. Collins, "but if she is really headstrong and foolish, I know not whether she would be a very desirable wife to a man in my situation, who naturally looks for happiness in the marriage state. If therefore she actually persists in rejecting my suit, perhaps it is better not to force her into accepting me, because she could not contribute much to my felicity if liable to such defects of temper."

"Sir, you quite misunderstand me," said Mrs. Bennet, alarmed. "Lizzy is only headstrong in such matters as these. In everything else she is as good-natured a girl as ever lived. I will go directly to Mr. Bennet, and we shall very soon settle it with her, I am sure."

She did not give him time to reply, but hurried instantly to her husband and called out as she entered the library, "Oh! Mr. Bennet, you are wanted immediately. We are all in an uproar. You must come and make Lizzy marry Mr. Collins, for she vows she will not have him, and if you do not make haste he will change his mind and not have *her*."

Mr. Bennet raised his eyes from his book as she entered,

and fixed them on her face with a calm unconcern which was not in the least altered by her communication.

"I have not the pleasure of understanding you," said he, when she had finished her speech.

"Mr. Collins wants to marry Lizzy! Lizzy declares she will not have Mr. Collins, and Mr. Collins begins to say that he will not have Lizzy."

"And what am I to do on the occasion? It seems a hopeless business."

"Speak to Lizzy about it yourself. Tell her that you insist upon her marrying him."

"Let her be called down. She shall hear my opinion."

Mrs. Bennet rang the bell, and Miss Elizabeth was summoned to the library.

"Come here, child," said her father as she appeared. "I understand Mr. Collins has made you an offer of marriage. Is it true?" Elizabeth replied that it was. "Very well. And this offer of marriage you have refused?"

"I have, sir."

"Very well. We now come to the point. Your mother insists upon your accepting it. Is it not so, Mrs. Bennet?"

"Yes, or I will never see her again."

"An unhappy alternative is before you, Elizabeth. From this day you must be a stranger to one of your parents. Your mother will never see you again if you do *not* marry Mr. Collins, and I will never see you again if you *do*."

Elizabeth could not but smile at such a conclusion, but Mrs. Bennet, who had persuaded herself that her husband regarded the affair as she wished, was excessively disappointed.

"What do you mean, Mr. Bennet, in talking this way? You promised me to insist upon her marrying him."

"My dear," replied her husband, "I have two small favors to

request. First, that you will allow me the free use of my under-standing on the present occasion. Secondly, of my room. I shall be glad to have the library to myself as soon as may be."

In spite of her disappointment in her husband, Mrs. Bennet did not give up the point. She talked to Elizabeth again and again, coaxing and threatening by turns. She endeavored to secure Jane in her interest; but Jane, with all possible mildness, declined to interfere. Elizabeth replied to her attacks, sometimes with real earnestness, and sometimes with playful gaiety. Though her manner varied, her determination did not.

Mr. Collins, meanwhile, meditated in solitude on what had passed. He thought too well of himself to comprehend on what motives his cousin could refuse him. Though his pride was hurt, he suffered in no other way. His regard for her was quite imagi-nary, and the possibility of her deserving her mother's reproach prevented his feeling any regret.

While the family was in this confusion, Charlotte Lucas came to spend the day with them. She was met in the vestibule by Lydia, who, flying to her, said in a half whisper, "I am glad you are come, for there is such fun here! Mr. Collins has made an offer to Lizzy this morning and she will not have him."

Charlotte hardly had time to answer, before they were joined by Kitty, who came to tell the same news. No sooner had they entered the breakfast room, where Mrs. Bennet was alone, than she likewise began on the subject, calling on Miss Lucas for her compassion, and entreating her to persuade her friend Lizzy to comply with the wishes of all her family. "Pray do, my dear Miss Lucas," she added in a melancholy tone, "for nobody is on my side, nobody takes part with me, nobody feels for my poor nerves."

Charlotte's reply was spared by the entrance of Jane and Elizabeth.

"Aye, there she comes," continued Mrs. Bennet, "looking as unconcerned as may be, and caring no more for us than if we were at York, provided she can have her own way. But I tell you, Miss Lizzy, if you take it into your head to go on refusing every offer of marriage in this way, you will never get a husband at all; and I will have had that conversation, you know which I speak of, for no reason. I am sure I do not know who is to maintain you when your father is dead. I shall not be able to keep you, and so I warn you. I am done with you from this very day. I told you that I should never speak to you again, and you will find me as good as my word. I have no pleasure in talking to undutiful children. Not that I have much pleasure in talking to anybody. People who suffer as I do from nervous complaints can have no great inclination for talking. Nobody can tell what I suffer! But it is always so. Those who do not complain are never pitied."

Her daughters listened in silence to this effusion, sensible that any attempt to reason with her would only increase the irritation. She talked on without interruption till they were joined by Mr. Collins, who entered the room with an air more stately than usual. On perceiving him, Mrs. Bennet said to the girls, "Now, I do insist that all of you hold your tongues and let me and Mr. Collins have a little conversation together."

Elizabeth passed quietly out of the room, Jane and Kitty followed, but Lydia stood her ground, determined to hear all she could. Charlotte, detained first by the civility of Mr. Collins, whose inquiries after herself and all her family were very minute, and then by a little curiosity, satisfied herself with walking to the window and pretending not to hear. In a doleful voice Mrs. Bennet began the projected conversation, "Oh, Mr. Collins!"

"My dear madam, let us be forever silent on this point. Far be it from me," he said in a voice that marked his displeasure, "to resent the behavior of your daughter. Resignation to inevitable evils is the duty of us all; the peculiar duty of a young man who has been so fortunate as I have been in early preferment, and I trust I am resigned. You will not, I hope, consider it a disrespect to your family by withdrawing my pretensions to your daughter's favor, without having paid yourself and Mr. Bennet the compliment of requesting you to interpose your authority on my behalf."

Charlotte found Mr. Collin's reflection in the window as he spoke, and she watched him carefully. She could see why Elizabeth refused him, but her friend had always been prone to romantic inclinations and would have judged solely on her emotions, not practicality. Charlotte was not so imprudent. She was past an age to be choosy and had never been considered pretty. With an idea forming in the back of her mind, she turned to Mr. Collins and smiled as the conversation behind her lagged. "I believe you mentioned, sir, that your abode is across the lane from Rosings? Tell me, is it a grand view?"

To her inquiry, Mr. Collins was most obliged to answer, and did so with much care to the minute details of the park surrounding the parsonage.

CHAPTER NINETEEN

THE DISCUSSION OF MR. COLLINS'S OFFER was now nearly at an end, and Elizabeth had only to suffer from the peevish allusions of her mother. As for the gentleman himself, his feelings were chiefly expressed, not by embarrassment or dejection, or by trying to avoid her, but by stiffness of manner and resentful silence. He scarcely ever spoke to her, and his assiduous attentions were transferred for the rest of the day to Miss Lucas, whose civility in listening to him was a seasonable relief to them all, and especially to her friend.

The morrow produced no abatement of Mrs. Bennet's ill humor or ill health. Mr. Collins was also in the same state of angry pride. Elizabeth had hoped that his resentment might shorten his visit, but his plan did not appear in the least affected by it. He was to have always gone on Saturday, and to Saturday he meant to stay.

After breakfast, the girls walked to Meryton to inquire if

Mr. Wickham had returned, and to lament over his absence from the Netherfield ball. He joined them on their entering town, and attended them to their aunt's where his regret and vexation, and the concern of everybody, was well talked over. To Elizabeth, however, he voluntarily acknowledged the necessity of his absence had been self-imposed.

"I found," said he, "as the time drew near that I had better not meet Mr. Darcy. To be in the same room, the same party with him for so many hours together, might be more than I could bear, and that scenes might arise unpleasant to more than myself."

She highly approved his forbearance, and they had leisure for a full discussion of it. Elizabeth, however, did not mention her interaction with Mr. Darcy, choosing to keep his strange behavior on the balcony completely to herself; for she did not even dare to mention the occurrence to Jane. As Wickham and another officer walked back with them to Longbourn, he particularly attended to her. His accompanying them was a double advantage. She felt all the compliment it offered to herself, and it was most acceptable as an occasion of introducing him to her father and mother.

Soon after their return, a letter was delivered to Miss Bennet from Netherfield. The envelope contained a sheet of elegant, little, hot-pressed paper, well covered with a lady's fair and flowing hand. Elizabeth saw her sister's countenance change as she read it, and saw her dwelling intently on some particular passages. Jane recollected herself, and putting the letter away, tried to join the general conversation with her usual cheerfulness. Elizabeth felt an anxiety on the subject which drew off her attention even from Wickham. No sooner had he and his companion taken leave, than a glance from Jane invited her to follow her upstairs.

When they had gained their own room, Jane, taking out the letter, said, "This is from Caroline Bingley. The whole party left Netherfield and they are on their way to town without any intention of returning. You shall hear what she says." She then read the first sentence aloud, which comprised the information of their having just resolved to follow their brother to town directly, and of their meaning to dine in Grosvenor Street, where Mr. Hurst had a house. Continuing to read, Jane said, "I do not pretend to regret anything I shall leave in Hertfordshire, except your society, my dearest friend. We will hope, at some future period, to enjoy many returns of that delightful intercourse we have known, and in the meanwhile may lessen the pain of separation by a very frequent and most unreserved correspondence. I depend on you for that."

Elizabeth listened to these high-flown expressions with distrust. The suddenness of their removal surprised her, but she saw nothing in it really to lament. It was not to be supposed that their absence from Netherfield would prevent Mr. Bingley's being there, and as to the loss of their society, she was persuaded that Jane must cease to regard it, in the enjoyment of his.

"It is unlucky," said Elizabeth, after a short pause, "that you should not be able to see your friends before they leave the country. But may we not hope that the period of future happiness to which Miss Bingley looks forward may arrive earlier than she is aware, and that the delightful intercourse you have known as friends will be renewed with greater satisfaction as sisters? Mr. Bingley will not be detained in London by them."

"Caroline decidedly says that none of the party will return into Hertfordshire this winter. I will read it to you." Jane again lifted the letter. "When my brother left us yesterday, he imagined that the business which took him to London might be concluded in three or four days, but we are certain it cannot be so. At the same time convinced that when Charles gets to town he will be in no hurry to leave it again, we have determined on following him thither, that he may not be obliged to spend his vacant hours in a comfortless hotel. Many of my acquaintances are already there for the winter. I wish you, my dearest friend, had an intention of making one of the crowd, but of that I despair. I sincerely hope your Christmas in Hertfordshire may abound in the gaieties which that season generally brings, and that your beaux will be so numerous as to prevent your feeling the loss of the three of whom we shall deprive you."

"It is evident by this," added Jane, "that he comes back no more this winter."

"It is only evident that Miss Bingley does not think he should come back."

"Why will you think so? It must be his own doing. He is his own master. But you do not know all. I will read you the passage which particularly hurts me. I will have no reserves from you." Again, she paused and lifted the letter. "Mr. Darcy is impatient to see his sister. To confess the truth, we are scarcely less eager to meet her again. I really do not think Georgiana Darcy has her equal for beauty, elegance, and accomplishments; and the affection she inspires in Louisa and myself is heightened into something still more interesting, from the hope we dare entertain of her being hereafter our sister. I do not know whether I ever before mentioned to you my feelings on this subject, but I will not leave the country without confiding them, and I trust you will not esteem them unreasonable. My brother admires her greatly already. He will have frequent opportunity now of seeing her on the most intimate footing and her relations all wish the connection as much as his own. With all these circumstances to favor an attachment, and nothing to prevent it, am I wrong in indulging a hope which will secure the happiness of so many?"

Elizabeth could think of nothing immediate to say, but that she severely disliked the author of such indulgences.

"What do you think of that, my dear Lizzy?" said Jane as she finished it. "Is it not clear enough? Does it not expressly declare that Caroline neither expects nor wishes me to be her sister? She is perfectly convinced of her brother's indifference, and if she suspects the nature of my feelings for him, she means to kindly put me on my guard. Can there be any other opinion on the subject?"

"Yes, there can for mine is totally different. Will you hear it?"

"Most willingly."

"You shall have it in a few words. Miss Bingley sees that her brother is in love with you, and wants him to marry Miss Darcy. She follows him to town in hope of keeping him there, and tries to persuade you that he does not care about you."

Jane shook her head.

"Indeed, Jane, you ought to believe me. No one who has ever seen you together can doubt his affection. Miss Bingley, I am sure, cannot. She is not such a simpleton. Could she have seen half as much love in Mr. Darcy for herself, she would have ordered her wedding clothes. But the case is this: We are not rich enough or grand enough for them. She is the more anxious to get Miss Darcy for her brother, from the notion that when there has been one intermarriage, she may have less trouble in achieving a second. In that scheme there is certainly some ingenuity, and I daresay it would succeed, if Miss de Bourgh were out of the way. But, my dearest Jane, you cannot seriously imagine that because Miss Bingley tells you her brother greatly admires Miss Darcy, he is in the smallest degree less sensible of your merit than when he took leave of you on Tuesday, or that it will be in her power to persuade him that, instead of being in love with you, he is very much in love with her friend."

"If we thought alike of Miss Bingley," replied Jane, "your representation of all this might make me quite easy. But I know the foundation is unjust. Caroline is incapable of willfully deceiving anyone. All that I can hope in this case is that she is deceiving herself."

"That is right. You could not have started a more happy idea, since you will not take comfort in mine. Believe her to be deceived, by all means. You have now done your duty by her, and must fret no longer."

"But can I be happy in accepting a man whose sisters and friends are all wishing him to marry elsewhere?"

"You must decide for yourself," said Elizabeth. "If, upon mature deliberation, you find that the misery of disobliging his two sisters is more than equivalent to the happiness of being his wife, I advise you by all means to refuse him."

"How can you talk so?" said Jane, faintly smiling. "You must know that though I should be exceedingly grieved at their disapprobation, I could not hesitate."

"I did not think you would. That being the case, I cannot consider your situation with much compassion."

"But if he returns no more this winter, my choice will never be required. A thousand things may arise in six months!"

Elizabeth treated the idea of his returning no more with the utmost contempt. It appeared to her merely the suggestion of Caroline's interested wishes, and she could not for a moment suppose that those wishes, however artfully spoken, could influence a young man so totally independent of everyone.

She told her sister as forcibly as possible what she felt on the subject, and soon had the pleasure of seeing its happy effect. Jane's temper was not despondent, and she was gradually led to hope that Bingley would return to Netherfield and answer every wish of her heart.

They agreed that Mrs. Bennet should only hear of the departure of the family, without being alarmed on the score of the gentleman's conduct. However, even this partial communication gave her a great deal of concern, and she bewailed it as exceedingly unlucky that the ladies should happen to go away just as they were all getting so intimate together. After lamenting it at some length, she had the consolation that Mr. Bingley would soon be down again and dining at Longbourn. The conclusion of all was the comfortable declaration, that though he had been invited only to a family dinner, she would take care to have two full courses.

CHAPTER TWENTY

THE BENNETS WERE ENGAGED TO DINE with the Lucases and again Miss Lucas was kind enough to listen to Mr. Collins. Elizabeth took an opportunity of thanking her. "It keeps him in good humor," said she, "and I am more obliged to you than I can express."

Charlotte assured her friend of her satisfaction in being useful, and that it amply repaid her for the little sacrifice of her time. This was very amiable, but Charlotte's kindness extended farther than Elizabeth had any conception of. Charlotte's object was nothing else than to secure her friend from any return of Mr. Collins's advances, by engaging them towards herself. Such was Miss Lucas's scheme; and appearances were so favorable, that when the opportunity arose, **she managed to get him alone. It was not hard, for none of the others showed any interest in talking to the man, and were indeed grateful for her attentions to him.**

Despite her pragmatic determination, Charlotte felt herself quite nervous as she walked alone with Mr. Collins. There was little need for her to speak, for he was happy to supply both sides of the conversation. In that way, her scheme proved itself to be easy. Though hardly practiced in the arts of flirtation, she did her best to send those subtle hints in his direction—batting her eyelashes, pursing her lips, swaying just a little. At one point, she allowed her hand to brush against the back of his; and, at another, she bent over to pick a flower, stumbling so that her gown lifted ever so slightly at the ankle. Mr. Collins, of course, was obliged to catch her and she allowed her chest to fall directly into his. The poor man seemed most flustered by the attention, and spent an improperly long time looking down at her chest, hand splayed as if he would pounce upon it in lecherous attention.

However, soon after, by the continued flow of his words, Charlotte would have assumed him to be unaffected by her efforts, if not for the strange way he carried his hands before his groin and walked with a wider than normal step. Never before had she been aware of having such a physical effect on a man, and with that awareness Charlotte felt a sense of power. Diligently, she listened to Mr. Collins prattle on. By his own admission he fancied himself too honorable to trifle with a woman's modesty, and Charlotte meant to use this information to her utmost advantage.

After purposefully tripping a second time, Charlotte fell backwards against him so that her back was to his chest. As she bent forward in an effort to right herself, the back of her skirt brushed indecently against him and she pretended not to notice. Mr. Collins, however, let loose a pained sigh and trembled, his cheeks puffing out with the effort it took to rein in his obvious arousal.

"Forgive me, sir," said she. "I must confess I am unused to

walking alone with a gentleman. However, I feel there is nothing to worry about with one such as yourself, being as you are a man with such a high and noble position."

This seemed to gratify him, and he assured her in the longest of terms that he did not think less of her for agreeing to walk with him. They continued on as they had before, him talking and Charlotte nodding in encouragement. When they parted that night, he went so far as to kiss her hand, rubbing his thumb against her palm, while staring briefly at her chest. She would have felt secure of her success if he was not to leave Hertfordshire so very soon, making it impossible to further pursue her cause. However, she did have hope that someday he would come back to visit, and perhaps then she could renew her efforts.

However, she did injustice to the depth of his affection, as well as the independence of his character, for it led him to escape out of Longbourn House the next morning with admirable slyness, and hasten to Lucas Lodge to throw himself at her feet. He was anxious to avoid the notice of his cousins, from a conviction that if they saw him depart, they could not fail to conjecture his design, and he was not willing to have the attempt known till its success might be known likewise; for though feeling almost secure, and with reason, for Charlotte had been tolerably encouraging, he was comparatively diffident since the adventure of Wednesday. His reception, however, was of the most flattering kind. Miss Lucas perceived him from an upper window as he walked towards the house, and instantly set out to meet him accidentally in the lane.

In as short a time as Mr. Collins's long speeches would allow everything was settled between them to the satisfaction of both. As they entered the house he earnestly entreated her to name the day that was to make him the happiest of men, and though such a solicitation must be waived for the present, the lady felt no inclination to trifle with his happiness. The same stupidity that he was favored with by nature must also guarantee a woman would not wish for a long continuance of his court-ship. Miss Lucas, who accepted him solely from the pure and disinterested desire of an establishment, cared not how soon that establishment was gained.

Sir William and Lady Lucas were speedily applied to for their consent, and it was bestowed with a most joyful alacrity. Mr. Collins's present circumstances made it a most eligible match for their daughter, to whom they could give little fortune; and his prospects of future wealth were exceedingly fair. Lady Lucas began to calculate, with more interest than the matter had ever excited before, how many years longer Mr. Bennet was likely to live; and Sir William gave it as his decided opinion, that whenever Mr. Collins should be in possession of the Longbourn estate, it would be highly expedient that both he and his wife should make their appearance at St. James's. The whole family, in short, was properly overjoyed on the occasion. The younger girls formed hopes of coming out a year or two sooner than they might otherwise have done. The boys were relieved from their apprehension of Charlotte's dying an old maid.

Charlotte herself was tolerably composed. She had gained her point, and had time to consider it. Her reflections were in general satisfactory. Mr. Collins, to be sure, was neither sensi-ble nor agreeable. His society was irksome and his attachment to her must be imaginary. But still he would be her husband. Without thinking highly either of men or matrimony, marriage had always been her object. It was the only provision for well-educated young women of small fortune, and however uncer-tain of giving happiness, must be their pleasantest preservative from want. This preservative she had now obtained; and at the age of twenty-seven, without having ever been handsome, she felt all the good luck of it.

The least agreeable circumstance in the business was the surprise the news would cause Elizabeth Bennet, whose friendship she valued beyond that of any other person. She resolved to give her friend the information herself, and therefore charged Mr. Collins to drop no hint of what had passed when he returned to Longbourn. A promise of secrecy was of course dutifully given, but it could not be kept without difficulty; for the curiosity excited by his long absence burst forth in such very direct questions on his return as required some ingenuity to evade, and he was at the same time exercising great self-denial, for he was longing to publish his prosperous love.

As he was to begin his journey too early on the morrow to see any of the family, the ceremony of leave-taking was performed when the ladies moved for the night. Mrs. Bennet, with great politeness and cordiality, said how happy they should be to see him at Longbourn again, whenever his engagements might allow him to visit them.

"My dear madam," he replied, "this invitation is particularly gratifying, because it is what I have been hoping to receive. You may be very certain that I shall avail myself of it as soon as possible."

They were all astonished. Mr. Bennet, who could by no means wish for so speedy a return, immediately said, "But is there no danger of Lady Catherine's disapprobation here, my good sir? You had better neglect your relations than run the risk of offending your patroness."

"My dear sir," replied Mr. Collins," I am particularly obliged to you for this friendly caution, and you may depend upon my not taking so material a step without her ladyship's concurrence."

"You cannot be too much upon your guard. Risk anything

rather than her displeasure. And if you find it likely to be raised by your coming to us again, which I should think exceedingly probable, stay quietly at home, and be satisfied that we shall take no offense."

"Believe me, my gratitude is warmly excited by such affectionate attention, Depend upon it, you will speedily receive from me a letter of thanks for this, and for every other mark of your regard during my stay in Hertfordshire. As for my fair cousins, though my absence may not be long enough to render it necessary, I shall now take the liberty of wishing them health and happiness, not excepting my cousin Elizabeth."

With proper civilities the ladies withdrew, all of them equally surprised that he meditated a quick return. Mrs. Bennet wished to understand by it that he thought of paying his addresses to one of her younger girls, and Mary might have been prevailed on to accept him. But on the following morning, every hope of this kind was done away. Miss Lucas called soon after breakfast, and in a private conference with Elizabeth related the event of the day before.

The possibility of Mr. Collins's fancying himself in love with her friend had once occurred to Elizabeth within the last day or two, but that Charlotte could encourage him seemed almost as far from possibility as she could encourage him herself, and her astonishment was consequently so great as to overcome at first the bounds of decorum, and she could not help crying out, "Engaged to Mr. Collins? My dear Charlotte, impossible!"

The steady countenance which Miss Lucas had commanded in telling her story, gave way to a momentary confusion here on receiving so direct a reproach. Though, as it was no more than she expected, she soon regained her composure, and calmly replied, "Do you think it incredible that Mr. Collins should be able to procure any woman's good opinion, because he was not so happy as to succeed with you?"

Elizabeth recollected herself, and making a strong effort, was able to assure with tolerable firmness that the prospect of their relationship was highly grateful to her, and that she wished her all imaginable happiness.

"I see what you are feeling," replied Charlotte. "You must be surprised, very much surprised—so lately as Mr. Collins was wishing to marry you. But when you have had time to think it over, I hope you will be satisfied with what I have done. I am not romantic, you know. I never was. I ask only a comfortable home and considering Mr. Collins's character, connection, and situation in life, I am convinced that my chance of happiness with him is as fair as most people can boast on entering the marriage state."

"Undoubtedly," Elizabeth quietly answered. After an awkward pause, they returned to the rest of the family. Charlotte did not stay much longer, and Elizabeth was then left to reflect on what she had heard. It was a long time before she became at all reconciled to the idea of so unsuitable a match. The strangeness of Mr. Collins's making two offers of marriage within three days was nothing in comparison of his being now accepted. She had always felt that Charlotte's opinion of matrimony was not exactly like her own, for Charlotte often said she was not romantic in nature and it had been subject of many friendly debates between them, but Elizabeth had not supposed it possible that, when called into action, her friend would have sacrificed every better feeling to worldly advantage. Charlotte the wife of Mr. Collins was a most humiliating picture.

Elizabeth sat with her mother and sisters, reflecting on what she had heard, and doubting whether she was authorized to mention it, when Sir William Lucas himself appeared, sent by his daughter to announce her engagement to the family. With many compliments to them, and much self-gratulation on the prospect of a connection between the houses, he unfolded the matter—to an audience not merely wondering, but incredulous. Mrs. Bennet, with more perseverance than politeness, protested he must be entirely mistaken. Lydia, always unguarded and often uncivil, boisterously exclaimed, "Good Lord, Sir William, how can you tell such a story? Do you not know that Mr. Collins wants to marry Lizzy?"

Nothing less than the complaisance of a courtier could have borne without anger such treatment, but Sir William's good breeding carried him through it all. Though he begged leave to be positive as to the truth of his information, he listened to all their impertinence with the most forbearing courtesy.

Elizabeth, feeling it incumbent on her to relieve him from so unpleasant a situation, now put herself forward to confirm his account, by mentioning her prior knowledge of it from Charlotte. She endeavored to put a stop to the exclamations of her mother and sisters by the earnestness of her congratulations to Sir William, in which she was readily joined by Jane, and by making a variety of remarks on the happiness that might be expected from the match, the excellent character of Mr. Collins, and the convenient distance of Hunsford from London.

Mrs. Bennet was too overpowered to say a great deal while Sir William remained, but no sooner had he left them than her feelings found a rapid vent. In the first place, she persisted in disbelieving the whole of the matter. Secondly, she was very sure that Mr. Collins had been taken in. Thirdly, she trusted they would never be happy together. And, fourthly, that the match might be broken off. Two inferences, however, were plainly deduced from the whole: one, that Elizabeth was the real cause of the mischief; and the other that she herself had been barbarously misused by them all. On these two points she principally dwelt during the rest of the day. Nothing could console and nothing could appease her. Nor did the day wear out her resentment. A week elapsed before she could see Elizabeth without scolding her, a month passed away before she could speak to Sir William or Lady Lucas without being rude, and many months were gone before she could at all forgive their daughter.

Mr. Bennet's emotions were much more tranquil on the occasion. It gratified him to discover that Charlotte Lucas, whom he had been used to think tolerably sensible, was as foolish as his wife and more foolish than his daughter.

Lady Lucas could not be insensible of triumph on being able to retort on Mrs. Bennet the comfort of having a daughter well married. She called at Longbourn rather oftener than usual to say how happy she was, though Mrs. Bennet's sour looks and ill-natured remarks might have been enough to drive happiness away.

Between Elizabeth and Charlotte there was a restraint which kept them mutually silent on the subject. Elizabeth felt persuaded that no real confidence could ever subsist between them again. For she never truly believed Charlotte cared so little for matters of the heart, and for their opinions on marriage to be so far apart caused her to reexamine many conversations throughout their friendship. Her disappointment in Charlotte made her turn with fonder regard to her sister, of whose rectitude and delicacy she was sure her opinion could never be shaken, and for whose happiness she grew daily more anxious as Bingley had now been gone a week and nothing more was heard of his return.

Jane had sent Caroline an early answer to her letter, and was counting the days till she might reasonably hope to hear again. The promised letter of thanks from Mr. Collins arrived on Tuesday, addressed to their father, and written with all the solemnity of gratitude which a twelvemonth's abode in the family might have prompted. After discharging his conscience on that head, he proceeded to inform them with many rapturous expressions of his happiness in having obtained the affection of their amiable neighbor, Miss Lucas. He then explained it was merely with the view of enjoying her society that he had been so ready to close with their kind wish of seeing him again at Longbourn, whither he hoped to be able to return on Monday fortnight; for Lady Catherine, he added, so heartily approved his marriage that she wished it to take place as soon as possible, which he trusted would be an unanswerable argument with his Charlotte to name an early day for making him the happiest of men.

Mr. Collins's return into Hertfordshire was no longer a matter of pleasure to Mrs. Bennet. It was very inconvenient and exceedingly troublesome. She hated having visitors in the house while her health was so indifferent, and lovers were the most disagreeable. Such were the gentle murmurs of Mrs. Bennet, and they gave way only to the greater distress of Mr. Bingley's continued absence.

Neither Jane nor Elizabeth were comfortable on this subject. Day after day passed away without bringing any other tidings of him than the report which shortly prevailed in Meryton of his coming no more to Netherfield the whole winter. Even Elizabeth began to fear—not that Bingley was indifferent—but that his sisters would be successful in keeping him away. Unwilling as she was to admit an idea so destructive of Jane's happiness, and so dishonorable to the stability of her lover, she could not prevent its frequently occurring. The united efforts of his two unfeeling sisters and of his overpowering friend, assisted by the attractions of Miss Darcy and the amusements of London might be too much, she feared, for the strength of his attachment.

As for Jane, her anxiety under this suspense was, of course, more painful than Elizabeth's, but whatever she felt she was desirous of concealing. Therefore between herself and Elizabeth the subject was never alluded to. No such delicacy restrained her mother and an hour seldom passed in which she did not talk of Bingley, express her impatience for his arrival, or even require Jane to confess that if he did not come back she would think herself very ill used. It took all Jane's steady character to bear these attacks with reasonable tranquility.

Mr. Collins returned most punctually on Monday fortnight, but his reception at Longbourn was not quite so gracious as it had been on his first introduction. He was too happy to need much attention, and the business of love-making relieved the family from a great deal of his company. The chief of every day was spent by him at Lucas Lodge, and he sometimes returned to Longbourn only in time to make an apology for his absence before the family went to bed.

Mrs. Bennet was in a most pitiable state. The very mention of anything concerning the match threw her into an agony of ill-humor. The sight of Miss Lucas was odious to her. As her successor in that house, she regarded her with jealous abhorrence. Whenever Charlotte came to see them, she concluded her to be anticipating the hour she was to take possession. Whenever the woman spoke in a low voice to Mr. Collins, she was convinced they talked of the Longbourn estate, and resolving to turn herself and her daughters out of the house as soon as Mr. Bennet was dead.

CHAPTER TWENTY-ONE

*M*ISS BINGLEY'S LETTER ARRIVED and put an end to doubt. The very first sentence conveyed the assurance of their being all settled in London for the winter, and concluded with her brother's regret at not having had time to pay his respects to his friends in Hertfordshire before he left the country.

Hope was over, entirely over. When Jane could attend to the rest of the letter, she found little, except the professed affection of the writer, that could give her any comfort. Miss Darcy's praise occupied the chief of it. Her many attractions were again dwelt on and Caroline boasted joyfully of their increasing intimacy, and ventured to predict the accomplishment of the wishes which had been unfolded in her former letter.

Elizabeth, to whom Jane very soon communicated the chief of all this, heard it in silent indignation. To Caroline's assertion of her brother's being partial to Miss Darcy she paid no credit.

That he was really fond of Jane, she doubted not. As much as she had always been disposed to like him, she could not think without anger, hardly without contempt, on that easiness of temper, that want of proper resolution, which now made him the slave of his designing friends and led him to sacrifice of his own happiness to the caprice of their inclination. Yet whether Bingley's regard had really died away, or were suppressed by his friends' interference; whether he had been aware of Jane's attachment, or whether it had escaped his observation; whatever were the case, though her opinion of him must be materially affected by the difference, her sister's situation remained the same.

A day or two passed before Jane had courage to speak of her feelings to Elizabeth. On Mrs. Bennet's leaving them together, after a longer irritation than usual about Netherfield and its master, she could not help saying, "Oh, that my dear mother had more command over herself. She can have no idea of the pain she gives me by her continual reflections on him. But I will not repine. It cannot last long. He will be forgotten and we shall all be as we were before."

Elizabeth looked at her sister, but said nothing.

"You doubt me?" Jane colored slightly. "Indeed, you have no reason. He may live in my memory as the most amiable man of my acquaintance, but that is all. I have nothing to reproach him with." With a stronger voice she soon added, "It has been no more than an error of fancy on my side."

"You are too good!" exclaimed Elizabeth. "Your sweetness and disinterestedness are really angelic. I do not know what to say to you. I feel as if I had never done you justice, or loved you as you deserve. There are few people whom I really love, and still fewer of whom I think well. The more I see of the world, the more I am dissatisfied with it. Every day confirms my belief of the inconsistency of all human characters, and of the little dependence that can be placed on the appearance of merit or sense. I have met with two instances lately, one I will not mention and the other is Charlotte's unaccountable marriage."

"Such feelings will ruin your happiness. You must make allowance for difference of situation and temper. Consider Mr. Collins's respectability, and Charlotte's steady, prudent character. Remember that she is one of a large family, and so as to fortune it is a most eligible match. She may feel something like regard and esteem for our cousin."

"If I were persuaded that Charlotte had any regard for him, I should only think worse of her understanding than I now do of her heart. Mr. Collins is a conceited, pompous, narrow-minded, silly man. You must feel the woman who marries him cannot have a proper way of thinking. You shall not defend her, though it is Charlotte Lucas."

"I think your language too strong," replied Jane, "and I hope you will be convinced otherwise by seeing them happy together. But enough of this. You alluded to something else. You mentioned two instances. I cannot misunderstand you, but I entreat you not to pain me by thinking that person to blame, and saying your opinion of him is sunk. We must not be so ready to fancy ourselves intentionally injured. It is very often nothing but our own vanity that deceives us. Women fancy admiration means more than it does."

"And men take care that they should."

"If it is designedly done, they cannot be justified. I have no idea of there being so much design in the world as some persons imagine."

Elizabeth sighed. "I am far from attributing any part of Mr. Bingley's conduct to design, but without scheming to do wrong there may be error and there may be misery. Thoughtlessness, want of attention to other people's feelings, and want of resolution, will do the business."

"And do you impute it to either of those?"

"Yes, to the last."

"You persist in supposing his sisters influence him?"

"Yes, in conjunction with his friend."

"I cannot believe it. They can only wish his happiness. If he is attached to me, no other woman can secure it."

"Your first position is false. They may wish many things besides his happiness. They may wish his increase of wealth and consequence. They may wish him to marry a girl who has all the importance of money, great connections, and pride."

"Beyond a doubt, they do wish him to choose Miss Darcy," replied Jane, "but this may be from better feelings than you suppose. They have known her much longer than they have known me. No wonder if they love her better. Whatever their own wishes, it is very unlikely they should have opposed their brother's. What sister would think herself at liberty to do it, unless there were something very objectionable? If they believed him attached to me, they would not try to part us. If he were so, they could not succeed."

From this time Mr. Bingley's name was scarcely ever mentioned between them.

Though Mrs. Bennet still continued to wonder and repine at his returning no more, Mr. Bennet treated the matter differently. "So, Lizzy," said he one day, "your sister is crossed in love, I find. I congratulate her. Next to being married, a girl likes to be crossed a little in love now and then. It is something to think of, and it gives her a sort of distinction among her companions. When is your turn to come? You will hardly bear to be long outdone by Jane. Let Wickham be your man. He is a pleasant fellow, and would jilt you creditably."

"We must not all expect Jane's good fortune."

"True," said Mr. Bennet, "but it is a comfort to think that, whatever may befall you, you have an affectionate mother who will make the most of it."

Mr. Wickham's society was of material service in dispelling the gloom which the late perverse occurrences had thrown on many of the Longbourn family. They saw him often, and to his other recommendations was now added that of general unreserve. The whole of what Elizabeth had already heard, his claims on Mr. Darcy, and all that he had suffered from him, was now openly acknowledged and publicly canvassed. Everybody was pleased to know how much they had always disliked Mr. Darcy before they had known anything of the matter.

Jane was the only creature who could suppose there might be any extenuating circumstances in the case, unknown to the society of Hertfordshire. Her mild and steady candor always pleaded for allowances, and urged the possibility of mistakes—but by everybody else Mr. Darcy was condemned as the worst of men.

Elizabeth was no exception, and her strong feelings against the gentleman were only intensified by the fact he was boorish enough to kiss her in her dreams upon occasion, forcing her to jilt any affections she might harbor for Mr. Wickham by presuming himself the object of her desires—a circumstance she added to his many known offenses, though he could hardly be responsible for the workings of her mind. Mr. Wickham, on the other hand, never entered her dreams beyond that of a secondary character.

On those unfortunate nights, she would awake to find herself breathing hard and her body aching. Never had she been put so out of sorts and she found she did not like the distraction. Though she did hope to someday have love and passion in marriage, it was most inconvenient to feel it when there was no immediate hope of such an event. Unengaged women could not

go about kissing whoever they pleased, at least not while retaining a hope of a pleasant future. Oh, but if they could! If society allowed such indecencies, she might have kissed Mr. Darcy on the balcony for the sole purpose of driving him out of her head. Then she could convince her mind that his kisses would be no great thing, and hardly worth dreaming about. Even as she thought it, a small shiver coursed over her, bringing with it a feverish heat. Though she was loathe to give up her logical conclusion, she could not help the tiny whisper in the back of her mind that assured her she was most wrong in her assessment of the skill of that man's lips.

CHAPTER TWENTY-TWO

*a*FTER A DAY SPENT IN PROFESSIONS OF LOVE and schemes of felicity, Mr. Collins worked up the courage to kiss his fiancée. He had been thinking of it most earnestly since their private walk. Preparing her for this advance in their relationship, he felt, was his solemn duty, and therefore spent several minutes lecturing on the state of an engagement, and how it was very like a marriage in the eyes of all, especially with steady characters such as theirs. Then, proceeding to wet his mouth, as to not make the experience unpleasant, he took her by the arms and pressed his mouth to hers.

Charlotte was by no means deficient in knowledge when it came to such matters. She had grown up on a farm, tending to animals, and had a fair bit of knowledge of husbandry. Though she did not suppose humans mated like sheep, she understood well how a child was conceived. And, her mother wishing to help her advance her engagement before the joyous event took place, had been obliged to suggest helpful hints into securing Mr. Collin's interest.

Though Charlotte hardly doubted Mr. Collin's intent, she knew one word from Lady Catherine, whom she had never met, would be sufficient in turning his regard and making him end the engagement before the wedding took place. Only a strong inducement on her part would secure her lot and she intended to see that her future was indeed hers. So it was, as Mr. Collins pressed his lips to hers on the private bench, she allowed her hand to slide onto his thigh, as if by unconscious design, and pretended to be so enraptured by his kiss that she did not know what she did. Her fingers kneaded into his leg, indecently high, and she felt the muscles stiffen beneath her hand.

Mr. Collins instantly took hold of her face, pressing most earnestly against her so that her teeth cut into the tender flesh of her mouth. There was no art to his lovemaking, for the indelicate fumblings of his hands were hardly adept for the task. However, this did not stop him from taking control of the situation, and so he took Charlotte's hand and moved it up to caress the heavy press of his manhood through his breeches. The sensation was all too pleasurable and he began to rock most insistently.

Trembling and sighing in great turn, he released her mouth, and quickly undid his breeches so that flesh might meet flesh. He felt no qualms in using his fiancée in such a way, for he had given the matter a great deal of thought in the time they were parted and determined that should such an occasion arise, he was well within his rights to take advantage of it. He led her hand to his shaft, and noted with great appreciation her look of modesty as she turned her eyes away from him. Applying pressure, he showed her how he wished for her to move.

To Charlotte, she thought of the task not unlike milking

a cow. Though such thoughts were not those of a proper bride-
to-be, she could not help them. She looked upon sex as another
chore that must be performed. Mr. Collins was quite content to
let her stroke him, as he buried his face into her chest and played
with her breasts through the barrier of her gown. He made
strange noises, breathing hard and fast, until finally she milked
him of his seed. Afterwards, she was pleasantly surprised to find
him so grateful for the service that he hardly said anything at all
and they were obliged to pass several hours in silence.

Therefore, throughout the rest of his week-long visit,
Charlotte often found her fiancé escorting her away to a private setting, where he would find some excuse to be close her.
After the first time these scenarios ended the same—Charlotte
would bare her breasts for him to lick and suck on, as she cra-
dled his erection in her hands. And, though curious as to what it
would be like to finish the deed in some other way, she did not
press to hurry the events of the wedding night. Her aim was met.
Mr. Collins felt very obligated to her for her services, and she
felt certain not even Lady Catherine could overthrow her as the
future Mrs. Collins.

Mr. Collins was called from his amiable Charlotte, and of
the private services she rendered him, by the arrival of Saturday.
The pain of separation was alleviated on his side, by preparations for the reception of his bride. He had reason to hope, that
shortly after his return into Hertfordshire, the day would be
fixed that was to make him the happiest of men. He took leave
of his relations at Longbourn with as much solemnity as before,
wished his fair cousins health and happiness, and promised
their father another letter of thanks.

On the following Monday, Mrs. Bennet had the pleasure of receiving her brother and his wife, who came as usual to spend the Christmas at Longbourn. Mr. Gardiner was a sensible, gentlemanlike man, greatly superior to his sister by nature as well as education. The Netherfield ladies would have had difficulty in believing that a man, who lived by trade, and within view of his own warehouses, could have been so well-bred and agreeable. Mrs. Gardiner, who was several years younger than Mrs. Bennet and Mrs. Philips, was an intelligent, elegant woman, and a great favorite with all her Longbourn nieces. Between the two eldest and herself especially, there subsisted a particular regard. They had frequently stayed with her in town.

The first part of Mrs. Gardiner's business on her arrival was to distribute her presents and describe the newest fashions. When this was done she had a less active part to play. It became her turn to listen. Mrs. Bennet had many grievances to relate, and much to complain of. They had all been very ill-used since she last saw her sister. Two of her girls had been upon the point of marriage, but nothing came of it.

"I do not blame Jane," she continued, "for Jane would have got Mr. Bingley if she could. But Lizzy! Oh, sister, it is very hard to think that she might have been Mr. Collins's wife by this time, had it not been for her own perverseness. He made her an offer in this very room, and she refused him. The consequence of it is that Lady Lucas will have a daughter married before I have, and that the Longbourn estate is just as much entailed as ever. The Lucases are very artful people indeed. They are all for what they can get. I am sorry to say it of them, but so it is. However, your coming is the greatest of comforts, and I am very glad to hear what you tell us of long sleeves."

Mrs. Gardiner, to whom the chief of this news had been given before in the course of Jane and Elizabeth's correspondence with her, made her sister a slight answer, and, in compassion to her nieces, turned the conversation.

When alone with Elizabeth afterwards, she spoke more on the subject. "It seems likely to have been a desirable match for Jane. I am sorry it went off, but these things happen so often. A young man, such as you describe Mr. Bingley, so easily falls in love with a pretty girl for a few weeks, and when accident separates them so easily forgets her. These sorts of inconsistencies are very frequent."

"An excellent consolation in its way," said Elizabeth, "but it will not do for us. We do not suffer by accident. It does not often happen that the interference of friends will persuade a young man of independent fortune to think no more of a girl whom he was violently in love with only a few days before."

"But that expression of 'violently in love' is so hackneyed, so doubtful, so indefinite, that it gives me very little idea. It is as often applied to feelings which arise from a half-hour's acquaintance, as to a real, strong attachment. Pray, how violent was Mr. Bingley's love?"

"I never saw a more promising inclination. He grew quite inattentive to other people and wholly engrossed by her. Every time they met, it was more decided and remarkable. At his own ball he offended two or three young ladies, by not asking them to dance. I spoke to him twice myself, without receiving an answer. Could there be finer symptoms? Is not general incivility the very essence of love?"

"Oh, yes, of that kind of love which I suppose him to have felt. Poor Jane! I am sorry for her. With her disposition, she may not get over it immediately. It had better have happened to you, Lizzy. You would have laughed yourself out of it sooner. Do you think she would be prevailed upon to go back with us? Change of scene might be of service, and perhaps a little relief from home may be as useful as anything."

Pleased with this proposal, Elizabeth felt persuaded of her sister's ready acquiescence.

"I hope," added Mrs. Gardiner, "that no consideration with regard to this young man will influence her. We live in so different a part of town, all our connections are so different, and we go out so little, that it is very improbable that they should meet at all unless he comes to see her."

"And that is quite impossible for he is now in the custody of his friend, Mr. Darcy, who would no more suffer him to call on Jane in such a part of London. Mr. Darcy may perhaps have heard of such a place as Gracechurch Street, but he would hardly think a month's ablution enough to cleanse him from its impurities, were he once to enter it. And depend upon it, Mr. Bingley never stirs without him."

"So much the better. I hope they will not meet at all. But his sister will not be able to help calling."

"She will drop the acquaintance entirely."

In spite of the certainty, Elizabeth felt a solicitude on the subject which convinced her, on examination, that she did not consider it entirely hopeless. It was possible, and sometimes she thought it probable, that his affection might be reanimated and the influence of his friends successfully combated by the more natural influence of Jane's attractions.

Jane accepted her aunt's invitation with pleasure. The Bingleys were in her thoughts at the same time. She hoped by Caroline's not living in the same house with her brother, she might occasionally spend a morning with her without any danger of seeing him.

The Gardiners stayed a week at Longbourn; and what with the Philipses, the Lucases, and the officers, there was not a day without its engagement. Mrs. Bennet had so carefully provided for the entertainment of her brother and sister that they did not once sit down to a family dinner. When the engagement was for home, some of the officers always made part of it—of which Mr. Wickham was sure to be one. On these occasions, Mrs. Gardiner rendered suspicious by Elizabeth's warm commendation, narrowly observed them both. Without supposing them, from what she saw, to be very seriously in love, their preference of each other was plain enough to make her a little uneasy. She resolved to speak to Elizabeth on the subject before she left Hertfordshire, and represent to her the imprudence of encouraging such an attachment.

To Mrs. Gardiner, Wickham had one means of affording pleasure, unconnected with his general powers. About ten or a dozen years ago, before her marriage, she had spent a considerable time in that very part of Derbyshire to which he belonged. They had, therefore, many acquaintances in common. Though Wickham had been little there since the death of Darcy's father, it was yet in his power to give her fresher intelligence of her former friends than she had been in the way of procuring.

Mrs. Gardiner had seen Pemberley, and had known the late Mr. Darcy by character perfectly well. Here consequently was an inexhaustible subject of discourse. In comparing her recollection of Pemberley with the minute description which Wickham could give, and in bestowing her tribute of praise on the character of its late possessor, she was delighting both him and herself. On being made acquainted with the present Mr. Darcy's treatment of him, she tried to remember some of that gentleman's reputed disposition when he was a lad which might agree with it, and was confident at last that she recollected having heard Mr. Fitzwilliam Darcy formerly spoken of as a very proud, ill-natured boy.

Mrs. Gardiner's caution to Elizabeth was punctually and kindly given on the first favorable opportunity of speaking to her alone. After honestly telling her what she thought, she went on, "You are too sensible a girl, Lizzy, to fall in love merely because you are warned against it. Therefore, I will speak openly. I would have you be on your guard. Do not involve yourself or endeavor to involve him in an affection which the want of fortune would make so very imprudent. I have nothing to say against him. He is a most interesting young man. If he had the fortune he ought to have, I should think you could not do better. But as it is, you must not let your fancy run away with you. You have sense, and we all expect you to use it. Your father would depend on your resolution and good conduct, I am sure. You must not disappoint."

"My dear aunt, you are serious indeed."

"Yes, and I hope to engage you to be serious likewise."

"Well, then, you need not be under any alarm. I will take care of myself and of Mr. Wickham too. He shall not be in love with me, if I can prevent it."

"Elizabeth, you are not serious now."

"I beg your pardon, I will try again. At present I am not in love with Mr. Wickham. He is, beyond all comparison, the most agreeable man I ever saw. I should be very sorry to be the means of making any of my family unhappy, but since we see every day that, where there is affection, young people are seldom withheld by immediate want of fortune from entering into engagements with each other. How can I promise to be wiser than so many of my fellow-creatures if I am tempted? All that I can promise you is not to be in a hurry to believe myself his first object. When I am in company with him, I will not be wishing."

"Perhaps it will be as well if you discourage his coming here so very often. At least, you should not remind your mother of inviting him."

"As I did the other day?" Elizabeth gave a conscious smile. "Very true. It will be wise in me to refrain from that. But do not imagine that he is always here so often. It is on your account that he has been so frequently invited this week. You know my mother's ideas as to the necessity of constant company for her friends. But upon my honor, I will try to do what I think to be the wisest. I hope you are satisfied."

Her aunt assured her that she was. **"And, now Lizzy, what is this you hinted at earlier about a lady's parlor? I will admit, your comment left me perplexed as to its source."**

Elizabeth, well used to the candid conversation of her aunt, and most grateful for it, relayed that conversation Mrs. Bennet had been insistent to give and vowed never talk about again.

"And that is how my sister described the marriage bed?" Mrs. Gardiner exclaimed. "If that is the way mothers tell their daughters about such matters, it is no wonder so many girls get into awful situations. If it were Jane, I would not speak so frankly, but since it is you and I know I can depend upon your discretion, I will explain it to you in better terms. What was alluded to was the pleasure a man finds in his wife's body, and some husbands enjoy the pleasure more often than others. In truth, it is not so horrible as your mother has painted it to be. As for the lying still, I will not comment, only to say that is not always the case, beyond that your husband will have to help you on." Then, going on to explain the mechanics behind such marital acts in the most tactful way possible, Mrs. Gardiner managed to answer several of her niece's questions before they parted.

Mr. Collins returned into Hertfordshire soon after it had been quitted by the Gardiners and Jane. However, as he took up his abode with the Lucases, his arrival was no great inconvenience to Mrs. Bennet. His marriage was now fast approaching, and she was so far resigned as to think it inevitable. Thursday was to be the wedding day, and on Wednesday Miss Lucas paid her farewell visit. When she rose to take leave, Elizabeth, ashamed of her mother's ungracious and reluctant good wishes, accompanied her out of the room. As they went downstairs together, Charlotte said, "I shall depend on hearing from you very often, Eliza."

"That you certainly shall."

"And I have another favor to ask you. Will you come and see me?"

"We shall often meet, I hope, in Hertfordshire."

"I am not likely to leave Kent for some time. Promise me, therefore, to come to Hunsford."

Elizabeth could not refuse, though she foresaw little pleasure in the visit.

"My father and Maria are coming to me in March," added Charlotte, "and I hope you will consent to be of the party. Indeed, Eliza, you will be as welcome as either of them."

The wedding took place. The bride and bridegroom set off for Kent from the church door, and everybody had as much to say on the subject as usual. Elizabeth soon heard from her friend and their correspondence was as regular and frequent as it had ever been, though that it should be equally unreserved was impossible. Elizabeth could never address her without feeling that all the comfort of intimacy was over. For the sake of what had been, she determined not to slacken as a correspondent. Charlotte wrote cheerfully, seemed surrounded with comforts, and mentioned nothing which she could not praise. The house, furniture, neighborhood, and roads, were all to her taste, and Lady Catherine's behavior was most friendly. It was Mr. Collins's picture of Hunsford and Rosings rationally softened, and Elizabeth perceived that she must wait for her own visit to know the truth.

Jane had already written a few lines to her sister to announce their safe arrival in London and, when she wrote again, Elizabeth hoped it would be in her power to say something of the Bingleys.

Her impatience for this second letter was as well rewarded as impatience generally is. Jane had been a week in town without either seeing or hearing from Caroline. She accounted for it by supposing that her last letter from Longbourn to her friend had by some accident been lost.

"My aunt," she continued, "is going tomorrow into that part of the town, and I shall take the opportunity of calling in Grosvenor Street."

She wrote again when the visit was paid and she had seen Miss Bingley. "I did not think Caroline in spirits," were her words, "but she was very glad to see me and reproached me for giving her no notice of my coming to London. I was right. My last letter never reached her. I inquired after their brother, of course. He was well, but so much engaged with Mr. Darcy that they scarcely ever saw him. I found Miss Darcy was expected to dinner. I wish I could see her. My visit was not long, as Caroline and Mrs. Hurst were going out. I daresay I shall have a return visit from them soon."

Elizabeth shook her head over this letter, convinced that only an accident would reveal to Mr. Bingley that her sister was in town.

Four weeks passed away, and Jane saw nothing of him. She endeavored to persuade herself that she did not regret it, but she could no longer be blind to Miss Bingley's inattention. After waiting at home every morning for a fortnight, and inventing every evening a fresh excuse, the visitor did at last appear. The shortness of her stay and the alteration of her manner would allow Jane to deceive herself no longer. The letter which she wrote on this occasion to her sister proved what she felt.

"My dearest Lizzy will, I am sure, be incapable of triumphing in her better judgment, at my expense, when I confess myself to have been entirely deceived in Miss Bingley's regard for me. But, though the event has proved you right, do not think me obstinate if I still assert that, considering what her behavior was, my confidence was as natural as your suspicion. I do not at all comprehend her reason for wishing to be intimate with me, but if the same circumstances were to happen again, I am sure I should be deceived again. Caroline did not return my visit till yesterday—not a note, not a line, did I receive in the meantime. When she did come, it was very evident that she had no pleasure in it. She made a slight, formal apology, for not calling before, said not a word of wishing to see me again, and was in every respect so altered a creature, that when she went away I was perfectly resolved to continue the acquaintance no longer. I pity, though I cannot help blaming her. She was very wrong in singling me out as she did. I can safely say that every advance to intimacy began on her side. But I pity her, because she must feel that she has been acting wrong, and because I am very sure that anxiety for her brother is the cause of it. I cannot but wonder at her having any such fears now, because, if he had at all cared about me, we must have met long ago. He knows of my being in town, I am certain, from something she said. Yet it would seem, by her manner of talking, as if she wanted to persuade herself that he is really partial to Miss Darcy. I cannot understand it. If I were not afraid of judging harshly, I should be almost tempted to say that there is a strong appearance of duplicity in all this. Miss Bingley said something of his never returning to Netherfield again, of giving up the house, but not with any certainty. We had better not mention it. I am extremely glad you have such pleasant accounts from our friends at Hunsford. Pray go to see them with Sir William and Maria. I am sure you will be very comfortable there. Yours, Jane."

This letter gave Elizabeth some pain, but her spirits returned as she considered Jane would no longer be duped, by the sister at least. All expectation from the brother was now absolutely over. She would not even wish for a renewal of his attentions. His character sunk on every review of it. As a punishment for him, as well as a possible advantage to Jane, she seriously hoped he might soon marry Mr. Darcy's sister. By Wickham's account, she would make him abundantly regret what he had thrown away.

Mrs. Gardiner about this time reminded Elizabeth of her promise concerning that gentleman, and required information. Elizabeth had such to send that might give contentment to her aunt rather than to herself. His apparent partiality had subsided, his attentions were over, he was the admirer of someone else. Elizabeth was watchful enough to see it all, but she could see it and write of it without material pain. Her heart had been but slightly touched, and her vanity was satisfied with believing that she would have been his only choice, had fortune permitted it. The sudden acquisition of ten thousand pounds was the most remarkable charm of the young lady to whom he was now rendering himself agreeable. Elizabeth, less clear-sighted perhaps in this case than in Charlotte's, did not quarrel with him for his wish of independence. Nothing, on the contrary, could be more natural. While able to suppose that it cost him a few struggles to relinquish her, she was ready to allow it a wise and desirable measure for both, and could very sincerely wish him happy.

Besides, one could hardly think of Mr. Wickham without soon after thinking of Mr. Darcy's treatment of him. Elizabeth wanted nothing more than to never think of Mr. Darcy again, or dream of him for that matter. Had she allowed it, her fantasies would have taken a turn for the day and the haunting kisses she suffered at night on balconies and in solitary gardens would have slipped into her conscious mind, causing the most unwelcome daydreams. Since she did not like Mr. Darcy, she could not account for the strange attraction, or for why her mind would

be so evil as to make her suffer through it. Though, forming an attachment to that man was entirely impossible and she contented herself with the idea that her mind would soon tire of its torture.

After relating the news about Mr. Wickham to Mrs. Gardiner, did she write, "I am now convinced that I have never been much in love. Had I really experienced that pure and elevating passion, I should at present detest his very name, and wish him all manner of evil. But my feelings are not only cordial towards him, they are even impartial towards Miss King. I cannot find that I hate her at all, or that I am in the least unwilling to think her a very good sort of girl. There can be no love in all this. My watchfulness has been effectual. Though I certainly should be a more interesting object to all my acquaintances were I distractedly in love with him, I cannot say that I regret my comparative insignificance. Importance may sometimes be purchased too dearly. Kitty and Lydia take his defection much more to heart than I do. They are young in the ways of the world, and not yet open to the mortifying conviction that handsome young men must have something to live on as well as the plain."

CHAPTER TWENTY-THREE

ITH NO GREATER EVENTS than these in the Longbourn family, and otherwise diversified by little beyond the walks to Meryton, sometimes dirty and sometimes cold, did January and February pass away. March was to take Elizabeth to Hunsford. At first, she had not thought very seriously of going, but Charlotte was depending on the plan and she gradually learned to consider it herself with greater pleasure. Absence had increased her desire of seeing Charlotte again, and weakened her disgust of Mr. Collins. There was novelty in the scheme, and, with such a mother and such uncompanionable sisters, home could not be faultless. A little change was not unwelcome. The journey would moreover give her a peep at Jane. As the time drew near, she would have been very sorry for any delay. Everything went on smoothly, and was finally settled according to Charlotte's first sketch. She was to accompany Sir William and his second daughter. The improvement of spending

a night in London was added in time, and the plan became perfect as plan could be.

The next day she was off with her fellow travelers. Sir
William Lucas, and his daughter Maria, a good-humored girl,
but as empty-headed as himself, had nothing to say that could be
worth hearing, and were listened to with about as much delight
as the rattle of the chaise. Elizabeth loved absurdities, but she
had known Sir William's too long. He could tell her nothing
new of the wonders of his presentation and knighthood. His
civilities were worn out, like his information.

It was a journey of only twenty-four miles, and they began
it so early as to be in Gracechurch Street by noon. As they drove
to Mr. Gardiner's door, Jane was at a drawing room window
watching their arrival. When they entered the passage she was
there to welcome them, and Elizabeth, looking earnestly in her
face, was pleased to see it healthful and lovely as ever. All was joy
and kindness. The day passed most pleasantly away—the morning in bustle and shopping, the evening at one of the theatres.

Elizabeth then contrived to sit by her aunt. Their first object
was her sister. She was more grieved than astonished to hear, in
reply to her minute inquiries, that though Jane always struggled
to support her spirits, there were periods of dejection. It was reasonable, however, to hope that they would not continue long.
Mrs. Gardiner gave her the particulars also of Miss Bingley's
visit in Gracechurch Street, and repeated conversations occurring at different times between Jane and herself, which proved
that the former had, from her heart, given up the acquaintance.

Mrs. Gardiner then rallied her niece on Wickham's deser-
tion, and complimented her on bearing it so well. "What sort
of girl is Miss King? I should be sorry to think our friend
mercenary."

"Pray, what is the difference in matrimonial affairs, between the mercenary and the prudent motive? Last Christmas you were afraid of his marrying me, because it would be imprudent. Now, because he is trying to get a girl with only ten thousand pounds, you want to find out that he is mercenary."

"If you will only tell me what sort of girl Miss King is, I shall know what to think."

"She is a very good kind of girl, I believe. I know no harm of her."

"But he paid her not the smallest attention till her grandfather's death made her mistress of this fortune."

"No, why should he? If it were not allowable for him to gain my affections because I had no money, what occasion could there be for making love to a girl whom he did not care about, and who was equally poor?"

"But there seems an indelicacy in directing his attentions towards her so soon after this event."

"A man in distressed circumstances has no time for all those elegant decorums which other people may observe. If she does not object to it, why should we?"

"Her not objecting does not justify him. It only shows her being deficient in something herself—sense or feeling."

"Well," cried Elizabeth, "have it as you choose. He shall be mercenary, and she shall be foolish."

"No, Lizzy, that is what I do not choose. I should be sorry to think ill of a young man who has lived so long in Derbyshire."

"Oh, if that is all, I have a very poor opinion of young men who live in Derbyshire." Elizabeth was not pleased to be reminded of Mr. Darcy, even though her aunt's comment had not been thus intended. She had gone most of the day without thinking of him and the mere mention of his name made her argumentative. "Their intimate friends who live in Hertfordshire are not much better. I am sick of them all. Thank Heaven! I am going tomorrow where I shall find a man who has not one agreeable quality, who has neither manner nor sense to recommend him. Stupid men are the only ones worth knowing, after all."

"Take care, Lizzy, that speech savors strongly of disappointment."

Before they were separated by the conclusion of the play, she had the unexpected happiness of an invitation to accompany her uncle and aunt in a tour of pleasure which they proposed taking in the summer.

"We have not determined how far it shall carry us," said Mrs. Gardiner, "but, perhaps, to the Lakes."

No scheme could have been more agreeable to Elizabeth, and her acceptance of the invitation was most ready and grateful. "Oh, my dear aunt," she rapturously cried, "what delight! You give me fresh life, for what are young men to rocks and mountains?"

CHAPTER TWENTY-FOUR

*E*VERY OBJECT IN THE NEXT DAY'S JOURNEY was new and interesting to Elizabeth. When they left the high road for the lane to Hunsford, every eye was in search of the Parsonage, and every turning expected to bring it in view. The palings of Rosings Park formed a boundary on one side. Elizabeth smiled at the recollection of all that she had heard of its inhabitants.

At length the Parsonage was discernible. The garden sloping to the road, the house standing in it, the green pales, and the laurel hedge, everything declared they were arriving. Mr. Collins and Charlotte appeared at the door, and the carriage stopped at the small gate which led by a short gravel walk to the house, amidst the nods and smiles of the whole party. In a moment they were all out of the chaise, rejoicing at the sight of each other. Mrs. Collins welcomed her friend with the liveliest pleasure. She saw instantly that her cousin's manners were not altered by his marriage. His formal civility was just what it had been, and he detained her some minutes at the gate to hear and satisfy his inquiries after all her family. They were then, with no other delay than his pointing out the neatness of the entrance, taken into the house. As soon as they were in the parlor, he welcomed them a second time, with ostentatious formality to his humble abode, and punctually repeated all his wife's offers of refreshment.

Elizabeth was prepared to see him in his glory, and she could not help in fancying that in displaying the good proportion of the room, its aspect and its furniture, he addressed himself particularly to her, as if wishing to make her feel what she had lost in refusing him. But though everything seemed neat and comfortable, she was not able to gratify him by any sigh of repentance, and rather looked with wonder at her friend that she could have so cheerful an air with such a companion. When Mr. Collins said anything of which his wife might reasonably be ashamed, which was not unseldom, she involuntarily turned her eye on Charlotte. Once or twice she could discern a faint blush, but in general Charlotte wisely did not hear. After sitting long enough to admire every article of furniture in the room, from the sideboard to the fender, to give an account of their journey, and of all that had happened in London, Mr. Collins invited them to take a stroll in the garden, which was large and well laid out, and to the cultivation of which he attended himself. To work in this garden was one of his most respectable pleasures. Elizabeth admired the command of countenance with which Charlotte talked of the healthfulness of the exercise, and owned she encouraged it as much as possible. Here, leading the way through every walk and cross walk, and scarcely allowing them an interval to utter the praises he asked for, every view was pointed out with a minuteness which left beauty entirely behind. He could number the fields in every direction, and could tell how many trees there were in the most distant clump. But of all the views which his garden, or which the country or kingdom could boast, none were to be compared with the prospect of Rosings, afforded by an opening in the trees that bordered the park nearly opposite the front of his house. It was a handsome modern building, well situated on rising ground.

From his garden, Mr. Collins would have led them round his two meadows; but the ladies, not having shoes to encounter the remains of a white frost, turned back. While Sir William accompanied him, Charlotte took her sister and friend around the house, extremely well pleased to have the opportunity of showing it without her husband's help. It was rather small, but well built and convenient. Everything was fitted up and arranged with a neatness and consistency of which Elizabeth gave Charlotte all the credit. When Mr. Collins could be forgotten, there was really an air of great comfort throughout, and by Charlotte's evident enjoyment of it, Elizabeth supposed he must be often forgotten.

She had already learned that Lady Catherine was still in the country. It was spoken of again while they were at dinner, when Mr. Collins observed, "Yes, Miss Elizabeth, you will have the honor of seeing Lady Catherine de Bourgh on the ensuing Sunday at church, and I need not say you will be delighted with her. I have scarcely any hesitation in saying she will include you and my sister Maria in every invitation with which she honors us during your stay here. Her behavior to my dear Charlotte is charming. We dine at Rosings twice every week, and are never allowed to walk home. Her ladyship's carriage is regularly ordered for us. I should say, one of her ladyship's carriages, for she has several."

"Lady Catherine is a very respectable, sensible woman indeed," added Charlotte, "and a most attentive neighbor."

"Very true, my dear, that is exactly what I say. She is the sort of woman whom one cannot regard with too much deference."

The evening was spent chiefly in talking over Hertfordshire news, and telling again what had already been written. When it closed, Elizabeth, in the solitude of her chamber, had to meditate upon Charlotte's degree of contentment, to understand her address in guiding, and composure in bearing with, her husband, and to acknowledge that it was all done very well. She had also to anticipate how her visit would pass, the quiet tenor of their usual employments, the vexatious interruptions of Mr. Collins, and the gaieties of their intercourse with Rosings. A lively imagination soon settled it all. **But, best of all, despite her ladyship being the aunt of that most exasperating intruder into her dreams, she had no hopes of being reminded of Mr. Darcy the whole of her visit. For other than her present company, of whom she had no intention of encouraging discourse of that sort, there was nothing about her present quarters that would remind her of him.**

The middle of the next day, as she was in her room getting ready for a walk, a sudden noise below seemed to send the whole house in confusion. After listening a moment, she heard somebody running upstairs in a violent hurry. She met Maria in the landing, who, breathless with agitation, said, "Oh, Eliza, pray make haste and come into the dining room, for there is such a sight to be seen!"

Elizabeth asked questions in vain. Maria would tell her nothing more, and down they ran into the dining room, which fronted the lane, in quest of this wonder. It was two ladies stopping in a low phaeton at the garden gate.

"Is this all?" asked Elizabeth. "I expected at least that the pigs had got into the garden, and here is nothing but Lady Catherine and her daughter."

"La! My dear," said Maria, quite shocked at the mistake, "it is not Lady Catherine. The old lady is Mrs. Jenkinson, who lives with them. The other is Miss de Bourgh. Only look at her. She is quite a little creature. Who would have thought that she could be so thin and small?"

"She is abominably rude to keep Charlotte out of doors in all this wind."

"Charlotte says she hardly ever does. It is the greatest of favors when Miss de Bourgh comes in."

"I like her appearance," said Elizabeth, struck with other ideas. "She looks sickly and cross. Yes, she will do very well for Mr. Darcy. She will make him a very proper wife."

Maria did not hear her, but since the words had been more for her own enjoyment and not for conversation, Elizabeth did not expect an answer. Though, it did not escape her that the very man she was determined never to think about during her visit was the first to come to her mind.

Mr. Collins and Charlotte were both standing at the gate in conversation with the ladies. Sir William was stationed in the doorway, in earnest contemplation of the greatness before him, and constantly bowing whenever Miss de Bourgh looked that way. **Elizabeth endeavored not to laugh at the whole scene and wished there might be one person with whom she could share her amusement.**

At length there was nothing more to be said. The ladies drove on and the others returned to the house. Mr. Collins no sooner saw the two girls than he began to congratulate them on their good fortune, which Charlotte explained by letting them know that the whole party was asked to dine at Rosings the next day.

CHAPTER TWENTY-FIVE

*M*R. COLLINS'S TRIUMPH, in consequence of this invitation, was complete. The power of displaying the grandeur of his patroness to his wondering visitors, and of letting them see her civility towards himself and his wife, was exactly what he had wished for.

"I confess," said he, "that I should not have been at all surprised by her ladyship's asking us on Sunday to drink tea and spend the evening at Rosings. I rather expected, from my knowledge of her affability that it would happen. But who could have foreseen such an attention as this? Who could have imagined that we all should receive an invitation to dine there so immediately after your arrival?"

Scarcely anything was talked of the whole day or next morning but their visit to Rosings. To Elizabeth, Mr. Collins assured, "Do not make yourself uneasy, my dear cousin, about your apparel. Lady Catherine is far from requiring that elegance of dress in us which becomes herself and her daughter. I would advise you merely to put on whatever of your clothes are superior to the rest—there is no occasion for anything more. Lady Catherine will not think the worse of you for being simply dressed. She likes to have the distinction of rank preserved."

When the time came, they had a pleasant walk of about half a mile across the park. Every park has its beauty and its prospects, and Elizabeth saw much to be pleased with, though the weather was fine she could not be in such raptures as Mr. Collins expected the scene to inspire.

When they ascended the steps to the hall, though the rest of the party seemed to be quite apprehensive of who they were about to face, Elizabeth's courage did not fail her. She had heard nothing of Lady Catherine that spoke of any extraordinary talents or miraculous virtue; rather than the mere stateliness of money or rank, both of which she thought she could witness without trepidation.

From the entrance hall they followed the servants through an antechamber, to the room where Lady Catherine, her daughter, and Mrs. Jenkinson were sitting. Her ladyship, with great aloofness, arose to receive them. Mrs. Collins had settled it with her husband that the responsibility of introduction should be hers, it was performed in a proper manner, without any of those apologies and thanks which he would have thought necessary.

In spite of having been at St. James's Sir William was so completely awed by the grandeur surrounding him, that he had just courage enough to make a very low bow, and take his seat without saying a word. His daughter, frightened almost out of her senses, sat on the edge of her chair, not knowing which way to look. Elizabeth found herself quite equal to the scene, and could observe the three ladies before her composedly. Lady Catherine was a tall, large woman, with strongly-marked features, which might once have been handsome. Her air was not conciliating, nor was her manner of receiving them such as to make her visitors forget their inferior rank. She was not rendered formidable by silence, but whatever she said was spoken in so authoritative a tone, as marked her self-importance, and brought Mr. Wickham immediately to Elizabeth's mind; and from the observation of the day altogether, she believed Lady Catherine to be exactly what he represented.

Examining the mother, Elizabeth soon found some resemblance of Mr. Darcy in countenance and deportment. If arrogance was an inheritable trait, it was a strong one in this family. **For a moment, Elizabeth almost felt sorry for Mr. Darcy, having grown up surrounded by the stately coldness of such as Lady Catherine, for it could be assumed that Lady Anne Darcy had been like her sister, having been raised with the same self-importance. It was a stark contrast to her own childhood filled with laughter and emotion.** She turned her eyes on the daughter, and could almost have joined in Maria's astonishment at her being so thin and small. There was neither in figure nor face any likeness between the ladies. Miss de Bourgh was pale and sickly; her features, though not plain, were insignificant; and she spoke very little, except in a low voice to Mrs. Jenkinson, who was entirely engaged in listening to what she said.

The dinner was exceedingly handsome, and there were all the servants and all the articles of plate which Mr. Collins had promised. As he had likewise foretold, he took his seat at the bottom of the table, by her ladyship's desire, and looked as if he felt that life could furnish nothing greater. He carved, and ate, and praised with delighted alacrity. Every dish was commended, first by him and then by Sir William, who was now recovered enough to echo whatever his son-in-law said. Elizabeth wondered how Lady Catherine could bear it; but the lady seemed gratified by their excessive admiration, especially when any dish on the table proved a novelty to them.

The party did not supply much conversation. Elizabeth was ready to speak whenever there was an opening, but she was seated between Charlotte and Miss de Bourgh—the former of whom was engaged in listening to Lady Catherine, and the latter said not a word to her all dinner. Mrs. Jenkinson was chiefly employed in watching how little Miss de Bourgh ate. Maria thought speaking out of the question. The gentlemen did nothing but eat and admire.

When the ladies returned to the drawing room, there was little to be done but to hear Lady Catherine talk, which she did without any intermission till coffee came in, delivering her opinion on every subject in so decisive a manner as proved that she was not used to having her judgment refuted. She inquired into Charlotte's domestic concerns familiarly and minutely, gave her a great deal of advice as to the management of them all. Elizabeth found nothing was beneath this great lady's attention, which could furnish her with an occasion of dictating to others. In the intervals of her discourse with Mrs. Collins, she addressed a variety of questions to Maria and Elizabeth, but especially to the latter, of whose connections she knew the least, and who she observed to Mrs. Collins was a very genteel, pretty kind of girl. She asked her, at different times, how many sisters she had, whether they were older or younger than her, whether any of them were likely to be married, whether they were handsome, where they had been educated, what carriage her father kept, and what had been her mother's maiden name. Elizabeth felt all the impertinence of her questions but answered them very composedly. **At least Mr. Darcy did not pry so readily into other's affairs, a family trait he did not share with his aunt. In contrast to her ladyship, his manners were not so disagreeable.**

Lady Catherine then observed, "Your father's estate is entailed on Mr. Collins, I think. For your sake," turning to Charlotte, "I am glad of it, but otherwise I see no occasion for entailing estates from the female line. It was not thought necessary in Sir Lewis de Bourgh's family. Do you play and sing, Miss Bennet?"

"A little."

"Our instrument is a capital one. You shall try it someday. Do your sisters play and sing?"

"One of them does."

"Why not all? You all ought to have learned. Do you draw?"

"No, not at all."

"What, none of you?"

"Not one."

"That is very strange. But I suppose you had no opportunity. Your mother should have taken you to town every spring for the benefit of masters."

"My mother would have had no objection, but my father hates London."

"Has your governess left you?"

"We never had any governess."

"No governess! How was that possible? Five daughters brought up at home without a governess? I never heard of such a thing. Your mother must have been quite a slave to your education."

Elizabeth could hardly help smiling. "I assure you, she was not."

"Then, who attended to you? Without a governess, you must have been neglected."

"Compared with some families, I believe we were, but those of us who wished to learn never wanted the means. We were always encouraged to read, and had all the masters that were necessary. Those who chose to be idle, certainly might."

"Aye, no doubt, but that is what a governess will prevent. Are any of your younger sisters out, Miss Bennet?"

"Yes, ma'am, all."

"All! What, all five out at once? Very odd! And you only the second. The younger ones out before the elder ones are married! Your younger sisters must be very young?"

"Yes, my youngest is not sixteen. Perhaps she is young to be in company. But really, ma'am, I think it would be very hard upon younger sisters that they should not have their share of society and amusement, because the elder may not have the means or inclination to marry early. The last born has as good a right to the pleasures of youth as the first. I think to have it otherwise would not be very likely to promote sisterly affection."

"Upon my word," said her ladyship, "you give your opinion very decidedly for so young a person. Pray, what is your age?"

"With three younger sisters grown up your ladyship can hardly expect me to own up to it."

Lady Catherine seemed quite astonished at not receiving a direct answer. Elizabeth suspected herself to be the first creature who had ever dared to trifle with so much dignified impertinence.

"You cannot be more than twenty, I am sure, therefore you need not conceal your age."

"I am not one-and-twenty."

When the gentlemen had joined them, and tea was over, the card tables were placed. And, only after Lady Catherine and her daughter had played as long as they chose, the carriage was immediately ordered. As soon as they had driven from the door, Elizabeth was called on by her cousin to give her opinion of all that she had seen at Rosings, which, for Charlotte's sake, she made more favorable than it really was. But her commendation, though costing her some trouble, could by no means satisfy Mr. Collins, and he was very soon obliged to take her ladyship's praise into his own hands.

CHAPTER TWENTY-SIX

*S*IR WILLIAM STAYED only a week at Hunsford, but his visit was long enough to convince him of his daughter being most comfortably settled, and of her possessing such a husband and such a neighbor as were not often met with. While Sir William was with them, Mr. Collins devoted his morning to driving him out in his gig, and showing him the country. When he went away, the whole family returned to their usual employments, and Elizabeth was thankful to find that they did not see more of her cousin by the alteration, for the chief of the time between breakfast and dinner was now passed by him either at work in the garden or in reading and writing, and looking out of the window in his own book room, which fronted the road. The room in which the ladies sat was backwards. Elizabeth had at first wondered why Charlotte did not prefer the dining parlor for common use. It was a better sized room, and had a more pleasant aspect, but she soon saw that her friend had an excellent reason for what she did, for Mr. Collins would undoubtedly have been much less in his own apartment, had they sat in one equally lively. She gave Charlotte credit for the arrangement.

From the drawing room they could distinguish nothing in the lane, and were indebted to Mr. Collins for the knowledge of what carriages went along, and how often especially Miss de Bourgh drove by in her phaeton, which he never failed coming to inform them of, though it happened almost every day. She frequently stopped at the Parsonage, and had a few minutes' conversation with Charlotte, but was scarcely ever prevailed upon to get out.

Very few days passed in which Mr. Collins did not walk to Rosings, and not many in which his wife did not think it necessary to go likewise; and till Elizabeth recollected that there might be other family livings to be disposed of, she could not understand the sacrifice of so many hours. **It was after these walks to Rosings, that Elizabeth observed a quietness to her cousin that seemed out of character. She wondered if he naturally fatigued during the day, but Charlotte merely smiled a secretive smile and assured her that it was merely the exercise that turned his thoughts inward.**

Now and then they were honored with a call from her ladyship, and nothing escaped her observation that was passing in the room during these visits. She examined into their employments, looked at their work, and advised them to do it differently. Elizabeth soon perceived that though this great lady was not in commission of the peace of the county, she was a most active magistrate in her own parish, the minutest concerns of which were carried to her by Mr. Collins. Whenever any of the cottagers were quarrelsome, discontented, or too poor, she sallied forth into the village to settle their differences, silence their complaints, and scold them into harmony and plenty.

The entertainment of dining at Rosings was repeated about twice a week. Their other engagements were few, as the style of living in the neighborhood in general was beyond Mr. Collins's reach. This, however, was no evil to Elizabeth, and upon the whole she spent her time comfortably enough. There were half-hours of pleasant conversation with Charlotte, and the weather was so fine for the time of year that she had often great enjoyment out of doors. Her favorite walk, and where she frequently went while the others were calling on Lady Catherine, was along the open grove which edged the side of the park, where there was a nice sheltered path, which no one seemed to value but herself, and where she felt beyond the reach of Lady Catherine's curiosity.

And then news came, by and by, that Mr. Darcy was expected at Rosings. At first Elizabeth did not know what to think of such an occurrence, but after assuring herself that the gentlemen would not seek out her company, she began to suspect that she might be amused in seeing how hopeless Miss Bingley's designs on him were by his behavior to his cousin. Lady Catherine evidently believed Mr. Darcy destined to marry her daughter. The lady talked of his coming with the greatest satisfaction, and seemed almost angry to find that he had already been frequently seen by Miss Lucas and herself.

The moment of Mr. Darcy's arrival was known at the Parsonage for Mr. Collins was walking the whole morning within view of the lodges opening into Hunsford Lane in order to have the earliest assurance of it. After making his bow as the carriage turned into the Park, he hurried home with the great intelligence, and on the following morning he hastened to Rosings to pay his respects. There were two nephews of Lady Catherine to require them, for Mr. Darcy had brought with him a Colonel Fitzwilliam, the younger son of his uncle Lord Brandon, and, to the great surprise of all the party, when Mr. Collins returned, the gentleman accompanied him. Charlotte had seen them from her husband's room, crossing the road, and immediately running into the other, told the girls what an honor they might expect, adding, "I may thank you, Eliza, for this piece of civility. Mr. Darcy would never have come so soon to wait upon me."

Elizabeth had scarcely time to disclaim all right to the compliment, before their approach was announced by the doorbell. **The sound of it caused her to jump a little, a reaction that surprised her in its strength for it was only Mr. Darcy, a man she should be of no real hurry to see.** Shortly afterwards the three gentlemen entered the room. Colonel Fitzwilliam, who led the way, was about thirty, not handsome, but in person and address most truly the gentleman. Mr. Darcy looked just as he had in Hertfordshire—paid his compliments to Mrs. Collins with his usual reserve, and met Elizabeth with every appearance of composure.

Elizabeth merely curtseyed to him without saying a word. It was not out of a desire to snub the gentleman that kept her quiet, but the sudden quickening of her heart when he entered. His eyes, so often seen in the shade of her dreams, struck her with their brilliant force, made all the more predominate by the blue color of his jacket. How could she have forgotten the exact shade of his eyes? For they were brilliant, even if they did belong to such a man.

Colonel Fitzwilliam entered into conversation directly with the ease of a well-bred man, and talked very pleasantly. Mr. Darcy, after having addressed a slight observation on the house and garden to Mrs. Collins, sat for some time without speaking to anybody. At length, however, his civility was awakened so far as to inquire of Elizabeth after the health of her family.

She answered him in the usual way, and after a moment's

pause, added, "My eldest sister has been in town these three months. Have you happened to see her there?"

She was perfectly sensible that he never had, but she wished to see whether he would betray any consciousness of what had passed between the Bingleys and Jane, and she thought he looked a little confused as he answered that he had never been so fortunate as to meet Miss Bennet. The subject was pursued no farther, and the gentlemen soon afterwards went away.

"Colonel Fitzwilliam seems very pleasant," observed Charlotte, as her husband went to watch the gentlemen depart. "Mr. Darcy looked well."

"Did he?" Elizabeth inquired, feigning ignorance. The effects of his presence had not completely worn off and now that he was gone, she took a deep breath to stop her stomach from quaking and her heart from pounding. "I had not noticed."

"I daresay he was very polite to you," Charlotte continued. "If you would like, I could give you advice that my mother gave me on how to fix a man's interest. I will now confess that it is what keeps Mr. Collins quiet after his walks, as you have often observed."

"I do not think it necessary. Mr. Darcy appeared the same to me. I did not notice much different in him." Elizabeth quickly changed the subject, noting the exact shape of a new hat she had seen in a London shop, and thus turning the course of their conversation to more frivolous pursuits.

CHAPTER TWENTY-SEVEN

*C*OLONEL FITZWILLIAM'S MANNERS were very much admired at the Parsonage, and the ladies felt he must add considerably to the pleasures of their engagements at Rosings. It was some days, however, before they received another invitation—for while there were visitors in the house, they could not be necessary. It was not till almost a week after the gentlemen's arrival, that they were honored by such an attention. They had seen very little of Lady Catherine or her daughter. Colonel Fitzwilliam had called at the Parsonage more than once during the time, but Mr. Darcy they had seen only at church.

The invitation was accepted of course, and at a proper hour they joined the party in Lady Catherine's drawing room. Her ladyship received them civilly, but it was plain their company was by no means as acceptable as when she could get nobody else. She was engrossed by her nephews, speaking to them, especially to Darcy, much more than to any other person in the room.

Colonel Fitzwilliam seemed glad to see them for anything was a welcome relief to him at Rosings, and Mrs. Collins's pretty friend had caught his fancy. He seated himself by her, and talked agreeably of Kent and Hertfordshire, of traveling and staying at home, of new books and music. Elizabeth had never been half so well entertained in that room before, and they conversed with so much spirit and flow, as to draw the attention of Lady Catherine, as well as of Mr. Darcy. *His* eyes repeatedly turned towards them with a look of curiosity and Elizabeth pretended not to notice his attention.

Her ladyship did not scruple to call out, "What is that you are saying, Fitzwilliam? What are you telling Miss Bennet? Let me hear what it is."

"We are speaking of music, madam," said he, when no longer able to avoid a reply.

"Of music! Then pray speak aloud. It is of all subjects my delight. There are few people in England who have more true enjoyment of music than myself, or a better natural taste. If I had ever learned, I should have been a great proficient. And so would Anne, if her health had allowed her to apply. How does Georgiana get on, Darcy?"

Mr. Darcy spoke with affectionate praise of his sister. **"She gets on exceedingly well. I daresay she is one of the few ladies I have heard with so obvious a natural talent."**

"I am very glad to hear such a good account of her," said Lady Catherine. "And pray tell her from me, that, though she has natural talent, she cannot expect to excel if she does not practice a good deal."

"I assure you, madam, that she does not need such advice," he replied. "She practices constantly."

"So much the better. It cannot be done too much. When I next write to her, I shall charge her not to neglect it on any account. I have told Miss Bennet several times, that she will never play really well unless she practices more; and though Mrs. Collins has no instrument, she is very welcome to come to Rosings every day and play on the pianoforte in Mrs. Jenkinson's room. She would be in nobody's way in that part of the house."

To his credit, and Elizabeth's surprise, Mr. Darcy looked a little ashamed of his aunt's ill-breeding, and made no answer.

When coffee was over, Colonel Fitzwilliam reminded Elizabeth of having promised to play to him, and she sat down directly to the instrument. He drew a chair near her. Lady Catherine listened to half a song, and then talked to her other nephew till the latter walked away from her. Making with his usual deliberation towards the pianoforte, Mr. Darcy stationed himself so as to command a full view of the fair performer's countenance.

Elizabeth saw what he was doing. At the first convenient pause, turned to him with a mischievous smile, and said, "You mean to frighten me, Mr. Darcy, by coming in all this state to hear me? I will not be alarmed though your sister does play so well."

"I shall not say you are mistaken," he replied, "because you could not really believe me to entertain any design of alarming you. I have had the pleasure of your acquaintance long enough to know that you find great enjoyment in occasionally professing opinions which in fact are not your own."

Elizabeth laughed heartily at this picture of herself, and said to Colonel Fitzwilliam, "Your cousin will give you a very pretty notion of me, and teach you not to believe a word I say. I am unlucky to meet with a person so able to expose my real character, in a part of the world where I had hoped to pass myself off with some degree of credit. Indeed, Mr. Darcy, it is very ungenerous in you to mention all that you knew to my disadvantage in Hertfordshire for you are provoking me to retaliate, and such things may come out as will shock your relations to hear."

"I am not afraid of you," said he, smilingly. **She quickly turned her eyes to her fingers as they stumbled across a few keys.**

"Pray let me hear what you have to accuse him of," said Colonel Fitzwilliam. "I should like to know how he behaves among strangers."

"Prepare yourself for something very dreadful. The first time of my ever seeing him in Hertfordshire was at a ball. He danced only four dances, though gentlemen were scarce and, to my certain knowledge, more than one young lady was sitting down in want of a partner."

"I had not at that time the honor of knowing any lady in the assembly beyond my own party."

"True, and nobody can ever be introduced in a ballroom." **She watched him from under her lashes, feeling somewhat light-hearted at their banter.**

"Perhaps," said Darcy, "I should have judged better, had I sought an introduction, but I am ill-qualified to recommend myself to strangers."

"Shall we ask your cousin the reason of this?" said Elizabeth, still addressing Colonel Fitzwilliam. "Shall we ask him why a man of sense and education, and who has lived in the world, is ill-qualified to recommend himself to strangers?"

"I can answer your question," said Fitzwilliam, "without applying to him. It is because he will not give himself the trouble."

"I certainly have not the talent which some people possess," said Darcy, "of conversing easily with those I have never seen before. I cannot catch their tone of conversation, or appear interested in their concerns, as I often see done."

"My fingers," said Elizabeth, "do not move over this

instrument in the masterly manner which I see so many women's do. Yet, I have always supposed it to be my own fault because I will not take the trouble of practicing. It is not that I do not believe my fingers as capable as any other woman's."

Darcy stared at her fingers as she spoke, watching them tap absently on the keys in tiny, delicate caresses. "You are perfectly right. You have employed your time much better. No one admitted to the privilege of hearing you can think anything wanting. We neither of us perform to strangers."

Here they were interrupted by Lady Catherine, who called out to know what they were talking of. Elizabeth immediately began playing again. Lady Catherine approached, and, after listening for a few minutes, said to Darcy, "Anne would have been a delightful performer, had her health allowed her to learn."

Elizabeth looked at Darcy to see how cordially he assented to his cousin's praise. Neither at that moment nor at any other could she discern any symptom of love. Not much else happened, and Elizabeth stayed at the instrument until her ladyship's carriage was ready to take them home,

CHAPTER TWENTY-EIGHT

*E*LIZABETH SAT BY HERSELF the next morning, writing to Jane while Mrs. Collins and Maria went on business into the village, when she was startled by a ring at the door. She had heard no carriage and worried it might be Lady Catherine, and under that apprehension put away her half-finished letter so she might escape any impertinent questions. When the door opened, to her very great surprise, Mr. Darcy, and Mr. Darcy alone, entered the room.

He seemed astonished too on finding her by herself, and apologized for his intrusion by letting her know that he had understood all the ladies were to be within.

They sat down, and when her inquiries after Rosings were made, seemed in danger of sinking into total silence. It was absolutely necessary, therefore, to think of something, and in this emergence recollecting when she had seen him last in Hertfordshire, and feeling curious to know what he would say on the subject of their hasty departure, she observed, "How very suddenly you all quitted Netherfield last November, Mr. Darcy. It must have been a most agreeable surprise to Mr. Bingley to see you all so soon. He and his sisters were well, I hope, when you left London?"

"Perfectly so, thank you."

She found that she was to receive no other answer, and, after a short pause added, "I think I have understood that Mr. Bingley will not be returning to Netherfield?"

"I have never heard him say so. It is probable that he may spend very little of his time there in the future. He has many friends, and is at a time of life when friends and engagements are continually increasing."

"If he means to be but little at Netherfield, it would be better for the neighborhood that he should give up the place entirely, for then we might possibly get a settled family there. But, perhaps, Mr. Bingley did not take the house so much for the convenience of the neighborhood as for his own, and we must expect him to keep it or quit it on the same principle."

"I should not be surprised," said Darcy, "if he were to give it up as soon as any eligible purchase offers."

Elizabeth made no answer. She was afraid of talking longer of his friend and, having nothing else to say, was now determined to leave the trouble of finding a subject to him. **She was not unaware that the last time she had been alone with him had been when they were on the balcony at Netherfield, and he had touched her cheek. There was something quite different to being completely alone with a man, than talking privately with him in the company of others. The room, once adequate in proportions, suddenly felt very small. Though a proper distance separated them and no one would think twice about their situation, should they be walked in on, Elizabeth felt herself resisting the urge to**

squirm in her seat. Their eyes met briefly. She pulled her gaze away to look at general objects in the room, only to find her way back to him. He studied her carefully, as if considering something gravely important—something she was sure she did not understand nor did she entertain herself to try.

When she did not again offer conversation, he took the hint, and said, "This seems a very comfortable house. Lady Catherine, I believe, did a great deal to it when Mr. Collins first came to Hunsford."

"I believe she did, and I am sure she could not have bestowed her kindness on a more grateful object."

"Mr. Collins appears to be very fortunate in his choice of a wife."

Elizabeth wondered at the way he said it. Was it possible he had heard of her rejecting the man? Since it would be too improper to ask him of it, she instead said, "Yes, indeed, his friends may well rejoice in his having met with one of the very few sensible women who would have accepted him, or have made him happy if they had. My friend has an excellent understanding. Though I am not certain I consider her marrying Mr. Collins as the wisest thing she ever did, she seems perfectly content. In a prudential light, it is certainly a very good match for her."

"It must be agreeable for her to be settled within so easy a distance of her family and friends."

"An easy distance, you call it? It is nearly fifty miles."

"And what is fifty miles of good road? Little more than half a day's journey. Yes, I call it a very easy distance."

"I never considered the distance as an advantage of the match," said Elizabeth. "I would never have said Mrs. Collins was settled near her family."

"It is a proof of your own attachment to Hertfordshire.

Anything beyond the very neighborhood of Longbourn appears far."

As he spoke there was a sort of smile which Elizabeth fancied she understood. He must suppose her to be thinking of Jane and Netherfield, and she blushed as she answered. "I do not mean to say that a woman may not be settled too near her family. The far and the near must be relative, and depend on many varying circumstances. Where there is fortune to make the expenses of traveling unimportant, distance becomes no evil. But that is not the case here. Mr. and Mrs. Collins have a comfortable income, but not such a one as will allow of frequent journeys and I am persuaded my friend would not call herself near her family under less than half the present distance."

Mr. Darcy drew his chair a little towards her. She noticed the room getting all the smaller. "You cannot have a right to such very strong local attachment. You cannot have been always at Longbourn."

Elizabeth could not hide her surprise. The gentleman experienced some change of feeling and drew back his chair. He took a newspaper from the table, and glancing over it, said, in a colder voice, "Are you pleased with Kent?"

A short dialogue on the subject of the county ensued, on either side calm and concise—and soon put an end to by the entrance of Charlotte and her sister, just returned from their walk. The tete-a-tete surprised them. Mr. Darcy related the mistake which had occasioned his intruding on Miss Elizabeth, and after sitting a few minutes longer without saying much to anybody, went away. Maria soon followed him out of the room to watch out the front window.

"What can be the meaning of this?" said Charlotte, as soon as they were alone. "My dear, Eliza, he must be in love with you, or he would never have called on us in this familiar way."

"Nonsense. I am quite certain Mr. Darcy does not feel the slightest inclination of love towards me. Undoubtedly, he was here by order of his aunt, to please her by calling on yourself and Mr. Collins. If anything, he was put out by the emptiness of the house and deigned to say not much to me at all." Elizabeth then explained in great detail the entire visit to a most eager listener.

"I do not flatter myself that Lady Catherine sent him to call upon us, though her ladyship is very gracious," said Charlotte "Perhaps his visit was merely a diversion from the difficulty of finding anything to do, which is the more probable explanation from the time of year."

Elizabeth was inclined to agree with her friend's estimation. All field sports were over. Within doors there was Lady Catherine, books, and a billiard table, but gentlemen cannot always be within doors; and in the nearness of the Parsonage, or the pleasantness of the walk to it, or of the people who lived in it, the two cousins found a temptation from this period of walking thither almost every day. They called at various times of the morning, sometimes separately, sometimes together, and now and then accompanied by their aunt. It was plain to them all that Colonel Fitzwilliam came because he had pleasure in their society, a persuasion which of course recommended him still more. Elizabeth was reminded by her own satisfaction in being with him, as well as by his evident admiration of her, of her former favorite George Wickham. Though, in comparing them, she saw there was less captivating softness in Colonel Fitzwilliam's manners, she believed he might have the best informed mind.

But why Mr. Darcy came so often to the Parsonage, it was more difficult to understand. **The frequent visits only enforced Elizabeth's belief that Mr. Darcy called out of boredom. What else could it be?** It could not be for society, as he frequently sat there ten minutes together without opening his lips. When he did speak, it seemed the effect of necessity rather than of choice—a sacrifice to propriety, not a pleasure to himself. He seldom appeared really animated.

Charlotte knew not what to make of him. Colonel Fitzwilliam's occasionally laughing at an anecdote of stupidity from his cousin's youth, proved that Mr. Darcy was generally different than how she now knew him. **The Darcy that Colonel Fitzwilliam talked about did not appear in the man who sat before them; but, then, perhaps there was a reason for so different a character.** She would liked to have believed this marked difference the effect of love, and the object of that love her friend Eliza, and she set herself seriously to work to find it out. She watched him whenever they were at Rosings, and whenever he came to Hunsford, but without much success. He certainly looked at her friend a great deal, but the expression of that look was disputable. It was an earnest, steadfast gaze, but she often doubted whether there were much admiration in it, and sometimes it seemed nothing but absence of mind.

She had once or twice suggested to Elizabeth the possibility of his being partial to her, but Elizabeth always laughed at the idea. Charlotte did not think it right to press the subject, from the danger of raising expectations which might only end in disappointment; for in her opinion it admitted not of a doubt, that all her friend's dislike would vanish, if she could suppose him to be in her power.

In her kind schemes for Elizabeth, Charlotte sometimes planned her marrying Colonel Fitzwilliam. He was beyond comparison the most pleasant man and he certainly admired her. His situation in life was most eligible, but to counterbalance these advantages Mr. Darcy had considerable patronage in the church, and his cousin could have none at all.

CHAPTER TWENTY-NINE

*M*ORE THAN ONCE DID ELIZABETH, in her aimless stroll within the park, unexpectedly meet Mr. Darcy. She felt all the perverseness of the mischance that brought him where no one else had come. To prevent its ever happening again, she took care to inform him at first that it was a favorite haunt of hers. How it could occur a second time, therefore, was very odd. Yet it did, and even a third. It seemed like willful ill-nature, or a voluntary penance, for on these occasions it was not merely a few formal inquiries and an awkward pause and then away, but he actually thought it necessary to turn back and walk with her. He never said a great deal, nor did she give herself the trouble of talking, but it struck her in the course of their third rencontre that he was asking some odd unconnected questions—about her pleasure in being at Hunsford, her love of solitary walks, and her opinion of Mr. and Mrs. Collins's happiness. However, what struck her as most peculiar

was when speaking of Rosings and her not perfectly understanding the layout of the house, he seemed to expect that
whenever she came into Kent again she would be staying *there*
instead of the Parsonage. His words seemed to imply it. Could
he have Colonel Fitzwilliam in his thoughts? She supposed, if
he meant anything, he must allude to what might arise in that
quarter. It distressed her a little, and she was quite glad to find
herself at the gate in the pales opposite the Parsonage.

**As she reached for the gate, intent on ending the conversa-
tion before aught else could be implied, he extended his hand at
the same time to open it for her. His hand slid over hers on the
latch and the shock of his warmth curled over her fingers. She
snatched her hand away a second too late and silently bowed her
head in thanks as he allowed her to pass into the yard. Reaching
the door, she turned only to find Mr. Darcy still stood, his hand
resting on the latch of the now closed gate. At her look, he nodded
once and quickly withdrew down the lane. Until that moment,
she'd been doing very well in keeping her strange attraction to
Mr. Darcy from her mind whenever he was around. She knew
the foolishness of such daydreams, and knew the fantasy did not
coincide with the reality of the man. She had even convinced herself that her attraction sprung from the mystery of his character
and naught else.**

Elizabeth was engaged one day in perusing Jane's last letter as she walked, dwelling on some passages which proved that
Jane had not written in spirits, when, instead of being again surprised by Mr. Darcy, she glanced up to find Colonel Fitzwilliam
was meeting her. Immediately, putting away the letter and forcing a smile, she said, "I did not know you ever walked this way."

"I have been making the tour of the park," he replied, "as
I generally do every year, and intend to close it with a call at the
Parsonage. Are you going much farther?"

"No, I should have turned in a moment."

And accordingly she did turn, and they walked towards the Parsonage together.

"Do you certainly leave Kent on Saturday?" she asked.

"Yes, if Darcy does not put it off again. But I am at his disposal. He arranges the business just as he pleases."

"And if not able to please himself in the arrangement, he has at least pleasure in the great power of choice. I do not know anybody who seems to enjoy the power of doing what he likes more than Mr. Darcy."

"He likes to have his own way very well," replied Colonel Fitzwilliam. "But so do we all. It is only that he has better means of having it than many others, because he is rich, and many others are poor. I speak feelingly. A younger son, you know, must be inured to self-denial and dependence."

"In my opinion, the younger son of an earl can know very little of either. Now seriously, what have you ever known of self-denial and dependence? When have you been prevented by want of money from going wherever you chose, or procuring anything you had a fancy for?"

"These are home questions—and perhaps I cannot say that I have experienced many hardships of that nature. But in matters of greater weight, I may suffer from want of money. Younger sons cannot marry where they like."

"Unless where they like are women of fortune, which I think they very often do."

"Our habits of expense make us too dependent, and there are too many in my rank of life who can afford to marry without some attention to money."

"Is this meant for me?" she thought, coloring at the idea. Recovering, she said in a lively tone, "And pray, what is the usual price of an earl's younger son? Unless the elder brother is very sickly, I suppose you would not ask above fifty thousand pounds."

He answered her in the same playful style, and the subject dropped.

To interrupt a silence which might make him fancy her affected with what had passed, she soon afterwards said, "I imagine your cousin brought you down with him chiefly for the sake of having someone at his disposal. I wonder he does not marry, to secure a lasting convenience of that kind. But, perhaps, his sister does as well for the present, and, as she is under his sole care, he may do what he likes with her."

"No," said Colonel Fitzwilliam, "that is an advantage which he must divide with me. I am joined with him in the guardianship of Miss Darcy."

"Are you indeed? And pray what sort of guardians do you make? Does your charge give you much trouble? Young ladies of her age are sometimes a little difficult to manage, and if she has the true Darcy spirit, she may like to have her own way."

As she spoke she observed him looking at her earnestly. The manner in which he immediately asked her why she supposed Miss Darcy likely to give them any uneasiness, convinced her that she had somehow gotten pretty near the truth.

She directly replied, "You need not be frightened. I never heard any harm of her. I daresay she is one of the most well-mannered creatures in the world. She is a very great favorite with some ladies of my acquaintance, Mrs. Hurst and Miss Bingley. I think I have heard you say that you know them."

"I know them a little. Their brother is a pleasant gentlemanlike man—he is a great friend of Darcy's."

"Oh, yes," said Elizabeth drily. "Mr. Darcy is uncommonly kind to Mr. Bingley, and takes extraordinary care of him."

"Care of him? Yes, I really believe Darcy does take care of him in those points where he most wants care. From something that he told me in our journey here, I have reason to think Bingley is very much indebted to him. But I ought to beg his pardon, for I have no right to suppose that Bingley was the person meant. It was all conjecture."

"What is it you mean?"

"It is a circumstance which Darcy could not wish to be generally known, because if it were to get round to the lady's family, it would be an unpleasant thing."

"You may depend upon my not mentioning it."

"And remember I have not much reason for supposing it to be Bingley. What he told me was merely this: that he congratulated himself on having lately saved a friend from the inconveniences of a most imprudent marriage. He did this without mentioning names or any other particulars. I only suspected it to be Bingley from believing him the kind of young man to get into a scrape of that sort, and from knowing them to have been together the whole of last summer."

It took all her self-control to remain calm. Her heart pounded violently. Blood rushed in her ears. "Did Mr. Darcy give you reasons for this interference?"

"I understood that there were some very strong objections against the lady."

"And what arts did he use to separate them?"

"He did not talk to me of his arts," said Fitzwilliam, smiling. "He only told me what I have now told you."

Elizabeth made no answer, and walked on, her heart swelling with indignation. **Out of all things she could have discovered about Mr. Darcy, she decided this singular piece of news determined once and for all her true opinion of him. She loathed him. He was a disagreeable, proud, insufferable man who thought the world at his disposal. His attraction of face and fortune, and those damnable blue eyes, could not make up for his having objected** to Jane. **All the unpleasantness and silence in the world could have been forgiven him, had he not injured a beloved sister so grievously.**

After watching her a little, Fitzwilliam asked her why she was so thoughtful.

"I am thinking of what you have been telling me," said she, endeavoring to keep her voice calm. "Your cousin's conduct does not suit my feelings. Why was he to be the judge?"

"You are rather disposed to call his interference officious?"

"I do not see what right Mr. Darcy had to decide on the propriety of his friend's inclination, or why, upon his own judgment alone, he was to direct in what manner his friend was to be happy. But," she continued, recollecting herself as best she could, "as we know none of the particulars, it is not fair to condemn him. It is not to be supposed that there was much affection in the case."

"That is not an unnatural surmise," said Fitzwilliam, "but it lessens the honor of my cousin's triumph."

This was spoken jestingly; but it appeared to her so just a picture of Mr. Darcy, that she would not trust herself with an answer. She abruptly changed the conversation to indifferent matters until they reached the Parsonage. There, shut into her own room, as soon as their visitor left them, she could think without interruption of all that she had heard.

Fitzwilliam undoubtedly talked of Bingley, even if he did not know for certain. There could not exist in the world two men over whom Mr. Darcy could have such boundless influence. That he had been involved in the measures taken to separate Bingley and Jane she had never doubted, but she had always attributed the principal design and arrangement of them to Miss Bingley. If his own vanity, however, did not mislead him to brag without cause, Mr. Darcy was the reason Jane had suffered, and still continued to suffer. He had ruined for a while every hope of happiness for the most affectionate, generous heart in the world, and no one could say how lasting an evil he might have inflicted.

"There were some very strong objections against the lady," were Colonel Fitzwilliam's words. Those strong objections were probably her having one uncle who was a country attorney, and another who was in business in London.

"To Jane herself," Elizabeth reasoned, "there could be no possibility of objection. She is loveliness and goodness, her understanding excellent, her mind improved, and her manners captivating. Neither could anything be said against my father, who, though with some peculiarities, has abilities Mr. Darcy himself need not disdain, and respectability which he will probably never reach." When she thought of her mother, her confidence gave way a little, but she would not allow that any objections there had material weight with Mr. Darcy, whose pride, she was convinced, would receive a deeper wound from the want of importance in his friend's connections, than from their want of sense. She decided, at last, that he had been partly governed by this worst kind of pride, and partly by the wish of retaining Mr. Bingley for his sister.

CHAPTER THIRTY

*E*LIZABETH'S MIND WAS FILLED **with thoughts of Jane, Bingley, and, worst of all, Mr. Darcy. She refused to leave her room.** The agitation and tears which the subject occasioned brought on a headache. It grew so much worse towards the evening that, added to her unwillingness to see Mr. Darcy, it determined her not to attend her cousins to Rosings where they were engaged to drink tea. Mrs. Collins, seeing she was really unwell, did not press her to go and as much as possible prevented her husband from pressing her. However, Mr. Collins could not conceal his apprehension of Lady Catherine's being rather displeased by her staying at home.

Elizabeth could not care about Lady Catherine or any disappointment she might feel. At the moment she wanted nothing more than to be far away from Rosings. Had there been a carriage at her disposal, she would have been off before her hosts were back from their engagement. However, there was not such

means of escape and she instead found refuge beneath the covers, hidden away from the world as she tried to find a solution to end her sister's suffering and reunite her with Mr. Bingley. Nothing came to mind.

When they were gone not quite the full of a half-an-hour, Elizabeth, intending to exasperate herself as much as possible against Mr. Darcy, examined all of the letters which Jane had written to her since arriving in Kent. They contained no actual complaint, nor was there any revival of past occurrences, or any communication of present suffering. But in all, and in almost every line of each, there was a want of that cheerfulness which had been used to characterize her style, and which, proceeding from the serenity of a mind at ease with itself and kindly disposed towards everyone, had been scarcely clouded. Elizabeth noticed every sentence conveyed the idea of uneasiness, with an attention which it had hardly received on the first perusal. Mr. Darcy's shameful boast of what misery he had been able to inflict, gave her a keener sense of her sister's sufferings. It was some consolation to think that his visit to Rosings was to end on the day after the next—and, a still greater, that in less than a fortnight she herself would be with Jane again to contribute to the recovery of her spirits, by all that affection could do.

She could not think of Darcy's leaving Kent without remembering that his cousin was to go with him. Colonel Fitzwilliam had made it clear that he had no intentions at all, and agreeable as he was, she did not mean to be unhappy about him. **Elizabeth would not pretend to love where she did not, nor because the option before her seemed a reasonable prospect. Though, had Colonel Fitzwilliam been inclined towards her, she might have begun to feel differently. But, he did not and she did not.**

While settling this point, she was suddenly roused by the sound of the doorbell. Her spirits were lifted by the idea of its being Colonel Fitzwilliam, who had once before called late in the evening, and might now come to inquire after her. However, this idea was soon banished, and her spirits were very differently affected, when, to her utter amazement, she saw Mr. Darcy walk into the room. In a hurried manner he immediately began an inquiry after her health, imputing his visit to a wish of hearing that she was better. She answered him with cold civility, **her stomach too knotted and her chest too tight for her to say much else beyond, "I am better, thank you."**

Though she did not offer, he sat down for a few moments. **She did not join him, did not dare, for her head swam with the memory of Jane's letter, and if she stepped too close she might say something imprudent.** He watched her expectantly, and then, in the same hurried manner, he got up and paced about the room. **Elizabeth's anger towards him was replaced by surprise, but she said not a word.**

After a silence of several minutes, he came towards her, agitated. **"Forgive my coming so late, but I had to see you, Miss Elizabeth."**

At his words she took a seat, unable to continue supporting herself in her amazement.

He came before her, standing straight with his hands stiffly at his side, as if forcing them to remain there. "In vain I have struggled and will do it no longer. My feelings will not be repressed. I have fought against what I know to be right, considering the inferiority of your birth and the expectations of my rank; the obstacles of your wont of connections, of its being a degradation to my—"

"What do you mean by telling me this, sir?" she interrupted, not caring if she were rude.

"You must allow me to tell you how ardently I admire and love you."

Elizabeth's astonishment was beyond expression **and she instantly pushed to her feet. He stood a little close to her chair and the action brought her directly before him. She had intended to move away from him, but her legs would not make the effort. She could not speak and found herself staring at him with what had to be a dumbfounded look of astonishment. When the initial words finally made their way through her brain, she began to doubt she had actually heard them. Surely, Mr. Darcy did not just say he loved her. Such a notion was inconceivable.**

He took a few steps back to put distance between them, studying her face as he waited for her to speak. She could not. Clearly considering her silence to be sufficient encouragement, he continued, "As I have said, I long struggled with these feelings for you. I came to you on the balcony at Netherfield with the idea that I might tell you, but knew such a declaration warranted full consideration. I took pains to suppress my feelings because of the improbability of such a match as ours, but they will be silenced no longer." Coming towards her once more, his hands lifted, hesitated, then firmly clasped hers. He drew them up, settling them against his chest so she could feel his heart beating. The rhythm was fast, and blended with the heat and lift of his chest. His words became soft, as he said, "I love you, and for this reason I am willing to overlook those things which render my regard illogical. I can forget common sense; forgive the difference of our ranks; and will forever put aside any disregard I have toward your family—for they can hardly be considered as to recommend my suit. Though my intention is not to be disrespectful on that matter, only honest in my telling you, for you have always seemed fond of a direct assertion of opinion."

He spoke well, though he was no more eloquent on the subject of tenderness than of pride, and there were feelings besides those of the heart he felt it necessary to be detailed. In spite of her deeply-rooted dislike, she could not be insensible to the compliment of such a man's affection, and though her intentions did not vary for an instant, she was at first sorry for the pain he was to receive. **His hands tightened on hers, his strong fingers stroking the backs of her hands in what could only be eager anticipation on his part. She found it hard to concentrate with him so close and pulled her hands gently away. He glanced down at the parting, but let her go, moving instead to lean against the mantelpiece with his eyes fixed on her face.**

Taking a deep breath, she thought of all he said, and all sympathy roused to resentment by his preceding language. She lost all compassion in anger. She tried, however, to compose herself to answer him with patience.

He concluded with, "I wish to represent to you the strength of my attachment which, in spite of all my endeavors, I have found it impossible to conquer; and do so express my hope that I should now be rewarded by your acceptance of my hand."

As he said this, she could easily see that he had no doubt of a favorable answer. He spoke of apprehension and anxiety, but his countenance expressed real security. Such a circumstance could only exasperate farther. The color rose into her cheeks, and she said, "In such cases as this, I believe the established mode is to express a sense of obligation for the sentiments avowed, however unequally they may be returned. It is natural that obligation should be felt, and if I could feel gratitude, I would now thank you."

"Could?" He stiffened visibly.

"But I cannot." She continued, as if he had not interrupted. "I have never desired your good opinion, and you have certainly bestowed it most unwillingly. I am sorry for the pain I have caused you. It has been most unconsciously done. However, I daresay it will be of short duration. The feelings which, you tell me, have long prevented the acknowledgment of your regard, can have little difficulty in overcoming it."

Mr. Darcy seemed to catch her words with no less resentment than surprise. His complexion became pale with anger, and the disturbance of his mind was visible in every feature. He was struggling for the appearance of composure, and would not open his lips till he believed himself to have attained it. The pause was, to Elizabeth's feelings, dreadful. **At length, he came closer to her, studying her expression, as if closer examination would somehow contradict her words.** With a voice of forced calmness, he said, "And this is all the reply which I am to have the honor of expecting? I might, perhaps, wish to be informed why, with so little endeavor at civility, I am thus rejected."

"I might as well inquire," replied she, her voice rising as she thought of what he had done to Jane, "why with so evident a desire of offending and insulting me, you chose to tell me that you liked me against your will, against your reason, and even against your character? This is some excuse for incivility, if I was uncivil, but I have other provocations. You know I have. Had not my feelings decided against you—had they been indifferent, or had they even been favorable, do you think any consideration would tempt me to accept the man who has been the means of ruining, perhaps forever, the happiness of a most beloved sister?"

As she spoke, Mr. Darcy's mouth parted slightly and his face colored, but the emotion was short, and he listened without attempting to interrupt her while she continued.

Elizabeth leaned aggressively towards him. "I have every reason in the world to think ill of you. No motive can excuse the unjust and ungenerous part you played there. You dare not, you cannot deny, that you have been the principal, if not the only means of dividing them from each other—of exposing one to the censure of the world for caprice and instability, and the other to its derision for disappointed hopes, and involving them both in misery of the acutest kind."

She paused, and saw with no slight indignation that he was listening with an air which proved him wholly unmoved by any feelings of remorse. He even looked at her with a smile of affected incredulity.

"Can you deny that you have done it?" she repeated.

With assumed tranquility, he replied, "I have no wish of denying that I did everything in my power to separate my friend from your sister, or that I rejoice in my success. Towards *him* I have been kinder than towards myself."

Elizabeth disdained the appearance of noticing this civil reflection, but its meaning did not escape, nor was it likely to conciliate her. **"You call your actions kind?"**

"I do." The words held a finality of subject and she knew he did not intend to explain himself further.

"Jane would have made him the best of wives, for her entire being would have been devoted to his every happiness. You may object to my family, but you cannot object to Jane's manners. She is sweet and good and harbors no ill will towards anyone. I daresay she would even forgive and make excuses for you should she ever learn of your role in her acute unhappiness. She loved Mr. Bingley, wholly and completely—and not for his superiority of position as you would be apt to call it, but for himself alone. When he was at Netherfield she could talk of nothing else, and even you had seen how her entire being lit up whenever he came near despite the fact she is painfully shy and guards her emotions even with me. How can you call severing such a love as a kindness?"

He did not have an answer.

"But it is not merely this affair," she continued, "on which my dislike is founded. Long before it had taken place my opinion of you was decided. Your character was unfolded many months ago by the words of Mr. Wickham. On this subject, what can you have to say? In what imaginary act of friendship can you here defend yourself? Or under what misrepresentation can you here impose upon others?"

"You take an eager interest in that gentleman's concerns," said Darcy, in a less tranquil tone, and with a heightened irritation. **He too leaned forward. Their faces came uncomfortably close. Every muscle in his body tensed and she was all too aware of his person.**

Her fists balled at her sides. "Knowing what his misfortunes have been, how can one but help feeling an interest in him?"

"His misfortunes!" repeated Darcy contemptuously. "Yes, his misfortunes have been great indeed."

"And of your infliction," cried Elizabeth with energy. "You have reduced him to his present state of comparative poverty. You have withheld the advantages which you must know to have been designed for him. You have deprived the best years of his life of that independence which was no less his due than his desert. You have done all this and yet you can treat the mention of his misfortune with contempt and ridicule."

"And this is your opinion of me!" **Darcy's eyes scanned over her cheeks and mouth, as if he could not decide between kissing and slapping her.** He walked with quick steps across the room, "This is the estimation in which you hold me! I thank you for explaining it so fully. My faults, according to this calculation, are heavy indeed. But perhaps," added he, stopping in his walk, and turning towards her. **His voice rose, matching the loud tone of hers.** "These offenses might have been overlooked, had not your pride been hurt by my honest confession of the scruples that had long prevented my forming any serious design. These bitter accusations might have been suppressed, had I, with greater policy, concealed my struggles, and flattered you into the belief of my being impelled by unqualified, unalloyed inclination; by reason, by reflection, by everything. But disguise of every sort is my abhorrence. Nor am I ashamed of the feelings I related. They were natural and just. Could you expect me to rejoice in the inferiority of your connections? To congratulate myself on the hope of relations, whose condition in life is so decidedly beneath my own?"

Elizabeth felt herself growing angrier by the moment, yet endeavored to speak with composure. "You are mistaken, Mr. Darcy, if you suppose that the mode of your declaration affected me in any other way, than as it spared the concern which I might have felt in refusing you, had you behaved in a more gentleman-like manner." She saw him start to respond to this, but he said nothing, and she continued, "You could not have made the offer of your hand in any possible way that would have tempted me to accept it."

Again his astonishment was obvious. He looked at her with an expression of mingled incredulity and mortification.

She went on, "From the very beginning—from the first moment of my acquaintance with you—your manners, impressing me with the fullest belief of your arrogance, your conceit, and your selfish disdain of the feelings of others, were such as to form the groundwork of disapprobation on which succeeding events have built so immovable a dislike. I had not known you a month before I felt that you were the last man in the world whom I could ever be prevailed on to marry."

The hard tone of his words that had inspired her responding yells suddenly went away. In manner, once again calm and cold, he answered, "You have said quite enough, madam. I perfectly comprehend your feelings, and have now only to be ashamed of what my own have been. Forgive me for having taken up so much of your time, and accept my best wishes for your health and happiness."

And with these words he hastily left the room, and Elizabeth heard him the next moment open the front door and quit the house.

The tumult of her mind was now painfully great. She knew not how to support herself, and from actual weakness sat down and cried for half-an-hour. Her astonishment, as she reflected on what had passed, was increased by every review of it. That she should receive an offer of marriage from Mr. Darcy! That he should have been in love with her for so many months, so much in love as to wish to marry her in spite of all the objections which had made him prevent his friend's marrying her sister, and which must appear at least with equal force in his own case was almost incredible. It was gratifying to have inspired unconsciously so strong an affection. But his pride, his abominable pride—his shameless avowal of what he had done with respect to Jane—his unpardonable assurance in acknowledging, though he could not justify it, and the unfeeling manner in which he had mentioned Mr. Wickham, his cruelty towards whom he had not attempted to deny, soon overcame the pity which the consideration of his attachment had for a moment excited. She continued in very agitated reflections till the sound of Lady Catherine's carriage made her feel how unequal she was to encounter Charlotte's observation of her state, and hurried her away to her room.

CHAPTER THIRTY-ONE

*E*LIZABETH AWOKE THE NEXT MORNING to the same thoughts and meditations which had at length closed her eyes. She could not recover from the surprise of what had happened. It was impossible to think of anything else. Totally indisposed for want of something productive to do, she resolved, soon after breakfast, to indulge herself in air and exercise. She was proceeding directly to her favorite walk, when the recollection of Mr. Darcy's sometimes coming there stopped her. Instead of entering the park, she turned up the lane, which led farther from the turnpike-road. The park paling was still the boundary on one side, and she soon passed one of the gates into the ground.

After walking two or three times along that part of the lane, she was tempted, by the pleasantness of the morning, to stop at the gates and look into the park. The five weeks which she had passed in Kent made a great difference in the country, and every day added to the verdure of the early trees. She was on the point of continuing her walk, when she caught a glimpse of a gentleman within the grove which edged the park. He was moving her way and, fearful of its being Mr. Darcy, she was directly retreating. But the person who advanced was now near enough to see her, and stepping forward with eagerness, pronounced her name. She had turned away but, on hearing herself called in a voice which proved it to be Mr. Darcy, she moved again towards the gate. He had by that time reached it also, and, holding out a letter, which she instinctively took, said, with a look of haughty composure, "I have been walking in the grove some time in the hope of meeting you. Will you do me the honor of reading that letter?" And then, with a slight bow, turned again into the plantation.

Elizabeth watched him walk away. The stiff set of his shoulders, and the length and pace of his gait gave nothing away but the steady purpose she often saw in him. He did not turn back around and she did not look away until he was again out of sight.

With no expectation of pleasure, but with the strongest curiosity, Elizabeth opened the letter. The envelope contained two sheets of letter-paper written quite through in a very close hand, and the envelope itself was likewise full. Pursuing her way absently along the lane, she began to read. It was dated from Rosings, at eight o'clock in the morning.

"Be not alarmed, madam, on receiving this letter, by the apprehension of its containing any repetition of those sentiments or renewal of those offers which were last night so disgusting to you. I write without any intention of paining you, or humbling myself, by dwelling on wishes which, for the happiness of both, cannot be too soon forgotten. The effort which the formation and the perusal of this letter must occasion, should have been spared, had not my character required it to be written and read. You must, therefore, pardon the freedom with which I demand your attention. Your feelings, I know, will bestow it unwillingly, but I demand it of your justice."

Elizabeth took a deep breath, glancing around to make sure she was quite alone. Her heart beat an unsteady rhythm in her chest. For the briefest moment, as a gentle breeze caressed her face, she thought to detect the scent of Mr. Darcy on the paper. A nervous flutter assaulted her stomach. She turned so the breeze was at her back and continued to read.

"Two offenses of a very different nature, and by no means of equal magnitude, you last night laid to my charge. The first mentioned was, that, regardless of the sentiments of either, I had detached Mr. Bingley from your sister. The other, that I had, in defiance of various claims, in defiance of honor and human-ity, ruined the immediate prosperity and blasted the prospects of Mr. Wickham. Willfully and wantonly to have thrown off the companion of my youth, the acknowledged favorite of my father, a young man who had scarcely any other dependence than on our patronage, and who had been brought up to expect its exertion, would be a depravity, to which the separation of two young persons, whose affection could be the growth of only a few weeks, could bear no comparison. But from the severity of that blame which was last night so liberally bestowed, respecting each circumstance, I shall hope to be in the future secured, when the following account of my actions and their motives has been read. If, in the explanation of them, which is due to myself, I am under the necessity of relating feelings which may be offensive to yours, I can only say that I am sorry. The necessity must be obeyed, and further apology would be absurd.

"I had not been long in Hertfordshire, before I saw that Bingley preferred your elder sister to any other young woman in the country. But it was not till the evening of the dance at Netherfield that I had any apprehension of his feeling a serious attachment. I had often seen him in love before. At that ball, while I had the honor of dancing with you, I was first made acquainted by Sir William Lucas's accidental information that Bingley's attentions to your sister had given rise to a general expectation of their marriage. He spoke of it as a certain event, of which the time alone could be undecided. From that moment I observed my friend's behavior attentively, and I could then perceive that his partiality for Miss Bennet was beyond what I had ever witnessed in him. Your sister I also watched. Her look and manners were open, cheerful, and engaging as ever, but without any symptom of particular regard. I remained convinced from the evening's scrutiny, that though she received his attentions with pleasure, she did not invite them by any participation of sentiment. If *you* have not been mistaken here, *I* must have been in error. Your superior knowledge of your sister must make the latter probable."

Elizabeth turned, pacing down a shaded part of the lane so as to remain hidden by trees.

"If it be so, if I have been misled by error to inflict pain on her, your resentment has not been unreasonable. But I shall not scruple to assert, that the serenity of your sister's countenance was such as might give the most acute observer a conviction that, however amiable her temper, her heart was not easily touched. That I was desirous of believing her indifferent is certain—but I will venture to say that my investigation and decisions are not usually influenced by my hopes or fears. I did not believe her to be indifferent because I wished it. I believed it on impartial conviction, as truly as I wished it in reason. My objections to the marriage were not merely those which I last night acknowledged to have, in my own case, the utmost force of passion to put aside. The want of connection could not be so great an evil to my friend as to me. But there were other causes

of repugnance—causes which, though still existing, and existing to an equal degree in both instances, I had myself endeavored to forget as they were not immediately before me. These
causes must be stated, though briefly. The situation of your
mother's family, though objectionable, was nothing in comparison to the total want of propriety so frequently, almost
uniformly betrayed by herself, by your three younger sisters,
and occasionally even by your father. Pardon me. It pains me
to offend you. Amidst your concern for the defects of your
nearest relations and your displeasure at this representation
of them, let it give you consolation to consider that you and
your eldest sister have conducted yourselves in such a way as
to avoid any share of the censure. This praise is bestowed on
you both, and I recognize the honorable sense and disposition
of you both. I will only add that from what passed that evening
of the ball, my opinion was confirmed, and every inducement
heightened which could have led me before, to preserve my
friend from what I esteemed a most unhappy connection. He
left Netherfield for London on the following day, as I am certain you remember, with the design of soon returning.

"I will now explain the part which I acted. His sisters' uneasiness had been equally excited with my own and our coincidence
of feeling was soon discovered. We agreed that no time should
be lost in detaching their brother, and we resolved on joining
him directly in London. There I readily engaged in the duty of
pointing out to my friend the certain evils of such a choice. I
described, and enforced them earnestly. However this remon-
strance might have staggered or delayed his determination, I do
not suppose it would ultimately have prevented the marriage,
had it not been seconded by my assurance of your sister's indifference, which I did not hesitate to give. He had before believed
her to return his affection with sincere, if not with equal regard.

But Bingley has great natural modesty, with a stronger dependence on my judgment than on his own. To convince him that he had deceived himself was no very difficult point. To persuade him against returning into Hertfordshire, when that conviction had been given, was scarcely the work of a moment. I cannot blame myself for having done thus much. There is but one part of my conduct in the whole affair on which I do not reflect with satisfaction. It is that I condescended to adopt the measures of art so far as to conceal from him your sister's being in town. I knew it myself, as it was known to Miss Bingley, but her brother is even yet ignorant of it. That they might have met without ill consequence is perhaps probable, but his regard did not appear to me enough extinguished for him to see her without some danger. Perhaps this concealment was beneath me. However, it is done and it was done for the best. On this subject I have nothing more to say, no other apology to offer. If I have wounded your sister's feelings, it was unknowingly done and though the motives which governed me may to you appear insufficient, I believed them at the time to be justified."

Again she paused, glancing around to ensure her privacy. Her hands trembled as she turned back to the letter.

"With respect to that other, weightier accusation, of having injured Mr. Wickham, I can only refute it by laying before you the whole of his connection with my family. Of what he has particularly accused me I am ignorant; but of the truth of what I shall relate, I can summon more than one witness of undoubted veracity.

"Mr. Wickham is the son of a very respectable man, who had for many years the management of all the Pemberley estates, and whose good conduct in the discharge of his trust naturally inclined my father to be of service to him. To George Wickham, who was his godson, his kindness was liberally bestowed. My

father supported him at school, and afterwards at Cambridge—
most important assistance, as his own father, always poor from
the extravagance of his wife, would have been unable to give
him a gentleman's education. My father was not only fond of
this young man's society, whose manner were always engaging;
he also had the highest opinion of him, and hoping the church
would be his profession, intended to provide for him in it. As for
myself, it is many, many years since I first began to think of him
in a very different manner. The cruel propensities—the want of
principle, which he was careful to guard from the knowledge of
his best friend, could not escape the observation of a young man
of nearly the same age with himself, and who had opportunities
of seeing him in unguarded moments, which my father could
not have. Here again shall give you pain—to what degree only
you can tell. But whatever may be the sentiments which Mr.
Wickham has created, a suspicion of their nature shall not prevent me from unfolding his real character—it adds even another
motive.

"My excellent father died about five years ago and his
attachment to Mr. Wickham was to the last so steady, that in
his will he particularly recommended it to me, to promote
his advancement in the best manner that his profession might
allow—and if he took orders, desired that a valuable family living
might be his as soon as it became vacant. There was also a legacy
of one thousand pounds. His own father did not long survive
mine, and within half a year from these events, Mr. Wickham
wrote to inform me that, having finally resolved against taking
orders, he hoped I should not think it unreasonable for him to
expect some more immediate pecuniary advantage, in lieu of the
preferment, by which he could not be benefited. He had some
intention, he added, of studying law, and I must be aware that
the interest of one thousand pounds would be a very insufficient

support for such an endeavor. I rather wished, than believed him to be sincere but, at any rate, was perfectly ready to accede to his proposal. I knew that Mr. Wickham ought not to be a clergyman and the business was therefore soon settled. He resigned all claim to assistance in the church, were it possible that he could ever be in a situation to receive it, and accepted in return three thousand pounds. All connection between us seemed now dissolved. I thought too ill of him to invite him to Pemberley, or admit his society in town. In town I believe he chiefly lived, but his studying the law was a mere pretence, and being now free from all restraint, his life was a life of idleness and dissipation. For about three years I heard little of him; but on the decease of the incumbent of the living which had been designed for him, he applied to me again by letter for the presentation. His circumstances, he assured me, and I had no difficulty in believing it, were exceedingly bad. He had found the law a most unprofitable study, and was now absolutely resolved on being ordained, if I would present him to the living in question—of which he trusted there could be little doubt, as he was well assured that I had no other person to provide for, and I could not have forgotten my revered father's intentions. You will hardly blame me for refusing to comply with this entreaty, or for resisting every repetition to it. His resentment was in proportion to the distress of his circumstances—and he was doubtless as violent in his abuse of me to others as in his reproaches to myself. After this period every appearance of acquaintance was dropped. How he lived I know not. But last summer he was again most painfully obtruded on my notice.

"I must now mention a circumstance which I would wish to forget myself, and which no obligation less than the present should induce me to unfold it to any human being. Having said as much, I feel no doubt of your secrecy. My sister, who is more than ten years my junior, was left to the guardianship of my mother's nephew, Colonel Fitzwilliam, and myself. About a year ago, she was taken from school, and an establishment formed for her in London. Last summer she went with the lady who presided over it, to Ramsgate; and there also went Mr. Wickham, undoubtedly by design; for there proved to have been a prior acquaintance between him and Mrs. Younge, in whose character we were most unhappily deceived. And by her connivance and aid, he so far recommended himself to Georgiana, whose affectionate heart retained a strong impression of his kindness to her as a child, that she was persuaded to believe herself in love, and to consent to an elopement. She was then but fifteen, which must be her excuse. After stating her imprudence, I am happy to add, that I owed the knowledge of it to herself. I joined them unexpectedly a day or two before the intended elopement, and then Georgiana, unable to support the idea of grieving and offending a brother whom she almost looked up to as a father, acknowledged the whole to me. You may imagine what I felt and how I acted. Regard for my sister's credit and feelings prevented any public exposure, but I wrote to Mr. Wickham, who left the place immediately, and Mrs. Younge was of course removed from her charge. Mr. Wickham's chief object was unquestionably my sister's fortune, which is thirty thousand pounds. I cannot help supposing that the hope of revenging himself on me was a strong inducement. His revenge would have been complete indeed.

"This, madam, is a faithful narrative of every event in which we have been concerned together. If you do not absolutely reject it as false, you will, I hope, acquit me henceforth of cruelty towards Mr. Wickham. I know not in what manner, under what form of falsehood he has imposed on you, but his success is not perhaps to be wondered at. Ignorant as you previously were of everything concerning either, detection could not be in your power, and suspicion certainly not in your inclination.

"You may possibly wonder why all this was not told to you last night. I was not then master enough of myself to know what could or ought to be revealed. For the truth of everything here related, I can appeal more particularly to the testimony of Colonel Fitzwilliam, who, from our near relationship and constant intimacy, and, still more, as one of the executors of my father's will, has been unavoidably acquainted with every particular of these transactions. If your abhorrence of me should make my assertions valueless, you cannot be prevented by the same cause from confiding in my cousin. So there may be the possibility of consulting him, I shall endeavor to find some opportunity of putting this letter in your hands in the course of the morning."

Elizabeth took a deep breath, softly reading the very last words aloud to herself: "Fitzwilliam Darcy."

CHAPTER THIRTY-TWO

HEN MR. DARCY gave her the letter, Elizabeth did not expect it to contain a renewal of his offer, and so had formed no expectation at all of its contents. Therefore, she had very eagerly gone through it once, then twice. She read with an eagerness which hardly left her power of comprehension. And impatient to know what the next sentence might bring, she was incapable of attending to the one before her eyes. As she read, her feelings were scarcely to be defined.

With a strong prejudice against everything he might say, she began his account of what had happened at Netherfield. Elizabeth instantly resolved to dismiss his belief of her sister's disinterest, for he freely admitted his real objections to the match. He expressed no regret for what he had done; his style was not penitent, but haughty. It was all pride and insolence.

"Insufferable man!" she whispered, staring at his words as if they should soon light on fire and engulf her hands in flames.

"Insufferable! How could he do it to poor Jane?"

However, this subject was succeeded by his account of Mr. Wickham. She read with somewhat clearer attention a relation of events which, if true, must overthrow every cherished opinion of Wickham's worth, and which bore so alarming an affinity to his own history of himself—her feelings were yet more acutely painful and more difficult to define. Astonishment, apprehension, and even horror, oppressed her. She wished to discredit it entirely, repeatedly exclaiming, "This must be false. It cannot be!" When she had gone through the whole letter twice, though scarcely knowing anything of the last page or two, she put it hastily away, protesting that she would not regard it and that she would never look in it again.

In this perturbed state of mind, with thoughts that could rest on nothing, she walked on. But it would not do. In half a minute the letter was unfolded again, and collecting herself as well as she could, she again began the mortifying perusal of all that related to Wickham, and commanded herself so far as to examine the meaning of every sentence. The account of his connection with the Pemberley family was exactly what he had related himself; and the kindness of the late Mr. Darcy, though she had not before known its extent, equally agreed with his own words. So far each recital confirmed the other, but when she came to the will the difference was great. What Wickham said of the living was fresh in her memory, and as she recalled his very words, it was impossible not to feel that there was gross duplicity on one side or the other. For a few moments, she flattered herself that her wishes did not err. But when she read and re-read with the closest attention, the particulars immediately following of Wickham's resigning all pretensions to the living, of his receiving in lieu so considerable a sum as three thousand pounds, again she was forced to hesitate. She put down the letter, weighed every circumstance with what she meant to be impartiality—deliberated on the probability of each statement—but with little success. On both sides it was only assertion. Again she read on. Every line laid out the affair more clearly and, whereas before reading she had believed it impossible that any contrivance could render Mr. Darcy's conduct less than infamous, she found his words capable of making him appear entirely blameless.

The extravagance and general profligacy which he scrupled not to lay at Mr. Wickham's charge, shocked her exceedingly because she could bring no proof of its injustice. She had never heard of him before his entrance into the militia, which he had engaged at the persuasion of a young man who, on meeting him accidentally in town, had renewed a slight acquaintance. Of his former way of life nothing had been known in Hertfordshire but what he, himself, told. As to his real character, had information been in her power, she had never felt the need to inquire. His countenance, voice, and manner had established him at once in the possession of every virtue. She tried to recollect some instance of goodness, some distinguished trait of integrity or benevolence, that might rescue him from the attacks of Mr. Darcy; or at least, by the predominance of virtue, atone for those casual errors under which she would endeavor to class what Mr. Darcy had described as the idleness and vice of many years' continuance. But she could think of nothing. She instantly imagined him before her, in every charm of air and manner of speaking; but she could remember no more substantial good than the general approbation of the neighborhood, and the regard which his social powers had gained him in the mess. After pausing on this point a considerable while, she once more continued to read. But, alas, the story which followed, of his designs on Miss Darcy, received some confirmation from what had passed between Colonel Fitzwilliam and herself only the morning before. At last she was referred for the truth of every particular to Colonel Fitzwilliam himself—from whom she had previously received the information of his near concern in all his cousin's affairs, and whose character she had no reason to question. At one time she had almost resolved on applying to him, but the idea was checked by the awkwardness of the application, and at length wholly banished by the conviction that Mr. Darcy would never have hazarded such a proposal, if he had not been well assured of his cousin's corroboration.

She perfectly remembered everything that had passed in conversation between Wickham and herself, in their first evening at Mr. Philips's. Many of his expressions were still fresh in her memory. She was now struck with the impropriety of such communications to a stranger, and wondered how it had escaped her before. She saw the indelicacy of putting himself forward as he had done, and the inconsistency of his professions with his conduct. He had boasted of having no fear of seeing Mr. Darcy—that Mr. Darcy might leave the country, but that he should stand his ground—yet he avoided the Netherfield ball the very next week. She remembered also that, till the Netherfield family had quitted the country, he had told his story to no one but herself. After their removal it had been discussed everywhere. He had then no scruples in sinking Mr. Darcy's character, though he had assured her that respect for the father would always prevent his exposing the son.

How differently did everything now appear where he was concerned. His attentions to Miss King were now the consequence of views solely and hatefully mercenary. The mediocrity of her fortune proved no longer the moderation of his wishes, but his eagerness to grasp at anything. His behavior to herself could now have had no tolerable motive. He had either been deceived with regard to her fortune, or had been gratifying his vanity by encouraging the preference which she believed she had most incautiously shown. Every lingering struggle in his favor grew fainter and fainter. And in farther justification of Mr. Darcy, she could not but allow Mr. Bingley, when questioned by Jane, had long ago asserted his blamelessness in the affair. Proud and repulsive as Mr. Darcy's manners were, she had never, in the whole course of their acquaintance seen anything that betrayed him to be unprincipled or unjust. Among his own connections he was esteemed and valued—that even Wickham had allowed him merit as a brother, and that she had often heard him speak so affectionately of his sister as to prove him capable of some amiable feeling.

Elizabeth took a deep, steadying breath, as her thoughts on the matter concluded. She grew ashamed of herself. Of neither Darcy nor Wickham could she think without feeling she had been blind, partial, prejudiced, and absurd.

"How despicably I have acted!" she whispered, ashamed by her role in defending Mr. Wickham's character at the expense of Mr. Darcy's. **She thought of all the little comments she had made to her friends and sisters, laughing at Darcy's behavior and pride while bolstering Wickham's.** "I, who have prided myself on my discernment. I, who have valued myself on my abilities, who have often disdained the generous candor of my sister, and gratified my vanity in useless or blamable mistrust. How humiliating is this discovery! Had I been in love, I could not have been more wretchedly blind; but vanity, not love, has been my folly. Pleased with the preference of one, and offended by the neglect of the other, on the very beginning of our acquaintance, I have courted ignorance, and driven reason away, where either were concerned. Till this moment I never knew myself."

From herself to Jane, from Jane to Bingley, her thoughts were in a line which soon brought to her recollection that Mr.

Darcy's explanation there had appeared very insufficient, and she read it again. Widely different was the effect of a third perusal. How could she refuse to credit his assertions in one instance, when she had been obliged to accept them in the other? He declared himself to be completely ignorant of her sister's attachment, and she could not help remembering what Charlotte's opinion had always been. Neither could she deny the justice of his description of Jane. She felt that Jane's feelings, though fervent, were little displayed, and there was a constant complacency in her air and manner not often united with great sensibility.

When she came to that part of the letter in which her family was mentioned in terms of such mortifying, yet merited reproach, her sense of shame was severe. The justice of the charge struck her too forcibly for denial, and the circumstances to which he particularly alluded as having passed at the Netherfield ball, and as confirming all his first disapprobation, could not have made a stronger impression on his mind than on hers; for her younger sisters and mothers, even her father, had acted in such a way as to expose themselves to censure.

The compliment to herself and her sister was not unfelt. It soothed, but it could not console her for the contempt which had thus been self-attracted by the rest of her family. **It was a wonder Mr. Darcy even asked for her hand at all. How great was his attachment to her? How could she have not seen it? For, to reconcile himself to accept her, must have taken a great struggle on his part. However, no matter how elegantly he spoke, once reconciled to his feelings and decision, he should have been able to express himself better than to tell her he liked her most unwillingly. The sting of his words warred with the declaration of his passions. How could she, even if she had been inclined to consider him, accept such a proposal, no matter how honestly given? Upon reflection, knowing what she now knew from the letter, she** might have been inclined to at least pause before declaring she would not have him.

It was too soon to regret her decision. She needed more time to think on it, more time to reconsider the whole of her acquaintance with Mr. Darcy, to form an opinion solely on her own, without having it spoiled by the falsity of others. Only then should she allow herself to rejoice or regret her hasty words.

"Not that it would matter," she told herself. "He will not renew the offer and what was said will remain said. There is no reason that I should doubt my first impression. However, I will allow that I must consider reframing my overall opinion of the gentleman, giving it the benefit of sound judgment."

"I love you, and for this reason I am willing to overlook those things which render my regard illogical," he had said.

The words caused a warmth to spread throughout her body. Love. What could a man like Mr. Darcy possibly know of love—at least the fine, stout love she craved? No, he could not love her, not truly, not deeply, not. . . .

"You must allow me to tell you how ardently I admire and love you." Each word he had spoken burned into her thoughts, as clear, if not clearer, than the first time he said them. Was she wrong in her assessment? Ardent admiration and love bespoke of passion. Did he hide his emotions? Just as Jane hid hers from Bingley? But if Elizabeth could see Jane's feelings, surely she could detect them in Darcy.

These thoughts led back around to her sister's suffering. As she considered that Jane's disappointment had been the work of their nearest relations, and how materially they were both hurt by the impropriety of the same, she felt depressed beyond anything she had ever known before.

After wandering along the lane for two hours, giving way to every variety of thought—re-considering events, determining probabilities, and reconciling herself, as well as she could, to a change so sudden and so important—fatigue, and the realization of her long absence, made her at length return home. She entered the house with the wish of appearing as cheerful as usual, and repressed all reflections that would make her unfit for conversation.

She was immediately told that the two gentlemen from Rosings had each called during her absence. Mr. Darcy came only for a few minutes to take leave. Colonel Fitzwilliam sat with them at least an hour, hoping for her return, and almost resolving to walk after her till she could be found. Elizabeth could but affect concern in missing him, though she really rejoiced at it. She could think only of her letter and did not trust herself around Colonel Fitzwilliam, for she would be tempted to mention Darcy's words.

CHAPTER THIRTY-THREE

THE FOLLOWING MORNING the two gentlemen left Rosings. **Though Darcy knew it would be torture to take his leave of Elizabeth after her refusal of him, he could not help but wonder at her reaction to his letter. It pained him to think she might not believe him, but he contented himself in knowing he had done all he could to relay the truth of passing events, and hope that any future meetings between them would be pleasant ones, without reproach or suspicion.**

Beyond the two offenses which he had explained at length in his letter—for he always seemed to do better expressing himself in the written word than in the conversation of the moment—he felt the sting of a rejection so acute he could scarcely put a name to it. Not once, in all his apprehensions about asking for Elizabeth's hand, did he consider *she* would not have *him*. The match, which caused him so much grief, should have caused within her a matching amount—if not more—joy. He was not

insensible to the luxury of his position and fortune. That she should reject him, even with the reasons she so laid out, took much reconciliation of mind on his part.

There could only be one reason for it. Her dislike of him must be great indeed for his fortune and power not to prove an inducement. No, she had not even hesitated in her refusal of him. His internal struggle had not allowed for the possibility of her not wanting him and the sudden knowledge left a hollow emptiness in his chest and a rock in his stomach. He had known his whole life the reason why a woman would want to marry him was for what he had, and not who he was. By rights, he could have any pick of female, from any family, and they would eagerly agree to his hand with little more inducement than his name. It was a fact of wealth that he had long ago resigned himself to.

She did not care for him and her abhorrence must be deep indeed for her to reject all he had to offer. And, yet, if she took him for his wealth or position, she would not be the woman he had fallen for. The look in her eyes as she declared she would not have him, that she could never be induced to have him, burned into his soul. He had never felt so dejected, so alone, so heartbroken. The pain only seemed to grow worse with each passing second. He would never have her, never possess her, never lie next to her, never wake her with his kisses, or fall asleep with the scent of her lingering around him, or discuss books and music, or travel, or argue with her about any number of mundane things. He felt the acute loss of the life he would not have. The urge to scream filled him, but he swallowed the emotion, hiding behind the only comforts he had left—propriety and pride.

With Elizabeth, he had wanted to be with her, wanted to speak to her though the words did not always come out the way he wished them to. Often, after walking with her in the park, he would think of things he should have said and would always determine to do better upon their next meeting. However, Elizabeth never seemed to mind his silence and allowed him time to gather his thoughts before expressing them. He had so convinced himself that she understood him and accepted him, for more than his wealth. She did not put herself forward as other women had in search of a husband, and thus he had concluded her attention to him came from her own enjoyment of his company and nothing else.

How he had been wrong!

"We can stop the carriage," said Colonel Fitzwilliam as they passed the Parsonage. "I can make some excuse if you would like to go in. A lost handkerchief perhaps?"

Seeing Mr. Collins waiting near the lodges to make them his parting obeisance, Darcy shook his head in denial. "No. I have nothing left to attend to at the Parsonage. I took my leave, I will not do it again."

"I do not know all that happened, and I will not ask you for the details, but Miss Elizabeth is a reasonable young lady. I am sure whatever you imagined she might need to have clarified from me has already been determined to your satisfaction."

"Indeed," he agreed simply to end the conversation. He leaned back his head, closed his eyes, and refused to say anything more.

Mr. Collins brought home news of the gentlemen's departure, particularly noting their appearance of good health. No sooner had he relayed his intelligence, did he hasten to Rosings to console Lady Catherine and her daughter.

While he was away, Elizabeth was happy to be alone with her friend. Charlotte was as close to her as her own sisters, though perhaps not so close as Jane, and she found the familiar ease with which they could converse to be a comfort.

"I remember, some days back, you were going to give me your mother's advice on how to keep your husband quiet," Elizabeth said. The thought had passed through her mind on more than one occasion, but until this moment she had not had the privacy to ask.

Charlotte laughed. "It is how she told me to fix Mr. Collins's interest, and is what gives me a few hours quiet when I should wish it."

Thoroughly interested, and in need of a good distraction, Elizabeth implored her to go on.

Charlotte, with whispering secrecy, though there was no one to overhear, said, "A man is not unlike an animal during its season—aggressive, distracted, and inclined to run about here and there. But, it is within a lady's power to control those habits, and make them more agreeable, not to mention the ability to settle things as they wish. Simply put, you must milk the energy from them."

"My dear Charlotte, your mother gives advice as obscurely as mine. Mine speaks of visiting parlors, your mother speaks of milking." Elizabeth laughed. "It is a wonder the world gets populated at all."

"You are not getting my meaning," said Charlotte. Then giving a slight, inappropriate gesture of her hands and a glance downward to the floor, she said, "You milk him. Down there. Though, it is not really milk, I daresay it works. It turns a man instantly docile and completely controllable, and what is the little chore when it assures I will have my way."

Elizabeth was not sure how to answer, and was prevented from even forming a gasp of shock by the return of Mr. Collins. She tried, unsuccessfully not to think of what Charlotte said and

the picture that formed was so disagreeable she could hardly respond to his news that they had an invitation from her ladyship to dine.

Elizabeth could not see Lady Catherine without recollecting that, had she chosen it, she might by this time have been presented to her as her future niece. Nor could she think, without a mischievous smile, of what her ladyship's indignation would have been. The idea was one of the few that brought her any amusement. **Most of the time, she had to make a conscious effort not to think of Mr. Darcy and his letter.**

Their first subject was the diminution of the Rosings party. "I assure you, I feel it exceedingly," said Lady Catherine. "I believe no one feels the loss of friends so much as I do. I am particularly attached to these young men, and know them to be much attached to me. They were excessively sorry to go."

Mr. Collins had one of his longwinded compliments to offer, which were kindly smiled on by the mother and daughter.

Lady Catherine observed, after dinner, that Miss Bennet seemed out of spirits, and immediately accounted for it by supposing that she did not like to go home again so soon. "But if that is the case, you must write to your mother and beg that you may stay a little longer. Mrs. Collins will be very glad of your company, I am sure."

"I am much obliged to your ladyship for your kind invitation," replied Elizabeth, "but it is not in my power to accept it. I must be in town next Saturday."

"Why, at that rate, you will have been here only six weeks. I expected you to stay two months. I told Mrs. Collins so before you came. There can be no occasion for your going so soon. Mrs. Bennet could certainly spare you for another fortnight."

"But my father cannot. He wrote last week to hurry my return."

"Oh, your father may spare you, if your mother can. Daughters are never of so much consequence to a father. If you will stay it will be in my power to take one of you as far as London, for I am going there for a week early in June. Indeed, if the weather should happen to be cool, I should not object to taking you both, as you are neither of you large."

"You are all kindness, madam, but I believe we must abide by our original plan."

Lady Catherine seemed resigned, and had many other questions to ask respecting their journey. As she did not answer them all herself, attention was necessary, which Elizabeth believed to be lucky for her. With a mind so occupied, she might have forgotten where she was. Reflection must be reserved for solitary hours. Whenever she was alone, she gave way to it as the greatest relief, and not a day went by without a solitary walk, in which she might indulge in all the delight of unpleasant recollections.

Mr. Darcy's letter she was in a fair way of soon knowing by heart. She studied every sentence and her feelings towards its writer were at times widely different. When she remembered the style of his address, she was still full of indignation; but when she considered how unjustly she had condemned and upbraided him, her anger was turned against herself; and his disappointed feelings became the object of compassion. His attachment excited gratitude, his general character respect. However, she could not for a moment repent her refusal, or allow herself the slightest inclination ever to see him again. **Her mind was too unsteady when it came to him and she had to err on the side of caution—not that he would renew his offer.**

In these solitary moments, she could not help wondering how things would be between them had she accepted him. There was a natural progression between a couple after the

announcement of an engagement. He had held her hands to his chest as he had made his sentiments known. What would he have done, had she exclaimed, "Yes! Yes, I will have you!"

Would those lips have brushed over her fingers as he lifted her hands to receive his mouth? Would he have taken it farther still, drawing her close? She knew him to be a man of honor, but would the certainty of their engagement have allowed him to kiss her? He would not back away from his word once it was given. If he had struggled to the point he had claimed, and at this point she did not doubt he believed all he said, then would he have felt propelled to end his own suffering as soon as she allowed? With the empty house and quiet evening, they would not have been disturbed.

Her thoughts traveled in such a way as to awaken all of her senses. She closed her eyes, aware that it was the middle of the day. She lay on her bed, having begged to be excused for a nap. No one would disturb her for hours.

Lifting the last page of the letter, she looked at his bold signature and whispered, "Fitzwilliam Darcy." As she traced the lines of it, she felt closer to him, and the sensation brought back all those small moment when he had touched her—her cheek, her hand, her arm.

She let the letter drop against her chest. The light weight of it felt heavy against her breasts. Without moving it, she bit her lip. Each breath became measured. Her legs moved over the coverlet in such a way that they became exposed from beneath her dress. As if possessed, her hips moved, rocking side to side. She pressed her thighs tightly together, aware of the ache building there.

"Fitzwilliam Darcy." What pleasure the words invoked. Elizabeth gave way to her longings, letting her mind play out what might have happened had she said yes. She licked her lips. What if all that anger he had shown in yelling at her had instead been passion? Would his lips have met hers, hard and sure? Or soft and probing?

He had strong hands, warm and capable. Elizabeth placed her hand on her exposed knee, pulling at her skirt to slide it up her thighs. What would such a moment feel like? To be claimed by a man in the most intimate of ways? She pictured those blue eyes watching her as he kissed her cheeks, trailing the warm caresses over her chin and neck. Letting her fingers play the part of his mouth, she touched her face before sliding them down to the front of her bodice. It did not take much to free the laces that would expose her chest.

Experience did not let her imagine the full effect of his love-making, but she was not so innocent as to not understand what would happen, and that men were not only of a nature, but of a shape to conquer women. Touching a breast, she massaged it in her palm as the nipple hardened. The pleasure of it shot through her, causing her toes to curl and her knees to lift.

"Fitzwilliam Darcy." The letter brushed her flesh, his signature to her naked chest. It was as if he touched her.

A harsh, ragged breath escaped her and she found her hand reaching to press against the ache of her sex. Rapturous delights greeted her fingers. Everywhere she looked she imagined him to be—watching her, touching her, taking her. By all that is blessed, he had the greatest eyes; and the masculine smell of him whenever he came too close was hardly forgotten. She guessed his scent would only be stronger if she peeled the jacket from his shoulders and the shirt from his chest. She wondered at the muscles she would find there—would they be tanned like his face from exposure to the sun? For a gentleman, he was not unaccustomed to vigorous exercise and pursuits. Surely his activities would translate themselves in the hidden length of his body. How hard he must feel compared to her softness, so much warmer than her cooler skin! The naughtiness of such thoughts caused her to blush, but the pleasure of them did not stay her fingers.

"Darcy," she gasped, opening her legs and pressing her feet to the bed. She rubbed her sex against her hand, seeking an end to the torment. In that second between torture and ecstasy, she considered she should have said yes if only to fulfill this one desire. Her base attraction to him was only enhanced by knowing he was attracted to her. She always supposed him indifferent to her charms, but if a man like Darcy asked for her hand, he who could have his pick of beautiful women, it must mean he felt for her the same need she sometimes felt for him.

Finally, release came, and a flood of trembling emotion followed the gratification of such a moment. Instantly, she knew it was wrong. She had rejected his suit and rightly so. This gave her no right to use him in such an intimate way, even if the gentleman would never know of the service he had just done her. Gasping, and more than a little embarrassed by the way she had allowed herself to get carried away without thought to her surroundings, she quickly righted her clothing.

At length, when her breath began to steady and her temperature to cool, she suffered herself to once again consider the recent events. In her own past behavior, there was a constant source of vexation and regret; and in the unhappy defects of her family, a subject of yet heavier chagrin. They were hopeless of remedy. Her father, contented with laughing at them, would never exert himself to restrain the wild giddiness of his youngest daughters; and her mother, with manners so far from right herself, was entirely insensible of the evil. Elizabeth had frequently united with Jane in an endeavor to check the imprudence of Catherine and Lydia. But while the young girls were supported by their mother's indulgence, what chance could there be of improvement? Catherine, weak-spirited, irritable, and completely under

Lydia's guidance, had been always affronted by their advice; and Lydia, self-willed and careless, would scarcely give them a hearing. They were ignorant, idle, and vain. While there was an officer in Meryton, they would flirt with him; and while Meryton was within a walk of Longbourn, they would be going there forever. **It was no wonder Mr. Darcy expressed concern. And, whereas she could not forgive his delivery out a sense of family principle, she could hardly wish him burdened with such a family as hers.**

Anxiety on Jane's behalf was another prevailing apprehension. Mr. Darcy's explanation, by restoring Bingley to all her former good opinion, heightened the sense of what Jane had lost. His affection was proved to have been sincere, and his conduct cleared of all blame, unless any could attach to the implicitness of his confidence in his friend. How grievous then was the thought that, of a situation so desirable in every respect, so replete with advantage, so promising for happiness, Jane had been deprived, by the folly and indecorum of her own family!

When to these recollections was added the development of Wickham's character, it may be easily believed that the happy spirits which had seldom been depressed before, were now so much affected as to make it almost impossible for Elizabeth to appear tolerably cheerful.

CHAPTER THIRTY-FOUR

ON SATURDAY MORNING Elizabeth and Mr. Collins met for breakfast a few minutes before the others appeared. He took the opportunity of paying the parting civilities which he deemed indispensably necessary.

"I know not, Miss Elizabeth, whether Mrs. Collins has yet expressed her sense of your kindness in coming to us, but I am very certain you will not leave the house without receiving her thanks. The favor of your company has been much felt, I assure you. We know how little there is to tempt anyone to our humble abode. Our plain manner of living, our small rooms and few domestics, and the little we see of the world, must make Hunsford extremely dull to a young lady like yourself. I hope you will believe us grateful for the condescension, and that we have done everything in our power to prevent your spending your time unpleasantly."

Elizabeth was eager with her thanks and assurances of

happiness. "I assure you, I have spent six weeks with great enjoyment."

Mr. Collins was gratified, and with a more smiling solemnity replied, "It gives me great pleasure to hear that you have passed your time agreeably. We have certainly done our best, and count it most fortunate to have it in our power to introduce you to very superior society. From our connection with Rosings, the frequent means of varying the humble home scene, I think we may flatter ourselves that your Hunsford visit cannot have been entirely irksome. Our situation with regard to Lady Catherine's family is indeed the sort of extraordinary advantage and blessing which few can boast."

Words were insufficient for the elevation of his feelings. He walked about the room, while Elizabeth tried to unite civility and truth in a few short sentences. **"The pleasure of being with my dear friend, and the kind attentions I have received from all, make me feel obliged. I will have nothing but fond stories to tell my sisters upon my return."**

"You may, in fact, carry a very favorable report of us into Hertfordshire, my dear cousin. I flatter myself that you will be able to do so. You have been a daily witness to Lady Catherine's great attentions to Mrs. Collins. Altogether I trust it does not appear your friend has drawn an unfortunate—but on this point it will be as well to be silent. Only let me assure you, that I can from my heart most cordially wish you equal felicity in marriage. My Charlotte and I have but one way of thinking. There is in everything a most remarkable resemblance of character and ideas between us. We seem to have been designed for each other."

Elizabeth was not sorry to have his words interrupted by the lady of the house. Poor Charlotte! It was melancholy to leave her to such society, but she had chosen it with her eyes open.

Though evidently regretting that her visitors were to go, she did not seem to ask for compassion. Her home and her housekeeping, her parish and her poultry, and all their dependent concerns, had not yet lost their charms.

At length the chaise arrived, the trunks were fastened on, the parcels placed within, and it was pronounced to be ready. After an affectionate parting between the friends, Elizabeth was attended to the carriage by Mr. Collins, and as they walked down the garden he was commissioning her with his best respects to all her family, not forgetting his thanks for the kindness he had received at Longbourn in the winter, and his compliments to Mr. and Mrs. Gardiner, though unknown. He then handed her in, Maria followed, and the door was on the point of being closed, when he suddenly reminded them, with some consternation, that they had hitherto forgotten to leave any message for the ladies at Rosings.

"But," he added, "you will of course wish to have your humble respects delivered to them, with your grateful thanks for their kindness to you while you have been here."

Elizabeth made no objection. The door was then allowed to be shut, and the carriage drove off.

"Good gracious," exclaimed Maria, after a few minutes' silence, "It seems but a day or two since we first came and yet how many things have happened!"

"A great many indeed," said her companion with a sigh.

"We have dined nine times at Rosings, besides drinking tea there twice. How much I shall have to tell!"

Elizabeth added privately, "And how much I shall have to conceal."

Their journey was performed without much conversation. Within four hours of their leaving Hunsford they reached Mr. Gardiner's house, where they were to remain a few days.

Jane looked well, and Elizabeth had little opportunity of studying her spirits, amidst the various engagements which the kindness of her aunt had reserved for them. But Jane was to go home with her, and at Longbourn there would be leisure enough for observation.

Meanwhile, she determined to wait until Longbourn before she told her sister of Mr. Darcy's proposal. The news would undoubtedly astonish Jane, and must at the same time gratify whatever of her own vanity Elizabeth had not yet been able to reason away. She was tempted at almost every moment to openly tell everything. However, in her state of indecision over what she should communicate, and her fear of being hurried into repeating something of Bingley which might only grieve her sister further, kept her silent.

The days passed quickly in Mr. Gardiner's house and with little events beyond visiting and news. It was the second week in May, in which the three young ladies set out together from Gracechurch Street for the appointed Hertfordshire inn where Mr. Bennet's carriage was to meet them. From there they traveled directly to Longbourn. Their reception at home was most kind. Mrs. Bennet rejoiced to see Jane in undiminished beauty, and more than once during dinner did Mr. Bennet say voluntarily to Elizabeth, "I am glad you are back, Lizzy."

In the afternoon Lydia wanted her sisters to walk to Meryton, to see how everybody went on. Elizabeth steadily opposed the scheme. It should not be said that the Miss Bennets could not be at home half a day before they were in pursuit of the officers. There was another reason too for her opposition. She dreaded seeing Mr. Wickham again, and was resolved to avoid it as long as possible. She took comfort in the regiment's approaching removal. In a fortnight they were to go—and once gone, she hoped there could be nothing more to plague her on his account.

"What has happened? Why have you not written me?" Georgiana Darcy demanded of her brother, nearly bouncing with her excitement. "Am I to have a sister?"

Darcy looked at his sister, not answering. The expression on his face conveyed the full depths of his pain, for hers instantly fell. Confusion filled her eyes, as if she could not believe any woman capable of refusing her brother. Instead, she reasoned, her brother must not have asked her. It was the only explanation her mind could accept.

CHAPTER THIRTY-FIVE

*E*LIZABETH'S IMPATIENCE to acquaint Jane with what had happened could no longer be overcome. At length, resolving to suppress every particular in which her sister was concerned, and preparing her to be surprised, she related to her the next morning the chief of the scene between Mr. Darcy and herself.

Jane's astonishment was soon lessened by the strong sisterly partiality, which made any admiration of Elizabeth appear perfectly natural, and all surprise was shortly lost in other feelings. "I am sorry that Mr. Darcy delivered his sentiments in a manner so little suited to recommend them, but still more am I grieved for the unhappiness which your refusal must have given him. His being so sure of succeeding was wrong, and certainly ought to have been better concealed, but consider how much it must increase his disappointment."

"Indeed," replied Elizabeth. "I am heartily sorry for him, but he has other feelings, which will probably soon drive away his regard for me. You do not blame me, however, for refusing him?"

"Blame you? Oh, no."

"But you blame me for having spoken so warmly of Wickham?"

"No, I do not know that you were wrong in saying what you did."

"Wait till I tell you what happened the very next day."

Elizabeth told Jane of the letter, repeating the whole of its contents as far as they concerned George Wickham. Jane would have willingly gone through her whole life without believing wickedness existed in all of mankind, as was here collected in one individual. Nor was Darcy's vindication capable of consoling her for such a discovery. She tried, most earnestly, to establish the probability of error and seek to clear the one without involving the other.

"This will not do," said Elizabeth. "You will never be able to make them both good. Take your choice, but you must be satisfied with only one. For my part, I am inclined to believe Darcy, but you shall do as you choose."

However, it was some time before a smile could be extorted from Jane. "I do not know when I have been more shocked. Wickham so very bad—it is almost past belief. And poor Mr. Darcy! Dear Lizzy, only consider what he must have suffered. He must have felt such a disappointment and with the knowledge of your ill opinion, too. Then having to relate such a thing about his sister. It is really too distressing. I am sure you must agree."

"Oh, no, my regret and compassion are all done away by seeing you so full of both. I know you will do his feelings ample justice that I am growing every moment more unconcerned and indifferent."

Jane sighed, refusing to be cheered by Elizabeth's jesting. "Poor Wickham, there is such an expression of goodness in his countenance and such an openness and gentleness in his manner."

"There certainly was some great mismanagement in the education of those two young men." **Elizabeth could not help but think of Darcy's stern countenance.** "One has got all the goodness, and the other all the appearance of it."

"I never thought Mr. Darcy so deficient in the appearance of it as you used to."

"I meant to be uncommonly clever in taking so decided a dislike to him, without any reason. Then I read his letter. With no one to speak to about what I felt, no Jane to comfort me and say that I had not been so very weak and vain and nonsensical as I knew I had. Oh, how I wanted you! You would have known just what I should have done to make it right."

"It is unfortunate that you used such very strong expressions in speaking of Wickham to Mr. Darcy, for now they do appear wholly undeserved."

"The misfortune of speaking with bitterness is a most natural consequence of the prejudices I had been encouraging. I do feel as if I ought to make our acquaintances understand Wickham's character. Though, I will not. Mr. Darcy has not authorized me to make his communication public. On the contrary, every particular relative to his sister was meant to be kept as much as possible to myself. Besides, who will believe me? The general prejudice against Mr. Darcy is so violent, that it would be the death of half the good people in Meryton to attempt to place him in an amiable light. Yet, I feel there is little justice in not redeeming his character."

"It would be an injustice to Mr. Darcy to reveal what he told you in confidence, even to hint at it. If he wishes to redeem his character, then I think he must be the one to do it—or at least charge the care to a friend."

"Thankfully, Wickham will soon be gone. It will be glad to forget him."

"To have Wickham's errors made public might ruin him forever. He is now, perhaps, sorry for what he has done, and anxious to re-establish a character. We must not make him desperate."

Elizabeth was not sure she wholly agreed with Jane's assessment. The fact that he tried to re-establish his character at the expense of a man who did not deserve it proved he was not sorry for what he had done. However, the tumult of her mind was allayed by their conversation. She had gotten rid of the two secrets that had weighed on her for a fortnight, and was certain of a willing listener in Jane whenever she might wish to talk again of either. But there were still a few things lurking in the back of her mind, both of which prudence forbade the disclosure. The first was that she dare not relate the other half of Mr. Darcy's letter. **The second was she dare not relate the unmentionable feelings she had for Mr. Darcy.** The first would only bring pain. **The second was not worth discussing for the feelings had nothing to do with considering marriage and everything to do with desiring an affair; and she could not bear to tell Jane she wanted Mr. Darcy in body only. Jane was kindness and good, and would only consider such happy desires as springing from marriage. Elizabeth knew such desires could spring from lust, but that marriage between Mr. Darcy and herself would be a mistake. They were both too proud, too stubborn, and would most likely argue until the end of time. And, lest she forget, he had ruined Jane's happiness—a most unforgivable offense.**

Now, being settled at home and at leisure to observe the real state of her sister's spirits, Elizabeth determined Jane was not happy. Her sister still cherished a very tender affection for Bingley. Having never fancied herself in love before, Jane's regard had all the warmth of first attachment and, from her age and disposition, greater steadiness than most first attachments often boast. So fervently did she remember him and prefer him to every other man.

"Well, Lizzy," said Mrs. Bennet one day. "What is your opinion of this sad business of Jane's? For my part, I am determined never to speak of it again to anybody. I told my sister Philips so the other day. But I cannot find out if Jane saw him in London. Has she mentioned it to you? Well, he is a very undeserving young man, and I do not suppose there's the least chance in the world of her ever getting him now. There is no talk of his coming to Netherfield in the summer. I have inquired of everybody, too, who is likely to know."

"I do not believe he will ever again live at Netherfield," Elizabeth said.

"Oh well, it is as he chooses. Nobody wants him to come. I shall always say he used my daughter extremely ill. I am sure Jane will die of a broken heart and then he will be sorry for what he has done."

As Elizabeth could not find comfort in such expectation, she made no answer.

"Well, Lizzy," continued her mother, "and so the Collinses live very comfortable, do they? Well, well, I only hope it will last. Charlotte is an excellent manager, I daresay. If she is half as sharp as her mother, she is saving enough. There is nothing extravagant in their housekeeping?"

"No, not at all."

"A great deal of good management, depend upon it. They will never be distressed for money. I suppose, they often talk of having Longbourn when your father is dead."

"It was a subject they did not mention before me."

"No, it would have been strange if they had. I do not doubt they often discuss it between themselves." **Mrs. Bennet continued to talk, supposing that Elizabeth should have been the current Mrs. Collins so that the entail would have been settled to their favor. Elizabeth did her best not to hear her and could not help but think of how her mother would react if she knew her daughter had refused a man with ten thousand a year. Prudence kept her from saying a word.**

CHAPTER THIRTY-SIX

*T*HE FIRST WEEK OF THEIR RETURN was soon gone and the second began. It was the last of the regiment's stay in Meryton, and all the young ladies in the neighborhood were feeling the sad effects. The dejection was almost universal. The elder Miss Bennets alone were still able to eat, drink, and sleep, and pursue the usual course of their employments. Very frequently were they reproached for this insensibility by Kitty and Lydia, whose own misery was extreme, and who could not comprehend such hard-heartedness. Their affectionate mother shared their grief.

"I cried for two days when Colonel Miller's regiment went away. I thought my heart broken," said Mrs. Bennet.

"I am sure I shall break mine," said Lydia.

"If one could but go to Brighton," observed Mrs. Bennet.

"Oh, yes, if one could but go to Brighton! But papa is so disagreeable."

"A little sea-bathing would set me up forever."

"And my aunt Philips is sure it would do *me* a great deal of good," added Kitty.

Such were the kind of lamentations resounding perpetually through Longbourn House. Elizabeth tried to be diverted by them, but all sense of pleasure was lost in shame. She felt anew the justice of Mr. Darcy's objections and never had she been so much disposed to pardon his interference in the views of his friend.

But Lydia's gloom was shortly cleared away for she received an invitation from Mrs. Forster, the wife of the colonel of the regiment, to accompany her to Brighton. This invaluable friend was a very young woman, and very lately married. A resemblance in good humor and good spirits had recommended her and Lydia to each other.

The rapture of Lydia on this occasion, her adoration of Mrs. Forster, the delight of Mrs. Bennet, and the mortification of Kitty, are scarcely to be described. Completely inattentive to her sister's feelings, Lydia flew about the house in restless ecstasy, calling for everyone's congratulations. The luckless Kitty complained about her fate, "I cannot see why Mrs. Forster should not ask me as well as Lydia. I have just as much right as she has. I am two years older."

In vain did Elizabeth attempt to make Kitty reasonable, and Jane to make her resigned. As for Elizabeth herself, this invitation was far from exciting in her the same feelings as in her mother and Lydia. She considered it as the death warrant of all possibility of common sense for the latter. Lydia would have detested her if she found out, but Elizabeth could not help secretly advising her father not to let her go. She represented to him all the improprieties of Lydia's general behavior, the little advantage she could derive from the friendship of such a woman as Mrs. Forster, and the probability of her being yet more imprudent with such a companion at Brighton, where the temptations must be greater than at home.

After listening attentively, he replied, "Lydia will never be easy until she has exposed herself in some public place or other, and we can never expect her to do it with so little expense or inconvenience to her family as under the present circumstances."

"If you were aware," Elizabeth said, "of the very great disadvantage to us all which must arise from the public notice of Lydia's unguarded and imprudent manner, I am sure you would judge differently."

"Has she frightened away some of your lovers? Poor little Lizzy! Do not be cast down. Such squeamish youths that cannot bear to be connected with a little absurdity are not worth a regret. Come, let me see the list of pitiful fellows who have been kept aloof by Lydia's folly."

"Indeed you are mistaken. I have no such injuries to resent." **Elizabeth refused to think of Mr. Darcy. There was no need to tell her father about the proposal.** "It is of general evils, which I am now complaining. Our importance, our respectability in the world must be affected by the wild volatility, and the disdain of all restraint that marks Lydia's character. If you will not take the trouble of checking her exuberant spirits, and of teaching her that her present pursuits are not to be the business of her life, she will soon be beyond the reach of correction. Her character will be fixed, and she will, at sixteen, be the most determined flirt that ever made herself or her family ridiculous. Kitty will follow wherever Lydia leads—vain, ignorant, idle, and absolutely uncontrolled. Can you suppose it possible that they will be censured and despised wherever they are known, and that their sisters will often be involved in the disgrace?"

Mr. Bennet saw that her whole heart was in the subject,

and affectionately taking her hand said in reply, "Do not make yourself uneasy, my love. Wherever you and Jane are known you must be respected and valued. You will not appear to less advantage for having a couple of very silly sisters. We shall have no peace at Longbourn if Lydia does not go to Brighton. Let her go, then. Colonel Forster is a sensible man, and will keep her out of any real mischief. She is luckily too poor to be an object of prey to anybody. At Brighton she will be of less importance than she has been here. Let us hope that her stay may teach her her own insignificance. At any rate, she cannot grow many degrees worse, without obliging us to lock her up for the rest of her life."

With this answer Elizabeth was forced to be content, but her own opinion continued the same and she left him disappointed and sorry.

During those last days before the soldiers were to leave Meryton, Elizabeth was frequently in the company of Mr. Wickham. Any agitation on her part did not last long. The very gentleness which had first delighted her, now filled her with disgust. The feeling was made all the more predominate by his testifying a renewal of those intentions which had marked the early part of their acquaintance. She had no wish to be the object of his idle and frivolous gallantry; and looked at him with renewed eyes at each and every meeting, and each time she found him lacking in another way.

On the very last day of the regiment's remaining at Meryton, he dined at Longbourn with some other officers. Elizabeth was so little disposed to part from him in good humor, that on his making some inquiry as to the manner in which her time had passed at Hunsford, she mentioned Colonel Fitzwilliam's and

Mr. Darcy's having both spent three weeks at Rosings, and asked him, if he was acquainted with the former.

He looked surprised, displeased, alarmed; but with a moment's recollection and a returning smile, replied that he had formerly seen him often. After observing that he was a very gentlemanlike man, asked her how she had liked him. Her answer was warmly in Fitzwilliam's favor.

With an air of indifference he added, "How long did you say he was at Rosings?"

"Nearly three weeks."

"And you saw him frequently?"

"Yes, almost every day."

"His manners are very different from his cousin's."

"Yes, very different. But I think Mr. Darcy improves upon acquaintance."

"Indeed!" said Mr. Wickham with a look which did not escape her. "And pray, may I ask . . . ?" But checking himself, he added, in a forced pleasant tone, "Is it in manners that he improves? Has he deigned to add civility to his ordinary style?"

"Oh, no," said Elizabeth, "in essentials, I believe, he is very much what he ever was."

Wickham looked as if scarcely knew whether to rejoice over her words, or to distrust their meaning. There was a something in her countenance which made him listen with an apprehensive and anxious attention.

Elizabeth could not resist. She would not say exactly what she meant, but let Wickham wonder at how much she knew. "When I said he improved on acquaintance, I did not mean that his mind or his manners were in a state of improvement, but that, from knowing him better, his disposition was better understood."

Wickham's alarm appeared in his heightened complexion, and she silently took the small victory. For a few minutes he did not speak. Then, shaking off his embarrassment, he turned to her again, and said, "You, who so well know my feeling towards Mr. Darcy, will readily comprehend how sincerely I must rejoice that he is wise enough to assume even the appearance of what is right. His pride in that direction may be of service, if not to himself then to others. It must deter him from repeating such foul misconduct as I have suffered. I only fear that the sort of cautiousness to which you have been alluding is merely adopted on his visits to his aunt, of whose good opinion and judgment he stands much in awe. His fear of her has always been evident when they were together, and a good deal is to be imputed to his wish of forwarding the match with Miss de Bourgh, which I am certain he has very much at heart."

Elizabeth could not repress a smile at this, but she answered only by a slight inclination of the head. She saw that he wanted to engage her on the old subject of his grievances, and she was in no humor to indulge him. The rest of the evening passed with the appearance, on his side, of usual cheerfulness, but with no further attempt to distinguish Elizabeth. They parted at last with mutual civility, and possibly a mutual desire of never meeting again.

When the party broke up, Lydia returned with Mrs. Forster to Meryton from whence they were to set out early the next morning. The separation between her and her family was more noisy than pathetic. Kitty was the only one who shed tears, but she wept from vexation and envy. Mrs. Bennet was diffuse in her good wishes for the felicity of her daughter, and impressive in her injunctions that she should not miss the opportunity of enjoying herself as much as possible—advice which there was every reason to believe would be well attended to.

CHAPTER THIRTY-SEVEN

*D*espite her protests to Jane otherwise, Elizabeth found her mind occupied with thoughts of marriage and Mr. Darcy—not necessarily because she was convinced she wanted to marry Mr. Darcy, but because his asking her and the succession of information that followed caused her to reconsider her opinions of herself and what she truly wanted in her life.

Had Elizabeth's opinion been all drawn from her own family, she could not have formed a very pleasing opinion of conjugal felicity or domestic comfort. **Her father married her mother because she was beautiful and had the appearance of a good nature. However, early in their marriage these qualities became tarnished by the reality of her weak mind and he lost what respect he had for her.** Now, he was fond primarily of the country and of books, and from these tastes had arisen his principal enjoyments. To his wife he was little indebted, other than the fact her ignorance and folly often contributed to his amusement. This is not the sort of happiness which a man would wish to owe to his wife but, where other powers of entertainment are wanting, the true philosopher will derive benefit from those that are given.

Elizabeth had never been blind to the impropriety of her father's behavior as a husband. She had always seen it with pain, but respecting his abilities, and grateful for his affectionate treatment of herself, she endeavored to forget what she could not overlook. She tried to banish from her thoughts that continual breach of conjugal obligation and decorum which, in exposing his wife to the contempt of her own children, was so highly reprehensible. But, till now, she had never felt so strongly the disadvantages which must befall the children of so unsuitable a marriage, nor ever been so fully aware of the evils arising from so ill-judged a direction of talents—talents, which, rightly used, might at least have preserved the respectability of his daughters, even if incapable of enlarging the mind of his wife.

On further contemplation, Elizabeth came to understand her own mind when it came to marriage. She had seen the folly of her parents' union and from it came a fear of meeting such an end for herself. She wanted there to be love in her marriage, a fine, stout love that lasted beyond youth; but her fear of never finding such happiness or mistaking it as her father had done— who she resembled in nature more so than her mother—kept her from seeking it out. Only, instead of a foolish wife, she would be trapped with a foolish husband, the much worse fate of the two. For a foolish wife could be laughed at. A foolish husband could drive a family into complete ruin and poverty.

When Elizabeth had rejoiced over Wickham's departure she found little other cause for satisfaction in the loss of the regiment. Their parties abroad were less varied than before, and at home she had a mother and sister constantly repining at the dullness of everything around them.

After three weeks of Lydia's absence, cheerfulness began to reappear at Longbourn. The families who had been in town for the winter came back again, and summer finery and summer engagements arose. Elizabeth had real reason to rejoice. The time fixed for their northern tour was fast approaching, when a letter arrived from Mrs. Gardiner, which at once delayed its commencement and curtailed its extent. Mr. Gardiner would be prevented by business from setting out till a fortnight later in July, and must be in London again within a month. As that left too short a period for them to go so far, they were obliged to give up the Lakes and substitute a more contracted tour. Accordingly, they were to go no farther northwards than Derbyshire. In that county there was enough to occupy the chief of their three weeks, and to Mrs. Gardiner it had a peculiarly strong attraction. The town where she had formerly passed some years of her life, and where they were now to spend a few days, was as great an object of her curiosity as all the celebrated beauties of Matlock, Chatsworth, Dovedale, or the Peak.

With the mention of Derbyshire there were many ideas connected. **Until the letter, Elizabeth had been able to convince herself that she might never see Mr. Darcy again, at least not for many years. He would not be coming back to Netherfield, she did not often go to London, and the chances of her visiting Charlotte while he was at Rosings were very slim.** But now, it was impossible for her to see the change in plans without thinking of Pemberley and its owner.

"But surely," thought she, "I may enter his county without impunity, and rob it of a few petrified spars without his perceiving me."

When Mr. and Mrs. Gardiner appeared at Longbourn with their four children, Elizabeth had about given up on the day ever arriving. The children, two girls and two younger boys, were to be left to the care of their cousin Jane, who was the general favorite, and whose steady sense and sweetness of temper adapted her for attending to them.

The Gardiners stayed one night at Longbourn and set off the next morning with Elizabeth in pursuit of novelty and amusement. Enjoyment was certain as was the suitableness of Elizabeth's companions. Their route took them through many remarkable places—Oxford, Blenheim, Warwick, Kenilworth, Birmingham—and, having seen all the principal wonders of the country, they settled in a small part of Derbyshire in the little town of Lambton. This was the scene of Mrs. Gardiner's former residence, and where she had lately learned some acquaintance still remained. But, to Elizabeth's concern, she learned from her aunt that Pemberley was situated within five miles of the very place they were staying. Mrs. Gardiner expressed an inclination to see the place again, Mr. Gardiner declared his willingness, and Elizabeth was applied to for her approbation.

"My love, should you not like to see a place which you have heard so much of?" inquired her aunt. "A place, too, with which so many of your acquaintances are connected? Wickham passed all his youth there, you know."

Distressed, Elizabeth felt she had no business at Pemberley and was obliged to assume a disinclination for seeing it. "I must own that I am tired of great houses, after going over so many. I really have no pleasure in fine carpets or satin curtains."

Mrs. Gardiner chuckled. "If it were merely a fine house richly furnished I should not care myself, but the grounds are delightful. They have some of the finest woods in the country."

**"Then perhaps we should merely wander the woods,"
Elizabeth said. "There is no reason to trouble the occupants of
Pemberley. It will surely be an imposition to the master of the
house."**

"Nonsense!" declared Mr. Gardiner. "The house is open for visitors."

"If that is your only objection, its being an imposition, than I shall consider it settled!" Mrs. Gardiner said.

Elizabeth said no more, but she worried of the possibility of meeting Mr. Darcy. The very idea was alarming. She would not know what to say to him or how to act. The last words they spoken were in anger. She had been mistaken about him, and his part in her sister's unhappiness was unforgiveable. It was unforgivable, right? She was not so sure anymore. Though she did not appreciate his reasons, she understood how he had come to his conclusions. However, sisterly affection dictated she defend Jane out of principle.

When she retired that night, she asked the chambermaid whether Pemberley were not a very fine place? What was the name of its proprietor? And, with no little apprehension, whether the family was down for the summer? A most welcome negative followed the last question—and, her worry now being removed, she was at leisure to feel a great deal of curiosity to see the house herself. So, when the subject was revived the next morning, and she was again applied to, she could readily answer with a proper air of indifference that she was quite up to the scheme. To Pemberley, therefore, they were to go.

CHAPTER THIRTY-EIGHT

*E*LIZABETH WATCHED for the first appearance of Pemberley Woods with some agitation. When at length their carriage turned in at the lodge, her spirits were in a state of high excitement. The park was very large, and contained great variety of ground. They entered it in one of its lowest points, and drove for some time through a beautiful wood stretching over a wide extent.

Elizabeth's mind was too full for conversation, but she saw and admired every remarkable spot and point of view. They gradually ascended for half-a-mile, and found themselves at the top of a considerable eminence, where the wood ceased, and the eye was instantly caught by Pemberley House situated on the opposite side of a valley, into which the road with some abruptness wound. It was a large, handsome stone building, standing well on rising ground, and backed by a ridge of high woody hills. In front, a stream of some natural importance was swollen with water. Its banks were neither formal nor falsely adorned. Elizabeth had never seen a place for which nature had done more, or where natural beauty had been so little counteracted by an awkward taste. They were all warm in their admiration and at that moment she felt that to be mistress of Pemberley might be something special indeed.

They descended the hill, crossed the bridge, and drove to the door. While examining the nearer aspect of the house, all her apprehension of meeting its owner returned. She dreaded lest the chambermaid had been mistaken. On applying to see the place, they were admitted into the hall to await the housekeeper; and Elizabeth had leisure to wonder at her being where she was. **Everywhere she looked seemed to be built on perfection—a perfection that awed and overwhelmed at the same time.**

The elderly housekeeper was a respectable-looking woman, much less fine and more civil than she had any notion of finding her. They followed her into the dining parlor. It was a large, well proportioned room, handsomely fitted up. Elizabeth, after surveying it, went to a window to enjoy its prospect. The hill, crowned with wood, which they had descended, receiving increased abruptness from the distance, was a beautiful object. Every disposition of the ground was good. As she looked on the whole scene, the river, the trees scattered on its banks and the winding of the valley, as far as she could trace it, with delight. As they passed into other rooms these objects were taking different positions, but from every window there were beauties to be seen. The rooms were lofty and handsome, and their furniture suitable to the fortune of its proprietor. Elizabeth saw, with admiration of his taste, that it was neither gaudy nor uselessly fine; with less of splendor, and more real elegance, than the furniture of Rosings. **This last fact took her by surprise. She had expected his home to reflect a different picture of himself than it did. She**

anticipated it to be beyond Rosings in grandeur, and surpassing
the most ostentatious of homes in grandiose design and presentation. Had she never met Mr. Darcy and only had his home to
judge him by, she would have instantly admired and envied him.
To be brought up surrounded by such beauty and knowledge! To
live surrounded by such nature! Elizabeth's heart raced. She took
a deep breath, endeavoring to look calm lest her aunt and uncle
suspect she was too overwhelmed to speak.

"I might have been the mistress of Pemberley," she thought,
"and Mr. Darcy my husband. What a life we would have lived in
such a home; with these rooms I might now have been familiarly acquainted. Instead of viewing them as a stranger, I might
have rejoiced in calling them my own. Even now, I might have
welcomed visitors like my uncle and aunt, and guided them
through the rooms. But no, that could never be. My uncle and
aunt would have been lost to me, as would the rest of my family,
except for perhaps Jane. I would not have been allowed to invite
them."

This was a lucky realization—it saved her from something
very like regret. She straightened her shoulders and determinedly
turned away from the picturesque view.

She longed to inquire of the housekeeper whether her
master was really absent, but had not the courage for it. At length
however, the question was asked by her uncle. She waited with
trepidation while Mrs. Reynolds replied that he was away, adding, "But we expect him tomorrow with a large party of friends."

One day. Elizabeth wondered why she should be so nervous
at the idea of being so close to meeting him. It was not like she
would still be there tomorrow. She was safe.

Her aunt called her to look at a picture. She approached
and saw the likeness of Mr. Wickham, suspended, amongst several other miniatures, over the mantelpiece. Her aunt asked her,

smilingly, how she liked it. The housekeeper came forward, and told them it was a picture of a young gentleman, the son of her late master's steward, who had been brought up by him at his own expense. "He is now in the army, but I am afraid he has turned out very wild."

Mrs. Gardiner looked at her niece with a smile, but Elizabeth could not return it.

Mrs. Reynolds pointed to another of the miniatures. "That is my master—and very like him. It was drawn at the same time as the other, about eight years ago."

"I have heard much of your master's fine person," said Mrs. Gardiner. "It is a handsome face. Lizzy, can you tell us whether it captures the gentleman?"

Mrs. Reynolds respect for Elizabeth seemed to increase on this intimation of her knowing her master. "Does the young lady know Mr. Darcy?"

Elizabeth colored, and said, "A little."

"And do not you think him a very handsome gentleman?"

Nervously, she stared at his likeness. Why had she never noticed that playful look in his eyes? Almost breathless, she said, "Very handsome."

Elizabeth did not expect to be struck so forcibly by his portrait when she had seen the man in the flesh often enough. There was something different about looking at his likeness, as if she could stare as long as she pleased without fear of offending him. She took her time, studying the lines of his face. The artists had captured him quite well, especially the shade of his eyes. They seemed bright against the tan of his face and the dark of his clothes. Now that her disposition towards him had changed, she noticed a kindness about his reserved features that she had not seen before. The pride was there, naturally, but the artist had depicted the softest of smiles on the side of his mouth.

"I am sure I know none so handsome, but in the gallery upstairs you will see a finer, larger picture of him than this. This room was my late master's favorite room, and these miniatures are just as they used to be then. He was very fond of them."

Elizabeth was not sure she wanted to see a larger picture of the master of the house. The small one was making her feel something altogether unwelcome—regret, apprehension, attraction, the stirrings of desire. How could she have been blind to his virtues while adding up his faults?

Mrs. Reynolds then directed their attention to one of Miss Darcy, drawn when she was only eight years old.

"Is Miss Darcy as handsome as her brother?" asked Mrs. Gardiner.

"Oh, yes, the handsomest young lady that ever was seen and so accomplished! She plays and sings all day long. In the next room is a new instrument just come down for her. It is a present from my master. She comes here tomorrow with him."

Mr. Gardiner, whose manners were very easy and pleasant, encouraged her communicativeness by his questions and remarks. Mrs. Reynolds, either by pride or attachment, evidently had great pleasure in talking of her master and his sister.

"Is your master much at Pemberley in the course of the year?"

"Not so much as I could wish, sir. I daresay he may spend half his time here and Miss Darcy is always down for the summer months."

"If your master would marry," said Mr. Gardiner, "you might see more of him."

"Yes, sir, but I do not know when that will be. I do not know who is good enough for him."

Elizabeth's stomach tightened. Much could be detected about a man by the dispositions of his servants when he was not

nearby. **If Mrs. Reynolds was to be his judge, he was the kindest, handsomest, most deserving of men. She could not help saying,** "It is very much to his credit that you think so."

"I say no more than the truth, and everybody that knows him will say the same," replied the woman. "I have never known a cross word from him in my life, and I have known him since he was four years old."

Though she had allowed her first opinion of Mr. Darcy to be altered, Mrs. Reynolds's high praise was going pretty far. She found herself resisting the woman's picture of her master. She could not allow herself to like him, not completely, or else she might start to regret her decision to refuse him. Still, Elizabeth's keenest attention was awakened and she longed to hear more. She was grateful to her uncle for obliging her curiosity.

"There are very few people of whom so much can be said," observed Mr. Gardiner. "You are lucky to have such a master."

"Yes, sir. If I were to go through the world, I could not meet with a better. But I have always observed that they who are good-natured when children are good-natured when they grow up. He was always the sweetest-tempered, most generous-hearted boy in the world."

"His father was an excellent man," said Mrs. Gardiner.

"Yes, ma'am, he was indeed. His son will be just like him— just as affable to the poor."

Elizabeth listened, wondered, doubted, and was impatient for more. Mrs. Reynolds could interest her on no other point. She related the subjects of the pictures, the dimensions of the rooms, and the price of the furniture, but in vain. Mr. Gardiner, highly amused by the kind of family prejudice to which he attributed her excessive commendation of her master, soon led again to the subject. The housekeeper dwelled with energy on Darcy's many merits as they proceeded together up the great staircase.

"He is the best landlord, and the best master," said she, "not like the wild young men nowadays, who think of nothing but themselves. There is not one of his tenants or servants but will give him a good name. Some people call him proud, but I am sure I never saw anything of it. To my fancy, it is only because he does not rattle away like other young men."

The nervous feeling returned to her stomach tenfold. Elizabeth's hand trembled and she touched the railing to steady herself. The height of the ceilings and fineness of their murals stared down at her, the cherub faces watching her ascent. She did not feel worthy of being lady of such a hall, and that its master had even thought to ask her took her by surprise as it never had before. She could scarcely imagine belonging in such a place and felt at once the awe and responsibility such a position would entail. Though she could not forgive his botched proposal, she now understood it more than before. How could he not feel the full extent of his worth when this had been his childhood home? And, as the housekeeper continued on about Mr. Darcy's many duties and his honorable undertaking of them with both benevolence and grace, Elizabeth felt as if she might not have known him at all. If such a representation were true, how could she have been so mistaken? It was a question she found herself repeating often, each time coming up with an unsatisfactory answer.

"This fine account of him," whispered her aunt as they walked, "is not quite consistent with his behavior to our poor friend."

"Perhaps we were deceived."

"That is not very likely. Our authority was good."

"Then perhaps events were misunderstood," said Elizabeth, **unwilling to go into the truth. For, to do so, would require her to reveal the proposal and letter.**

On reaching the spacious lobby above they were shown

into a very pretty sitting room, lately fitted up with greater elegance and lightness than the apartments below. They were informed that it was done for Miss Darcy, who had taken a liking to the room when last at Pemberley.

"He is certainly an attentive brother." Elizabeth walked towards one of the windows.

Mrs. Reynolds anticipated Miss Darcy's delight, when she should enter the room. "And this is always the way with him. Whatever can give his sister any pleasure is sure to be done in a moment. There is nothing he would not do for her. **When he marries, I imagine he will dote on his bride with as much care. She will indeed be a lucky woman.**"

The picture-gallery, and two or three of the principal bedrooms, were all that remained to be shown. In the former were many good paintings, but Elizabeth knew little of the art beyond its being very fine and she willingly turned to look at some of Miss Darcy's crayon drawings, whose subjects were more interesting and more intelligible.

In the gallery there were many family portraits, but they had little to fix the attention of a stranger. Elizabeth walked in quest of the only face whose features would be known to her. At last it arrested her—and she beheld a striking resemblance to Mr. Darcy, with such a smile over the face as she remembered to have sometimes seen when he looked at her. She stood several minutes before the picture in earnest contemplation, and returned to it again before they quitted the gallery. Mrs. Reynolds informed them that it had been taken in his father's lifetime.

There was certainly at this moment, in Elizabeth's mind, a more gentle sensation towards the original than she had ever felt at the height of their acquaintance. **Though she tried to resist them, the last of her defenses began to crack. From the first moment she saw him, she had felt something shift inside her** chest. **That first meeting had caused her world to spin and her body to float. If not for the events that followed, who knew what kind of journey her emotions would have taken.**

The commendation bestowed on him by Mrs. Reynolds was of no trifling nature, and the surety of it convinced her throughout the course of their tour that she was telling the truth. What praise is more valuable than the praise of an intelligent servant? As a brother, a landlord, a master, she considered how many people's happiness were in his guardianship, how much of pleasure or pain was it in his power to bestow, how much of good or evil must be done by him. Every idea that had been brought forward by the housekeeper was favorable to his character, and as she stood before the canvas on which he was represented, and fixed his eyes upon hers, she thought of his regard with a deeper sentiment of gratitude than it had ever risen before. She remembered its warmth, and that softened its impropriety of expression.

When all of the house open to general inspection had been seen, they returned downstairs, and, taking leave of the housekeeper, were consigned over to the gardener, who met them at the hall door. As they walked across the hall towards the river, her uncle and aunt stopped while the former was conjecturing as to the date of the building. **Elizabeth turned back to look again, fighting the sudden urge to run as fast and far as she could away from Pemberley. Emotions swirled inside her chest, not the least of which was doubt. Then, as if fate itself had come to mock her torment,** the owner of Pemberley suddenly came forward from the road, which led behind the stables.

They were within twenty yards of each other, and so abrupt was his appearance, that it was impossible to avoid his sight. Their eyes instantly met, and the cheeks of both were overspread with the deepest blush. He came to an abrupt stop, and for a moment seemed immovable from surprise. However, he shortly thereafter recovered himself and advanced towards the party.

Elizabeth instinctively turned away, **considering her options. Should she walk on as if she had not noticed him? Run away and deal with the impropriety of such an act later? Unsure, she took too long to decide.**

"Miss Elizabeth," Mr. Darcy acknowledged, forcing her to face him. He spoke, if not in terms of perfect composure, at least of perfect civility.

She received him with an embarrassment impossible to be overcome. Astonished and confused, Elizabeth scarcely dared lift her eyes to his face. **By way of an excuse as to her presence in his home, she said, "We are touring the house."**

She looked at her aunt and uncle. They stood a little aloof while Darcy talked to their niece, affording her an unintentional privacy with the gentleman. Had his first appearance, or his resemblance to the picture they had just examined, been insufficient to assure the other two who they now saw, the gardener's expression of surprise on beholding his master immediately told it.

Mr. Darcy turned, glancing at the estate before giving her his attention once more. "Would you like to see inside? I have recently acquired new paintings."

"We have already been," she answered quickly. "The paintings were lovely."

The compliment, so automatically spoken, brought to mind the one painting that had captured her above the others—his. She blushed at the very thought.

"Of course." His hand lifted and then fell. "And how is your family?"

"They are well, thank you. Lydia is away to Brighton with friends, but everyone else is home."

The few minutes in which they politely continued were some of the most uncomfortable in her life. Amazed at the alteration of his manner since they last parted, every sentence that he uttered was increasing her embarrassment, and every idea of the impropriety of her being found there recurred to her mind. Nor did he seem much more at ease. His words had none of their usual sedateness, and he repeated his inquiries as to the time of her having left Longbourn, and of her having stayed in Derbyshire, so often and in so hurried a way, as to plainly reveal the distraction of his thoughts. At length every idea seemed to fail him.

Ensuring her aunt and uncle had not come closer, she said softly, "I did not mean to impose upon your privacy. I was of the understanding you were away. My aunt and uncle. . . ." She could say no more, as he shook his head to stop her apology.

He studied her and looked as if he would speak. However, after standing a few moments without saying a word, he suddenly recollected himself, and took leave. "Enjoy your trip, Miss Elizabeth."

She curtsied to his bow, and watched him stride away. The others then joined her, and expressed admiration of him. Elizabeth heard not a word, and wholly engrossed by her own feelings, followed them in silence. She was overpowered by shame and vexation. Her coming there was the most unfortunate, the most ill-judged thing in the world. How strange it must appear to him, her at his home after rejecting his proposal. In what a disgraceful light it painted her, for it might seem as if she had purposely thrown herself in his way again. Oh, why did he come home a day before he was expected? Had they been only ten minutes sooner, they should have been beyond the reach of his discrimination, for it was plain he just arrived. She blushed over the perverseness of the meeting. And his behavior, so strikingly altered—what could it mean? That he should even speak to her was amazing, but to speak with such civility, to inquire after her family? Never in her life had she seen his manners so little dignified, never had he spoken with such gentleness as on this unexpected meeting. What a contrast it offered to his last address in Rosings Park, when he put his letter into her hand. She knew not what to think, or how to account for it.

Darcy hurried through his home, having taken just enough time to greet his housekeeper and a few other servants before seeking the sanctuary of his library. Elizabeth, there, in his home! He could hardly account for his conversation with her, but suspected it had not been spoken eloquently on his side. She was the last person he had expected to see at Pemberley.

What did it mean? Why had she come? He did not dare hope it had been out of a desire to see him. She looked quite out of sorts when he approached her, and for a moment Darcy thought she might actually run away from him. Then there was her tone. It was not as he had expected. It had been soft, gentle, apologetic. Had his letter had the desired effect? He often wondered since handing it to her if her thoughts towards him had changed. It took all his willpower not to ask her about it.

Watching as his gardener led the guests toward the pathway around the fish pond, he resisted the urge to go after her. His feelings had not lessened and they were not to be trusted in her presence. He could not, would not, renew the sentiments that she had so decidedly rejected. Yet, he could not get her out of his mind. To have her so close, to have within his reach a possible hint as to what she now thought of him. Did she believe him? Had his letter vindicated himself to her? Had her feelings towards him softened into the romantic? He did not dare to hope for the latter, but once thought the idea would not leave him.

He had to see her again. He had to know, if only by some small indication, that she believed him. Her opinion of him mattered, even if she would not have him. As he thought it, he knew that was not the only reason. He needed to see her again, needed to be near her if only for a moment. One laugh, one smile, one word he could take with him to remember. That was all he would ask of her, and even that he would ask in silence.

Elizabeth took a deep, cleansing breath. They had entered a beautiful walk by the side of the water, and every step brought forward a nobler fall of ground, or a finer reach of the woods to which they were approaching. But it was some time before Elizabeth was sensible of any of it. Though she answered mechanically to the repeated appeals of her uncle and aunt, and seemed to direct her eyes to such objects as they pointed out, she distinguished no part of the scene. Her thoughts were all fixed on that one spot of Pemberley House, whichever it might be, where Mr. Darcy then was. She longed to know what at the moment was passing in his mind—in what manner he thought of her, and whether, in defiance of everything, she was still dear to him. Perhaps he had been civil only because he felt himself at ease. Yet there had been that in his voice which was not like ease. Whether he had felt more of pain or of pleasure in seeing her she could not tell, but he certainly had not seen her with composure. **And, she daresay, she had been just as flustered to see him.**

At length her companions remarked on her absentmindedness and she felt it necessary to appear more like herself.

They entered the woods, and bidding adieu to the river for

a while, ascended some of the higher grounds. In spots the opening of the trees gave the eye power to wander. There were many
charming views of the valley, the opposite hills, with the long
range of woods overspreading many, and occasionally part of the
stream. Mr. Gardiner expressed a wish of going round the whole
park, but feared it might be beyond a walk. With a triumphant
smile they were told that it was ten miles round. It settled the
matter and they pursued the accustomed circuit, which brought
them to the edge of the water. They crossed it by a simple bridge,
in character with the general air of the scene. Elizabeth longed to
explore, but when they perceived their distance from the house
Mrs. Gardiner, who was not a great walker, could go no farther
and thought only of returning to the carriage as quickly as possible. Her niece was, therefore, obliged to submit. Their progress towards the house was slow for Mr. Gardiner was very fond
of fishing and was engaged in talking to the man about the occasional appearance of trout in the water that he advanced but little.

While wandering in this slow manner, they were again
surprised by the sight of Mr. Darcy approaching. Elizabeth's
astonishment was equal to what it had been the first time she
encountered him that day. Though, however astonished, she
was at least more prepared for a conversation than before and
resolved to appear calm and to speak intelligently. For a few
moments, she worried that he would strike into some other path
as the walk concealed him from their view.

She held her breath until he took a turn and came immediately before them. He had lost none of his recent civility, and
to imitate his politeness she began to admire the beauty of the
place. However, she had not got beyond the words "delightful,"
and "charming," when some unlucky recollections obtruded,
and she fancied that praise of Pemberley from her might be
mischievously construed. Her color changed, and she said no

more. **She did not dare to imagine what he must think of her. His opinion of her family's lack of propriety was still fresh in her mind. Now he must think she shared the same trait. He had made allowances for herself and Jane, but would he do so again after seeing how ineptly she spoke just now?**

Mrs. Gardiner stood a little behind and, as she paused, he asked if she would do him the honor of introducing him to her friends. This was a stroke of civility for which she was quite unprepared. She could hardly suppress a smile at his seeking the acquaintance of some of those very people against whom his pride had revolted in his offer to herself.

The introduction was immediately made and as she named their relationship to herself, she stole a sly look at him to see how he bore it. She expected him to decamp as fast as he could from such disgraceful companions. That he was surprised by the connection was evident, but he sustained it with fortitude. Joining them in their walk, he immediately entered into conversation with Mr. Gardiner. Pleased, Elizabeth found it consoling that he should meet some of her relations for whom there was no need to be embarrassed over.

The conversation soon turned to fishing and she heard Mr. Darcy invite him to fish there as often as he chose while he continued in the neighborhood, offering at the same time to supply him with fishing tackle, and pointing out those parts of the stream where there was usually most sport. Mrs. Gardiner, who was walking arm-in-arm with Elizabeth, gave her a look expressive of wonder. Elizabeth said nothing, but her astonishment was extreme.

She could not help thinking, "Why is he so altered? It cannot be for my sake that his manners are thus softened. My reproofs at Hunsford could not work such a change as this." Then, almost trembling visibly at the thought, she whispered to herself, "It is impossible that he still loves me."

Mrs. Gardiner glanced at her in wonder, but Elizabeth did not repeat the words louder. After walking some time, her aunt, who, fatigued by the exercise of the morning, found Elizabeth's arm inadequate to support her, and consequently preferred her husband's. Mr. Darcy took her place by her niece, and they walked on together.

After a short silence, she said, "I wish you to know that I had been assured of your absence before we came here, and your housekeeper informed us that you would certainly not be here till tomorrow. I would not have intruded—"

"I arrived early," he said. "Business with my steward occasioned my coming ahead of the rest of my party—Mr. Bingley and his sisters included. They will join me early tomorrow."

Elizabeth answered only by a slight bow. Her thoughts were instantly driven back to the time when Mr. Bingley's name had been the last mentioned between them. If she might judge by his complexion, his mind was not very differently engaged.

"There is also one other person in the party," he continued after a pause, "who particularly wishes to be known to you. Will you allow me to introduce my sister during your stay at Lambton? Or do I ask too much?"

The surprise of such a request was great indeed. Elizabeth nodded, barely managing to accede to the wish. "I would be honored."

Whatever desire Miss Darcy might have of being acquainted with her must be the work of her brother, and, without looking too deeply at his words, it was gratifying to know that his resentment had not made him think ill of her. They walked on in silence, each of them deep in thought. Elizabeth did not know what to say, though she was flattered and pleased. His wish of introducing his sister to her was a compliment of the highest kind. When they reached the carriage, Mr. and Mrs. Gardiner were half a quarter of a mile behind.

He invited her into the house to rest, but she declared herself not tired, and they stood together on the lawn. The silence was very awkward. She wanted to talk, but there seemed to be an embargo on every subject. At last she recollected that she had been traveling, and they talked of Matlock and Dovedale with great perseverance. Yet time and her aunt moved slowly— and her patience and her ideas were nearly worn out before the tete-a-tete was over. On Mr. and Mrs. Gardiner's coming up, Mr. Darcy offered refreshment. They declined and parted on each side with utmost politeness. Mr. Darcy handed the ladies into the carriage. When it drove off, Elizabeth saw him walking slowly towards the house.

The observations began almost as once. Her uncle and aunt pronounced him to be infinitely superior to anything they had expected. "He is perfectly well behaved, polite, and unassuming," said her uncle.

"There is something a little stately in him, to be sure," replied her aunt, "but it is confined to his air, and is not unbecoming. I can now say with the housekeeper, that though some people may call him proud, I have seen nothing of it."

"I was never more surprised than by his behavior to us. It was more than civil. It was really attentive and there was no necessity for such attention. His acquaintance with Elizabeth was very trifling."

"To be sure, Lizzy," said her aunt, "he is not so handsome as Wickham. Rather, he has not Wickham's countenance, for his features are perfectly good. But how came you to tell me that he was so disagreeable?"

Elizabeth excused herself as well as she could. She said that she had liked him better when they had met in Kent, and that she had never seen him so pleasant as this morning.

"But perhaps he may be a little whimsical in his civilities," replied her uncle. "Your great men often are. Therefore I shall not take him at his word about the fishing, as he might change his mind another day, and warn me off his grounds."

Elizabeth felt that they had entirely misunderstood his character, but said nothing.

"From what we have seen of him," continued Mrs. Gardiner, "I am not sure he could have behaved in so cruel a way by anybody as he has done by poor Wickham. He has not an ill-natured look. On the contrary, there is something pleasing about his mouth when he speaks. And there is something of dignity in his countenance that would not give one an unfavorable idea of his heart. But, to be sure, the good lady who showed us his house did give him a most flattering character, I could hardly help laughing."

Elizabeth felt herself called on to say something in vindication of his behavior to Wickham. **How could she stand by and allow him to be unjustly attacked because of the lies of another?** Trusting her aunt and uncle, she therefore gave them to understand, in as guarded a manner as she could, that by what she had heard from his relations in Kent, his actions were capable of a very different construction; and that his character was by no means so faulty, nor Wickham's so amiable, as they had been considered in Hertfordshire. In confirmation of this, she related the particulars of all the pecuniary transactions in which they had been connected, without actually naming her authority, but stating it to be reliable.

CHAPTER THIRTY-NINE

*E*LIZABETH HAD DETERMINED that Mr. Darcy would most likely bring his sister to visit her the day after her reaching Pemberley, and was consequently resolved not to be out of sight of the inn the whole of that morning. But her conclusion was false. On the very morning after their arrival at Lambton, the visitors came. They were just returning to the inn from a walk to dress themselves for dining with some of their new friends, when the sound of a carriage drew them to a window. They saw a gentleman and a lady in a curricle driving up the street. Elizabeth immediately recognizing the livery, guessed what it meant, and imparted no small degree of her surprise to her relations by acquainting them with the honor which she expected. Her uncle and aunt were astonished. Elizabeth was quite amazed at her own discomposure and dreaded the partiality of Mr. Darcy should have said too much in her favor. Anxious to please, she naturally suspected that every power of pleasing would fail her.

She retreated from the window, fearful of being seen. Walking up and down the room, she endeavored to compose herself. The inquiring looks of her uncle and aunt made everything worse.

Miss Darcy and her brother appeared, and with astonishment Elizabeth saw that her new acquaintance was at least as embarrassed as herself. Since her being at Lambton, she had heard that Miss Darcy was exceedingly proud, but the observation of a very few minutes convinced her that she was only exceedingly shy. She found it difficult to obtain even a word from her beyond a monosyllable.

Though little more than sixteen, Miss Darcy was taller than Elizabeth and had a womanly, graceful figure. She was less handsome than her brother, but there was sense and good humor in her face, and her manners were perfectly unassuming and gentle. Elizabeth, who had expected to find in her as acute and unembarrassed an observer as ever Mr. Darcy had been, was much relieved by discerning such different feelings. She instantly liked the girl.

They had not long been together before Mr. Darcy told her that Bingley was also coming to wait on her. She barely had time to express her satisfaction, and prepare, when Bingley's quick step was heard on the stairs and he entered the room. All Elizabeth's anger against him had been long done away, but had she still felt any, it could hardly have stood its ground against the unaffected cordiality with which he expressed himself on seeing her again. He inquired in a friendly, though general way, after her family, and looked and spoke with the same good-humored ease that he had ever done.

To Mr. and Mrs. Gardiner he was scarcely a less interesting personage for they had long wished to see him. Though, suspicions had begun to arise in them of Mr. Darcy and their niece. They directed their observation towards each with an earnest though guarded inquiry, and soon drew the full conviction that one of them knew what it was to be in love. Of the lady's sensations they remained a little in doubt, but that the gentleman was overflowing with admiration was evident.

Elizabeth wanted to ascertain the feelings of each of her visitors, and she wanted to compose her own to make herself agreeable to all. In seeing Bingley, her thoughts naturally flew to her sister. Oh, how she longed to know whether his were directed in a like manner. Sometimes she fancied that he talked less than on former occasions, but, though this might be imaginary, she could not be deceived in his behavior to Miss Darcy, who had been set up as a rival to Jane. No look appeared on either side that spoke a particular regard, nothing occurred between them that could justify the hopes of his sister.

It was not often that she could turn her eyes on Mr. Darcy. Whenever she did catch a glimpse, she saw an expression of general complaisance, and in all that he said she heard an accent so removed from hauteur or disdain of his companions. When she saw him thus seeking the acquaintance and courting the good opinion of people with whom any intercourse a few months ago would have been a disgrace—when she saw him thus civil, not only to herself, but to the very relations whom he had openly disdained, and recollected their last lively scene in Hunsford Parsonage—the difference was so great, and struck so forcibly on her mind, that she could hardly restrain her astonishment. Never, even in the company of his dear friends at Netherfield, or his dignified relations at Rosings, had she seen him so desirous to please, so free from self-consequence or unbending reserve, as now, when no importance could result from the success of his endeavors, when even the acquaintance of those to whom his attentions were addressed would draw down the ridicule and censure of the ladies both of Netherfield and Rosings.

Their visitors stayed with them above half-an-hour. When they arose to depart, Mr. Darcy called on his sister to join him in expressing their wish of seeing Mr. and Mrs. Gardiner, and Miss Elizabeth, to dinner at Pemberley, before they left the country. Miss Darcy, though with a diffidence which marked her little in the habit of giving invitations, readily obeyed. Mrs. Gardiner looked at her niece, desirous of knowing how *she*, whom the invitation most concerned, felt disposed as to its acceptance, but Elizabeth had turned away her head. Presuming however, that this studied avoidance spoke rather a momentary embarrassment than any dislike of the proposal, and seeing in her husband, who was fond of society, a perfect willingness to accept it, she ventured to engage for her attendance, and the day after the next was fixed on.

Bingley expressed great pleasure in the certainty of seeing Elizabeth again, having a great many inquiries to make after all their Hertfordshire friends. Elizabeth, construing all this into a wish of hearing her speak of her sister, was pleased. Eager to be alone, and fearful of inquiries or hints from her uncle and aunt, she stayed with them only long enough to hear their favorable opinion of Bingley, and then hurried away to dress.

But she had no reason to fear Mr. and Mrs. Gardiner's curiosity. They did not wish to force her communication. It was evident that she was much better acquainted with Mr. Darcy than they had before any idea of; it was evident that he was very much in love with her. They saw much to interest, but nothing to justify inquiry.

With respect to Wickham, the travelers soon found that he was not held in much estimation. For though the chief of his concerns with the son of his patron were imperfectly understood, it was a well-known fact that, on his quitting Derbyshire, he had left many debts behind him, which Mr. Darcy afterwards discharged.

As for Elizabeth, her thoughts were at Pemberley this evening more than the last; and the evening, though as it passed seemed long, was not long enough to determine her feelings towards *one* in that mansion. She lay awake two whole hours endeavoring to make them out. She certainly did not hate him. No, hatred had vanished long ago. She had almost as long been ashamed of ever feeling a dislike against him. The respect created by the conviction of his valuable qualities, though at first unwillingly admitted, had for some time ceased to be repugnant to her feeling. It was now heightened into somewhat of a friendlier nature, by the testimony so highly in his favor, and bringing forward his disposition in so amiable a light, which yesterday had produced. But above all, above respect and esteem, there was a motive within her of goodwill which could not be overlooked. It was gratitude—gratitude, not merely for having once loved her, but for loving her still well enough to forgive all the petulance of her manner in rejecting him, and all the unjust accusations accompanying her rejection. She had convinced herself that he would avoid her as his greatest enemy. But on this accidental meeting, he appeared most eager to preserve the acquaintance, and without any indelicate display of regard, or any peculiarity of manner. He was soliciting the good opinion of her friends, and bent on making her known to his sister. Such a change in a man of so much pride excited not only astonishment but gratitude—for to love, ardent love, such a change must be attributed. She respected, she esteemed, she was grateful to him, she felt a real interest in his welfare; and she only wanted to know how far she wished that welfare to depend upon herself.

It had been settled in the evening between the aunt and the

niece, that such a striking civility as Miss Darcy's in coming to see them on the very day of her arrival at Pemberley, for she had reached it only to a late breakfast, ought to be imitated, though it could not be equaled, by some exertion of politeness on their side. Consequently, it would be highly expedient to wait on her at Pemberley the following morning. They were, therefore, to go. Elizabeth was pleased. Though, when she asked herself the reason, she had very little to say in reply.

Mr. Gardiner left them soon after breakfast. The fishing scheme had been renewed the day before, and a positive engagement made of his meeting some of the gentlemen at Pemberley before noon.

Convinced that Miss Bingley's dislike of her had originated in jealousy, Elizabeth could not help feeling how unwelcome her appearance at Pemberley must be to her, and was curious to see how civil she would now be.

On reaching the house, they were shown through the hall into the saloon, whose northern aspect rendered it delightful for summer. Its windows opening to the ground admitted a most refreshing view of the high woody hills behind the house, and of the beautiful oaks and Spanish chestnuts which were scattered over the intermediate lawn.

In this house they were received by Miss Darcy, who sat with Mrs. Hurst and Miss Bingley, and the lady with whom she lived in London. Georgiana's reception of them was very civil, but attended with all the embarrassment which, though proceeding from shyness and the fear of doing wrong, would easily give those who felt themselves inferior the belief of her being proud and reserved. Mrs. Gardiner and her niece, however, did her justice, and pitied her.

By Mrs. Hurst and Miss Bingley they were noticed only by a curtsey. On their being seated, a pause, awkward as such pauses must always be, succeeded for a few moments. It was first broken by Mrs. Annesley, a genteel, agreeable-looking woman, whose endeavor to introduce some kind of discourse proved her to be more truly well-bred than either of the others. She spoke chiefly to Mrs. Gardiner, with occasional help from Elizabeth, the conversation was carried on. Miss Darcy looked as if she wished for courage enough to join in and sometimes did venture a short sentence when there was least danger of its being heard.

Elizabeth soon saw that she was herself closely watched by Miss Bingley, and that she could not speak a word, especially to Miss Darcy, without calling her attention. This observation would not have prevented her from trying to talk to the latter, had they not been seated at an inconvenient distance. She expected every moment that some of the gentlemen would enter the room, and she wished, she feared, that the master of the house might be amongst them. Whether she wished or feared it most, she could scarcely determine. After sitting in this manner a quarter of an hour without hearing Miss Bingley's voice, Elizabeth was roused by receiving from her a cold inquiry after the health of her family. She answered with equal indifference and brevity, and the others said no more.

The next variation which their visit afforded was produced by the entrance of servants with cold meat, cake, and a variety of all the finest fruits in season. This did not take place till after many significant looks and a smile from Mrs. Annesley to Miss Darcy reminded the latter of her of her post. There was now employment for the whole party—for though they could not all talk, they could all eat. The beautiful pyramids of grapes, nectarines, and peaches soon collected them round the table.

While thus engaged, Elizabeth had a fair opportunity of deciding whether she most feared or wished for the appearance of Mr. Darcy by the feelings which prevailed on his entering the room. She began to regret that he came. He had been some time engaged by the river with Mr. Gardiner and two or three other gentlemen from the house. On learning that the ladies of the family intended a visit to Georgiana that morning, he had left them. No sooner did he appear than Elizabeth wisely resolved to be perfectly easy and unembarrassed—a necessary resolution to be made, but not the most easily kept. There was a wildness about him, from being outdoors. **Wind had tousled his hair and ruffled the normally fine press of his clothing. It was not unattractive to say the least, for the look gave him the appearance of vitality and health; and when he walked near her, she smelled the fresh country air on his person.**

She saw the suspicions of the whole party were awakened against them, and there was scarcely an eye which did not watch his behavior. In no curiosity was so strongly marked as in Miss Bingley's, in spite of the smiles which overspread her face whenever she spoke, for jealousy had not yet made her desperate, and her attentions to Mr. Darcy were by no means over. Miss Darcy, on her brother's entrance, exerted herself much more to talk. Elizabeth saw he was anxious for his sister and herself to get acquainted, and forwarded as much as possible, every attempt at conversation on either side.

Likewise, Miss Bingley saw this and, in the imprudence of anger, took the first opportunity of saying, with sneering civility, "Pray, Miss Eliza, are not the militia removed from Meryton? They must be a great loss to *your* family."

In Darcy's presence she dared not mention Wickham's name, but Elizabeth instantly comprehended that he was uppermost in his thoughts. The various recollections connected with him gave her a moment's distress, but exerting herself vigorously to repel the ill-natured attack, she presently answered the question in a tolerably detached tone. While she spoke, an involuntary glance showed her Darcy, with a heightened complexion, earnestly looking at her. Had Miss Bingley known what pain she was giving, she undoubtedly would have refrained from the hint. She had merely intended to discompose Elizabeth by bringing forward the idea of a man to whom she believed her partial, to make her betray a sensibility which might injure her in Darcy's opinion, and, perhaps, to remind the latter of all the follies and absurdities by which some part of her family were connected with that corps. Not a syllable had ever reached her of Miss Darcy's meditated elopement. To no creature had it been revealed, where secrecy was possible, except to Elizabeth.

As Miss Bingley, vexed and disappointed, dared not approach nearer to Wickham, in time Georgiana also recovered her stunned senses, though not enough to be able to speak any more. Her brother, whose eye she feared to meet, scarcely recollected her interest in the affair, and the very circumstance which had been designed to turn his thoughts from Elizabeth seemed to have fixed them on her more and more cheerfully.

Their visit did not continue long after Miss Bingley's question. While Mr. Darcy was attending them to their carriage Miss Bingley vented her feelings in criticisms on Elizabeth's person, behavior, and dress. But Georgiana would not join her. Her brother's recommendation was enough to ensure her favor, for his judgment could not err. And he had spoken in such terms of Elizabeth as to leave Georgiana without the power of finding her otherwise than lovely and amiable. When Darcy returned to the saloon, Miss Bingley could not help repeating to him some part of what she had been saying to his sister.

"How very ill Miss Eliza Bennet looks this morning, Mr. Darcy," she said. "I never in my life saw anyone so much altered as she is since the winter. She is grown so brown and coarse."

However little Mr. Darcy liked such an address, he

contented himself with coolly replying that he perceived no other alteration than her being rather tanned, no miraculous consequence of traveling in the summer.

"For my own part," she rejoined, "I must confess that I never could see any beauty in her. Her face is too thin, her complexion has no brilliancy, and her features are not at all handsome. Her nose wants character—there is nothing marked in its lines. Her teeth are tolerable, but not out of the common way. As for her eyes, which have sometimes been called fine, I could never see anything extraordinary in them. They have a sharp, shrewish look, which I do not like at all."

Persuaded as Miss Bingley was that Darcy admired Elizabeth, this was not the best method of recommending herself. But angry people are not always wise and in seeing him at last look somewhat nettled, she had all the success she expected. He was resolutely silent, however, and, from a determination of making him speak, she continued, "When we first knew her in Hertfordshire, how amazed we all were to find that she was a reputed beauty. I particularly recollect your saying one night, after they had been dining at Netherfield, that you did not find her so handsome. However, she seemed to improve on you, and I believe you thought her rather pretty at one time."

Darcy could contain himself no longer. "For many months, I have considered her as one of the handsomest women of my acquaintance."

He then went away, and Miss Bingley was left to all the satisfaction of having forced him to say what gave no one any pain but herself.

CHAPTER FORTY

*E*LIZABETH WAS DISAPPOINTED in not finding a letter from Jane on their arrival at Lambton. This disappointment had been renewed on each of the mornings until the third when two letters arrived at one time, one of which was marked that it had been missent elsewhere. Elizabeth was not surprised, as Jane had written the direction remarkably ill.

They had just been preparing to walk as the letters came in. Her uncle and aunt, leaving her to enjoy them in quiet, set off by themselves. She attended to the missent one first, as it was five days old. The beginning contained an account of all their little parties and engagements, with such news as the country afforded; but the latter half, which was dated a day later, and written in evident agitation, gave more important intelligence.

Elizabeth read, "Since writing the above, dearest Lizzy, something has occurred of a most unexpected and serious nature. I am afraid of alarming you—be assured that we are all

well. What I have to say relates to poor Lydia. An express came at
twelve last night from Colonel Forster, just as we were all gone
to bed, to inform us that she has gone off to Scotland with one of
his officers. To own the truth, with Wickham! Imagine our surprise. To Kitty, however, it does not seem so wholly unexpected.
I am very sorry. So imprudent a match on both sides! But I am
willing to hope the best, and that his character has been misunderstood. Thoughtless and indiscreet I can easily believe him,
but this step marks nothing bad at heart. His choice is disinterested at least, for he must know my father can give her nothing. Our poor mother is sadly grieved. My father bears it better.
How thankful am I that we never let them know what has been
said against him, and we must forget it ourselves. They were
off Saturday night about twelve, but were not missed till yesterday morning at eight. The express was sent off directly. Colonel
Forster gives us reason to expect him here soon. Lydia left a few
lines for his wife, informing her of their intention. I must conclude, for I cannot be long from my poor mother."

Without allowing herself time for consideration, and
scarcely knowing what she felt, Elizabeth instantly seized the
other letter, and opening it with the utmost impatience, read that
it had been written a day after the conclusion of the first.

"By this time, my dearest sister, you have received my
hurried letter. I wish this may be more intelligible, but though
not confined for time, my head is so bewildered that I cannot
answer for being coherent. Dearest Lizzy, I hardly know what
I would write, but I have bad news for you, and it cannot be
delayed. Imprudent as the marriage between Mr. Wickham and
our poor Lydia would be, we are now anxious to be assured it
has taken place, for there is but too much reason to fear they are
not gone to Scotland. Colonel Forster came yesterday, having
left Brighton the day before, not many hours after the express.

Though Lydia's short letter to Mrs. F. gave them to understand that they were going to Gretna Green, something was dropped by Denny expressing his belief that W. never intended to go there, or to marry Lydia at all, which was repeated to Colonel F., who, instantly taking the alarm, set off from Brighton intending to trace their route. He did trace them easily to Clapham, but no further, for on entering that place they removed into a hackney coach, and dismissed the chaise that brought them from Epsom. All that is known after this is that they were seen to continue the London road. I know not what to think. After making every possible inquiry on that side London, Colonel F. came to Hertfordshire, anxiously renewing them at all the turnpikes, and at the inns in Barnet and Hatfield, but without any success. With the kindest concern he came on to Longbourn, and broke his apprehensions to us in a manner most creditable to his heart. I am sincerely grieved for him and Mrs. F., but no one can throw any blame on them. Our distress, my dear Lizzy, is very great. My father and mother believe the worst, but I cannot think so ill of him. Many circumstances might make it more eligible for them to be married privately in town than to pursue their first plan. Even if he could form such a design against a young woman of Lydia's connections, which is not likely, can I suppose her so lost to everything? I grieve to find Colonel F. is not disposed to depend upon their marriage. He said he feared W. was not a man to be trusted. My poor mother is really ill, and keeps her room. Could she exert herself, it would be better, but this is not to be expected. As to my father, I never in my life saw him so affected. Poor Kitty has their anger for concealing their attachment, but as it was a matter of confidence, one cannot wonder. I am truly glad you have been spared something of these distressing scenes. But now, as the first shock is over, shall I own I long for your return? I am not so selfish as to press for

it, if inconvenient. Adieu! Oh, Lizzy, I take up my pen again to
do what I have just told you I would not, but circumstances are
such that I cannot help earnestly begging you all to come here
as soon as possible. I know my dear uncle and aunt so well, that
I am not afraid of requesting it, though I have still something
more to ask of the former. My father is going to London with
Colonel Forster to try to discover her. What he means to do I am
not sure, but his excessive distress will not allow him to pursue
any measure in the best and safest way, and Colonel Forster is
obliged to be at Brighton again tomorrow evening. In such and
exigency, my uncle's advice and assistance would be everything
in the world. He will immediately comprehend what I must feel,
and I rely upon his goodness."

"Oh, where is my uncle?" Elizabeth cried, darting from
her seat as she finished the letter. She eagerly intended to follow him, without losing a precious moment, but as she reached
the door it was opened by a servant and Mr. Darcy appeared.
Her pale face and impetuous manner made him start, and before
he could recover himself to speak, she, in whose mind every
idea was superseded by Lydia's situation, hastily exclaimed, "I
beg your pardon, but I must leave you. I must find Mr. Gardiner
this moment, on business that cannot be delayed. I have not an
instant to lose."

"Good God! What is the matter?" he asked, with more feeling than politeness. Then recollecting himself, "I will not detain
you a minute, but let me, or let the servant go after Mr. and Mrs.
Gardiner. You are not well enough. You cannot go yourself."

Elizabeth hesitated, but her knees trembled under her and
she felt how little would be gained by her attempting to pursue
them. Calling back the servant, she commissioned him, though
in so breathless a way as made her almost unintelligible, to fetch
his master and mistress home instantly.

On his quitting the room she swayed on her feet and looked helplessly at Darcy. **Before she knew what she was doing, she had reached for his arm and was gripping it tightly. His arm stiffened, but he placed his hand over hers with a gentle pat.** Elizabeth felt faint and instantly swayed towards his heat. Unable to support herself, and looking so miserably ill, it was impossible for Darcy to leave her **as her forehead hit the center of his chest. Darcy slipped his arm along her waist to hold her up. She pressed tight against him, feeling a kind of comfort she would have thought impossible in so a dire moment.**

"You must sit," he said, the words more of an order than a request. He led her to a chair and she did as he commanded her. He leaned next to her, letting her keep hold of his arm, as she had yet to release him.

In a tone of gentleness and commiseration, he said, "Let me call your maid. Is there nothing you could take to give you present relief? A glass of wine? Shall I get you one?"

"No, I thank you," she replied, endeavoring to recover herself. "There is nothing the matter with me. I am quite well."

He glanced down to where she clutched his arm and she instantly let go, mumbling an incoherent apology. Darcy straightened, taking a seat across from her.

"I am only distressed by some dreadful news which I have just received from Longbourn." She burst into tears as she alluded to it, and for a few minutes could not speak another word. Darcy, in wretched suspense, could only say something indistinctly of his concern, and observe her in compassionate silence. At length she spoke again. "I have just had a letter from Jane, with such dreadful news that it cannot be concealed from anyone. My younger sister has thrown herself into the power of—of Mr. Wickham. They are gone off together from Brighton. You know him too well to doubt the rest. She has no money, no connections, nothing that can tempt him to—she is lost forever."

Darcy was fixed in astonishment. He wanted to reach for her and pull her close, but it was not his place to do so.

"When I consider," she added in a yet more agitated voice, "that I might have prevented it! I, who knew what he was. Had I but explained some part of what I learned to my own family. Had his character been known, this could not have happened. But it is too late now."

"I am grieved indeed," Darcy said. "Is it absolutely certain?"

"Yes. They left Brighton together on Sunday night and were traced almost to London, but not beyond. They are certainly not gone to Scotland."

"And what has been done to recover her?"

"My father is gone to London, and Jane has written to beg my uncle's immediate assistance. We shall be off, I hope, in half-an-hour. But nothing can be done—I know very well that nothing can be done. How are they even to be discovered? I have not the smallest hope."

Darcy shook his head in silent acquiescence and made no answer. He seemed scarcely to hear her, and was walking up and down the room in earnest meditation, his brow contracted, his air gloomy. Elizabeth soon observed, and instantly understood it. Her power was sinking. Everything must sink under such a proof of family weakness, such an assurance of the deepest disgrace. She could neither wonder nor condemn, but the belief of his self-conquest brought nothing to her consolatory to her bosom, afforded no palliation of her distress. It was, on the contrary, exactly calculated to make her understand her own wishes. Never had she so honestly felt that she could have loved him completely, as now, when all love must be vain.

In each of his pacing steps, she felt a kind of pounding atop her heart, beating it down into her chest. The pain consumed her

and for an instant, she thought that she might die from it. But self-pity, though it would intrude, could not engross her. Lydia— the humiliation, the misery she was bringing on them all—soon swallowed up every private care. Covering her face with her handkerchief, Elizabeth was soon lost to everything else.

After several minutes, she was only recalled to a sense of her situation by the voice of her companion, who, though it spoke compassion, spoke likewise restraint, said, "I am afraid you have been long desiring my absence, nor have I anything to plead in excuse of my stay, but real, though unavailing concern. Would to Heaven that anything could be either said or done on my part that might offer consolation. But I will not torment you with vain wishes, which may seem purposely to ask for your thanks. This unfortunate affair will, I fear, prevent my sister's having the pleasure of seeing you at Pemberley today."

"Oh, yes. Be so kind as to apologize for us to Miss Darcy. Say that urgent business calls us home immediately. Conceal the unhappy truth as long as it is possible, I know it cannot be long."

He readily assured her of his secrecy, again expressed his sorrow for her distress, wished it a happier conclusion than there was at present reason to hope, and leaving his compliments for her relations, with only one serious, parting look, went away.

As he quitted the room, Elizabeth felt how improbable it was that they should ever see each other again on such terms of cordiality as had marked their several meetings in Derbyshire. As she threw a retrospective glance over the whole of their acquaintance, so full of contradictions and varieties, she sighed at the perverseness of those feelings which would now have promoted its continuance, and would formerly have rejoiced in its termination.

If gratitude and esteem are good foundations of affection, Elizabeth's change of sentiment will be neither improbable nor faulty. But if otherwise—if regard springing from such sources is unreasonable or unnatural, in comparison of what is so often described as arising on a first interview with its object, and even before two words have been exchanged, nothing can be said in her defense, except that she had given somewhat of a trial to the latter method in her partiality for Wickham, and that its ill success might authorize her to seek the other less interesting mode of attachment. Be that as it may, she saw him go with regret, and in this early example of what Lydia's infamy must produce, found additional anguish as she reflected on that wretched business. Never, since reading Jane's second letter, had she entertained a hope of Wickham's meaning to marry her. No one but Jane could flatter themselves with such an expectation. Surprise was the least of her feelings. While the contents of the first letter remained in her mind, she was all astonishment that Wickham should marry a girl whom it was impossible he could marry for money. How Lydia could ever have attached him had appeared incomprehensible. But now it was all too natural. For such a sordid attachment as this she might have sufficient charms, and though she did not suppose Lydia to be deliberately engaging in an elopement without the intention of marriage, she had no difficulty in believing that neither her virtue nor her understanding would preserve her from falling an easy prey.

She was wild to be at home—to hear, to see, to share with Jane in the cares that must now fall wholly upon her, in a family so deranged, a father absent, a mother incapable of exertion and requiring constant attendance. Though almost persuaded that nothing could be done for Lydia, her uncle's interference seemed of the utmost importance, and till he entered the room her impatience was severe. Mr. and Mrs. Gardiner had hurried back in alarm, supposing by the servant's account that their niece was taken suddenly ill. But, satisfying them instantly on that head, she eagerly communicated the cause of their summons, reading the two letters aloud, and dwelling on the postscript of the last with trembling energy. Though Lydia had never been a favorite with them, Mr. and Mrs. Gardiner could not but be deeply afflicted. Not Lydia only, but all were concerned in it. After the first exclamations of surprise and horror, Mr. Gardiner promised every assistance in his power. Elizabeth, though expecting no less, thanked him with tears of gratitude.

"But what is to be done about Pemberley?" asked Mrs. Gardiner. "John told us Mr. Darcy was here when you sent for us."

"Yes, and I told him we should not be able to keep our engagement. That is all settled."

Everything relating to their journey was speedily arranged and they were to be off as soon as possible. Elizabeth, after all the misery of the morning, found herself, in a shorter space of time than she could have supposed, seated in the carriage, and on the road to Longbourn.

CHAPTER FORTY-ONE

"I HAVE BEEN THINKING IT OVER again, Elizabeth," said her uncle, as they drove from the town, "and upon serious consideration, I am much more inclined to judge as your eldest sister does on the matter. It appears to me so very unlikely that any young man should form such a design against a girl who is by no means unprotected or friendless, and who was actually staying with his colonel's family. I am strongly inclined to hope the best. Could he expect that her friends would not step forward? Could he expect to be noticed again by the regiment, after such an affront to Colonel Forster? His temptation is not adequate to the risk."

"Do you really think so?" Elizabeth brightened for a moment.

"Upon my word," said Mrs. Gardiner, "I begin to be of your uncle's opinion. Can you yourself, Lizzy, so wholly believe Wickham capable of it?"

"Not of neglecting his own interest, but of every other neglect I can believe him capable. Why should they not go on to Scotland if that had been the case?"

"There is no absolute proof that they are not gone to Scotland," replied Mr. Gardiner.

"Oh, but their removing from the chaise into a hackney coach is such a presumption," said Elizabeth. "And, besides, no traces of them were to be found on the Barnet road."

"Well, then, suppose them to be in London. They may be there, though for the purpose of concealment, for no more exceptional purpose. It is not likely that money should be very abundant on either side. It might strike them that they could be more economically, though less expeditiously, married in London than in Scotland."

"But why all this secrecy? Why any fear of detection? Why must their marriage be private? Oh, no, no—this is not likely. His most particular friend, you see by Jane's account, was persuaded of his never intending to marry her. Wickham will never marry a woman without some money. He cannot afford it. And what claims has Lydia—what attraction has she beyond youth, health, and good humor that could make him, for her sake, forego every chance of benefiting himself by marrying well? As to what restraint the apprehensions of disgrace in the corps might throw on a dishonorable elopement with her, I am not able to judge for I know nothing of the effects that such a step might produce. But as to your other objection, I am afraid it will hardly hold good. Lydia has no brothers to step forward, and he might imagine, from my father's indolence and the little attention he has ever seemed to give to what was going forward in his family that he would do as little, and think as little about it, as any father could do in such a matter."

"But can you think Lydia is so lost to everything but love

of him as to consent to live with him on any terms other than marriage?"

"It does seem, and it is most shocking indeed," replied Elizabeth, with tears in her eyes, "that a sister's sense of decency and virtue in such a point should admit of doubt. But, really, I know not what to say. Perhaps I am not doing her justice. But she is very young. She has never been taught to think on serious subjects, and for the last half-year, nay, for a twelvemonth, she has been given up to nothing but amusement and vanity. She has been allowed to dispose of her time in the most idle and frivolous manner, and to adopt any opinions that came in her way. Since the militia was first quartered in Meryton, nothing but love, flirtation, and officers have been in her head. She has been doing everything in her power by thinking and talking on the subject to give greater susceptibility to her feelings, which are naturally lively enough. And we all know Wickham has every charm that can captivate a woman."

"Jane does not think so very ill of Wickham as to believe him capable of the attempt," said her aunt.

"Of whom does Jane ever think ill? And who is there, whatever might be their former conduct, that she would think capable of such an attempt, till it was proved against them? But Jane knows, as well as I do, what Wickham really is. He has been profligate in every sense of the word. He has neither integrity nor honor and is as false and deceitful as he is insinuating."

"And do you really know all this?" asked Mrs. Gardiner, whose curiosity as to the mode of her intelligence was all alive.

"I do indeed," replied Elizabeth, coloring. "I told you, the other day, of his infamous behavior to Mr. Darcy. You yourself, when last at Longbourn, heard in what manner he spoke of the man who had behaved with such forbearance and liberality towards him. And there are other circumstances which I am not at liberty—which it is not worthwhile to relate—but his lies about the whole Pemberley family are endless. From what he said of Miss Darcy I was thoroughly prepared to see a proud, reserved, disagreeable girl. Yet he knew to the contrary himself. He must know that she was as amiable and unpretending as we have found her."

"But does Lydia know nothing of this? Can she be ignorant of what you and Jane seem so well to understand?"

"Oh, yes, that, that is the worst of all. Till I was in Kent, and saw so much both of Mr. Darcy and his relation Colonel Fitzwilliam, I was ignorant of the truth myself. And when I returned home, the Militia was to leave Meryton in a week or fortnight's time. As that was the case, neither Jane, to whom I related the whole, nor I, thought it necessary to make our knowledge public. What use could it apparently be to any one, that the good opinion which all the neighborhood had of him should then be overthrown? And even when it was settled that Lydia should go with Mrs. Forster, the necessity of opening her eyes to his character never occurred to me."

"When they all removed to Brighton you had no reason to believe them fond of each other?"

"Not the slightest. I can remember no symptom of affection on either side. When first he entered the corps, she was ready enough to admire him, but so we all were. Every girl in or near Meryton was out of her senses about him for the first two months, but he never distinguished her by any particular attention. Consequently, after a moderate period of extravagant and wild admiration, her fancy for him gave way, and others of the regiment, who treated her with more distinction, again became her favorites."

It may be easily believed, that however little of novelty could be added to their fears, hopes, and conjectures, on this subject, by its repeated discussion, no other could detain them from it long, during the whole of the journey.

Lydia did not care about anything outside the small confines of the room. She did not see the dust along the corners of the rough-hewn wood floorboards, nor the bare walls, nor did she detect the foul smoke that had permanently settled into the air. To her, all of these things did not matter for she felt like the most perfect of queens; for she was in love with Wickham, and even more so with the romantic idea of her having run away with him. How jealous her sisters would be when they found out! That was her only regret, not seeing their jealous expressions when it had been discovered what she had done—for surely they would be jealous, especially Elizabeth who had tried to get Wickham for herself and failed. Oh, how Lizzy liked to lecture her. Well, let that haughty sister see her now! And, Kitty, poor Kitty would be so shocked—almost as badly as the time she'd caught Lydia in flagrante delicto. Lydia had to threaten Kitty to keep her quiet, telling her she would inform their mother that she saw Kitty on her knees in front of the married Colonel.

Lydia looked down her naked body and giggled. "Well, perhaps not at this exact moment I should like my sisters to see me."

Crossing the room, she took up Wickham's discarded jacket and slipped it over her shoulders. She loved wearing his uniform, even if doing so made him a little cross with her. The thick material rubbed along her breasts, sending small ripples of pleasure throughout her body. She liked keeping herself aroused for her Wickham, for the rewards of such a scheme were great. No man could resist a woman once they discovered her sex was wet and ready. Their cockerels simply would not allow it.

Out of all her lovers, Wickham was by far the best—though he did not know of the others and she had no intention of ever telling him. Men seemed to enjoy thinking themselves the first to conquer her virginity—though on the rare occasion, she took a lover like Sykes, who she did not have to pretend with. Perhaps it was the soldier in them, but they all wore the same expression of pride and vanity on their face as they lay claim to her maidenhead. Sometimes, when she had nothing better to do, she would think over their words and deeds, comparing how they made love. The first time was often tutorial, as they taught her how to be with a man. The next times were better, each time a little more eager and rough, and all the more daring. For by that time, after a half dozen promiscuous undertakings, she could subtly look at them in a way that made them know what she was thinking. She did it purposefully when they were unable to get to her—across crowded ballrooms, while dining, while marching. She liked knowing her lovers thought of her all day, and when finally they came together, the man was already mad with the itch, and would take her in the most peculiar places. Her favorite was when Wickham took her behind the curtain at a ball in Brighton. That is the moment she knew she loved him, when she had teased him to the point of being overbold.

"Where are you?" she muttered, imagining herself quite miserable without him. He had been gone for nearly half-an-hour to retrieve food. Pacing the floor, she let the uniform jacket tease her flesh, caressing nipples, brushing along her ass. It smelled of Wickham and the sensations combined forced a small shutter of excitement to course through her.

At that moment, the door opened and the object of her lust appeared carrying a tray with bread and cheese. He frowned slightly to see her in his jacket, but said nothing as he locked them in and sat down the tray. He, himself, wore only his shirt, breeches and boots, for the walk to the inn's kitchen was not far.

"Mm, Wickham, what took you so long? I am famished!" She pouted her lower lip, not bothering to pull the jacket closed to hide her body from view. "I almost went after you to scold you for keeping me waiting."

"Perhaps you should eat then, Miss Bennet," he answered.

Lydia gave him a wicked smile as she marched towards him in exaggerated steps. When she came face to chest with him, she looked up at him through her lashes. "I suppose then I have no choice but to obey your orders, sir."

Before he could speak, she reached for his pants and pretended to fumble as she undid them. Her hand slid onto his hard arousal and squeezed. She licked her lips, slowly stroking them with her tongue. His pants fell to his feet. Guiding him by his hips, she turned him toward the bed and made him walk backwards to it. His legs hit the mattress and she pushed, aggressively forcing him onto his back.

She crawled next to him. Wickham breathed heavily. His body was ready, his arousal towering from his hips. He reached for her, pulling her by the back of her head so that her mouth met the tip of his desire. When she endeavored to speak, he pushed her down, and said, "There is a good soldier."

Lydia obliged him for a moment, letting her mouth pull against his shaft. But, she was greedy and did not want to give all the passion away. As soon as his fingers loosened their hold, she pulled her lips off him and instantly moved to straddle his waist. She tugged at his shirt, wrinkling it in her fists. Warm hands ran along the backs of her thighs and she threw back her head to laugh, reveling in her wicked behavior. Her heart pounded and she was rather more interested in the arching and thrust of her own body than his. She pouted her lips, loving the power she felt over men; it was almost better than the pleasure they gave her. As she took him into her body, she knew the ultimate woman's control. When they had sex she could get him to agree to anything. That is how she persuaded him to buy her pretty things, like ribbons and gloves. That is how she got him to say he loved her. That is how she got him to agree to run away with her—a most thrilling idea if she did think so herself.

"Oh, my Wickham," she purred, laughing at what she perceived to be her own cleverness and authority. The pressure inside her built, forcing her to close her eyes as all thoughts flittered out of her head. She rocked her hips, rolling them in small circles. When finally she came, pleasure and tension washing over her in perfect unison, Lydia collapsed against his chest. She did not care that he still moved beneath her, that he had not finished his own release. She had gotten what she wanted from him. Now, perhaps, she would demand they marry. Or, perhaps, she would demand a new hat or dress. They could always get married on the morrow, and she imagined having a secret lover was much more exciting than having a husband, for every pretty woman eventually had one of those and Lydia fancied herself more special than other pretty ladies.

CHAPTER FORTY-TWO

*E*LIZABETH, HER AUNT, and her uncle travelled as expeditiously as possible, even sleeping one night on the road so they could reach Longbourn by dinner time the next day. It was a comfort to Elizabeth to consider that Jane would not have to be worried by long expectations.

The little Gardiners, attracted by the sight of a chaise, were standing on the steps of the house as they entered the paddock. When the carriage drove up to the door, the joyful surprise lighted up their faces, and displayed itself over their whole bodies, in a variety of capers and frisks, showed the pleasing earnestness of their welcomes. Elizabeth jumped out and, after giving each of them a hasty kiss, hurried into the vestibule where Jane had come running down from her mother's apartment.

Elizabeth had tears in her eyes as she affectionately embraced her. "Have you heard anything of the fugitives?"

"Not yet," replied Jane. "But now that my dear uncle has

come, I hope everything will be well."

"Is father in town?"

"Yes, he went on Tuesday, as I wrote you word."

"And have you heard from him often?"

"We have heard only twice. He wrote me a few lines on Wednesday to say that he had arrived in safety, and to give me his directions, which I particularly begged him to do. He merely added that he should not write again till he had something of importance to mention."

"And mother—how is she? How are you all?"

"Mother is tolerably well, though her spirits are greatly shaken. She is upstairs and will have great satisfaction in seeing you. She does not yet leave her dressing room. Mary and Kitty are, thank Heaven, are quite well."

"But you—how are you?" insisted Elizabeth. "You look pale. How much you must have gone through!"

Her sister assured her of her being perfectly well. Their conversation, which had been passing while Mr. and Mrs. Gardiner were engaged with their children, was now put an end to by the approach of the whole party. Jane ran to her uncle and aunt, and welcomed and thanked them both, with alternate smiles and tears.

Mrs. Bennet, to whose apartment they all repaired, after a few minutes' conversation together, received them exactly as might be expected, with tears and lamentations of regret, invectives against the villainous conduct of Wickham, and complaints of her own sufferings and ill-usage. She blamed everybody but the person to whose ill-judging indulgence principally contributed to the errors of her daughter.

"If I had been able," said she, "to carry my point in going to Brighton, with all my family, this would not have happened. Poor Lydia had nobody to take care of her. Why did the Forsters ever let her out of their sight? I am sure there was some great neglect or other on their side, for she is not the kind of girl to do such a thing if she had been well looked after. I always thought they were very unfit to have the charge of her, but I was over-ruled, as I always am. Poor child! And now Mr. Bennet has gone away, and I know he will fight Wickham, wherever he meets him and then he will be killed, and what is to become of us all? The Collinses will turn us out before he is cold in his grave, and if you are not kind to us, brother, I do not know what we shall do."

They all exclaimed against such terrific ideas. Mr. Gardiner, after general assurances of his affection for her and all her family, told her that he meant to be in London the very next day, and would assist Mr. Bennet in every endeavor for recovering Lydia.

"Do not give way to useless alarm," added he, "though it is right to be prepared for the worst, there is no occasion to look on it as certain. It is not quite a week since they left Brighton. In a few days more we may gain some news of them. Till we know they are not married, and have no design of marrying, do not let us give the matter over as lost. As soon as I get to town I shall go to my brother, and make him come home with me to Gracechurch Street. Then we may consult together as to what is to be done."

In the afternoon, the two elder Miss Bennets were able to be by themselves for half-an-hour. When Elizabeth asked for the particulars of the event, Jane was happy to oblige. "Colonel Forster did own that he had often suspected some partiality, especially on Lydia's side, but nothing to give him any alarm. Kitty, however, finally owned, with a very natural triumph on knowing more than the rest of us, that in Lydia's last letter she had prepared her for such a step. It seems she had known of their being in love with each other for many weeks."

"But not before they went to Brighton?" Elizabeth frowned.

**She could throttle Kitty for not revealing the scheme the second
she heard of it.**

"No, I believe not."

"Could Colonel Forster repeat the particulars of Lydia's
note to his wife?"

"He brought it with him for us to see." Jane then took it
from her pocket-book, and gave it to Elizabeth.

Elizabeth read, "My dear Harriet, you will laugh when you
know where I am gone, and I cannot help laughing myself at
your surprise tomorrow morning, as soon as I am missed. I am
going to Gretna Green, and if you cannot guess with who I shall
think you a simpleton, for there is but one man in the world I
love, and he is an angel. I should never be happy without him,
so think it no harm to be off. You need not send them word at
Longbourn of my going, for it will make the surprise the greater
when I write to them and sign my name 'Lydia Wickham.' What
a good joke it will be! I can hardly write for laughing. Pray make
my excuses to Pratt for not keeping my engagement, and dancing with him to-night. Tell him I hope he will excuse me when
he knows all, and tell him I will dance with him with great pleasure at the next ball we meet. I shall send for my clothes when I
get to Longbourn. I wish you would tell Sally to mend a great slit
in my worked muslin gown before it is packed up, for I would
not like my mother to see it and form the wrong opinion of how
it got there. Goodbye. Give my love to Colonel Forster. I hope
you will drink to our good journey. Your affectionate friend,
Lydia Bennet."

"Oh, thoughtless Lydia!" exclaimed Elizabeth. "What a letter is this, to be written at such a moment? But at least it shows
that she was serious on the subject of their journey. Whatever
he might afterwards persuade her to, it was not on her side a
scheme of infamy."

"I never saw anyone so shocked as father. He could not speak a word for full ten minutes. Mother was taken ill immediately, and the whole house in such confusion." Jane thought a moment, then added, "Lady Lucas has been very kind. She walked here on Wednesday morning to condole with us."

Elizabeth hated the idea of everyone knowing their family shame. There was nothing to be done for it, as Lydia handled herself very badly. Inquiries needed to be made by their father and Colonel Forster, servants would know of Lydia's disappearance, soldiers would know of Wickham's intent. This was the kind of gossip people loved to spread.

For the briefest moment, she thought of Mr. Darcy, and felt how lost he was to her. She may never see him again, and could not blame him for not taking back up their acquaintance. She hated Lydia in that moment. How could a sister throw away her entire family's reputation so carelessly and selfishly? How could she forever ruin the hopes and futures of all her sisters?

"It would have been better, had Lady Lucas stayed at home," said Elizabeth. "Perhaps she meant well, but, under such a misfortune as this, one cannot see too little of one's neighbors. Assistance is impossible and condolence insufferable. Let them triumph over us at a distance, and be satisfied."

The whole party hoped for a letter from Mr. Bennet the next morning, but the post came in without bringing a single line from him. His family knew him to be, on all common occasions, a most negligent and dilatory correspondent, but at such a time they had hoped for exertion. They were forced to conclude that he had no pleasing intelligence to send.

Mr. Gardiner had waited only for the letters before he set

off. When he was gone, they were certain at least of receiving constant information of what was going on, and at parting their uncle promised to prevail on Mr. Bennet to return to Longbourn.

Mrs. Gardiner and the children were to remain in Hertfordshire a few days longer. She shared in their attendance on Mrs. Bennet, and was a great comfort to them in their hours of freedom. Their other aunt also visited them frequently, and always, as she said, with the design of cheering and heartening them up—though, as she never came without reporting some fresh instance of Wickham's extravagance or irregularity, she seldom went away without leaving them more dispirited than she found them.

All Meryton seemed striving to blacken the man who, but three months before, had been an angel of light. He was declared to be in debt to every tradesman in the place, and his intrigues, all honored with the title of seduction, had been extended into every tradesman's family. Everybody declared that he was the wickedest young man in the world, and everybody began to find out that they had always distrusted the appearance of his goodness. Elizabeth, though she did not credit half of what was said, believed enough to make her former assurance of her sister's ruin more certain.

Mr. Gardiner left Longbourn on Sunday, and on Tuesday his wife received a letter from him. On his arrival, he had immediately found his brother and persuaded him to come to Gracechurch Street. Before his arrival, Mr. Bennet had been to Epsom and Clapham, but without gaining any satisfactory information. He was now determined to inquire at all the principal hotels in town, as Mr. Bennet thought it possible they might have gone to one of them on their first coming to London before they procured lodgings. Mr. Gardiner himself did not expect any success from this measure, but as his brother was eager in it, he meant to assist him in pursuing it. He added that Mr. Bennet seemed wholly disinclined at present to leave London and promised to write again very soon.

Every day at Longbourn was filled with anxiety. Before they again heard from Mr. Gardiner, a letter arrived for their father from Mr. Collins. As Jane had received directions to open all that came for him in his absence, she accordingly read aloud to Elizabeth, "My dear sir, I feel myself called upon by our relationship, and my situation in life, to condole with you on the grievous affliction you are now suffering under, of which we were yesterday informed by a letter from Hertfordshire. Be assured that Mrs. Collins and myself sincerely sympathize with you and all your respectable family, in your present distress, which must be of the bitterest kind, because proceeding from a cause which no time can remove."

As Jane kept reading, Elizabeth looked over her shoulders, eager to skip the longwinded sentiments of her cousin to learn what, if anything, was said to Darcy's aunt. As Jane continued, Elizabeth read silently to herself, "The death of your daughter would have been a blessing in comparison of this." **She frowned, scanning forward past his pious words as to the licentiousness of behavior in Lydia that proceeded from a faulty degree of indulgence. Then, coming to the part she was most anxious to hear, and read,** "You are grievously to be pitied, in which opinion I am not only joined by Mrs. Collins, but likewise by Lady Catherine and her daughter, to whom I have related the affair. They agree with me in apprehending that this false step in one daughter will be injurious to the fortunes of all the others. For who, as Lady Catherine herself condescendingly says, will connect themselves with such a family? And this consideration leads me moreover to reflect, with augmented satisfaction, on a certain event of last November; for had it been otherwise, I must have been involved in all your sorrow and disgrace. Let me then advise you, dear sir, to console yourself as much as possible, to throw off your unworthy child from your affection for ever, and leave her to reap the fruits of her own heinous offense."

"He is insufferable," Elizabeth exclaimed. "How superior he acts, as if now somehow redeemed against the imaginary slight of my not marrying him! He, who asked another within days of receiving said rejection. Of course, he went to Lady Catherine, happy to report everything to her."

Jane looked curiously at her, for she had not gotten to that part of the letter. Elizabeth, by way of answer, pointed to the hateful lines. Seeing she did not have a willing listener, Jane proceeded to read in silence.

Mr. Gardiner wrote when he had received word from Colonel Forster, and then he had nothing of a pleasant nature to send. It was not known if Wickham had a single relationship with whom he kept up any connection, and it was certain that he had no near one living. And in the wretched state of his own finances, there was a very powerful motive for secrecy, in addition to his fear of discovery by Lydia's relations, for it had just transpired that he had left gaming debts behind him to a very considerable amount. Colonel Forster believed that more than a thousand pounds would be necessary to clear his expenses at Brighton. He owed a good deal in town, but his debts of honor were still more formidable. Mr. Gardiner did not attempt to conceal these particulars from the Longbourn family.

Jane heard them with horror. "A gamester! This is wholly unexpected. I had no idea of it."

Rendered spiritless by the ill-success of all their endeavors, Mr. Bennet yielded to his brother-in-law's entreaty that he would return to his family, and leave it to him to do whatever occasion might suggest to be advisable for continuing their pursuit.

As Mrs. Gardiner began to wish to be at home, it was settled that she and the children should go to London, at the same time that Mr. Bennet came from it. The coach took them the first stage of their journey, and brought its master back to Longbourn.

The present unhappy state of the family rendered any other excuse for the lowness of Elizabeth's spirits unnecessary. She was tolerably well acquainted with her own feelings, and was perfectly aware that, had she known nothing of Darcy, she could have borne the dread of Lydia's infamy somewhat better.

When Mr. Bennet arrived, he had all the appearance of his usual philosophic composure. He said as little as he had ever been in the habit of saying, made no mention of the business that had taken him away, and it was some time before Elizabeth had courage to speak of it. On her briefly expressing her sorrow for what he must have endured, he replied, "Say nothing of that. Who should suffer but myself? It has been my own doing, and I ought to feel it." Then after a short silence he continued, "Lizzy, I bear you no ill-will for being justified in your advice to me last May, which, considering the event, shows some greatness of mind."

CHAPTER FORTY-THREE

TWO DAYS AFTER MR. BENNET'S RETURN, Jane and Elizabeth were walking together in the shrubbery behind the house when they saw their father walking with a letter. Eager to find out what it said, they ran after him, as he deliberately pursued his way towards a small wood on one side of the paddock.

Jane, who was not so light nor so much in the habit of running as Elizabeth, soon lagged behind, while her sister, panting for breath, caught up with him, and eagerly cried out, "Oh, papa, what news? Is that letter from my uncle?"

"Yes I have had a letter from him by express."

"Well, and what news does it bring—good or bad?"

"What is there of good to be expected?" said he, taking the letter from his pocket. "But perhaps you would like to read it."

Elizabeth impatiently caught it from his hand. Jane now came up.

"Read it aloud," said their father, "for I hardly know myself what it is about."

Elizabeth obliged, "Gracechurch Street, Monday, August 2. My dear brother, at last I am able to send you some tidings of my niece, and such as, upon the whole, I hope it will give you satisfaction. Soon after you left me on Saturday, I was fortunate enough to find out in what part of London they were. The particulars I reserve till we meet. It is enough to know they are discovered. I have seen them—"

"Then it is as I always hoped," cried Jane. "They are married!"

Elizabeth read on, "I have seen them both. They are not married, nor can I find there was any intention of being so, but if you are willing to perform the engagements which I have ventured to make on your side, I hope it will not be long before they are. All that is required of you is, to assure to your daughter, by settlement, her equal share of the five thousand pounds secured among your children after the decease of yourself and my sister. Moreover, to enter into an engagement of allowing her, during your life, one hundred pounds per annum. These are conditions which, considering everything, I had no hesitation in complying with, as far as I thought myself privileged, for you. I shall send this by express, that no time may be lost in bringing me your answer. Yours, Edw. Gardiner."

"Is it possible?" cried Elizabeth, when she had finished.

"Wickham is not so undeserving, then, as we thought him," said her sister. "My dear father, I congratulate you."

"And have you answered the letter?" asked Elizabeth.

"No, but it must be done soon."

She earnestly entreated him to lose no more time before he wrote.

"I dislike it very much, but it must be done." And so saying, he turned back with them, and walked towards the house.

Elizabeth followed him. "But the terms, I suppose, must be complied with."

"Complied with? I am only ashamed of his asking so little. But, they must marry. There is nothing else to be done. However there are two things that I want very much to know. One, how much money your uncle has laid down to bring it about. And the other, how am I ever to repay him."

"What do you mean?" Jane asked.

"I mean, that no man in his senses would marry Lydia on so slight a temptation as one hundred a year during my life, and fifty after I am gone. Wickham's a fool if he takes her with a farthing less than ten thousand pounds. I should be sorry to think so ill of him, in the very beginning of our relationship."

"Ten thousand pounds!" Jane exclaimed. "Heaven forbid!"

It now occurred to the girls that their mother was in all likelihood perfectly ignorant of what had happened. They followed their father to the library and asked whether he would not wish them to make it known to her. He coolly replied, "Just as you please."

"May we take my uncle's letter to read to her?"

"Take whatever you like, and get away."

Elizabeth took the letter from his writing table, and they went upstairs together. Mary and Kitty were both with Mrs. Bennet. After a slight preparation for good news, the letter was read aloud. Mrs. Bennet could hardly contain herself. As soon as Jane had read Mr. Gardiner's hope of Lydia's being soon married, her joy burst forth, and every following sentence added to its exuberance.

"My dear, dear Lydia!" she exclaimed. "This is delightful indeed. She will be married at sixteen and I shall see her again. My good, kind brother, I knew he would manage everything.

How I long to see her and dear Wickham! But the wedding clothes? I will write to my sister Gardiner about them directly. Lizzy, my dear, run down to your father, and ask him how much he will give her. Stay, stay, I will go myself. I will put on my things in a moment. My dear Lydia! How merry we shall be when we meet!"

Her eldest daughter endeavored to give some relief to the violence of these transports, by leading her thoughts to the obligations which Mr. Gardiner's behavior laid them all under.

"For we must attribute this happy conclusion," she added, "in a great measure to his kindness. We are persuaded that he has pledged himself to assist Mr. Wickham with money."

"Well," cried her mother, "it is all very right. Who should do it but her own uncle? If he had not had a family of his own, I and my children must have had all his money, you know. It is the first time we have ever had anything from him, except a few presents."

Elizabeth, sick of the folly of her mother's thoughts, took refuge in her own room so she might think with freedom. Poor Lydia's situation was bad enough, but that it was no worse, she had need to be thankful. **However, she found it hard to rejoice, for though what family reputation could be salvaged, would be, it would not be enough to undo the loss of Elizabeth's heart. For, though a man of lesser worth might someday marry her despite Lydia's actions, the one man she had come to desire to marry her would never be able to. Lady Catherine would see to it if the world did not.**

CHAPTER FORTY-FOUR

*M*R. BENNET HAD VERY OFTEN WISHED before this period of his life that, instead of spending his whole income, he had laid by an annual sum for the better provision of his children, and of his wife, if she survived him. He now wished it more than ever. Had he done his duty in that respect, Lydia need not have been indebted to her uncle for whatever of honor or credit could now be purchased for her. The satisfaction of prevailing on one of the most worthless young men in Great Britain to be her husband might then have rested in its proper place.

He was seriously concerned that a cause of so little advantage to anyone should be forwarded at the sole expense of his brother-in-law, and he was determined, if possible, to find out the extent of his assistance, and to discharge the obligation as soon as he could.

When first Mr. Bennet had married, economy was held to

be perfectly useless, for, of course, they were to have a son. The son was to join in cutting off the entail, as soon as he should be of age, and the widow and younger children would by that means be provided for. Five daughters successively entered the world and the event of a son had at last been despaired of, but then it was too late to be saving. Mrs. Bennet had no turn for economy, and her husband's love of independence had alone prevented their exceeding their income.

Five thousand pounds was settled by marriage articles on Mrs. Bennet and the children. But in what proportions it should be divided amongst the latter depended on the will of the parents. This was one point, with regard to Lydia, at least, which was now to be settled, and Mr. Bennet could have no hesitation in acceding to the proposal before him. In terms of grateful acknowledgment for the kindness of his brother, though expressed most concisely, he then delivered on paper his perfect approbation of all that was done, and his willingness to fulfill the engagements that had been made for him. He had never before supposed that, could Wickham be prevailed on to marry his daughter, it would be done with so little inconvenience to himself as by the present arrangement. He would scarcely be ten pounds a year the loser by the hundred that was to be paid them; for, what with her board and pocket allowance, and the continual presents in money which passed to her through her mother's hands, Lydia's expenses had been very little within that sum.

That it would be done with such trifling exertion on his side, too, was another very welcome surprise. His wish at present was to have as little trouble in the business as possible. When the first transports of rage which had produced his activity in seeking her were over, he naturally returned to all his former indolence. His letter was soon dispatched, in which he begged to know further particulars of what he was indebted to his brother, but was too angry with Lydia to send any message to her.

The good news spread quickly through the house, and with proportionate speed through the neighborhood. It was borne in the latter with decent philosophy. To be sure, it would have been more for the advantage of conversation had Miss Lydia Bennet come upon the town; or, as the happiest alternative, been secluded from the world, in some distant farmhouse. But there was much to be talked of in her marrying. All the spiteful old ladies in Meryton lost but little of their spirit in this change of circumstances, because with such a husband her misery was considered certain.

It was a fortnight since Mrs. Bennet had been downstairs, but on this happy day she again took her seat at the head of her table. No sentiment of shame dampened her triumph. The marriage of a daughter, which had been the first object of her wishes since Jane was sixteen, was now on the point of accomplishment, and her thoughts and her words ran wholly on those attendants of elegant nuptials, fine muslins, new carriages, and servants. She was busily searching through the neighborhood for a proper situation for her daughter, and, without knowing or considering what their income might be, rejected many as deficient in size and importance.

"Haye Park might do," said she, "if the Gouldings could quit it—or the great house at Stoke, if the drawing room were larger. Ashworth is too far off. I could not bear to have her ten miles from me. As for Pulvis Lodge, the attics are dreadful."

Her husband allowed her to talk on without interruption while the servants remained. But when they had withdrawn, he said to her, "Mrs. Bennet, before you take any or all of these houses for your son and daughter, let us come to a right understanding. Into one house in this neighborhood they shall never have admittance. I will not encourage the impudence of either, by receiving them at Longbourn."

A long dispute followed this declaration, but Mr. Bennet was firm. It soon led to another. Mrs. Bennet found, with amazement and horror, that her husband would not advance a guinea to buy clothes for his daughter. He protested that she should receive from him no mark of affection whatever on the occasion. Mrs. Bennet could hardly comprehend it. That his anger could be carried to such a point of inconceivable resentment as to refuse his daughter a privilege, without which her marriage would scarcely seem valid, exceeded all she could believe possible. She was more alive to the disgrace which her want of new clothes must reflect on her daughter's nuptials, than to any sense of shame at her eloping and living with Wickham a fortnight before they took place.

Elizabeth was now most heartily sorry that she had, from the distress of the moment, been led to make Mr. Darcy acquainted with their fears for her sister. Since her marriage would so shortly give the proper termination to the elopement, they might hope to conceal its unfavorable beginning from all those who were not immediately on the spot.

She had no fear of its spreading farther through his means. There were few people on whose secrecy she would have more confidently depended. Yet, at the same time, there was no one whose knowledge of a sister's frailty would have mortified her so much—not from any fear of it being a disadvantage to herself, for there seemed an impassable gulf between them. Had Lydia's marriage been concluded on the most honorable terms, it was not to be supposed that Mr. Darcy would connect himself with a family who would now be aligned with a man whom he justly scorned.

He would shrink from such a connection. The wish of procuring her regard, which she had assured herself of his feeling in

Derbyshire, could not survive such a blow as this. She was humbled, she was grieved; she repented, though she hardly knew of what. She became jealous of his esteem, when she could no longer hope to be benefited by it. She wanted to hear of him, when there seemed the least chance of gaining intelligence. She was convinced that she could have been happy with him, when it was no longer likely they should meet.

What a triumph for him, she often thought, if he knew that the proposals which she had proudly spurned only four months ago, would now have been most gladly and gratefully received! He was as generous, she doubted not, as the most generous of his sex, but he was also mortal, and where man is mortal there must also be triumph.

The pain in her chest when she thought of him was unbearable. Longing filled her—longings of the heart, and more physical longings of her body. She could understand, in some small way, the attraction Lydia must have felt for Wickham to drive her to act so impractically, not that she forgave her sister. When she thought of Darcy, Elizabeth felt a warm tingling erupt all along her body, centering low in her belly. She would give anything to be held by him just one time. Of course, that could never happen. She would never disgrace herself like that outside of marriage, or at least a solid engagement. Still, if the world could but fall away for one moment, and such a desire could be realized, she would promise to never regret another thing in her life.

More practically, she began to comprehend that Darcy was exactly the man who, in disposition and talents, would most suit her as a husband. His understanding and temper, though unlike her own, would have answered all her wishes. It was a union that would have been to the advantage of both. With her ease and liveliness, his mind might have been softened and his manners improved. From his judgment, information, and knowledge of

the world, she must have received benefit of a greater importance. But no such happy marriage was in her future to show her
what connubial felicity really was.

A union of a different tendency, and precluding the possibility of the other, was soon to be formed in their family. How
Wickham and Lydia were to be supported in tolerable independence, she could not imagine. But how little of permanent happiness could belong to a couple who were only brought together
because their passions were stronger than their virtue, she could
easily conjecture.

Mr. Gardiner soon wrote again to his brother. To Mr.
Bennet's acknowledgments he briefly replied, with assurance of
his eagerness to promote the welfare of any of his family, and
concluded with entreaties that the subject might never be mentioned to him again. The principal purport of his letter was to
inform them that Mr. Wickham had resolved on quitting the
Militia.

"It was greatly my wish that he should do so," he added, "as
soon as his marriage was fixed on. And I think you will agree with
me, in considering the removal from that corps as highly advisable, both on his account and my niece's. It is Mr. Wickham's
intention to go into the Regulars. Among his former friends,
there are still some who are able and willing to assist him in the
army. He has the promise of an ensigncy in a regiment now quartered in the North. It is an advantage to have it so far from this
part of the kingdom. I hope among different people, where they
may each have a character to preserve, they will both be more
prudent. I have written to Colonel Forster, to inform him of
our present arrangements, and to request that he will satisfy the

various creditors of Mr. Wickham in and near Brighton, with assurances of speedy payment, for which I have pledged myself. And will you give yourself the trouble of carrying similar assurances to his creditors in Meryton, of whom I shall subjoin a list according to his information? He has given in all his debts, or at least I hope he has not deceived us. Haggerston has our directions, and all will be completed in a week. They will then join his regiment, unless they are first invited to Longbourn. I understand from Mrs. Gardiner, that my niece is very desirous of seeing you all before she leaves the South. She is well, and begs to be dutifully remembered to you and her mother. Yours, Edw. Gardiner."

Mr. Bennet and his daughters saw all the advantages of Wickham's removal from the Militia as clearly as Mr. Gardiner. Mrs. Bennet was not pleased with it. Lydia's being settled in the North, just when she had expected most pleasure and pride in her company, for she had by no means given up her plan of their residing in Hertfordshire, was a severe disappointment. Besides, it was such a pity that Lydia should be taken from a regiment where she was acquainted with everybody, and had so many favorites.

His daughter's request, for such it might be considered, of being admitted into her family again before she set off for the North, received at first an absolute negative. But Jane and Elizabeth, who agreed in wishing, for the sake of their sister's feelings and consequence, that she should be noticed on her marriage by her parents, urged him so earnestly yet so rationally and so mildly, to receive her and her husband at Longbourn, as soon as they were married. From this he was prevailed on to think as they thought, and act as they wished. Their mother had the satisfaction of knowing that she would be able to show her married daughter in the neighborhood before she was banished to the North.

CHAPTER FORTY-FIVE

*L*YDIA'S WEDDING DAY ARRIVED. Jane and Elizabeth felt for her probably more than she felt for herself. The carriage was sent to meet the newlyweds, and they were to return in it by dinnertime. When they arrived, the family assembled in the breakfast room to receive them. A smile decked the face of Mrs. Bennet as the carriage drove up to the door. Her husband looked impenetrably grave; her daughters, alarmed, anxious, and uneasy.

Lydia's voice was heard in the vestibule as the door was thrown open. She ran into the room. Her mother stepped forward, embraced her, and welcomed her with rapture. Mrs. Bennet then gave her hand, with an affectionate smile, to Wickham, who followed his lady. She wished them both joy with an alacrity which showed no doubt of their happiness.

Their reception from Mr. Bennet was not quite so cordial. His countenance gained in austerity and he scarcely opened his lips. The easy assurance of the young couple was enough to provoke him. Elizabeth was disgusted, and even Jane was shocked. Lydia was Lydia still; untamed, unabashed, wild, noisy, and fearless. She turned from sister to sister, demanding their congratulations.

When at length they all sat down, Lydia looked eagerly round the room, took notice of some little alteration in it, and observed, with a laugh, that it was a great while since she had been there. Wickham was not at all more distressed than herself. His manners were always so pleasing, that had his character and his marriage been exactly what they ought, his smiles and his easy address would have delighted them all.

There was no want of discourse. The bride and her mother could neither of them talk fast enough. Wickham, who happened to sit near Elizabeth, began inquiring after his acquaintances in that neighborhood, with a good humored ease which she felt very unable to equal in her replies. They seemed each of them to have the happiest memories in the world. Nothing of the past was recollected with pain, and Lydia led voluntarily to subjects which her sisters would not have alluded to for the world.

"Only think of its being three months," she said, "since I went away. It seems but a fortnight I declare, and yet there have been things enough that have happened in that time. Good gracious, when I went away I am sure I had no more idea of being married till I came back again—though I thought it would be very good fun if I was."

Her father lifted up his eyes. Jane was distressed. Elizabeth looked expressively at Lydia, but she, who never heard nor saw anything of which she chose to be insensible, gaily continued, "Oh, mamma, do the people hereabouts know I am married today? I was afraid they might not. When we overtook William Goulding in his curricle, I was determined he should know it and so I let down the side-glass next to him, and took off my glove, and let my hand just rest upon the window frame, so that he might see the ring, and then I bowed and smiled."

Elizabeth could bear it no longer. She got up and left the room, not bothering to rejoin the party until she heard them passing through the hall to the dining parlor. She then joined them soon enough to see Lydia, with anxious parade, walk up to her mother's right hand, and say to her eldest sister, "Ah! Jane, I take your place now, and you must go lower, because I am a married woman."

It was not to be supposed that time would give Lydia the embarrassment which she currently lacked. Her ease and good spirits increased. She longed to see Mrs. Philips, the Lucases, and all their other neighbors, and to hear herself called "Mrs. Wickham" by each of them. In the mean time, she went after dinner to show her ring, and boast of being married, to Mrs. Hill and the two housemaids.

"Well, mamma," said she, when they were all returned to the breakfast room, "and what do you think of my husband? Is he not a charming man? I am sure my sisters must envy me. I only hope they may have half my good luck. They must all go to Brighton. That is the place to get husbands."

"Lydia, I do not like that you are going such a way off. Must it be so?"

"Oh, yes, there is nothing in that. You and papa, and my sisters, must come down and see us. We shall be at Newcastle all winter, and I daresay there will be some balls, and I will take care to get good partners for them all."

"I should like it beyond anything!" said her mother.

"And when you go away, you may leave one or two of my sisters behind you. I shall get husbands for them before the winter is over."

"I thank you for my share of the favor," said Elizabeth, "but I do not particularly like your way of getting husbands."

Their visitors were not to remain above ten days with them. Mr. Wickham had received his commission before he left London, and he was to join his regiment at the end of a fortnight.

No one but Mrs. Bennet regretted that their stay would be so short. She made the most of the time by visiting about with her daughter, and having very frequent parties at home.

Wickham's affection for Lydia was just as Elizabeth had expected to find it—not equal to Lydia's for him. Their elopement had been brought on by the strength of her love, rather than by his. She would have wondered why, without violently caring for her, he chose to elope with her at all, had she not felt certain that his flight was rendered necessary by distress of circumstances.

One morning, soon after their arrival, as she was sitting with her two elder sisters, she said to Elizabeth, "Lizzy, I never gave you an account of my wedding, I believe. You were not by, when I told mamma and the others all about it. Are not you curious to hear how it was managed?"

"Not really," replied Elizabeth. "I think there cannot be too little said on the subject."

"La! You are so strange! I must tell you how it went off. We were married, you know, at St. Clement's, because Wickham's lodgings were in that parish. It was settled that we should all be there by eleven o'clock. My uncle and aunt and I were to go together, and the others were to meet us at the church. Well, Monday morning came, and I was in such a fuss. I was so afraid something would happen to put it off. And there was my aunt, all the time I was dressing, preaching and talking away just as if she was reading a sermon. However, I did not hear above one word, for I was thinking of my dear Wickham. I longed to know whether he would be married in his blue coat."

"I will not listen," insisted Elizabeth.

"We breakfasted at ten as usual and I thought it would never be over, for my uncle and aunt were horrid unpleasant all the time I was with them. I did not once put my foot out of doors, though I was there a fortnight. Not one party, or scheme, or anything. To be sure London was rather thin, but the Little Theatre was open."

"Can you not comprehend the necessity of it?" Elizabeth demanded, only to again be ignored by Lydia's telling of her story.

"So just as the carriage came to the door, my uncle was called away upon business to that horrid man Mr. Stone. You know when once they get together there is no end of it. I was so frightened I did not know what to do, for my uncle was to give me away. If we were beyond the hour, we could not be married all day. But, luckily, he came back again in ten minutes' time, and then we all set out. However, I recollected afterwards that if he had been prevented going, the wedding need not be put off for Mr. Darcy might have done as well."

"Mr. Darcy?" repeated Elizabeth, in utter amazement.

"Oh, yes! He was to come there with Wickham, you know. But gracious me! I quite forgot! I ought not to have said a word about it. It was to be a secret!"

"If it was to be secret," said Jane, "say not another word on the subject. You may depend upon my seeking no further."

"Oh, certainly," said Elizabeth, though burning with curiosity. "We will ask you no questions."

"Thank you," said Lydia, "for if you did, I should certainly tell you all, and then Wickham would be angry."

On such encouragement to ask, Elizabeth was forced to put it out of her power, by leaving the room. But to live in ignorance on such a point was impossible, or at least it was impossible not to try for information. Mr. Darcy had been at her sister's wedding. It was exactly a scene, and exactly among people, where he had apparently least to do, and least temptation to go. Conjectures as to the meaning of it, rapid and wild, hurried into her brain, yet she was satisfied with none. Those that best pleased her, as placing his conduct in the noblest light, seemed most improbable. She could not bear such suspense and, hastily seizing a sheet of paper, wrote a short letter to her aunt to request an explanation of what Lydia had hinted at, if it were compatible with the secrecy which had been intended.

"You may readily comprehend," she added, "what my curiosity must be to know how a person unconnected with any of us, and—comparatively speaking—a stranger to our family, should have been among you at such a time. Pray write instantly, and let me understand it—unless it is, for very cogent reasons, to remain in the secrecy which Lydia seems to think necessary. Then I must endeavor to be satisfied with ignorance."

"Not that I shall," she added to herself, as she finished the letter, "and my dear aunt, if you do not tell me in an honorable manner, I shall certainly be reduced to tricks and stratagems to find it out."

Elizabeth had the satisfaction of receiving an answer to her letter as soon as she possibly could. She was no sooner in possession of it than, hurrying into the little copse, where she was least likely to be interrupted, she sat down on one of the benches and prepared to be happy for the length of the letter convinced her that it did not contain a denial.

She read, "Gracechurch Street, Sept. 6. My dear niece, I have just received your letter, and shall devote this whole morning to answering it, as I foresee that a little writing will not comprise what I have to tell you. I must confess myself surprised by your application. I did not expect it from *you*. Do not think me angry, for I only mean to let you know that I had not imagined such inquiries to be necessary on your side. If you do not choose to understand me, forgive my impertinence. Your uncle is as much surprised as I am—and nothing but the belief of your being a party concerned would have allowed him to act as he has done. But if you are really innocent and ignorant, I must be more explicit.

"On the very day of my coming home from Longbourn, your uncle had a most unexpected visitor. Mr. Darcy called, and was shut up with him several hours. It was all over before I arrived, so my curiosity was not so dreadfully racked as yours seems to have been. He came to tell Mr. Gardiner that he had found out where your sister and Mr. Wickham were, and that he had seen and talked with them both—Wickham repeatedly, Lydia once. From what I can collect, he left Derbyshire only one day after ourselves, and came to town with the resolution of hunting for them. The motive professed was his conviction of its being owing to himself that Wickham's worthlessness had not been so well known as to make it impossible for any young woman of character to love or confide in him. He generously imputed the whole to his mistaken pride, and confessed that he had before thought it beneath him to lay his private actions open to the world. His character was to speak for itself. He called it, therefore, his duty to step forward, and endeavor to remedy an evil which had been brought on by himself. If he had another motive, I am sure it would never disgrace him. He had been some days in town, before he was able to discover them, but he had something to direct his search, which was more than we had, and the consciousness of this was another reason for his resolving to follow us.

"There is a lady, it seems, a Mrs. Younge, who was some time ago governess to Miss Darcy, and was dismissed from her charge on some cause of disapprobation, though he did not say what. She then took a large house in Edward Street, and has since maintained herself by letting lodgings. This Mrs. Younge was, he knew, intimately acquainted with Wickham, and he went to her for intelligence of him as soon as he got to town. But it was two or three days before he could get from her what he wanted. She would not betray her trust, I suppose, without bribery and corruption, for she really did know where her friend was to be found. Wickham indeed had gone to her on their first arrival in London, and had she been able to receive them into her house, they would have taken up their abode with her. At length, however, our kind friend procured the wished-for direction. They were in Bailey Street. He saw Wickham, and afterwards insisted on seeing Lydia. His first object with her, he acknowledged, had been to persuade her to quit her present disgraceful situation, and return to her friends as soon as they could be prevailed on to receive her, offering his assistance, as far as it would go. But he found Lydia absolutely resolved on remaining where she was. She cared for none of her friends, wanted no help of his, and she would not hear of leaving Wickham. She was sure they should be married some time or other, and it did not much signify when. Since such were her feelings, it only remained, he thought, to secure and expedite a marriage, which, in his very first conversation with Wickham, he easily learned had *never* been his design. He confessed himself obliged to leave the regiment, on account of some debts of honor, which were very pressing, and scrupled not to lay all the ill-consequences of Lydia's flight on her own folly alone. He meant to resign his commission immediately and as to his future situation, he could conjecture very little about it. He must go somewhere, but he did not know where, and he knew he should have nothing to live on.

"Mr. Darcy asked him why he had not married your sister at once. Though Mr. Bennet was not imagined to be very rich, he would have been able to do something for him, and his situation must have been benefited by marriage. But he found, in reply to this question, that Wickham still cherished the hope of more effectually making his fortune by marriage in some other country. Under such circumstances, however, he was not likely to be proof against the temptation of immediate relief.

"They met several times, for there was much to be discussed. Wickham of course wanted more than he could get, but at length was reduced to be reasonable.

"Everything being settled between them, Mr. Darcy's next step was to make your uncle acquainted with it, and he first called in Gracechurch Street the evening before I came home. But Mr. Gardiner could not be seen, and Mr. Darcy found, on further inquiry, that your father was still with him, but would quit town the next morning. He did not judge your father to be a person whom he could so properly consult as your uncle, and therefore readily postponed seeing him till after the departure of the former. He did not leave his name, and till the next day it was only known that a gentleman had called on business.

"On Saturday he came again. Your father was gone, your uncle at home, and, as I said before, they had a great deal of talk together.

"They met again on Sunday, and then *I* saw him too. It was not all settled before Monday, but as soon as it was, the express was sent off to Longbourn. But our visitor was very obstinate. I fancy, Lizzy, that obstinacy is the real defect of his character. He has been accused of many faults at different times, but this is the true one. Nothing was to be done that he did not do himself, though I am sure your uncle would most readily have settled the whole affair.

"They battled it together for a long time, which was more than either the gentleman or lady concerned in it deserved. But at last your uncle was forced to yield, and instead of being allowed to be of use to his niece, was forced to put up with only having the probable credit of it, which went sorely against the grain. I really believe your letter this morning gave him great pleasure, because it required an explanation that would rob him of his borrowed feathers, and give the praise where it was due. But, Lizzy, this must go no farther than yourself, or Jane at most.

"You know pretty well, I suppose, what has been done for the young people. His debts are to be paid, amounting, I believe, to considerably more than a thousand pounds, another thousand in addition to her own settled upon her, and his commission purchased. The reason why all this was to be done by him alone, was such as I have given above. It was owing to him, to his reserve and want of proper consideration, that Wickham's character had been so misunderstood, and consequently that he had been received and noticed as he was. Perhaps there was some truth in this, though I doubt whether his reserve, or anybody's reserve, can be answerable for the event. But in spite of all this fine talking, my dear Lizzy, you may rest perfectly assured that your uncle would never have yielded, if we had not given him credit for *another interest* in the affair.

"When all this was resolved, he returned again to his friends, who were still staying at Pemberley. It was agreed that he should be in London once more when the wedding took place, and all money matters were then to receive the last finish.

"I believe I have now told you everything. It is a relation, which you tell me is to give you great surprise. I hope at least it will not afford you any displeasure. Lydia came to us and

Wickham had constant admission to the house. He was exactly what he had been, when I knew him in Hertfordshire, but I would not tell you how little I was satisfied with her behavior while she stayed with us, if I had not perceived, by Jane's letter last Wednesday, that her conduct on coming home was exactly the same, and therefore what I now tell you can give you no fresh pain. I talked to her repeatedly in the most serious manner, representing to her all the wickedness of what she had done, and all the unhappiness she had brought on her family. If she heard me, it was by good luck, for I am sure she did not listen. I was sometimes quite provoked, but then I recollected my dear Elizabeth and Jane, and for their sakes had patience with her.

"Mr. Darcy was punctual in his return, and as Lydia informed you, attended the wedding. He dined with us the next day, and was to leave town again on Wednesday or Thursday. Will you be very angry with me, my dear Lizzy, if I take this opportunity of saying—what I was never bold enough to say before—how much I like him? His behavior to us has, in every respect, been as pleasing as when we were in Derbyshire. His understanding and opinions all please me. He wants nothing but a little more liveliness, and that, if he marry prudently, his wife may teach him. I thought him very sly, for he hardly ever mentioned your name. But slyness seems the fashion.

"Pray forgive me if I have been very presuming, or at least do not punish me so far as to exclude me from P. I shall never be quite happy till I have been all round the park. A low phaeton, with a nice little pair of ponies, would be the very thing.

"But I must write no more. The children have wanted me this half hour. Yours, very sincerely, M. Gardiner."

The contents of this letter threw Elizabeth into a flutter of spirits, in which it was difficult to determine whether pleasure or pain bore the greatest share. The vague and unsettled suspicions of what Mr. Darcy might have been doing to forward her sister's match, which she had feared to encourage as an exertion of goodness too great to be probable, and at the same time dreaded being just, were proved beyond their greatest extent to be true! He had followed them purposely to town, he had taken on himself all the trouble and mortification attendant on such a research; in which supplication had been necessary to a woman whom he must loathe and despise, and where he was reduced to frequently meet, reason with, persuade, and finally bribe, the man whom he always most wished to avoid, and whose very name it was punishment to him to pronounce. He had done all this for a girl whom he could neither regard nor esteem. Her heart did whisper that he had done it for her. But it was a hope shortly checked by other considerations, and she soon felt that even her vanity was insufficient, when required to depend on his affection for her—for a woman who had already refused him—as able to overcome a sentiment so natural as abhorrence against relationship with Wickham. Every kind of pride must revolt from the connection of him as brother-in-law. Darcy had, to be sure, done much. She was ashamed to think how much. But he had given a reason for his interference, which asked no extraordinary stretch of belief. It was reasonable that he should feel he had been wrong. He had liberality, and he had the means of exercising it. She would not place herself as his principal inducement, but could believe that a remaining partiality for her might assist his endeavors in a cause where her peace of mind must be materially concerned. It was exceedingly painful to know they were under obligations to a person who could never receive a return. They owed the restoration of Lydia, her character, everything, to him. Oh, how heartily did she grieve over every ungracious sensation she had ever encouraged, every saucy speech she had ever directed towards him. For herself she was humbled, but she was proud of him. Proud that in a cause of compassion and honor, he had been able to get the better of himself. She read over her aunt's commendation of him again and again. It was hardly enough, but it pleased her. She was even sensible of some pleasure, though mixed with regret, on finding how steadfastly both she and her uncle had been persuaded that affection and confidence subsisted between Mr. Darcy and herself.

She was roused from her seat, and her reflections, by some one's approach. Before she could strike into another path, she was overtaken by Wickham.

"I am afraid I interrupt your solitary ramble, my dear sister," said he, as he joined her.

"You certainly do," she replied with a smile that had nothing to do with him, "but it does not follow that the interruption must be unwelcome."

"I should be sorry indeed, if it were. We were always good friends, and now we are better."

"True. Are the others coming out?" **She made a move to walk back to the house, so as not to be forced too long in his company.**

"I do not know. Mrs. Bennet and Lydia are going in the carriage to Meryton. And so, my dear sister, I find, from our uncle and aunt, that you have actually seen Pemberley."

She replied in the affirmative.

"I almost envy you the pleasure, and yet I believe it would be too much for me, or else I could take it in my way to Newcastle. And you saw the old housekeeper, I suppose? Poor Reynolds, she was always very fond of me. But of course she did not mention my name to you."

"Yes, she did."

"And what did she say?"

"That you were gone into the army, and she was afraid you

had not turned out well. At such a distance as that, you know, things are strangely misrepresented."

"Certainly," he replied, biting his lips. Elizabeth hoped she had silenced him, but he soon afterwards he said, "I was surprised to see Darcy in town last month. We passed each other several times. I wonder what he can be doing there."

"Perhaps preparing for his marriage with Miss de Bourgh," said Elizabeth. "It must be something particular, to take him there at this time of year."

"Undoubtedly. Did you see him while you were at Lambton? I thought I understood from the Gardiners that you had."

"Yes, he introduced us to his sister."

"And do you like her?"

"Very much."

"I have heard, indeed, that she is uncommonly improved within this year or two. When I last saw her, she was not very promising. I am very glad you liked her. I hope she will turn out well."

"I daresay she will. She has got over the most trying age."

"Did you go by the village of Kympton?"

"I do not recollect that we did."

"I mention it, because it is the living which I ought to have had. A most delightful place, an excellent parsonage house. It would have suited me in every respect."

"How should you have liked making sermons?"

"Exceedingly well. I should have considered it as part of my duty, and the exertion would soon have been nothing. One ought not to repine, but, to be sure, it would have been such a thing for me. The quiet, the retirement of such a life would have answered all my ideas of happiness. But it was not to be. Did you ever hear Darcy mention the circumstance, when you were in Kent?"

"I have heard from authority, which I thought as good, that it was left you conditionally only, and at the will of the present patron."

"You have. Yes, there was something in that. I told you so from the first, you may remember."

"I did hear, too, that there was a time, when sermon-making was not so palatable to you as it seems to be at present, that you actually declared your resolution of never taking orders, and that the business had been compromised accordingly."

"You did? It was not wholly without foundation. You may remember what I told you on that point, when first we talked of it."

They were now almost at the door of the house, for she had walked fast to get rid of him; and unwilling, for her sister's sake, to provoke him, she only said in reply, with a good-humored smile, "Come, Mr. Wickham, we are brother and sister, you know. Do not let us quarrel about the past. In future, I hope we shall be always of one mind."

She held out her hand. He kissed it with affectionate gallantry, though he hardly knew how to look, and they entered the house.

CHAPTER FORTY-SIX

*M*R. WICKHAM WAS SO PERFECTLY SATISFIED with this conversation that he never again distressed himself, or provoked Elizabeth, by introducing the subject of it. She was pleased to find that she had said enough to keep him quiet. The day of his and Lydia's departure soon came. Mrs. Bennet was forced to submit to a separation, which, as her husband by no means entered into her scheme of their all going to Newcastle, was likely to continue at least a twelvemonth.

"Oh, my dear Lydia," she cried. "Write to me very often, my dear."

"As often as I can. But you know married women have never much time for writing. My sisters may write to me. They will have nothing else to do."

Mr. Wickham's adieus were much more affectionate than his wife's. He smiled, looked handsome, and said many pretty things.

"He is as fine a fellow," said Mr. Bennet, as soon as they were out of the house, "as ever I saw. He simpers, and smirks, and makes love to us all. I am prodigiously proud of him. I defy even Sir William Lucas himself to produce a more valuable son-in-law when it comes to absurdities."

The loss of her daughter made Mrs. Bennet very dull for several days.

"I often think," said she, "that there is nothing so bad as parting with one's children. One seems so forlorn without them."

"This is the consequence, you see, Madam, of marrying a daughter," said Elizabeth. "It must make you better satisfied that your other four are single."

"It is no such thing. Lydia does not leave me because she is married, but because her husband's regiment happens to be so far off. If that had been nearer, she would not have gone so soon."

But the spiritless condition which this event threw her into was shortly relieved, and her mind opened again to the agitation of hope, by an article of news which then began to be in circulation. The housekeeper at Netherfield had received orders to prepare for the arrival of her master, who was coming down in a day or two, to shoot there for several weeks. Mrs. Bennet was quite in the fidgets. She looked at Jane, and smiled and shook her head by turns.

When Mrs. Philips first brought her the news, Mrs. Bennet replied, "Well, so much the better. Not that I care about it. He is nothing to us, you know, and I am sure *I* never want to see him again. But, he is very welcome to come to Netherfield, if he likes it. And who knows what may happen? But that is nothing to us. You know, sister, we agreed long ago never to mention a word about it. And so, is it quite certain he is coming?"

"You may depend on it," replied the other, "for Mrs. Nicholls was in Meryton last night. I saw her passing by, and went out myself on purpose to know the truth of it. She told me that it was certain. He comes down on Thursday at the latest, very likely on Wednesday. She was going to the butcher's to order in some meat on Wednesday, and she has got three couple of ducks just fit to be killed."

Miss Bennet had not been able to hear of his coming without changing color. It was many months since Jane had mentioned his name to Elizabeth, but now, as soon as they were alone together, she said, "I saw you look at me today, Lizzy, when my aunt told us of the present report. I know I appeared distressed. But do not imagine it was from any silly cause. I was only confused for the moment. I do assure you that the news does not affect me either with pleasure or pain. I am glad of one thing, that he comes alone, because we shall see the less of him. Not that I am afraid of myself, but I dread other people's remarks."

Elizabeth did not know what to make of it. Had she not seen him in Derbyshire, she might have supposed him capable of coming there with no other view than what was acknowledged. However, she still thought him partial to Jane, and she wavered as to the greater probability of his coming there with his friend's permission, or being bold enough to come without it.

"Yet it is hard," she sometimes thought, "that this poor man cannot come to a house which he has legally hired, without raising all this speculation. I will leave him to himself."

In spite of what her sister declared, and really believed to be her feelings in the expectation of his arrival, Elizabeth could easily perceive that her spirits were affected by it. They were more disturbed, more unequal, than she had often seen them. The subject which had been so warmly canvassed between their parents, about a twelvemonth ago, was now brought forward again.

"As soon as ever Mr. Bingley comes, my dear," said Mrs. Bennet, "you will wait on him of course."

"No, no. You forced me into visiting him last year, and promised if I went to see him, he should marry one of my daughters. But it ended in nothing, and I will not be sent on a fool's errand again."

His wife represented to him how absolutely necessary such an attention would be from all the neighboring gentlemen, on his returning to Netherfield.

"'Tis an etiquette I despise," said he. "If he wants our society, let him seek it. He knows where we live. I will not spend my hours in running after my neighbors every time they go away and come back again."

"Well, all I know is that it will be abominably rude if you do not wait on him. But, however, that shan't prevent my asking him to dine here. We must have Mrs. Long and the Gouldings soon. That will make thirteen with ourselves, so there will be just room at table for him."

Consoled by this resolution, she was the better able to bear her husband's incivility, though it was very mortifying to know that her neighbors might all see Mr. Bingley before they did.

As the day of his arrival drew near, Jane said to her sister, "I begin to be sorry that he comes at all. It would be nothing for I could see him with perfect indifference, but I can hardly bear to hear it thus perpetually talked of. My mother means well, but she does not know, no one can know, how much I suffer from what she says. Happy shall I be, when his stay at Netherfield is over."

"I wish I could say anything to comfort you," replied Elizabeth, "but it is wholly out of my power."

Mr. Bingley arrived. Mrs. Bennet, through the assistance of servants, contrived to have the earliest tidings of it. She counted the days that must intervene before their invitation could be sent, hopeless of seeing him before. But on the third morning after his arrival in Hertfordshire, she saw him, from her dressing room window, enter the paddock and ride towards the house.

Her daughters were eagerly called to partake of her joy. Jane resolutely kept her place at the table. Elizabeth, to satisfy her mother, went to the window and that saw Mr. Darcy with him. Breathless, she sat down again by her sister.

"There is a gentleman with him, mamma," said Kitty. "Who can it be?"

"Some acquaintance or other I suppose, my dear. I am sure I do not know."

"La!" replied Kitty, "it looks just like that man that used to be with him before. Mr. what's-his-name. That tall, proud man."

"Good gracious, Mr. Darcy! So it does, I vow. Well, any friend of Mr. Bingley's will always be welcome here, to be sure, but I must say I hate the very sight of him."

Jane looked at Elizabeth with surprise and concern. She knew but little of their meeting in Derbyshire, and therefore felt for the awkwardness which must attend her sister, in seeing him almost for the first time after receiving his explanatory letter. Both sisters were uncomfortable enough. Each felt for the other, and of course for themselves. Their mother talked on, of her dislike of Mr. Darcy, and her resolution to be civil to him only as Mr. Bingley's friend, without being heard by either of them. But Elizabeth had sources of uneasiness which could not be suspected by Jane, to whom she had never yet had courage to show Mrs. Gardiner's letter, or to relate her own change of sentiment towards him. To Jane, he could be only a man whose proposals she had refused, and whose merit she had undervalued. But to her own more extensive information, he was the person to whom the whole family were indebted for the first of benefits, and whom she regarded herself with an interest, if not quite so tender, at least as reasonable and just as what Jane felt for Bingley. Her astonishment at his coming—at his coming to Netherfield, to Longbourn, and voluntarily seeking her again, was almost equal to what she had known on first witnessing his altered behavior in Derbyshire.

The color which had been driven from her face, returned for half a minute with an additional glow, and a smile of delight added luster to her eyes, as she thought for that space of time that his affection and wishes must still be unshaken. But she would not be secure.

"Let me first see how he behaves," thought she, "It will then be early enough for expectation."

She sat intently at work, striving to be composed, and without daring to lift up her eyes till anxious curiosity carried them to the face of her sister as the servant approached the door. Jane looked a little paler than usual, but more sedate than Elizabeth had expected. On the gentlemen's appearing, her color increased. Yet she received them with tolerable ease, and with a propriety of behavior equally free from any symptom of resentment or any unnecessary complaisance.

Elizabeth said as little to either as civility would allow. She ventured only one glance at Darcy. He looked serious, as usual, more as he had been used to look in Hertfordshire, than as she had seen him at Pemberley. But, perhaps he could not in her mother's presence be what he was before her uncle and aunt. It was a painful, but not an improbable, conjecture.

Bingley, she had likewise seen for an instant, and in that short period saw him looking both pleased and embarrassed. He was received by Mrs. Bennet with a degree of civility which made her two daughters ashamed, especially when contrasted with the cold and ceremonious politeness of her curtsey and address to his friend.

Elizabeth, particularly, who knew that her mother owed to the latter the preservation of her favorite daughter from irremediable infamy, was hurt and distressed to a most painful degree by a distinction so ill applied.

Darcy, after inquiring of her how Mr. and Mrs. Gardiner did, a question which she could not answer without confusion, said scarcely anything. He was not seated by her, and perhaps that was the reason of his silence. Several minutes elapsed without bringing the sound of his voice, and when she was unable to resist the impulse of curiosity she raised he eyes to his face. She as often found him looking at Jane as at herself, and frequently on no object but the ground. More thoughtfulness and less anxiety to please, than when they last met, were plainly expressed. She was disappointed, and angry with herself for being so.

"Could I expect it to be otherwise?" she thought.

She was in no humor for conversation with anyone but himself, and to him she had hardly courage to speak.

She inquired after his sister, but could do no more.

"It is a long time, Mr. Bingley, since you went away," said Mrs. Bennet.

He readily agreed to it. "Yes, it is."

"I began to fear you would never come back again. People did say you meant to quit the place entirely at Michaelmas. However, I hope it is not true. A great many changes have happened in the neighborhood since you went away. Miss Lucas is married and settled. And one of my own daughters. I suppose you have heard of it. Indeed, you must have seen it in the papers. It was in *The Times* and *The Courier*, I know, though it was not put in as it ought to be. It was only said, 'Lately, George Wickham, Esq. to Miss Lydia Bennet,' without there being a syllable said of

PRIDE AND PREJUDICE

her father, or the place where she lived, or anything. It was my
brother Gardiner's drawing up too, and I wonder how he came
to make such an awkward business of it. Did you see it?"

Bingley replied that he did, and made his congratulations.
Elizabeth dared not lift up her eyes. How Mr. Darcy looked,
therefore, she could not tell. **Every fiber of her being seemed
pulled in his direction and she wanted nothing more than to
banish the others from the room so that she may speak freely to
him. But, what would she say? How to begin such a conversation?
Insecurity thickened her tongue and she merely stared at the tips
of her shoes.**

"It is a delightful thing, to be sure, to have a daughter
well married," continued her mother, "but at the same time,
Mr. Bingley, it is very hard to have her taken from me. They
are gone down to Newcastle, a place quite northward, and there
they are to stay. His regiment is there. I suppose you have heard
of his leaving the militia, and of his being gone into the regulars. Thank Heaven, he has some friends, though perhaps not so
many as he deserves."

Elizabeth, who knew this to be leveled at Mr. Darcy, was
in such misery of shame, that she could hardly keep her seat. It
drew from her, however, the exertion of speaking, which nothing else had so effectually done before. She asked Bingley, "Do
you mean to stay in the country?"

"A few weeks," he answered with a boyishly charming smile.

"When you have killed all your own birds, Mr. Bingley,"
said her mother, "I beg you will come here, and shoot as many
as you please on Mr. Bennet's manor. I am sure he will be vastly
happy to oblige you, and will save all the best of the covies for
you."

Elizabeth's misery increased, at such unnecessarily officious attention. At that instant, she felt that years of happiness

could not make Jane or herself amends for moments of such painful confusion. Yet the misery, for which years of happiness were to offer no compensation, received material relief, as Elizabeth observed how much her sister's beauty rekindled the admiration of her former lover. When first he came in, he had spoken to her but little, but every five minutes seemed to be giving her more of his attention. He found her as handsome as she had been last year, as good natured, as unaffected, though not quite so talkative. Jane was anxious that no difference should be perceived in her at all, and was really persuaded that she talked as much as ever. But her mind was so busily engaged, that she did not always know when she was silent.

When the gentlemen rose to go away, Mrs. Bennet was mindful of her intended civility, and they were invited and engaged to dine at Longbourn in a few days time.

"You will remember, Mr. Bingley," she added, "when you went to town last winter, you promised to take a family dinner with us, as soon as you returned. I have not forgot, you see. I assure you, I was very much disappointed that you did not come back and keep your engagement."

Bingley looked a little silly at this reflection, and said something of his concern at having been prevented by business. They then went away.

Mrs. Bennet had been strongly inclined to ask them to stay and dine there that day. Though she always kept a very good table, she did not think anything less than two courses could be good enough for a man on whom she had such anxious designs, or satisfy the appetite and pride of one who had ten thousand a year.

As soon as they were gone, Elizabeth walked out to recover her spirits; or in other words, to dwell without interruption on those subjects that must deaden them more. Mr. Darcy's behavior astonished and vexed her. Quite alone, she said, "Why, if he came only to be silent, grave, and indifferent did he come at all?"

She could settle it in no way that gave her pleasure.

"He could be still amiable to my uncle and aunt when he was in town, why not to me? If he fears me, why come hither? If he no longer cares for me, why silent? Teasing, teasing, man! I will think no more about him."

Her pathetic resolution was for a short time involuntarily kept by the approach of her sister, who joined her with a cheerful look, which showed her better satisfied with their visitors, than Elizabeth.

"Now," said Jane, "that this first meeting is over, I feel perfectly easy. I know my own strength, and I shall never be embarrassed again by his coming. I am glad he dines here on Tuesday. It will then be publicly seen that, on both sides, we meet only as common and indifferent acquaintance."

"Yes, very indifferent indeed," said Elizabeth, laughingly. "Oh, Jane, take care."

"My dear Lizzy, you cannot think me so weak as to be in danger now?"

"I think you are in very great danger of making him as much in love with you as ever."

They did not see the gentlemen again till Tuesday. Mrs. Bennet, in the meanwhile, was giving way to all the happy schemes, which the good humor and common politeness of Bingley in half-an-hour's visit, had revived.

On Tuesday there was a large party assembled at Longbourn. The two who were most anxiously expected, to the credit of their punctuality as sportsmen, were in very good time. When they went to the dining room, Elizabeth eagerly watched to see whether Bingley would take the place, which in all their former parties had belonged to him, by her sister. Her prudent mother, occupied by the same ideas, forbore to invite him to sit by herself. On entering the room, he seemed to hesitate, but Jane happened to look round, and happened to smile. It was decided. He placed himself by her.

Elizabeth, with a triumphant sensation, looked towards his friend. He bore it with noble indifference, and she would have imagined that Bingley had received his sanction to be happy, had she not seen his eyes likewise turned towards Mr. Darcy, with an expression of half-laughing alarm.

His behavior to her sister showed an admiration of her, which, though more guarded than formerly, persuaded Elizabeth that, if left wholly to himself, Jane's happiness and his own would be speedily secured. Though she dared not depend upon it, she received pleasure from observing them. It gave her all the animation that her spirits could boast, for she was in no cheerful humor. Mr. Darcy was almost as far from her as the table could divide them. He was on one side of her mother. She knew how little such a situation would give pleasure to either, or make either appear to advantage. She was not near enough to hear any of their discourse, but she could see how seldom they spoke to each other, and how formal and cold was their manner whenever they did. Her mother's ungraciousness, made the sense of what they owed him more painful to Elizabeth's mind. At times, she would have given anything to be privileged to tell him that his kindness was neither unknown nor unfelt by the whole of the family.

She hoped the evening would afford some opportunity of bringing them together, and that the visit would not pass without

enabling them to enter into conversation beyond the mere ceremonious salutation attending his entrance. Anxious and uneasy,
the period which passed in the drawing room, before the gentlemen came, was wearisome and dull to a degree that almost
made her uncivil. She looked forward to their entrance as all her
chance of pleasure for the evening depended on it.

To herself, she whispered, "If he does not come to me, I
shall give him up forever."

The gentlemen came in. She thought Darcy looked as if he
would answer her hope, but, alas, the ladies had crowded round
the table where Miss Bennet was making tea and Elizabeth
pouring coffee. There was not a single vacancy near her which
would admit of a chair. And on the gentlemen's approaching,
Kitty moved closer to her than ever, and said, in a whisper, "The
men shan't come and part us, I am determined. We want none
of them, do we?"

Darcy walked to another part of the room. She followed
him with her eyes, envied everyone to whom he spoke, and had
scarcely patience enough to help anybody to coffee.

She became enraged against herself for being silly. How
could she expect a man who had been once refused to seek her
out? How could she be foolish enough to expect a renewal of
his love? Was there one among the male sex, who would not
protest against such a weakness as a second proposal to the same
woman?

She was a little revived from her dejection when he brought
back his coffee cup. She seized the opportunity by saying, "Is
your sister at Pemberley still?"

"Yes, she will remain there till Christmas."

"And quite alone? Have all her friends left her?"

"Mrs. Annesley is with her. The others have been gone on
to Scarborough, these three weeks."

She could think of nothing more to say. If he wished to converse with her, he might have better success, but he stood by her for some minutes in silence. Then, on Kitty's whispering to Elizabeth again, he walked away.

Mrs. Bennet had designed to keep the two Netherfield gentlemen for supper, but their carriage was unluckily ordered before any of the others, and she had no opportunity of detaining them.

"Well girls," said she, as soon as they were left to themselves, "What say you to the day? I think everything has passed off uncommonly well. The dinner was as well dressed as any I ever saw. The venison was roasted to a turn—and everybody said they never saw so fat a haunch. The soup was fifty times better than what we had at the Lucases' last week. Even Mr. Darcy acknowledged that the partridges were remarkably well done, and I suppose he has two or three French cooks at least. And, my dear Jane, I never saw you look in greater beauty. Mrs. Long said so too, for I asked her whether she agreed with me."

Mrs. Bennet was in very great spirits. She had seen enough of Bingley's behavior towards Jane to be convinced that she would get him at last, and her expectations of advantage to her family were so far beyond reason, that she was disappointed at not seeing him there again the next day to make his proposals.

"It has been a very agreeable day," said Jane to Elizabeth. "The party seemed well selected, so suitable one with the other. I hope we may often meet again."

Elizabeth smiled.

"Lizzy, you must not do so. You must not suspect me. I assure you that I have now learned to enjoy his conversation as an agreeable and sensible young man, without having a wish beyond it. I am perfectly satisfied, from what his manners now are, that he never had any design of engaging my affection. It is only that he is blessed with greater sweetness of address, and a stronger desire of generally pleasing, than any other man."

"You are very cruel," said her sister, "you will not let me smile, and are provoking me to it every moment."

"How hard it is in some cases to be believed!"

"And how impossible in others!"

"But why should you wish to persuade me that I feel more than I acknowledge?"

"That is a question which I hardly know how to answer. We all love to instruct, though we can teach only what is not worth knowing. Forgive me, and if you persist in indifference, do not make me your confidante."

CHAPTER FORTY-SEVEN

a FEW DAYS AFTER THIS VISIT, Mr. Bingley called again, and alone. His friend had left him that morning for London, but was to return home in ten days' time. He sat with them above an hour, and was in remarkably good spirits. Mrs. Bennet invited him to dine with them, but with many expressions of concern he confessed himself engaged elsewhere.

"Next time you call," said she, "I hope we shall be more lucky."

"I should be particularly happy at any time, and if you would give me leave, I will take an early opportunity of accepting your offer."

"Can you come tomorrow?"

"Yes," Mr. Bingley agreed. "I have no engagement at all for tomorrow. I would be delighted."

When he arrived the following day, the ladies were not dressed. Mrs. Bennet ran into her daughter's room in her dressing gown, and with her hair half finished, cried out, "My dear Jane, make haste. He is come—Mr. Bingley is come. Make haste, make haste. Here, Sarah, come to Miss Bennet this moment, and help her on with her gown. Never mind Miss Lizzy's hair."

"We will be down as soon as we can," said Jane, "but I daresay Kitty is forwarder than either of us, for she went up stairs half-an-hour ago."

"Oh, hang Kitty! What has she to do with it? Come be quick, be quick! Where is your sash, my dear?"

But when her mother was gone, Jane would not be prevailed on to go down without one of her sisters.

The same anxiety to get them by themselves was visible again in the evening. After tea, Mr. Bennet retired to the library, as was his custom, and Mary went up stairs to her instrument. Two obstacles of the five being thus removed, Mrs. Bennet sat looking and winking at Elizabeth and Catherine for a considerable time, without making any impression on them. Elizabeth would not observe her. When at last Kitty did, she very innocently said, "What is the matter mamma? What do you keep winking at me for? What am I to do?"

"Nothing child, nothing. I did not wink at you." She then sat still five minutes longer; but unable to waste such a precious occasion, she suddenly got up, and said to Kitty, "Come here, my love, I want to speak to you," and took her out of the room. Jane instantly gave a look at Elizabeth which spoke her distress at such premeditation, and her entreaty that she would not give in to it. In a few minutes, Mrs. Bennet half-opened the door and called out, "Lizzy, my dear, I want to speak with you."

Elizabeth was forced to go.

"We may as well leave them by themselves you know," said her mother, as soon as she was in the hall. "Kitty and I are going upstairs to sit in my dressing room."

Elizabeth made no attempt to reason with her mother, but remained quietly in the hall, till she and Kitty were out of sight, then returned into the drawing room.

Mrs. Bennet's schemes for this day were ineffectual. Bingley was everything that was charming, except the professed lover of her daughter. His ease and cheerfulness rendered him a most agreeable addition to their evening party, and he bore with the ill-judged officiousness of the mother, and heard all her silly remarks with a forbearance and command of countenance particularly grateful to the daughter.

He scarcely needed an invitation to stay for supper. Before he went away, an engagement was formed, chiefly through his own and Mrs. Bennet's means, for his coming next morning to shoot with her husband.

After this day, Jane said no more of her indifference. Not a word passed between the sisters concerning Bingley, but Elizabeth went to bed in the happy belief that all must speedily be concluded, unless Mr. Darcy returned within the stated time. Seriously, however, she felt tolerably persuaded that all this must have taken place with that gentleman's concurrence.

Bingley was punctual to his appointment, and he and Mr. Bennet spent the morning together as had been agreed on. The latter was much more agreeable than his companion expected. There was nothing of presumption or folly in Bingley that could provoke his ridicule, or disgust him into silence. Mr. Bennet was more communicative, and less eccentric, than the other had ever seen him. Bingley of course returned with him to dinner, and in the evening Mrs. Bennet's invention was again at work to get everybody away from him and her daughter. Elizabeth, who had a letter to write, went into the breakfast room for that purpose soon after tea, for as the others were all going to sit down to cards, she could not be wanted to counteract her mother's schemes.

With her dear sister gone to write a letter, and the others of the house banished by the schemes of her mother, Jane found herself alone with Mr. Bingley. When he was not around, she tried to tell herself she was happy with their friendship. But, whenever she was in his presence, her heart would beat and her world would become a dizzying spin that only settled when she looked upon his face.

As he stood from the couch, he did not move for a long time. He alternated between gazing into her eyes with his mouth half-open in silenced speech, and staring at the floor as if trying to reclaim the words that had fallen out unspoken. She wondered at his manner, but was patient enough to give him time, for she could not imagine what was putting such a charming man so out of sorts.

When he did not quickly speak, she ventured to say, "It is good the weather stayed warm for your sport this morn—"

"Marry me," Bingley blurted. Jane instantly stood. Her face must have been very pale in her surprise for he instantly stepped back from her and began to apologize. "Forgive me, Miss Bennet, that was not well said at all. I find each time when I try to get the nerve to ask you, I cannot think in a logical way."

"You," she managed breathlessly, but no more followed.

"I had prepared a speech," he said more to himself than her. Then, looking at her in earnest, he asked, "Should you like to hear it?"

Jane smiled, nodding eagerly. Her heart fluttered in her chest as she stepped closer to him. He was near the hearth, outlined by the orange light of fire.

He opened his mouth, and then laughed, the same happy sound that had first stirred her heart towards him. "I look at you and I cannot remember. However, I will promise you that if you have me, I will endeavor to remember every complement I wished to pay you and will write it down so I may read it to you later."

She smiled. "I would like to hear it read."

Then, giving a nervous laugh, he glanced around the room and took a knee. Jane looked down at his face, hardly able to believe he was looking up at her. She trembled violently as he reached to take her hand in his. "First, I must again beg your forgiveness. This event is not going as I have wished it to in my head. However, if you can see fit to forgive me, and will have me as your husband, I will endeavor to say all the right things in the future, though I can hardly promise to do as much as you will often fluster me with just one of your smiles. You see, my dear Miss Bennet, I am—I have been since the very first moment I saw you—deeply in love with you. I want to spend the rest of my life making you smile at me. I was incomprehensibly foolish to have left you before, but I cannot stand to lose you again. I love you. I love you and I am asking that you marry me."

It was not the most perfect of speeches, but there was something to his rush of eager words that captured Jane's heart and she did not notice a single flaw in its delivery. Happily, she nodded her head, whispering a faint, "Yes, yes."

Bingley grinned, surging to his feet. She naturally drew closer to him, and his hands went effortlessly to her waist, drawing her closer still. His lips met hers and she gasped at that first intimate contact to pass between them. At first, they did not move, but slowly, as she learned the feel of a man's kiss, she let the sensations of it overtake her. Just as they began to move their lips, the sound of the door latch opening pried them quickly apart. Stunned, Jane automatically smoothed her skirts along her waist, though they were not wrinkled. Bingley laughed nervously, but took a step back, unable to hide his happy grin.

Elizabeth, having finished her letter, returned to the drawing room, and saw, to her infinite surprise, there was reason to fear that her mother had been too ingenious in her plans to leave Jane and Mr. Bingley alone. On opening the door, she perceived her sister and Bingley standing together over the hearth, as if engaged in earnest conversation. This led to no suspicion for, as they hastily turned round and moved away from each other to sit down, the faces of both told it all. Their situation was awkward enough, but Elizabeth thought hers was still worse. Not a syllable was uttered by either. Elizabeth was on the point of going away again, when Bingley suddenly rose and, whispering a few words to her sister, ran out of the room.

Jane could have no reserves from Elizabeth, where confidence would give pleasure. Instantly embracing her sister, Jane acknowledged, with the liveliest emotion, "I am the happiest creature in the world. Bingley has asked and I have accepted. I wish I could remember every line of what he said, but it was very prettily done and—'tis by far too much! I cannot deserve it. Oh, why is everybody not as happy?"

Elizabeth's congratulations were given with a sincerity, a warmth, a delight, which words could but poorly express. Every sentence of kindness was a fresh source of happiness to Jane. But she would not allow herself to stay with her sister, or say half that remained to be said for the present.

"I must go instantly to my mother," Jane declared. "I would not on any account trifle with her affectionate solicitude, or allow her to hear it from anyone but myself. He is gone to my father already. Oh, Lizzy, to know that what I have to relate will give such pleasure to all my dear family. How shall I bear so much happiness?"

She then hastened away to her mother, who had purposely

broken up the card party, and was sitting up stairs with Kitty.

Elizabeth, who was left by herself, now smiled at the rapidity and ease with which the affair was finally settled, especially since it had given them so many previous months of suspense and vexation.

"And this," said she, "is the end of all his friend's anxious circumspection, of all his sister's falsehood and contrivance. This, the happiest, wisest, most reasonable end!"

In a few minutes she was joined by Bingley, whose conference with her father had been short and to the purpose.

"Where is your sister?" said he hastily, as he opened the door.

"With my mother up stairs. She will be down in a moment."

He then shut the door, and, coming up to her, claimed the good wishes and affection of a sister. Elizabeth honestly and heartily expressed her delight in the prospect of their relationship. They shook hands with great cordiality. Then, till her sister came down, she listened to all he had to say of his own happiness, and of Jane's perfections. In spite of his being so deeply in love, Elizabeth really believed all his expectations of felicity to be rationally founded, because they had for basis the excellent understanding, and super-excellent disposition of Jane, and a general similarity of feeling and taste between her sister and himself.

It was an evening of no common delight to them all. The satisfaction of Jane's mind gave a glow of such sweet animation to her face, as made her look handsomer than ever. Kitty simpered and smiled, and hoped her turn was coming soon. Mrs. Bennet could not give her consent or speak her approbation in terms warm enough to satisfy her feelings, though she talked to Bingley of nothing else for half-an-hour. Mr. Bennet joined them at supper, his voice and manner plainly showed how really happy he was.

Not a word, however, passed his lips in allusion to it, till their visitor took his leave for the night. As soon as he was gone, he turned to his daughter, and said, "Jane, I congratulate you. You will be a very happy woman."

Jane went to him instantly, kissed him, and thanked him for his goodness.

"You are a good girl," he replied, "and I have great pleasure in thinking you will be so happily settled. I have not a doubt of your doing very well together. Your tempers are by no means unlike. You are each of you so complying, that nothing will ever be resolved on; so easy, that every servant will cheat you; and so generous, that you will always exceed your income."

Jane could but smile.

"Exceed their income! My dear Mr. Bennet," cried his wife, "what are you talking of? Why, he has four or five thousand a year, and very likely more." Then addressing her daughter, "Oh, my dear, dear Jane, I am so happy! I am sure I shan't get a wink of sleep all night. I knew how it would be. I always said it must be so. I was sure you could not be so beautiful for nothing! I remember, as soon as ever I saw him, when he first came into Hertfordshire last year, I thought how likely it was that you should come together. Oh, he is the handsomest young man that ever was seen!"

Wickham and Lydia were forgotten. Jane was beyond competition her favorite child. At that moment, she cared for no other. Her younger sisters soon began to make interest with her for objects of happiness which she might in future be able to dispense. Mary petitioned for the use of the library at Netherfield, and Kitty begged very hard for a few balls there every winter.

Bingley, from this time, was of course a daily visitor at Longbourn; coming frequently before breakfast, and always remaining till after supper; unless some barbarous, detestable neighbor had given him an invitation which he thought himself obliged to accept.

Elizabeth had little time for conversation with her sister for, while he was present, Jane had no attention to bestow on anyone else. However, she found herself considerably useful to both of them in those hours of separation that must sometimes occur. In the absence of Jane, he always attached himself to Elizabeth, for the pleasure of talking of her; and when Bingley was gone, Jane constantly sought the same means of relief.

"He has made me so happy," said she, one evening, "by telling me that he was totally ignorant of my being in town last spring. I had not believed it possible."

"I suspected as much," replied Elizabeth. "But how did he account for it?"

"It must have been his sister's doing. They were certainly no friends to his acquaintance with me, which I cannot wonder at, since he might have chosen so much more advantageously in many respects. But when they see, as I trust they will, that their brother is happy with me, they will learn to be contented, and we shall be on good terms again. Though we can never be what we once were to each other."

"That is the most unforgiving speech I ever heard you utter," said Elizabeth. "Good girl! It would vex me, indeed, to see you again the dupe of Miss Bingley's pretended regard."

"Would you believe it, Lizzy, when he went to town last November, he really loved me? Nothing but a persuasion of my being indifferent would have prevented his coming down again!"

"He made a little mistake to be sure, but it is to the credit of his modesty."

This naturally introduced a panegyric from Jane on his diffidence, and the little value he put on his own good qualities. Elizabeth was pleased to find that he had not betrayed the

interference of his friend; for, though Jane had the most generous and forgiving heart in the world, she knew it was a circumstance which must prejudice her against Mr. Darcy.

"I am certainly the most fortunate creature that ever
existed!" exclaimed Jane. "Oh, Lizzy, why am I thus singled from
my family, and blessed above them all? If I could but see you as
happy! If there were but such another man for you!"

"If you were to give me forty such men, I never could be so
happy as you. Till I have your disposition, your goodness, I never
can have your happiness. Perhaps, if I have very good luck, I may
meet with another Mr. Collins."

**Jane's laughter joined Elizabeth's and neither one of them
could speak for many minutes.**

**The situation of affairs in the Longbourn family could not
be kept secret for long. Mrs. Bennet was privileged to whisper it to
Mrs. Philips, and she ventured, without any permission, to do the
same by all her neighbors in Meryton. The Bennets were speedily
pronounced to be the luckiest family in the world, though only a
few weeks before, when Lydia had first run away, they had been
generally proved to be marked out for misfortune.**

CHAPTER FORTY-EIGHT

ONE MORNING, about a week after Bingley's engagement with Jane had been formed, as he and the females of the family were sitting together in the dining room, their attention was suddenly drawn to the window by the sound of a carriage. They perceived a chaise and four driving up the lawn. It was too early in the morning for visitors, and besides, the equipage did not answer to that of any of their neighbors. The horses were post, and neither the carriage nor the livery of the servant who preceded it were familiar to them. As it was certain that somebody was coming, Bingley instantly prevailed on Miss Bennet to avoid the confinement of such an intrusion, and walk away with him into the shrubbery. They both set off, and the conjectures of the remaining three continued, though with little satisfaction, till the door was thrown open and their visitor entered. It was Lady Catherine de Bourgh.

They were of course all intending to be surprised, but their astonishment was beyond their expectation; and on the part of Mrs. Bennet and Kitty, though she was perfectly unknown to them, even inferior to what Elizabeth felt.

She entered the room with an air more than usually ungracious, made no other reply to Elizabeth's salutation than a slight inclination of the head, and sat down without saying a word. Elizabeth had mentioned her name to her mother on her ladyship's entrance, though no request of introduction had been made.

Mrs. Bennet, all amazement, though flattered by having a guest of such high importance, received her with the utmost politeness. After sitting for a moment in silence, Lady Catherine said very stiffly to Elizabeth, "I hope you are well, Miss Bennet. That lady, I suppose, is your mother."

"She is, my lady," Elizabeth replied very concisely.

"And *that* I suppose is one of your sisters."

"Yes, madam," said Mrs. Bennet, delighted to speak to Lady Catherine. "She is my youngest girl but one. My youngest of all is lately married, and my eldest is somewhere about the grounds, walking with a young man who, I believe, will soon become a part of the family."

"You have a very small park here," returned Lady Catherine after a short silence.

"It is nothing in comparison of Rosings, my lady, I daresay," answered Mrs. Bennet, "but I assure you it is much larger than Sir William Lucas's."

"This must be a most inconvenient sitting room for the evening, in summer. The windows are full west."

Mrs. Bennet assured her that they never sat there after dinner, and then added, "May I take the liberty of asking your ladyship whether you left Mr. and Mrs. Collins well."

"Yes, very well. I saw them the night before last."

Elizabeth now expected that she would produce a letter for her from Charlotte, as it seemed the only probable motive for her calling. But no letter appeared, and she was completely puzzled.

Mrs. Bennet, with great civility, begged her ladyship to take some refreshment. Lady Catherine very resolutely, and not very politely, declined eating anything. Then, rising up, said to Elizabeth, "Miss Bennet, there seemed to be a prettyish kind of a little wilderness on one side of your lawn. I should be glad to take a turn in it, if you will favor me with your company."

"Go, my dear," urged her mother, "and show her ladyship about the different walks. I think she will be pleased with the hermitage."

Elizabeth obeyed, and hurrying into her own room for a parasol, attended her noble guest downstairs. As they passed through the hall, Lady Catherine opened the doors into the dining parlor and drawing room, and after a short survey pronounced them to be decent looking rooms, and walked on.

Her carriage remained at the door, and Elizabeth saw that her waiting woman was in it. They proceeded in silence along the gravel walk that led to the copse. Elizabeth was determined to make no effort for conversation with a woman who was now more than usually insolent and disagreeable.

"How could I ever think her like her nephew?" thought she, as she looked in the woman's face.

As soon as they entered the copse, Lady Catherine began in the following manner, "You can be at no loss, Miss Bennet, to understand the reason of my journey hither. Your own heart, your own conscience, must tell you why I come."

Elizabeth looked with unaffected astonishment. "Indeed, you are mistaken, madam. I have not been at all able to account for the honor of seeing you here."

"Miss Bennet," replied her ladyship, in an angry tone, "you ought to know that I am not to be trifled with. But however insincere you may choose to be, you shall not find me so. My character has ever been celebrated for its sincerity and frankness, and in a cause of such moment as this, I shall certainly not depart from it. A report of a most alarming nature reached me two days ago. I was told that not only your sister was on the point of being most advantageously married, but that you, that Miss Elizabeth Bennet, would, in all likelihood, be soon afterwards united to my nephew, Mr. Darcy. Though I *know* it must be a scandalous falsehood, though I would not injure him so much as to suppose the truth of it possible, I instantly resolved on setting off for this place so that I might make my sentiments known to you."

"If you believed it impossible," said Elizabeth, coloring with astonishment and disdain, "I wonder you took the trouble of coming so far. What could your ladyship propose by it?"

"At once to insist upon having such a report universally contradicted."

"Your coming to Longbourn, to see me and my family," said Elizabeth coolly, "will be rather a confirmation of it—if, indeed, such a report is in existence."

"If! Do you then pretend to be ignorant of it? Has it not been industriously circulated by yourselves? Do you not know that such a report is spread abroad?"

"I never heard that it was."

"And can you likewise declare that there is no foundation for it?"

"I do not pretend to possess equal frankness with your ladyship. You may ask questions which I shall choose not to answer."

Lady Catherine looked to be near the point of stamping her feet upon the ground like a petulant child. Her entire body stiffened with her irritation. "This is not to be borne. Miss Bennet,

I insist on being satisfied. Has my nephew made you an offer of marriage?"

"Your ladyship has declared it to be impossible." **Elizabeth endeavored to keep an even tone, though she knew she was being somewhat insolent. How could she not? Such an unwelcome attack on a subject so freshly wounding to her heart!**

"It ought to be so—must be so, while he retains the use of his reason. But your arts and allurements may, in a moment of infatuation, have made him forget what he owes to himself and to all his family. You may have drawn him in."

"If I have, I shall be the last person to confess it."

This was not the humble, apologetic answer the lady had been seeking. With each breath her anger became more apparent. "Miss Bennet, do you know who I am? I have not been accustomed to such language as this. I am almost the nearest relation he has in the world, and am entitled to know all his dearest concerns."

"But you are not entitled to know mine, nor will such behavior as this, ever induce me to be explicit."

"Let me be rightly understood. This match, to which you have the presumption to aspire, can never take place. Mr. Darcy is engaged to my daughter. Now what have you to say?"

"Only this. That, if he is so engaged, you can have no reason to suppose he will make an offer to me."

Lady Catherine hesitated for a moment. "The engagement between them is of a peculiar kind. From their infancy, they have been intended for each other. It was the favorite wish of his mother, as well as myself. While in their cradles, we planned the union. Now, at the moment when the wishes of both sisters would be accomplished in their marriage, to be prevented by a young woman of inferior birth, of no importance in the world, and wholly unallied to the family! Do you pay no regard to the wishes of his friends? To his tacit engagement with Miss de Bourgh? Are you lost to every feeling of propriety and delicacy? Have you not heard me say that from his earliest hours he was destined for his cousin?"

"Yes, and I had heard it before. But what is that to me? If there is no other objection to my marrying your nephew, I shall certainly not be kept from it by knowing that his mother and aunt wished him to marry Miss de Bourgh. You both did as much as you could in planning the marriage. Its completion depended on others. If Mr. Darcy is neither by honor nor inclination confined to his cousin, why is not he to make another choice? And if I am that choice, why may not I accept him?" **She did not mean to say so much, as the event of her marriage to Mr. Darcy may never, in fact, take place, but she had hope. It was a small hope that was sparked to life by the anger radiating from his aunt. Her outrage gave Elizabeth an optimism she had never allowed herself to feel. Not to mention her ladyship's rudeness and presumption in arriving at all caused a defense to build behind each of Elizabeth's words.**

"Because honor, decorum, prudence, nay, interest, forbid it. Yes, Miss Bennet, interest! Do not expect to be noticed by his family or friends, if you willfully act against the inclinations of all. You will be censured, slighted, and despised, by everyone connected with him. Your alliance will be a disgrace. Your name will never even be mentioned by any of us."

"These are heavy misfortunes," replied Elizabeth with just a touch of sarcasm. "But the wife of Mr. Darcy must have such extraordinary sources of happiness necessarily attached to her situation that she could, upon the whole, have no cause to repine."

"Obstinate, headstrong girl! I am ashamed of you! Is this your gratitude for my attentions to you last spring? Is nothing due to me on that score? Let us sit down. You are to understand, Miss Bennet that I came here with the determined resolution of carrying my purpose. I will not be dissuaded from it. I have not been used to submit to any person's whims. I have not been in the habit of brooking disappointment."

"That will make your ladyship's situation at present more pitiable, but it will have no effect on me."

"I will not be interrupted. Hear me in silence. My daughter and my nephew are formed for each other. They are descended, on the maternal side, from the same noble line; and, on the father's, from respectable, honorable, and ancient—though untitled—families. Their fortune on both sides is splendid. They are destined for each other by the voice of every member of their respective houses. And what is to divide them? The upstart pretensions of a young woman without family, connections, or fortune? Is this to be endured? It must not, shall not be. If you were sensible of your own good, you would not wish to quit the sphere in which you have been brought up."

"In marrying your nephew, I should not consider myself as quitting that sphere. He is a gentleman. I am a gentleman's daughter. So far we are equal."

"True. You are a gentleman's daughter. But who was your mother? Who are your uncles and aunts? Do not imagine me ignorant of their condition."

"Whatever my connections may be," said Elizabeth, "if your nephew does not object to them, they can be nothing to you."

"Tell me once for all, are you engaged to him?"

Though Elizabeth would not, for the mere purpose of obliging Lady Catherine, have answered this question, she could not but say, after a moment's deliberation, "I am not."

Lady Catherine seemed pleased. "And will you promise me never to enter into such an engagement?"

"I will make no promise of the kind."

"Miss Bennet I am shocked and astonished. I expected to find a more reasonable young woman. But do not deceive yourself into a belief that I will ever recede. I shall not go away till you have given me the assurance I require."

"And I certainly never shall give it." **This was more than a person should have to bear. Elizabeth stood, intent on ending forever the distasteful and rude conversation. If her ladyship chose to stay on the bench to await an answer that was not forthcoming, so be it. She would make a miserable fixture to the family property and a curiosity for the neighbors to gawk at.** "I am not to be intimidated into anything so wholly unreasonable. Your ladyship wants Mr. Darcy to marry your daughter, but would my giving you the wished-for promise make their marriage at all more probable? Supposing him to be attached to me, would my refusing to accept his hand make him wish to bestow it on his cousin? Allow me to say, Lady Catherine, that the arguments with which you have supported this extraordinary application have been as frivolous as the application was ill-judged. You have widely mistaken my character, if you think I can be worked on by such persuasions as these. How far your nephew might approve of your interference in his affairs, I cannot tell, but you have certainly no right to concern yourself in mine. I must beg, therefore, to be importuned no farther on the subject."

When Elizabeth would give a small bow of her head in preparation to leave, Lady Catherine ordered, "Not so hasty, if you please. I have by no means done. To all the objections I have already urged, I have still another to add. I am no stranger to the particulars of your youngest sister's infamous elopement. I know it all. That young man's marrying her was a patched-up business, at the expense of your father and uncles. And is such a girl to be my nephew's sister? Is her husband, is the son of his late father's steward, to be his brother? Heaven and earth, of what are you thinking? Are the shades of Pemberley to be thus polluted?"

"You can now have nothing further to say to me," she resentfully answered. "You have insulted me by every possible means. I will now return to the house."

Lady Catherine rose as Elizabeth turned to leave and followed her back. Her ladyship was highly incensed, and would not quit the conversation. "You have no regard, then, for the honor and credit of my nephew. Unfeeling, selfish girl! Do you not consider that a connection with you must disgrace him in the eyes of everybody?"

"Lady Catherine, I have nothing further to say. You know my sentiments." **Elizabeth quickened her pace and had some satisfaction in seeing her ladyship's effort to keep up.**

"You are then resolved to have him?"

"I have said no such thing. I am only resolved to act in that manner, which will, in my own opinion, constitute my happiness, without reference to you or to any person so wholly unconnected with me."

"It is well. You refuse, then, to oblige me. You refuse to obey the claims of duty, honor, and gratitude. You are determined to ruin him in the opinion of all his friends, and make him the contempt of the world."

"Neither duty, nor honor, nor gratitude," replied Elizabeth, "have any possible claim on me, in the present instance. No principle of either would be violated by my marriage with Mr. Darcy. And with regard to the resentment of his family, or the indignation of the world, if the former were excited by his marrying me, it would not give me one moment's concern—and the world in general would have too much sense to join in the scorn."

"And this is your real opinion? This is your final resolve?

Very well. I shall now know how to act. Do not imagine, Miss
Bennet, that your ambition will ever be gratified. I came to try
you. I hoped to find you reasonable, but depend upon it, I will
carry my point." In this manner Lady Catherine talked on, till
they were at the door of the carriage, when, turning hastily
round, she added, "I take no leave of you, Miss Bennet. I send
no compliments to your mother. You deserve no such attention.
I am most seriously displeased."

Elizabeth made no answer. Without attempting to persuade her ladyship to return into the house, she walked quietly
into it herself. She heard the carriage drive away as she ran up
stairs. Her mother impatiently met her at the door of the dressing room to ask why Lady Catherine would not come in again
and rest herself.

"She did not choose it," said her daughter, "she would go."

"She is a very fine-looking woman. Her calling here was
prodigiously civil for she only came, I suppose, to tell us the
Collinses were well. She is on her road somewhere, I daresay,
and so, passing through Meryton, thought she might as well
call on you. I suppose she had nothing particular to say to you,
Lizzy?"

Elizabeth was forced to give in to a little falsehood here for
to acknowledge the substance of their conversation was impossible. **Whatever she mumbled must have been sufficient, though
she hardly knew what came out of her own mouth. She wanted
nothing more than to escape to the privacy of her room. Once
there, she threw her parasol and bit her lip in an effort to keep
from crying out. Every muscle in her body was tense and she had
never felt the urge to hit someone so much in her life.**

**"How dare she accost me thus!" She whispered to herself,
pacing the length of the room. "To insult my family, myself and
threaten me with every tool within her power!" Then, suddenly,**

she stopped as she thought of the subject of meeting. Mr. Darcy.
How did the rumors come to be spread of them? Had someone
observed a moment passing between them? For Elizabeth had
told no one of her feelings. Only Jane knew of the proposal, and
a more secure vault than Jane's discretion did not exist. Had Mr.
Darcy himself spoke of it? With his naturally secretive nature, it
did not seem likely, and in knowing him she knew that she had no
reason to hope that the rumors Lady Catherine had heard were
circulated by a creditably informed source. Undoubtedly, it was
Mr. Collins who heard such a thing, and had run to Rosings to
instantly tell Lady Catherine the news, for he could hardly see a
bird fly overhead without feeling the need to describe the event
to her ladyship.

"Detestable cousin," she muttered, thinking of Mr. Collins.
"Poor Charlotte, I wonder if you now regret your hasty decision
to marry so poor a choice."

Then, remembering each word of Lady Catherine's speech,
she began to pace anew and did not think to stop for quite some
time.

CHAPTER FORTY-NINE

THE DISCOMPOSURE OF SPIRITS which this extraordinary visit threw Elizabeth into could not be easily overcome, nor could she for many hours learn to think of it less than incessantly. Lady Catherine had actually taken the trouble of journeying from Rosings for the sole purpose of breaking off her supposed engagement with Mr. Darcy. It was a rational scheme, to be sure, but from what the report of their engagement could originate, Elizabeth was at a loss to imagine—till she recollected that *his* being the intimate friend of Bingley, and *her* being the sister of Jane, was enough to supply the idea at a time when the expectation of one wedding made everybody eager for another. It had not escaped her hopeful mind that the marriage of her sister must bring them more frequently together. Furthermore, she concluded that her neighbors at Lucas Lodge, through their communication with the Collinses, had instigated the report that reached Lady Catherine, and had set down as almost certain and immediate, which she had looked forward to as possible at some future time.

In revolving Lady Catherine's expressions, she could not help feeling some uneasiness as to the possible consequence of her persisting in this interference. From what she had said of her resolution to prevent their marriage, it occurred to Elizabeth that she must meditate an application to her nephew. How *he* might take a similar representation of the evils attached to a connection with her, she dared not pronounce. She knew not the exact degree of his affection for his aunt, or his dependence on her judgment, but it was natural to suppose that he thought much higher of her ladyship than she could do; and it was certain that, in enumerating the miseries of a marriage with one, whose immediate connections were so unequal to his own, his aunt would address him on his weakest side. With his notions of dignity, he would probably feel that those arguments, which to Elizabeth had appeared weak and ridiculous, contained much good sense and solid reasoning.

If he had been wavering before as to what he should do, which had often seemed likely, the advice and entreaty of so near a relation might settle every doubt, and determine him at once to be as happy as unblemished dignity could make him. In that case he would return no more. Lady Catherine might see him in her way through town, and his engagement to Bingley of coming again to Netherfield must give way.

"If, therefore, an excuse for not keeping his promise should come to his friend within a few days," she added, "I shall know how to understand it. I shall then give over every expectation, every wish of his constancy. If he is satisfied with only regretting me, when he might have obtained my affections and hand, I shall soon cease to regret him at all."

The assertion was much easier said than felt. In truth, if all

hope of Mr. Darcy was taken away from her, she feared her heart may never love again and she would be miserable in her old age, either a burden on her parents and sisters or the unlucky bride to an undesirable man. The thought instantly brought Charlotte to mind and Elizabeth felt she understood her friend's motivations better than she ever had in the past. Oh, to have such a heartless fate! She never considered herself destined to a life of heartbreak and misery, yet that is what she felt must be her fate if Darcy did not come back to Netherfield and give her the smallest reason to hope.

The surprise of the rest of the family, on hearing who their visitor had been, was very great, and they obligingly satisfied it with the same kind of supposition which had appeased Mrs. Bennet's curiosity. Elizabeth was spared from much teasing on the subject.

The next morning, as she was going downstairs, she was met by her father, who came out of his library with a letter in his hand. "Lizzy, I was going to look for you. Come into my room."

She followed him back into the library. Her curiosity to know what he had to tell her was heightened by the supposition of its being in some manner connected with the letter he held. It suddenly struck her that it might be from Lady Catherine, and she anticipated with dismay all the consequent explanations.

She followed her father to the fire place, and they both sat down. He then said, "I have received a letter this morning that has astonished me exceedingly. As it principally concerns yourself, you ought to know its contents. I did not know before that I had two daughters on the brink of matrimony. Let me congratulate you on a very important conquest."

The color now rushed into Elizabeth's cheeks in the instantaneous conviction of its being a letter from the nephew, instead of the aunt. She was undetermined whether most to be pleased that he explained himself at all, or offended that his letter was not rather addressed to herself; when her father continued, "You look conscious. Young ladies have great penetration in such matters as these, but I think I may defy even your sagacity, to discover the name of your admirer. This letter is from Mr. Collins."

"From Mr. Collins! What can he have to say?"

"Something very much to the purpose of course. He begins with congratulations on the approaching nuptials of my eldest daughter, of which, it seems, he has been told by some of the good-natured, gossiping Lucases. I shall not sport with your impatience, by reading what he says on that point. What relates to yourself, is as follows, 'Having thus offered you the sincere congratulations of Mrs. Collins and myself on this happy event, let me now add a short hint on the subject of another; of which we have been advertised by the same authority. Your daughter Elizabeth, it is presumed, will not long bear the name of Bennet, after her elder sister has resigned it, and the chosen partner of her fate may be reasonably looked up to as one of the most illustrious personages in this land.' Can you possibly guess, Lizzy, who is meant by this?"

Her father looked at her expectantly. Elizabeth did not answer, merely stared with a feeling of wonder and apprehension at what might come.

At her silence, her father continued, "Listen, my dear and all will be revealed. 'This young gentleman is blessed, in a peculiar way, with everything the heart of mortal can most desire—splendid property, noble kindred, and extensive patronage. Yet in spite of all these temptations, let me warn my cousin Elizabeth, and yourself, of what evils you may incur by a precipitate closure with this gentleman's proposals, which, of course, you will be inclined to take immediate advantage of.' Have you any idea, Lizzy, who this gentleman is?"

Again she remained silent.

And he continued, "But now it comes out. 'My motive for cautioning you is as follows. We have reason to imagine that his aunt, Lady Catherine de Bourgh, does not look on the match with a friendly eye.' You see, Lizzy, Mr. Darcy is the man! I think I *have* surprised you. Could he, or the Lucases, have pitched on any man within the circle of our acquaintance, whose name would have given the lie more effectually to what they related? Mr. Darcy, who never looks at any woman but to see a blemish, and who probably never looked at you in his life! It is an admirable rumor to be sure!"

Elizabeth tried to join in her father's pleasantry, but could only force one most reluctant smile. Never had his wit been directed in a manner so little agreeable to her.

"Are you not diverted?" he inquired.

"Oh, yes. Pray read on."

"'After mentioning the likelihood of this marriage to her ladyship last night, she immediately, with her usual condescension, expressed what she felt on the occasion. When it became apparent that on the score of some family objections on the part of my cousin, she would never give her consent to what she termed so disgraceful a match. I thought it my duty to give the speediest intelligence of this to my cousin, that she and her noble admirer may be aware of what they are about, and not run hastily into a marriage which has not been properly sanctioned.' Mr. Collins moreover adds, 'I am truly rejoiced that my cousin Lydia's sad business has been so well hushed up, and am only concerned that their living together before the marriage took place should be so generally known. I must not, however, neglect the duties of my station, or refrain from declaring my amazement at hearing that you received the young couple into your house as soon as they were married. It was an encouragement of vice, and had I been the rector of Longbourn, I should very strenuously have opposed it. You ought certainly to forgive them, as a Christian, but never to admit them in your sight, or allow their names to be mentioned in your hearing.' Ha! That is his notion of Christian forgiveness. The rest of his letter is only about his dear Charlotte's situation, and his expectation of a young olive-branch. But, Lizzy, you look as if you did not enjoy it. You are not going to be *missish*, I hope, and pretend to be affronted at an idle report. For what do we live for but to make sport for our neighbors and laugh at them in our turn?"

"Oh," said Elizabeth. "I am excessively diverted. But it is so strange!"

"Yes, *that* is what makes it amusing. Had they fixed on any other man it would have been nothing. But *his* perfect indifference, and *your* pointed dislike, make it so delightfully absurd! Much as I abominate writing, I would not give up Mr. Collins's correspondence for any consideration. Nay, when I read a letter of his, I cannot help giving him the preference even over Wickham, much as I value the impudence and hypocrisy of my son-in-law. And pray, Lizzy, what said Lady Catherine about this report? Did she call to refuse her consent?"

To this question his daughter replied only with a laugh, and as it had been asked without the least suspicion, she was not distressed by his repeating it. Elizabeth had never been more at a loss to make her feelings appear what they were not. It was necessary to laugh, when she would rather have cried. Her father had most cruelly mortified her, by what he said of Mr. Darcy's indifference, and she could do nothing but wonder at such a want of penetration, or fear that perhaps, instead of his seeing too little, she might have fancied too much.

CHAPTER FIFTY

*I*NSTEAD OF RECEIVING ANY LETTER of excuse
from his friend, as Elizabeth half expected Mr. Bingley to
do, he was able to bring Darcy with him to Longbourn before
many days had passed after Lady Catherine's visit. The gentlemen arrived early. Before Mrs. Bennet had time to tell him of
their having seen his aunt, of which her daughter sat in momentary dread, Bingley, who wanted to be alone with Jane, proposed their all walking out. It was agreed to. Mrs. Bennet was
not in the habit of walking, and Mary could never spare time,
but the remaining five set off together. Bingley and Jane soon
allowed the others to outstrip them. They lagged behind, while
Elizabeth, Kitty, and Darcy were to entertain each other. Very
little was said by either. Kitty was too much afraid of him to talk.
Elizabeth was secretly forming a desperate resolution, and perhaps he might be doing the same.

They walked towards the Lucases, because Kitty wished to

call upon Maria. As Elizabeth saw no occasion for making it a general concern, when Kitty left them she went boldly on with him alone. Now was the moment for her resolution to be executed, and, while her courage was high, she immediately said, "Mr. Darcy, I am a very selfish creature. For the sake of giving relief to my own feelings, care not how much I may be wounding yours. I can no longer help thanking you for your unexampled kindness to my poor sister. Ever since I have known it, I have been most anxious to acknowledge to you how gratefully I feel it. Were it known to the rest of my family, I should not have merely my own gratitude to express."

"I am sorry, exceedingly sorry," replied Darcy, in a tone of surprise and emotion, "that you have ever been informed of what may, in a mistaken light, have given you uneasiness. I did not think Mrs. Gardiner was so little to be trusted."

"You must not blame my aunt. Lydia's thoughtlessness first betrayed to me that you had been concerned in the matter. Of course, I could not rest till I knew the particulars. Let me thank you again and again, in the name of all my family, for that generous compassion which induced you to take so much trouble, and bear so many mortifications, for the sake of discovering them."

"If you will thank me," he replied, not pausing in their walk, "let it be for yourself alone."

His words were soft, but she heard them perfectly. Her mind raced with thoughts, urging her to pay close attention to everything he said, to cherish this moment that they could be alone, to speak well and clear, and to give no hint—by accident or mistake—that she was contrary to being in his company.

He continued, not lifting his eyes to meet hers as he stared into the distance. "That the wish of giving happiness to you might add force to the other inducements which led me on, I shall not attempt to deny. But your family owes me nothing.

Much as I respect them, I believe I thought only of you."

Elizabeth could not take another step. She stopped on the worn path and watched his back before he was forced to turn and look at her. She was too much embarrassed to say a word, and too struck by the way the sunlight hit upon his face to draw a deep breath. For a moment, she was content to look into his blue eyes, letting the familiar tingle of longing and anticipation fill her body. She could look into those eyes forever and be perfectly contented. How could she have ever thought to hate him? What a silly fool she had been. Even now, she might have been his wife—with all the rights of a wife to touch her husband. Finally, she glanced away.

Darcy took a step towards her to close the small distance and, as if mustering some inner courage, said, "You are too generous to trifle with me. If your feelings are still what they were last April, tell me so at once. My affections and wishes are unchanged, but one word from you will silence me on this subject forever."

Elizabeth, feeling all the common awkwardness and anxiety of his situation, now forced herself to speak, though not very fluently, saying, "I do not wish for your silence. Since you did honor me with your proposal and corrected so many errors, which I was wont to shamefully and regretfully believe, my sentiments have undergone a drastic and material change."

His mouth opened as if he would speak, but his eyes said he hardly believed what his ears had heard. And, for all her assurances that she would have him speak, he could not give her an answer.

Elizabeth, knowing it should rightfully fall to her to express that which he had freely given to her in the past, continued, "Perhaps saying my sentiments have undergone a material change will not do." When his expression fell, she hurried on. "What I mean to say is, though my logical thoughts of you were mistaken and led my mind to choose which my heart would have otherwise done, such an explanation is not sufficient." Her hand shook as she lifted it to take his. She lifted his fingers before her, holding his hand in both of her own. "I was struck by you the first moment I saw you, but I was too proud and your manners too stubborn for me to admit to it. I fancy I was too proud to like a man with your wealth and position, just for the sake of such materialistic things, and this, along with my general misconceptions of your character, caused my stubbornness to know no bounds. You see, I always determined I would not love someone simply because they were rich or titled. I prided myself on my strength of heart and determination of fine character to not do as was expected simply because it was expected. As you went through the struggle you first described to me, I determined that I could not love you for I had very strong notions about marriage and love which those sentiments you so truthfully expressed did not fit into. So, I hid my initial feelings from you in what I determined to be practical matters."

"And am I not to take it you have changed your views?" An expression of heartfelt delight diffused over his face, tinged with hope and pleasure.

"As difficult as it may seem," she laughed lightly, "yes, I admit that I was mistaken in my views—even as such admissions go against my stubborn nature. I will speak bluntly, for I know not else how I should wish to talk to you. My parents set a very poor example as to what a marriage could be, and though it pains me to admit it, and though I dread doing so for fear it will alter your opinion of matters by mentioning such a grievous subject, I feel it must be openly said between us. Their example hindered me in ways I had not realized before meeting you. I feared ending up as they have. I will say no more, for it would only be to state the obvious to the discomfort of yourself, and the embarrassment of myself."

Darcy's head had angled down towards hers, and she naturally gravitated closer to him.

"You see, Mr. Darcy," she whispered, "what I am trying to tell you, though very longwindedly done, is that I am struck by you still. You are everything that I never knew to want in a man, and the greatest pain of my life has been thinking that I threw it all away on foolishness and pride." Her eyes held his. "I love you, sir, more than I have ever loved anything. It is with gratitude and pleasure that I have heard your present assurances, for my feelings for you are now openly acknowledged if not so much changed. However, to be fair, one word from you will silence me on this subject forever."

His smile was fast in coming and she was sure she had never seen such a happy look upon his face. Elizabeth was not mindful of where they were, or who might see. Instinctively, she tugged his hands towards herself and lifted up on her toes. Their lips met and it was like nothing her imaginings of such a moment might produce. The warm, silky texture of his mouth greeted hers and she sighed against him.

The happiness which this reply produced was unlike anything Darcy had felt before. That he was madly and violently in love with Elizabeth he had no doubt. **He had carried her in his heart for many months now, and to hear her own struggle in coming to admit a love for him only strengthened his resolve to make her his wife. Every happiness he could imagine contained at its center his dear Elizabeth and he would not let her slip from him again. Her soft lips offered themselves to him so easily and surely. He felt her love in that kiss, the openness in which she gave herself to him. His body stirred and he had to pull away before he disgraced both of them with his passion.**

Taking her face in his hands, he smiled at her. "I cannot

express how happy you have made me. I have longed to hear you say half as much to me and never dared to hope there could be more. I have understood for some time that every happiness I might have in life is tied to you."

Elizabeth listened joyously as he continued to tell her of his feelings, which, in proving of what importance she was to him, made his affection every moment more valuable. She soon learned that they were indebted for their present good understanding to the efforts of his aunt, who did call on him in her return through London, and there relate her journey to Longbourn, its motive, and the substance of her conversation with Elizabeth. Believing such a relation must assist her endeavors to obtain a promise from her nephew which Elizabeth had refused to give, Lady Catherine dwelled emphatically on every expression of the young lady which, in her ladyship's apprehension, peculiarly denoted her perverseness and assurance. But, unluckily for her ladyship, its effect had been exactly contrariwise.

"It taught me to hope," said he, stroking her cheek, "as I had scarcely ever allowed myself to hope before. I knew enough of your disposition to be certain that, had you been absolutely, irrevocably decided against me, you would have acknowledged it to Lady Catherine, frankly and openly."

Elizabeth colored and laughed, as she replied, "Yes, you know enough of my frankness to believe me capable of *that*." They walked on, without knowing in what direction. There was too much to be thought, and felt, and said, for attention to any other objects. "After abusing you so abominably to your face, I could have no scruple in abusing you to all your relations."

"What did you say of me that I did not deserve? For, though your accusations were ill-founded, formed on mistaken premises, my behavior to you at the time had merited the severest reproof. It was unpardonable. I cannot think of it without abhorrence."

"We will not quarrel for the greater share of blame annexed to that evening," said Elizabeth, affectionately taking his arm. "The conduct of neither, if strictly examined, will be irreproachable. But such being the case, we have both, I hope, improved in civility."

"I cannot be so easily reconciled to myself. The recollection of what I then said, of my conduct, my manners, my expressions during the whole of it, is now, and has been many months, inexpressibly painful to me. Your reproof, so well applied, I shall never forget. 'Had you behaved in a more gentlemanlike manner.' Those were your words. You know not, you can scarcely conceive, how they have tortured me. Though, I confess, it was some time before I was reasonable enough to allow their justice."

"I was certainly very far from expecting them to make so strong an impression. I had not the smallest idea of their being ever felt in such a way."

"I can easily believe it. You thought me then devoid of every proper feeling, I am sure you did. The turn of your countenance I shall never forget, as you said that I could not have addressed you in any possible way that would induce you to accept me."

"Oh, do not repeat what I said. These recollections will not do at all. I assure you that I have long been most heartily ashamed of it."

Darcy slid his hand over hers, holding it to his arm. "And what of the letter I wrote you? Did it soon make you think better of me? Did you, on reading it, give any credit to its contents?"

She explained what its effect on her had been, and how gradually all her former prejudices had been removed.

"I knew what I wrote must give you pain, but it was necessary," he said. "I hope you have destroyed the letter. There was one part especially, the opening of it, which I should dread your having the power of reading again. I can remember some expressions which might justly make you hate me."

"The letter shall certainly be burned, if you believe it essential to the preservation of my regard, but, though we have both reason to think my opinions not entirely unalterable, they are not, I hope, quite so easily changed as that implies."

"When I wrote that letter," replied Darcy, "I believed myself perfectly calm and cool, but I am since convinced that it was written in a dreadful bitterness of spirit."

"The letter, perhaps, began in bitterness, but it did not end so. The adieu is charity itself. But think no more of the letter. The feelings of the person who wrote, and the person who received it, are now so widely different from what they were then, that every unpleasant circumstance attending it ought to be forgotten. You must learn some of my philosophy. Think only of the past as its remembrance gives you pleasure."

"I cannot give you credit for any philosophy of the kind. Your retrospections must be so totally void of reproach, that the contentment arising from them is not of philosophy, but, what is much better, of innocence. But with me, it is not so. Painful recollections will intrude which cannot, which ought not, to be repelled. I have been a selfish being all my life, in practice, though not in principle. As a child I was taught what was right, but I was not taught to correct my temper. I was given good principles, but left to follow them in pride and conceit. Unfortunately an only son and for many years an only child, I was spoiled by my parents, who, though good themselves—my father, particularly, all that was benevolent and amiable—allowed, encouraged, almost taught me to be selfish and overbearing; to care for none beyond my own family circle; to think meanly of all the rest of the world; to wish at least to think meanly of their sense and worth compared with my own. Such I was, from eight to eight and twenty;

and such I might still have been but for you, dearest, loveliest Elizabeth. What I owe you! You taught me a lesson, hard indeed at first, but most advantageous. By you, I was properly humbled. I came to you without a doubt of my reception. You showed me how insufficient were all my pretensions to please a woman worthy of being pleased."

"Had you then persuaded yourself that I should?"

"Indeed I had. What will you think of my vanity? I believed you to be wishing, expecting my addresses."

"My manners must have been in fault, but not intentionally, I assure you. I never meant to deceive you, but my spirits might often lead me wrong. How you must have hated me after *that* evening?"

"Hate you! I was angry perhaps at first, but my anger soon began to take a proper direction."

"I am almost afraid of asking what you thought of me, when we met at Pemberley. You thought it very wrong of me in coming?"

"No indeed. I felt nothing but surprise."

"Your surprise could not be greater than mine in being noticed by you. My conscience told me that I deserved no extraordinary politeness, and I confess that I did not expect to receive more than my due."

"My object then," replied Darcy, "was to show you, by every civility in my power, that I was not so mean as to resent the past. I hoped to obtain your forgiveness, to lessen your ill opinion, by letting you see that your reproofs had been attended to. How soon any other wishes introduced themselves I can hardly tell, but I believe in about half-an-hour after I had seen you."

He then told her of Georgiana's delight in her acquaintance, and of her disappointment at its sudden interruption; which naturally leading to the cause of that interruption, she soon learned that his resolution of following her from Derbyshire in quest of her sister had been formed before he quitted the inn, and that his gravity and thoughtfulness there had arisen from no other struggles than what such a purpose must comprehend.

She expressed her gratitude again, but it was too painful a subject to each, to be dwelt on farther. **Besides, there was no more reason to speak of it. Each understood the other perfectly on the matter and it was forever settled.**

After walking several miles in a leisurely manner, and too busy to know anything about it, they found at last, on examining their watches, that it was time to be at home.

"What has become of Mr. Bingley and Jane?" **Elizabeth asked, realizing it had been quite some time before she bothered to look back to see if her sister still followed. This introduced the discussion of her sister and Bingley's affairs.**

"Bingley wrote to me with the earliest information of it. I am delighted with their engagement and believe they will be as happy as any couple with such goodness in them must be," Darcy said.

"I must ask whether you were surprised?" Elizabeth inquired.

"Not at all. When I went away, I felt that it would soon happen."

"That is to say, you had given your permission. I guessed as much." And though he exclaimed at the term, she found that it had been pretty much the case.

"On the evening before my going to London," said he, "I made a confession to him, which I believe I ought to have made long ago. I told him of all that had occurred to make my former interference in his affairs absurd and impertinent. His surprise was great. He had never had the slightest suspicion. I told him, moreover, that I believed myself mistaken in supposing, as I had done, that your sister was indifferent to him. As I could easily perceive that his attachment to her was unabated, I felt no doubt of their happiness together."

Elizabeth could not help smiling at his easy manner of directing his friend.

"Did you speak from your own observation," said she, "when you told him that my sister loved him, or merely from my information last spring?"

"From the former. I had narrowly observed her during the two visits which I had lately made here. I was convinced of her affection."

"And your assurance of it, I suppose, carried immediate conviction to him."

"It did. Bingley is most unaffectedly modest. His diffidence had prevented his depending on his own judgment in so anxious a case, but his reliance on mine made everything easy."

Elizabeth longed to observe that Mr. Bingley had been a most delightful friend, so easily guided that his worth was invaluable, but she checked herself. She remembered that Mr. Darcy had yet learned to be laughed at, and it was rather too early to begin. In anticipating the happiness of Bingley, which of course was to be inferior only to his own, he continued the conversation till they came within distant sight of the house.

"I was obliged to confess one thing," he said, "which for a time, and not unjustly, offended him. I could not allow myself to conceal that your sister had been in town three months last winter, that I had known it, and purposely kept it from him. He was angry. But his anger, I am persuaded, lasted no longer than he remained in any doubt of your sister's sentiments. He has heartily forgiven me now, **and I have promised never to intercede in his life in such a way again. I am clearly not born to be a matchmaker.**"

"On that point I would have to agree," Elizabeth said. At his surprised look, she added, "Look at all this way we have walked, and all we have talked about, but you have yet to secure from me a promise that will make both of our happiness's complete."

Understanding filled his gaze and he returned her smile. "Shall I get down on one knee then? Or do you not trust me to make a better showing for myself this time?"

Elizabeth slipped her hand over his chest, feeling the beat of his heart against her palm. Everything about him filled her with a longing she wanted so badly to fill. His smell drew her instinctively closer. "Would you do me the honor of your hand, Mr. Darcy?"

"I believe that is what I am supposed to say." He touched her cheek and the tender caress sent a shiver along her entire body.

"No," Elizabeth denied. "All you are supposed to say is 'yes.'"

"Then, yes. Eternally and forever, yes."

This time when they kissed, there was more passion between their lips. She wanted to do more and knew that he wanted to as well.

"Soon," she thought, almost desperately. "Soon we will have no reason to part."

As if reading her mind, he pulled back and led her towards the house. Their steps quickened as lively as if they had not just walked miles around the countryside. When they reached the house, they parted in the front hall before any could suspect what they had been about.

CHAPTER FIFTY-ONE

"MY DEAR LIZZY, where can you have been walking to?" Jane asked as soon as Elizabeth entered their room, and from all the others when they sat down to table. She had only to say in reply, that they had wandered about, till she was beyond her own knowledge. She colored as she spoke but neither that, nor anything else, awakened a suspicion of the truth.

The evening passed quietly, unmarked by anything extraordinary. The acknowledged lovers talked and laughed, the unacknowledged were silent. Darcy was not of a disposition in which happiness overflows in mirth. Elizabeth, agitated and confused by his silence, and by the anticipation of what would be felt in the family when her situation became known. She was aware that no one liked him but Jane, and even feared that with the others it was a dislike which not all his fortune and consequence might do away.

Regardless of this pain, she did not for a second doubt her decision and it was only the stolen glances she shared with Mr. Darcy that kept her sprits somewhat lively, even if she was not at liberty to let them show. When the gentlemen left for home, Jane and Bingley openly spoke all of that longing and joy which was in their hearts. Elizabeth could but bow to Mr. Darcy and wish him well in the most amiable of words.

However, that night she opened her heart to Jane. Though suspicion was very far from her sister's general habits, Jane was absolutely incredulous at the news, "You are joking, Lizzy. This cannot be. Engaged to Mr. Darcy! No, no, you shall not deceive me. I know it to be impossible."

"This is a wretched beginning indeed! My sole dependence was on you, and I am sure nobody else will believe me, if you do not. Yet, indeed, I am in earnest. I speak nothing but the truth. He still loves me, and we are engaged."

Jane looked at her doubtingly. "Oh, Lizzy, it cannot be. I know how much you dislike him."

"You know nothing of the matter. That is all to be forgotten. Perhaps I did not always love him so well as I do now, or rather as openly as I am willing to now admit. But in such cases as these, a good memory is unpardonable. This is the last time I shall ever remember it myself."

Jane still looked all amazement. Elizabeth again, and more seriously, assured her of its truth. **"I have longed all evening to have someone as happy as myself to share this news with. Though I am happy for you, it has been agony to see you able to express to Bingley what I feel for Darcy. Every fiber of my being wished to show how happy I am."**

"Good Heaven, can it be really so? Yet now I must believe you," said Jane. "My dear, dear Lizzy, I would—I do congratulate you—but are you certain? Forgive the question, but are you quite certain that you can be happy with him?"

"There can be no doubt of that. It is settled between us already, that we are to be the happiest couple in the world. But are you pleased, Jane? Shall you like to have such a brother?"

"Very much. Nothing could give either Bingley or myself more delight. I confess, we considered it, but we talked of it as impossible. And do you really love him quite well enough? Oh, Lizzy, do anything rather than marry without affection. Are you quite sure that you feel what you ought to do?"

"Oh, yes! You will only think I feel more than I ought to do, when I tell you all."

"What do you mean?"

"Why, I must confess that I love him better than I do Bingley. I am afraid you will be angry."

"My dearest sister, now be serious and stop bouncing around like that. I want to talk very seriously. Let me know everything that I am to know, without delay. Will you tell me how long you have loved him?"

"It has been coming on so gradually, that I hardly know when it began. **Sometimes I think from the very beginning, though perhaps I did dislike him and then like him again. My emotions have been in chaos and yet now I can hardly imagine not liking him at all. Oh, Jane, I know I make little sense, but you must take that as a sign that I truly love him.** But I believe if I must date it then it most likely stemmed from my first seeing his beautiful grounds at Pemberley."

Elizabeth, of course, was joking and Jane knew it as well. Elizabeth could never be compelled to like a man for his house, let alone love him. Another entreaty that she would be serious, however, produced the desired effect. She soon satisfied Jane by her solemn assurances of attachment.

"In truth, dear sister, I believe it began in earnest after I

learned the truth from his letter, even if that first proposal was not very well done. It just took me a while to admit my feelings to myself."

Convinced on that article, Jane had nothing further to wish for. "Now I am quite happy, for you will be as happy as myself. I always had a value for him. Were it for nothing but his love of you, I must always have esteemed him; but now, as Bingley's friend and your husband, there can be only Bingley and yourself more dear to me. But Lizzy, you have been very sly, very reserved with me. How little did you tell me of what passed at Pemberley and Lambton? I owe all that I know of it to another, not to you."

Elizabeth told her the motives of her secrecy. She had been unwilling to mention Bingley, and the unsettled state of her own feelings had made her equally avoid the name of his friend. But now she would no longer conceal from her his share in Lydia's marriage. All was acknowledged, and half the night spent in conversation.

"Good gracious!" cried Mrs. Bennet, as she stood at a window the next morning, "if that disagreeable Mr. Darcy is not coming here again with our dear Bingley! What can he mean by being so tiresome as to be always coming here? I had no notion but he would go a-shooting, or something or other, and not disturb us with his company. What shall we do with him? Lizzy, you must walk out with him again, that he may not be in Bingley's way."

Elizabeth could hardly help laughing at so convenient a proposal, yet was really vexed that her mother should be always giving him such an epithet.

As soon as they entered, Bingley looked at her so expressively, and shook hands with such warmth, as left no doubt of his good information. He soon afterwards said aloud, "Mrs. Bennet, have you no more lanes hereabouts in which Lizzy may lose her way again today?"

"I advise Mr. Darcy, and Lizzy, and Kitty," said Mrs. Bennet, "to walk to Oakham Mount this morning. It is a nice long walk, and Mr. Darcy has never seen the view."

"It may do very well for the others," replied Mr. Bingley, "but I am sure it will be too much for Kitty. Won't it, Kitty?" Kitty owned that she had rather stay at home. Darcy professed a great curiosity to see the view from the Mount, and Elizabeth silently consented.

As she went up stairs to get ready, Mrs. Bennet followed her, saying, "I am quite sorry, Lizzy, that you should be forced to have that disagreeable man all to yourself. But I hope you will not mind it, for it is all for Jane's sake, you know. There is no occasion for talking to him, except just now and then. So, do not put yourself to inconvenience."

Elizabeth could hardly contain her excitement, yet said nothing. Her mother apologized at the necessity a few more times, thinking it essential to follow Elizabeth to her room and back out again. The unacknowledged couple left the house in silence, taking the prescribed path. The seclusion would fit their purpose in being alone quite well and Elizabeth could not help but laugh as she thought of how her mother's plans had the rare effect of working to her daughter's compete advantage.

"Please, share your amusement," Darcy said.

Knowing the path by heart, she knew the exact tree that would take them completely out of sight of everyone. As they passed it, she took his arm. "I was thinking how brilliant my mother's suggestion was in our coming out here alone. I can think of nothing more that I wanted to do today than see you."

As if emboldened by her touch, he took her hand from his

arm and lifted it to his mouth. He placed a gentle kiss on it. "Then a night has not changed your mind?"

"Changed it?" she exclaimed. "If anything my mind is fixed. I can think of nothing else but becoming your wife."

"I hear ladies are often excited for the festivities of the wedding, and can think of nothing else until the event is over."

Leading him, she directed him off the path to a seclusion within the trees. "It is not the wedding I think of, but afterwards."

Surprise instantly lit his features and for a stunned moment he did not speak. His eyes dipped down, skimming over her frame as if by involuntary action. After a long moment of studying her figure, he managed to get control of himself and drew his gaze back to her face. She blushed profusely to know he thought she meant to imply the wedding night itself. Though she was naturally anxious—and curiously excited—for that event to take place, she had not meant to imply it so boldly.

Worried that such a forthright statement would put him off, she tried to think of something to say to steer the subject away from her faux pas. "I did not mean that exactly as it sounded, but rather I think mostly of our life together. I—"

"I," he broke in, hesitating slightly before admitting in a clearer tone, "I have thought of my life with you, and our wedding night as well. Often."

The confession took her by surprise, so sincerely was it said. Elizabeth nervously looked away. For lack of anything better to say, she whispered, "You have? That is to say, I have wondered what it would be—but, I. . . ."

She knew she blushed profusely. All normal forthrightness faded and she hardly knew how to finish or what to say next. Propriety would tell her to be quiet, to never admit to such emotions and desires, but she did not want a marriage like that. She wanted honesty and passion and a husband who wanted to kiss her, ardently and often.

"You?" he prompted, as if holding his breath for her to finish.

"I do not want to be unseemly, but . . . ."

"You could never be unseemly to me. I know enough of your character and reputation, and from knowing you, that you are a woman of honor."

Encouraged by the openness of his expression, she admitted, "I cannot stop thinking of your mouth." The blush deepened, heating her cheeks. "When you kissed me I thought my legs might not support me. I have never felt anything like it. Yesterday, as we dined, I could think of little else—beyond the obvious frustration of not being able to shout our happiness to the room, but alas it was not the time or the place for such announcements."

Darcy could not describe the masculine pleasure he felt at her words. He saw the innocence in her expression, unable to artfully conceal the eager yearnings of her body. As she spoke, he watched her tongue dart out over her lips. To know she wanted him was a heady aphrodisiac indeed, and he could not help himself from taking another taste. He pulled her to him, wrapping his arms lightly around her waist as he kissed her. She moaned softly, accepting his embrace. Her body swayed, a small movement that brushed her skirts against his hips. Instantly, he became aroused, the full force of his long felt frustrations and unfulfilled desires coming to a head.

Her scent, like fresh wildflowers, surrounded him, and he breathed her in. His mind whispered that he should stop, that she was not quite his to take, not yet, but he could not command his mouth to move from hers for she parted her lips, and the warm caress of her breath as she exhaled urged him to deepen the embrace. He knew she was inexperienced, yet her enthusiasm to follow his lead was beyond anything he could have hoped.

His tongue edged into her mouth and she gasped, opening her lips wider so that he could dip inside. He did. How could he not? Logic and reason could not convince him that she did not belong to him. Every part of him felt the conqueror, tired of being denied the claim of what was destined to be his.

"My sweet Elizabeth," he whispered, withdrawing his mouth so they could breath. She leaned fully against him now, clinging to his shoulders. He tightened his hold, pressing her soft body into his harder one. Oh, the pleasure! A man could die from such as this.

"No one will come this way," she told him. "I do not want to leave you just yet."

The softly whispered plea caused an answering moan to escape him. Damn propriety! Elizabeth belonged to him, if not in name, in soul and spirit. She was his match, his perfect equal—nay, more than his equal for he was in her complete power. Delicate hands slid beneath his jacket, stroking the peaks and valleys of his chest. He shivered, desperate for more.

"I have longed for you." He trailed his mouth over her cheek. His hand, mindless of any other command, skimmed up her side to cup a breast. So soft and yielding it was, molding against his palm, protected only by her dress. "You cannot begin to understand the distress I feel."

"Ah," she answered, tipping her head back as she crumpled his shirt in her fists. "I think I may have some idea. I ache all over—my flesh, my mouth, deep inside. No man has ever made me feel like this. The world is spinning away and I feel as if nothing else matters but us and this moment."

Elizabeth could not think enough to stop her words. She trusted him, wanted to tell him everything. She thought of those private moments when she had touched herself to the memory of his eyes. This felt so much better. His larger body engulfed hers and she felt the contrasting differences between them—in the size and heat of his chest, the solid build of his muscles, and most poignantly in the mysteriously large pressure against her stomach. His hands slid over her chest and shoulders, along her neck, into her hair, down her back, until he had explored every curve within his reach.

"I am at your command," he said. "I am helpless against you. Tell me, lady, what would you have of me?"

"Everything," she answered, before she could form a better thought. Then, pulling away so she could look at his handsome face, she saw the strange straining of his expression. He looked to be in great pain. The same feeling echoed inside her stomach.

Elizabeth moved her hands under his jacket, pushing the thicker material off his shoulders. It slid behind them to the ground. She kept her eyes on his, carefully studying him for any clue as to his changing thoughts. His grip on her loosened and she reached to unbutton his shirt as far as it would go. Then, tugging it from his breeches, she pulled the looser material free. Tanned flesh met her fingers, only slightly lighter than his face and hands. Lifting the shirt and undershirt, she looked at his waist, seeing for the first time the narrow trail of hair leading downward, sprinkled over the strength of his stomach.

With shaking fingers, she touched him there, just below his navel. His entire body jerked, but he did not pull away. Growing bolder, she ran her hand up his chest endeavoring to memorize such undiscovered terrain. There was an addiction to the texture of his skin that forced her hand to rub up and down along the center of his chest. When his clothes impeded her travels, he pulled the bottom hem to lift them over his head.

Elizabeth explored every inch of exposed flesh and after her fingers had conquered there, they drew to his waistband. Darcy stood very still, letting her touch him, letting her learn what his body had to reveal. Curiosity became great as she looked between them to the bulge between his thighs. Did she dare touch? Look? After staring for a long moment, undecided, she was hampered from any lower exploration by his hands on her arms.

"Take off your dress," he urged her. Elizabeth shivered, glancing around though she knew they were quite alone. He continued, "I will not dishonor you to your family by getting it dirty. No one will ever know what we do here, but us."

Modesty caused her to turn her back to him. He chuckled, but did not move from his place as she did as he bid her. First, her gown was loosened and pulled over her head, stripping until she stood in her chemise. Cool air tickled her flesh. He appeared behind her, jerking her back to his chest. His hands moved freely now, over her stomach and chest, both of which were scantly protected by the thin material of her underclothes. He paid special notice to her nipples, rubbing them in small circles as his hips mimicked the gesture along her buttocks. She reached behind her, taking hold of his outer thighs.

Then, he groaned, letting his hand trail by small degrees down the front of her body. She knew where he would touch her next and waited for that first contact with the nervous anticipation of a woman unused to such situations. Elizabeth pressed her legs tightly together, worried about the dampness between them. It was a weak defense, but one he felt. His journey stopped and he took her by the shoulders and turned her to face him.

Breathing hard, he held her back from him when she would lean forwards. The harsh rasp capturing his words was like nothing she had ever heard from him. "We do nothing that you do not want."

The ache in her female sex nearly caused her to scream. It was unbearable that she had stopped him with her nervousness, for now his hand was far away from that needy place. "I want—I want you. I do not know what I am doing, but if you will deign to show me, I will be a willing student." Then, as if to prove her sincerity, she took his hand and drew it down to its former place. "I do not know if there is an acceptable end to such torment, but I cannot walk back like this."

The desire had never been so pronounced when she explored her own body. She concentrated on leaving her thighs open and he obligingly slipped his hand between them. She lost her footing, but he held her up. The thick press of his finger was nothing like the strumming of hers. He knew just where to rub, first soft, then harder, finding the bud of nerves buried within her folds, until she found herself rocking against him in feverish need.

Suddenly, he stopped, swept her feet off the ground and gently laid her on the grass. As her body sprawled along the earth, he reached for his waistband, making quick work of the breeches. Elizabeth leaned on her elbows to see the length of his manhood only to discover tight, naked flesh towering above a nest of hair. It was not as she imagined a man might look and she stared at it overlong. Then, reaching out curious fingers, she touched him. He groaned, letting his head roll back as he looked to the alcove of trees. Tiny dots of sunlight made it through the limbs, dancing on his flesh in a chaotic waltz.

"You are so warm," she observed, fascinated by the firm texture. She touched him more fully, wrapping her fingers around his shaft. "Almost hot. How do you manage to hide this under your clothing?"

His laugh was pained. "It is not always like this. Normally it is at rest. I should not be able to get a great many things done if I walked about in such a fevered state." Darcy took his hand over hers, closing her fingers more fully and showed her how to touch him, running her hand up and down the full length. Then, returning to his place between her thighs, he stroked her sex until she was again writhing against his hand. Moisture had soaked the thin barrier of material, but she no longer worried about it for he did not seem to mind the reaction.

"Will you kiss me again?" she asked, looking up at him through a shade of lashes.

It was too much. He was only a mortal man passed beyond his limits. Mindlessly, he pulled at the material guarding her sex from his eyes. The material ripped and she gave a small jump of surprise as she looked down at what he had done.

"I will buy you a thousand more if you wish it," he assured her. Before she could answer, he delved a finger along the naked petals of her sex, parting the wet folds. The softness of her engulfed his fingers and he could not resist pressing it inside the tight canal of her sex. Oh, how it gripped him, wondrously tight and gloriously wet. Darcy wiggled his finger, stretching her tight sheath. Seeing the dusky hint of a nipple straining against her chemise, he leaned down to take it into his mouth, wetting the material as he sucked.

"Oh," she gasped. Her cheeks were flushed, her eyes opened wide, and her hand had stopped moving on his shaft.

Her disheveled body proved the most erotic sight he had ever seen in his life. Knowing what was to come might cause her discomfort, he begged his body to go slow, to fight the primitive instincts coursing in his blood. He moved over her, putting his legs between hers. He bent a knee, forcing her legs wider apart. The torn entrance at the apex of her thighs beckoned him. She did not try to stop him as he guided his arousal forward. The tip pressed into the wet opening and already he knew untold pleasures awaited him. Leaning down, he whispered against her throat, "I have no wish to hurt you, but this might cause you some pain. Hold on to me."

She obeyed without hesitation or question, and the trust she had in him amazed him. She grabbed his arms. Darcy captured her lips, and thrust half way in. Elizabeth moaned softly. Her nails dug into his flesh but the small sting actually felt nice. Oh, glorious moment, as he laid claim to her body! The tight, wet, heat of her sex clung to him. He pushed deeper, wanting the full length of him buried within her. As the sensitive flesh of his balls met her buttocks, he groaned.

"You were made for me in every way," he said, hardly considering the admission. Darcy pushed up so he could look at her beneath him. A stunned expression became shaded with inquisitiveness as she looked down. He tested her, pulling out slowly, and then pressing back in. She made a weak noise. He did it again. "Tell me when the pain lessens and you feel the pleasure build."

Despite his baser instincts, he took her slow—in, out, in, out. By degrees she began to respond, trying to move her hips to test the feel of it. Darcy took hold of her hip and showed her how to rock against him. She ran her hand down his arms, the nails scratching lighter than before. Not once did she cry out in protest. Instead, small noises arose from the back of her throat.

An idea struck him and he artfully moved onto his back, rolling with her so she was then seated above him. The position shoved him deeper until she pulled up. Taking her hips, he lifted and released, teaching her the rhythm until she found her own control. She pressed her hands into his chest.

Elizabeth gasped, as pleasure overtook the dull pain. When he helped her to move, she was sure there was nothing more satisfying in the whole of Britain than the sensations building low in her stomach. The small dots of light danced around them; whimsical yet striking, as a mythical scene taken right from ancient Grecian marble, come to flesh and blood life. She had never in her life imagined herself in such a position, Darcy sprawled beneath her. They were surrounded by the countryside, serenaded by the call of birds, and caressed by the fresh air.

Darcy was perfection and she could not close her eyes, as she wanted to take in every moment. Her knees pressed into the ground. His hands moved over her sides, her breasts, her backside, tangling in her underclothes and finding peaks of flesh where he could. Tension built, a rapturous sensation that overtook all the others before releasing a wave of relief throughout her entire being. Soon after, Darcy stiffened, his face frozen in what looked like agony.

She endeavored to catch her breath, overwhelmed with sensations. There was the pleasure in her body, but it was nothing compared to the love in her heart. Elizabeth never expected such a rush of feeling. Was this how everyone felt when they were in love? She leaned down against his chest and he wrapped his arms around her, holding her close. His body supported hers, cushioning her from the ground with solid muscle.

"I know honor dictates that I should feel contrition for seducing you before our wedding," said Darcy, "but I find I do not have the energy nor the desire to apologize for something I have wanted for so long a time."

"I should be offended if you did," answered Elizabeth. He pushed the hair from her face, letting his fingers trail down the nape of her neck. "It is unfathomable to me that I once turned down your proposal. I feel as if we have been meant for this moment."

Elizabeth settled next to him, enjoying the pleasure of being in his arms. The newness of it filled her with wonder, and she could hardly concentrate as her mind grasped the different sensations and impressions. Much time passed before they were compelled to gather their clothes and right their appearances for the walk back to the house.

It was resolved that Mr. Bennet's consent should be asked in the course of the evening. Elizabeth reserved to herself the application for her mother's. She could not determine how her mother would take it; sometimes doubting whether all his wealth and grandeur would be enough to overcome her abhorrence of the man. But whether she were violently set against the match, or violently delighted with it, it was certain that her manner would be equally ill adapted to do credit to her sense. Elizabeth could no more bear that Mr. Darcy should hear the first raptures of her joy, than the first vehemence of her disapprobation.

As the house came into view, they did not speak and kept a respectable distance. Elizabeth worried that her father would deny Mr. Darcy her hand, thus ruining forever her greatest joy. She could not think of what would happen to her reputation if such a thing were to occur. Though she could admit, she did feel a sort of understanding towards Lydia she had never known before.

Darcy smiled at her and there was a softness in his gaze. He looked as if he wanted to say something, but instead looked to the house where Kitty could be seen at the door watching for them. Elizabeth wanted nothing more than to be free to take his hand, if only for the security of his touch after such a shared moment. He let her walk ahead of him towards the door and any such moment for contact was lost as Kitty began to demand accounts of their walk, for she had been quite bored in the house with only the lovebirds and her mother to entertain.

In the evening, soon after Mr. Bennet withdrew to the library, Elizabeth saw Mr. Darcy rise also and follow him. Her agitation was extreme, growing more so as he left the room. **It was hard to concentrate after knowing what they did, knowing she could not tell a soul—especially not Jane, for her dear sister would never look at her the same. When he moved, Elizabeth found she had a new appreciation for his body, a curious urge to look at it as if seeing it for the first time, and she was sure the warmth she felt inside her body while doing so would surely translate itself upon her face.**

Bingley smiled at her from across the room. The look sobered her thoughts from the impure and she turned her attention back to Kitty, pretending to listen to the senseless story she told of new gloves and a cut of lace. As Kitty rambled, Elizabeth did not listen. She had come to realize she did not fear her father's opposition, but did regret that he was going to be made unhappy. That it should be through her means—that she, his favorite child, would distress him by her choice, would fill him with fears and regrets in disposing of her—was a wretched reflection. She sat in misery, unable to concentrate. **There was so much to think about, and she would not be free to fully recollect on the unexpected turn that day's walk had brought till the house was quiet with sleep and she had time to think without fear of revealing the results of her stolen pleasure with Mr. Darcy.**

She almost jumped up when Mr. Darcy appeared again, but, looking at him, she was a little relieved by his smile. In a few minutes he approached the table where she was sitting with Kitty. Pretending to admire her work, he said in a whisper, "Go to your father, he wants you in the library." She was gone directly.

Her father was walking about the room, looking grave and anxious. "Lizzy, what are you doing? Are you out of your senses, to be accepting this man? Have not you always hated him?"

Now was not the time to think of their walk or the fact she

had not changed from her torn undergarments, so she pushed it out of her mind, instead concentrating on how to best explain what it was she really felt. How earnestly did she then wish that her former opinions had been more reasonable, her expressions more moderate. It would have spared her from explanations and professions which it was exceedingly awkward to give. But they were now necessary, and she assured him, with some confusion as to best how to speak, of her attachment to Mr. Darcy. "I promise you, I am very pleased with the match."

"Or, in other words, you are determined to have him. He is rich, to be sure, and you may have more fine clothes and fine carriages than Jane. But will they make you happy?"

"Have you any other objection than your belief of my indifference?"

"None at all. We all know him to be a proud, unpleasant sort of man," her father answered, studying her in his quiet manner, "but this would be nothing if you really liked him."

"I do, I do like him," she replied, with tears forming in her eyes. "I love him. Indeed he has no improper pride. He is perfectly amiable. You do not know what he really is, then pray do not pain me by speaking of him in such terms."

"Lizzy," said her father, "I have given him my consent. He is the kind of man, indeed, to whom I should never dare refuse anything, which he condescended to ask. I now give it to you, if you are resolved on having him. But let me advise you to think better of it. I know your disposition, Lizzy. I know that you could be neither happy nor respectable, unless you truly esteemed your husband, unless you looked up to him as a superior. Your lively talents would place you in the greatest danger in an unequal marriage. You could scarcely escape discredit and misery. My child, let me not have the grief of seeing you unable to respect your partner in life. You know not what you are about."

Elizabeth was still more affected by the open admittance of her father on the state of his own marriage and wanting to save her from the same ridiculous fate. She was earnest and solemn in her reply. At length, by repeated assurances that Mr. Darcy was really the object of her choice, by explaining the gradual change which her estimation of him had undergone, relating her absolute certainty that his affection was not the work of a day, but had stood the test of many months suspense, and enumerating with energy all his good qualities, she did conquer her father's incredulity, and reconcile him to the match.

"Well, my dear, it appears you are quite certain," said he, when she ceased speaking, "I have no more to say."

"But you might when I tell you the rest," she said, and then told him what Mr. Darcy had voluntarily done for Lydia.

He heard her with astonishment.

"This is an evening of wonders, indeed! And so, Darcy did everything? He made up the match, gave the money, paid the fellow's debts, and got him his commission? Had it been your uncle's doing, I must and would have paid him in time. I shall offer to pay Mr. Darcy tomorrow."

"No," Elizabeth denied. "You must not. He did it as a gift to me, for his love. In fact, he did not wish for me to know what he had done. It was only Lydia's impudence in accidently telling me that I learned of it at all."

"Nevertheless, the offer should be made on my part," said Mr. Bennet, but this time there was an ease to his words. "These violent young lovers carry everything their own way. Undoubtedly, Mr. Darcy will rant and storm about his love for you, and there will be an end of the matter. I will have offered and he, very obligingly, will decline that offer. It will all be settled quite nicely. I can see that you do love him, Lizzy. If this be the case, he deserves you. I could not have parted with you, my

Lizzy, to anyone less worthy."

He then recollected her embarrassment a few days before, on his reading Mr. Collins's letter. After laughing at her some time, allowed her at last to go—saying, as she quitted the room, "If any young men come for Mary or Kitty, send them in, for I am quite at leisure."

Elizabeth's mind was now relieved from a very heavy weight. After a few minute's quiet reflection in her own room, she was able to join the others with tolerable composure. **She would not announce the news to her mother until they were alone, but she did let her love know the outcome with a slight smile in his direction. Bingley seemed to pick up on it as well, or perhaps he had detected his good friend's happy mood, for he grinned as if on the point of yelling his congratulations to her as she entered. To his credit, he remained quiet.** Everything was too recent for familial gaiety, and so the evening passed tranquilly away with the secret mostly intact. There was no longer anything material to be dreaded, and the comfort of ease and familiarity would come in time.

When her mother went up to her dressing room at night, she followed her, and made the important communication. Its effect was most extraordinary. For on first hearing it, Mrs. Bennet sat quite still, and unable to utter a syllable. Nor was it under many, many minutes that she could comprehend what she heard. She began at length to recover, to fidget about in her chair, get up, sit down again, wonder, and bless herself.

"Good gracious! Lord bless me! Only think, dear me, Mr. Darcy! Who would have thought it? And is it really true? Oh, my sweetest Lizzy! How rich and how great you will be. What pin-money, what jewels, what carriages you will have. Jane's is nothing to it—nothing at all. I am so pleased—so happy. Such a charming man, so handsome, so tall. Oh, my dear Lizzy, pray apologize for my having disliked him so much before. I hope he will overlook it. Dear, dear Lizzy. A house in town—how delightful that will be for all of us! Everything that is charming! Three daughters married. Ten thousand a year. Oh, Lord, what will become of me? I shall become distracted."

This was enough to prove that her approbation need not be doubted. Elizabeth, rejoicing that such an effusion was heard only by herself, soon went away. But before she had been three minutes in her own room, her mother followed her.

"My dearest child," she cried, "I can think of nothing else. Ten thousand a year, and very likely more! 'Tis as good as a Lord! And a special license. You must and shall be married by a special license. But my dearest love, tell me what dish Mr. Darcy is particularly fond of, that I may have it tomorrow."

This was a sad omen of what her mother's behavior to the gentleman himself might be. Elizabeth found that, though in the certain possession of his warmest affection, and secure of her relations' consent, there was still something to be wished for. But the morrow passed off much better than she expected. Mrs. Bennet luckily stood in such awe of her intended son-in-law that she ventured not to speak to him, unless it was in her power to offer him any attention, or mark her deference for his opinion.

Elizabeth had the satisfaction of seeing her father taking pains to get acquainted with him, and Mr. Bennet soon assured her that he was rising every hour in his esteem.

"I admire all my three sons-in-law highly," said he. "Wickham, perhaps, is my favorite for his acquaintance will prove the most diverting to me, but I think I shall like your husband quite as well as Jane's."

CHAPTER FIFTY-TWO

*E*LIZABETH, with spirits soon rising to playfulness, wanted
Mr. Darcy to account for his having ever fallen in love with
her. **They sat on the garden bench outside her home. He had
come to visit and assure her that his affections had not changed,
and that he would keep himself within proper distance relative
to her family until the wedding vows were spoken. For, he had
assured her, should he be given the opportunity of getting her
alone, he would not hesitate to repeat the events of their glorious walk.**

**Elizabeth, though very eager to rejoin him in their passions,
knew that the anticipation of the wedding night would have to
feed her desires until she could have him again. Besides, with
Kitty always watching them with wide eyes and eagerly listening
for the slightest chance to follow them in their conversation, such
alone time was impossible.**

"How could you begin?" she continued. "I can comprehend

your going on charmingly, when you had once made a beginning, but what could set you off in the first place?"

He gave her a mischievous look. "I cannot fix on the hour, or the spot, or the look, or the words, which laid the foundation. It is too long ago. I was in the middle before I knew that I had begun."

"My beauty you had early withstood, and as for my manners—my behavior to you was at least always bordering on the uncivil, and I never spoke to you without rather wishing to give you pain than not. Now be sincere, did you admire me for my impertinence?"

"For the liveliness of your mind, I did."

"You may as well call it impertinence. It was very little less. The fact is you were sick of civility, of deference, of officious attention. You were disgusted with the women who were always speaking, and looking, and thinking for your approbation alone. I roused, and interested you, because I was so unlike them. Had you not been really amiable, you would have hated me for it. But in spite of the pains you took to disguise yourself, your feelings were always noble and just, and in your heart you thoroughly despised the persons who so assiduously courted you. There—I have saved you the trouble of accounting for it. Really, all things considered, I begin to think it perfectly reasonable. **In fact, I believe from this accounting I shall be persuaded to treat you dreadfully, and be impertinent to you at least once a fortnight or else you might get bored with me." She tried to look serious, but could not keep the smile from her face as she teased him. "Yes, I think the only way to assure I have your love is to ensure that I am neither civil, nor deferential, nor giving of too much attention."**

"Bored with you?" He glanced around to assure they were not being spied upon, before reaching to touch her cheek. A small shiver stirred through her. What little ache there had been from

losing her virginity paled with the memory of her release. Darcy's eyes held a passionate storm in their depths and she knew he felt it too. "There is not a thing in you that could ever bore me. But, if it pleases you, treat me very atrociously. I am yours to abuse. Do with me what you wish."

"To be sure, at the beginning you knew no actual good of me—but nobody thinks of that when they fall in love."

"Was there no good in your affectionate behavior to Jane while she was ill at Netherfield?"

"Dearest Jane! Who could have done less for her? But make a virtue of it by all means. **And, if that is the case, I guess I will be saved from having to mistreat you. It is a relief, for I do find I dearly like loving you."** With this, she licked her lips and offered her mouth to him. It only seemed natural that she do so.

He gave her a brief kiss before pulling back. **"Your temptations are great indeed, my love. And I find there are too many good qualities in you, so I shall not worry about how our marriage will be. If you should dislike me in time, I will be in love for the both of us and will never allow myself to see it."**

"Then we will both be fools, for I think my love will blind me to your ever disliking me. We will be foolish and in love and will make everyone sick to look at how happy we are. Therefore, my good qualities are under your protection, and you are to exaggerate them as much as possible. In return, it belongs to me to find occasions for teasing and quarrelling with you as often as may be, and I shall begin directly by asking you what made you so unwilling to come to the point at last. What made you so shy of me, when you first called, and afterwards dined here? Why, especially, when you called, did you look as if you did not care about me?"

"Because you were grave and silent, and gave me no encouragement."

"But I was embarrassed."

"And so was I."

"You might have talked to me more when you came to dinner."

"A man who had felt less, might."

"How unlucky that you should have a reasonable answer to give, and that I should be so reasonable as to admit it! But I wonder how long you would have gone on, if you had been left to yourself. I wonder when you would have spoken, if I had not asked you. My resolution of thanking you for your kindness to Lydia had certainly great effect. Too much, I am afraid," **she blushed, even as she wanted to kiss him again. The ache became great and she wished to ask him to touch her as he had, between the thighs, fingers rubbing, lips touching. She shivered, whispering,** "I ought not to have mentioned the subject. This will never do."

"You need not distress yourself about mentioning Lydia. The moral will be perfectly fair. Lady Catherine's unjustifiable endeavors to separate us were the means of removing all my doubts. I am not indebted for my present happiness to your eager desire of expressing your gratitude. I was not in a humor to wait for any opening of yours. My aunt's intelligence had given me hope, and I was determined at once to know everything."

"I shall insert a quick thanks for purposefully misunderstanding that last comment," said Elizabeth, before rushing to answer. "I agree, Lady Catherine has been of infinite use, which ought to make her happy, for she loves to be of use. But tell me, what did you come down to Netherfield for? Was it merely to ride to Longbourn and be embarrassed? Or had you intended any more serious consequence?"

"My real purpose was to see you, and to judge, if I could, whether I might ever hope to make you love me. My avowed one, or what I avowed to myself, was to see whether your sister was still partial to Bingley, and if she was, to make the confession to him which I have since made."

"Shall you ever have courage to announce to Lady Catherine what is to befall her?"

"I am more likely to want more time than courage, sweet Elizabeth. But it ought to be done, and if you will give me a sheet of paper, it shall be done directly."

"And if I had not a letter to write myself, I might sit by you and admire the evenness of your writing, as another young lady once did. But I have an aunt, too, who must not be longer neglected."

However, despite their resolve, Elizabeth kissed him again. She moaned, coming to stand before him as he sat on the bench. His legs parted and she stood between them. Her hands rediscovered those parts that had captivated their interest before. And, when neither of them could stand the torment, they imprudently rushed from the house to come together in a small gathering of trees. It was neither a wise or good decision, but it could not be helped. Their bodies would not be denied, and so it was that Darcy pressed her against a trunk to keep her steady and lifted her legs to wrap his waist. A rip freed her sex, and he quickly found hold within her body. Thrusting and straining, they came to release. Elizabeth was confounded that the second time should so outshine the first in pleasure, and Darcy could scarcely believe his luck in finding a bride so willing to meet his every desire. He determined that as soon as they could be wed, he would teach all he knew of pleasing a woman.

After long minutes of catching their breath, she righted her clothing and prompted him to do the same. They walked inside to attend the business of their letters. Her cheeks were flush and she could not help glancing up at him. Before they went inside, she

said, "I had a dream of you last night. It was delightfully wicked of my mind to torture me with it."

He cleared his throat, but was unable to answer as she went inside. She knew it was wrong to tease him, but there was some pleasure in knowing he ached for her as she suffered for him. They sat down to write their letters.

From an unwillingness to confess how much her intimacy with Mr. Darcy while in Derbyshire had been over-rated, Elizabeth had never yet answered Mrs. Gardiner's long letter. However now, having that to communicate which she knew would be most welcome, she was almost ashamed to find that her uncle and aunt had already lost three days of happiness, and immediately wrote, "I would have thanked you before, my dear aunt, as I ought to have done, for your long, kind, satisfactory, detail of particulars. To say the truth, I was too cross to write. You supposed more than really existed. But now suppose as much as you choose and give a loose rein to your fancy, and unless you believe me actually married, you cannot greatly err. You must write again very soon, and praise him a great deal more than you did in your last. I thank you, again and again, for not going to the Lakes. Your idea of the ponies is delightful. We will go round the Park every day. I am the happiest creature in the world. Perhaps other people have said so before, but not one with such justice. I am happier even than Jane. She only smiles. I laugh. Mr. Darcy sends you all the love in the world that he can spare from me. You are all to come to Pemberley at Christmas. Yours, Elizabeth."

Mr. Darcy's letter to Lady Catherine was in a different style.

Still different from either was what Mr. Bennet sent to Mr. Collins, in reply to his last letter, "Dear Sir, I must trouble you once more for congratulations. Elizabeth will soon be the wife of Mr. Darcy. Console Lady Catherine as well as you can. But, if I were you, I would stand by the nephew. He has more to give."

Miss Bingley's congratulations to her brother, on his approaching marriage, were all that was affectionate and insincere. She wrote even to Jane on the occasion, to express her delight, and repeat all her former professions of regard. Jane was not deceived, but she was affected. Though feeling no reliance on her, could not help writing her a much kinder answer than she knew was deserved.

The joy which Miss Darcy expressed on receiving similar information was as sincere as her brother's in sending it. Four sides of paper were insufficient to contain all her delight, and all her earnest desire of being loved by her sister.

Before any answer could arrive from Mr. Collins, or any congratulations to Elizabeth from his wife, the Longbourn family heard that the Collinses were come themselves to Lucas Lodge. The reason of this sudden removal was soon evident. Lady Catherine had been rendered so exceedingly angry by the contents of her nephew's letter, that Charlotte, really rejoicing in the match, was anxious to get away till the storm was blown over. At such a moment, the arrival of her friend was a sincere pleasure to Elizabeth, though in the course of their meetings she must sometimes think the pleasure dearly bought, when she saw Mr. Darcy exposed to all the parading and obsequious civility of her husband. He bore it, however, with admirable calmness.

Mrs. Philips's vulgarity was another, and perhaps a greater, tax on his forbearance. Though Mrs. Philips, as well as her sister, stood in too much awe of him to speak with the familiarity which Bingley's good humor encouraged, whenever she did speak, she must be vulgar. Nor was her respect for him, though it made her quieter, at all likely to make her more elegant. Elizabeth did all she could to shield him from the frequent notice of either, and was ever anxious to keep him to herself. Although the uncomfortable feelings arising from all this took from the season of courtship much of its pleasure, it added to the hope of the future. When they could not be alone, she tried to ensure they were around those of her family with whom he might converse without mortification.

She looked forward with delight to the time when they should be removed from society so little pleasing to either, to all the comfort and elegance of their family party at Pemberley. **For, it was only when they were alone that she could truly relax, and explore the full depth of her feelings which were not allowed to show themselves when others were in attendance. She kissed him often, thought of him always, and could barely wait to again explore the passion that had unfolded those brilliant days outside Longbourn.**

CHAPTER FIFTY-THREE

HE TWO MISS BENNETS could think of nothing more perfect than to marry on the same day, for then they would have reason to celebrate their good fortune every year at the same time with a ball, for the rest of their lives. As Mrs. Bennet had hoped, both her daughters were married by special license obtained from the Archbishop of Canterbury. Mr. Darcy, with all the connections and none of the desire to wait to claim his bride, did willingly apply for it, going so far as to have Bingley do the same at his own expense. Mrs. Bennet spent the whole day of the wedding informing all in the neighborhood of the fact, while engaging in many loud conversations during the wedding breakfast about the cost of the material used in her daughters' dresses and her sorrow in that the girls were not marrying in London.

"But I suppose it is very well that they shall depart here for their bridal tour, for it saves us the trip in coming home. Very practical of my Jane to think of it, for she is always thinking of others," said Mrs. Bennet to Lady Lucas. "You have heard that Mr. Darcy proposed that they travel all the way to the Italy for the bridal tour, but my Lizzy insisted she would rather go north to see the Lakes and to Italy another time. I daresay they will travel often, since the gentleman can well afford that and more."

Not even the chattering of her mother could ruin Elizabeth's happiness, which was only improved by seeing Jane settled as perfectly. After taking her leave of her friends and family, Elizabeth took her new husband's arm and let him lead her to the carriage. Though Mr. and Mrs. Bingley and Mr. and Mrs. Darcy were to share in their travels, two separate carriages were ordered for the trip. Elizabeth leaned from the window and waved until the sight of her family could no longer be discerned from the fading landscape.

Any anxiety she might have felt in leaving her childhood home was soon lost as she looked at her new husband. Darcy had a peculiar look on his face, as he studied her from across the carriage. Elizabeth asked, "What are you thinking just now, Mr. Darcy?"

"Of how lucky I am to have married you, Mrs. Darcy," answered he.

She smiled brightly, loving the sound of her new name, even as it was still unusual to hear herself addressed as such. "And what kind of life do you see us living, Mr. Darcy? Shall we be happy?"

His answer was to pull the carriage curtains and join her on her seat and take her face into his hands. He smiled, his eyes filled with tenderness, as he joined his lips with hers. The passion he had stirred inside her on their walk was easily rekindled into a burning flame that ignited every nerve in her body. She instantly grabbed hold of his arms, keeping him close, digging her fingers into his jacket. Lips moved down her jaw to her neck. She shivered to feel the intimate kiss.

Darcy drew his hands down her throat to her chest. A warm palm cupped her breast, massaging her through her gown. Elizabeth ran her fingers into his hair, sighing in pleasure. There was freedom in knowing they had every right to come together and need not fear retribution for their passion, just as there was pleasure in knowing that Mr. Darcy was hers—forever and completely.

"You have made me the happiest of men," he whispered, nipping at her earlobe, "and I will spend my life making sure you are the happiest of women. All you have to do is ask me and, if it is within my power to give, it shall be yours."

Elizabeth sighed, thinking of all the years they had ahead of them. The touch of his hand, his lips, his breath, all begged for a response. Her body obliged with heat and moisture between her thighs. She trembled, moaning weakly. The feelings she had suppressed during most of their official engagement surged forth, combining all of her late night fantasies of him with the reality of the moment.

She thrust her hands beneath his jacket, pushing it from his shoulders. "I want to look at you."

Darcy did not hesitate to grant her request. He undressed, slowly, allowing her to see him; each inch of hard flesh revealed to the harsh line of sunlight streaming into the carriage window where the curtains were slightly parted. She touched his chest, tracing the lines of it with her fingertip, learning the texture of his skin and the reactions of his body.

When he wore only his breeches, he set to work on her gown. She blushed in modesty, but did not stop his exploration, did not take her eyes from his face. With precision, he revealed her flesh as he had his, slowly and steadily until all that remained of her clothing was the thin linen of her chemise. A hand brushed across her nipple, hardening it.

"Elizabeth," he whispered as if that one word caused him great pain and great joy. "You cannot know how much I long for you. I should endeavor to wait until I can lay you in a proper bed, but I find myself compelled to be near you. Knowing you are my wife, and that there is nothing keeping us apart is more than a mortal can resist."

"I am not asking you to resist," she assured him, reaching to take off her chemise. His eyes took in her naked form with pleasure. "You know me too well to expect me to express feelings I do not have. I know not how to give false modesty. I want you to touch me, and kiss me, and make love to me again. You cannot know how much I long for you, and I shall not pretend to want to wait for a proper bed when, in truth, it does not matter to me where we are so long as I can have you."

She watched his reaction to her soft speech through the dark sweep of her lashes, hoping she did not disappoint him. A mild surprise followed the forthright statement, but was soon replaced by a look that combined all the masculine pride and husbandly joy imaginable.

"I am pleased you desire me. It is more than I could have hoped. You may have me whenever you wish, my love," he assured her. "You have but to ask."

Elizabeth maneuvered the best she could manage in the carriage. Darcy made quick work of his breeches, pulling them from his hips. She found her eyes instantly on that point of interest that had occupied much of her thoughts since their first time together. Now, seeing the thick member, standing tall and proud from his hips, she smiled.

He touched her chest, naked flesh to flesh. She gasped, pressing her hand onto his thigh. Several minutes passed in the gentle exploration of their bodies. Elizabeth learned his feel, and watched his reactions. Finally, her hand moved to the stiff arousal, taking the firm mass in hand.

Darcy rejoiced in his great luck in finding not only love, but passion. Thinking of how many times it was spoken throughout society that young wives lacked the passion of mistresses, he chuckled. It would appear in this instance that society was wrong.

At his laugh, Elizabeth's hand stilled. He leaned back on the seat, beckoning her to sit astride him. She obeyed, unquestioningly. When she looked at him, love and trust shone in her eyes. He knew that no man would ever be able to count himself as fortunate. For in his wife he had found something better than perfection. He had found the other half of his soul.

They came together, bodies joining and moving in time with the rocking of the carriage. In that moment, nothing else mattered. Their pleasure built, coursing through them as they moved towards a shared purpose. Then it happened, a beautiful eruption; muscles tensed, bodies strained, rocking and thrusting as they met with the sweet release that only such primal acts could give. They were perfection.

EPILOGUE

*H*APPY FOR ALL HER MATERNAL FEELINGS was the day on which Mrs. Bennet got rid of her two most deserving daughters. With what delighted pride she afterwards visited Mrs. Bingley, and talked of Mrs. Darcy, may be guessed. Unfortunately it could not be said, for the sake of her family, that the accomplishment of her earnest desire in the establishment of so many of her children produced so happy an effect as to make her a sensible, amiable, well-informed woman for the rest of her life. Though perhaps it was lucky for her husband, who might not have relished domestic felicity in so unusual a form, that she still was occasionally nervous and invariably silly.

Mr. Bennet missed his second daughter exceedingly. His affection for her drew him oftener from home than anything else could. He delighted in going to Pemberley, especially when he was least expected.

Mr. Bingley and Jane remained at Netherfield only a twelvemonth. So near a vicinity to her mother and Meryton relations was not desirable even to his easy temper, or her affectionate heart. The darling wish of his sisters was then gratified. He bought an estate in a neighboring county to Derbyshire, and Jane and Elizabeth, in addition to every other source of happiness, were within thirty miles of each other.

Kitty, to her very material advantage, spent the chief of her time with her two elder sisters. In society so superior to what she had generally known, her improvement was great. She was not of so ungovernable a temper as Lydia and, removed from the influence of Lydia's example, she became, by proper attention and management, less irritable, less ignorant, and less insipid. From the further disadvantage of Lydia's society she was carefully kept, and though Mrs. Wickham frequently invited her to come and stay, with the promise of balls and young men, her father would never consent to it.

Mary was the only daughter who remained at home. She was necessarily drawn from the pursuit of accomplishments by Mrs. Bennet's being unable to sit alone. Mary was obliged to mix more with the world, but she could still moralize over every morning visit. As she was no longer mortified by comparisons between her sisters' beauty and her own, it was suspected by her father that she submitted to the change without much reluctance.

As for Wickham and Lydia, their characters suffered no revolution from the marriage of her sisters. He bore with philosophy the conviction that Elizabeth must now become acquainted with whatever of his ingratitude and falsehood had before been unknown to her, and was not wholly without hope that Darcy might yet be prevailed on to make his fortune. The congratulatory letter which Elizabeth received from Lydia on her marriage, explained to her that, by his wife at least, if not by himself, such a hope was cherished. The letter was in part to this effect, "My dear Lizzy, I wish you joy. If you love Mr. Darcy half as well as I do my dear Wickham, you must be very happy. It is a great comfort to have you so rich, and when you have nothing else to do, I hope you will think of us. Wickham would like a place at court, and I do not think we shall have quite money enough to live upon without help. Any place would do, of about three or four hundred a year. However, do not speak to Mr. Darcy about it, if you had rather not. Yours, Lydia Wickham."

As it happened that Elizabeth had much rather not, she endeavored in her answer to put an end to every entreaty and expectation of the kind. Such relief, however, as it was in her power to afford, by the practice of what might be called economy in her own private expenses, she frequently sent them. It had always been evident to her that such an income as theirs, under the direction of two persons so extravagant in their wants, and heedless of the future, must be very insufficient to their support. Whenever they changed their quarters, either Jane or herself were sure of being applied to for some little assistance towards discharging their bills. They were always moving from place to place in quest of a cheap situation, and always spending more than they ought. His affection for her soon sunk into indifference. Hers lasted a little longer, and in spite of her youth and her manners, she retained all the claims to reputation which her marriage had given her. **For, the skills of her youth were aptly applied in marriage and she was able to take many more secret lovers than her husband, and never be caught outright at it. To Lydia's pleasure, her new station made the ruse of virginity and innocence completely unnecessary, and she could be as wild and varied in her tastes as ever she wanted.**

Though Darcy could never receive Wickham at Pemberley, for Elizabeth's sake he assisted him further in his profession. Lydia was occasionally a visitor there, when her husband was gone to enjoy himself in London or Bath, and with the Bingleys they both of them frequently stayed so long, that even Bingley's good humor was overcome, and he proceeded so far as to talk of giving them a hint to be gone.

Miss Bingley was very deeply mortified by Darcy's marriage, but as she thought it advisable to retain the right of visiting at Pemberley, she dropped all her resentment, was fonder than ever of Georgiana, almost as attentive to Darcy as heretofore, and paid off every arrear of civility to Elizabeth.

Pemberley was now Georgiana's home, and the attachment of the sisters was exactly what Darcy had hoped. They were able to love each other as well as they intended. Georgiana had the highest opinion in the world of Elizabeth, though at first she often listened with an astonishment bordering on alarm at her lively, sportive, manner of talking to her brother. He, who had always inspired in herself a respect which almost overcame her affection, she now saw the object of open pleasantry. Her mind received knowledge which had never before fallen in her way. By Elizabeth's instructions, she began to comprehend that a woman may take liberties with her husband which a brother will not always allow in a sister more than ten years younger than himself.

Lady Catherine was extremely indignant on the marriage of her nephew, and as she gave way to all the genuine frankness of her character in her reply to the letter which announced its arrangement, she sent him language so very abusive, especially of Elizabeth, that for some time all intercourse was at an end. But at length, by Elizabeth's persuasion, he was prevailed on to overlook the offense, and seek a reconciliation. After a little further resistance on the part of his aunt, her resentment gave way, either to her affection for him, or her curiosity to see how his wife conducted herself. She waited on them at Pemberley, in spite of that pollution which its woods had received, not merely from the presence of such a mistress, but the visits of her uncle and aunt from the city.

With the Gardiners, they were always on the most intimate terms. Darcy, as well as Elizabeth, really loved them. They were both ever sensible of the warmest gratitude towards the persons who, by bringing her into Derbyshire, had been the means of uniting them.

It was after one such happy visit drew to an end that Elizabeth found herself quite in raptures with her husband, which in itself was not unusual. The familiarity of marriage had not lessened one bit of her affection for him, nor her desire to be next to him whenever possible. They found a great many things to discuss, never lacking in the daily pleasures, and never had to find a reason to be in each other's company, for that is where they were whenever they could be.

Threading her arm through his, as the Gardiners' carriage took them away, she waited for him to shut the door and walk with her into their home. "And how was your fishing this morning, Mr. Darcy? Did you catch our supper or will we starve?"

"I did not catch a thing, Mrs. Darcy," he answered, smiling in a way that sent shivers down her spine. "But it is something I will soon rectify." Then, mindless of where they were, he spun around, lifting her into his arms to carry her up the large sweep of stairs. "For now I have caught you."

"Yes, you have captured me, my darling husband." She giggled. "I only hope you do not intend on throwing me back."

"Never," he swore. "I shall never let you escape."

Though they had separate rooms, they spent every night in the same bed, and sometimes, like he now intended, they spent the afternoons there as well. With all company gone and Georgiana practicing her music, they were at leisure to enjoy each other fully until supper.

Darcy's hands held her tightly, carrying her as if she did not weigh a thing. His lips brushed her temple and she wrapped her arms around his neck. Deep inside, she knew it would always be this way with them. Every second seemed to make her love him more, and every day she settled more comfortably into her role as his wife—though by no means were they perfect, they were happy and in love, and such things were a perfection all their own.

Running her fingers into his hair, she turned to him. As their lips touched, he quickened his pace, causing her to giggle against his mouth. So sweet were these moments! Elizabeth forgot everything but him, his kiss, his touch, his love. When their lips parted and her feet hit the ground, they were alone in his room. The place smelled of him, and had become one of her favorite rooms in the house, for it was where they could disappear into each other's arms.

Darcy pulled at his cravat, loosening it. The intent in his eyes mirrored her feelings. "Have I told you how much I love you, Mrs. Darcy?"

"Not half so much as I love you, Mr. Darcy." Happiness filled them as they came together, and they both knew that nothing in the world would ever keep them apart.

ABOUT THE AUTHORS

MICHELLE M. PILLOW, is one of the authors writing under the pseudonym of Annabella Bloom. She is the author of *All Things Romance* and a multipublished, award-winning author writing in many romance fiction genres. She has won the 2006 *Romantic Times BOOKreviews Magazine*'s Reviewers' Choice Award for her historical romance, *Maiden and the Monster*. Her love of history has led her to pursuing a degree in that field, as well as an appreciation for the classical novel. Michelle has a monthly column with Paranormal Underground Magazine, co-owns *www.ravenhappyhour.com* that hosts contests and free reads, and is actively seeking that next great adventure. She is married (madly in love) and has a wonderful family.

Michelle would love to hear from you and tries to answer her emails in a timely fashion. That is, if the current hero will let her go long enough to check the computer. Readers are welcome to contact her through her website, *www.MichellePillow.com*.

JANE AUSTEN was an English novelist whose works of romantic fiction remain some of the most beloved in all of literature and have inspired hundreds of adaptations in both print and film. She never married and, as far as we know, she died a virgin. More's the pity.